Blessed Trinity

Blessed Trinity

VANESSA DAVIS GRIGGS

Kensington Publishing Corp.
http://www.kensingtonbooks.com

DAFINA BOOKS are published by

Kensington Publishing Corp.
119 West 40th Street
New York, NY 10018

All Kensington Titles, Imprints, and Distributed Lines are available at special quantity discounts for bulk purchases for sales promotions, premiums, fund-raising, educational or institutional use. Special book excerpts or customized printings can also be created to fit specific needs. For details, write or phone the office of the Kensington special sales manager: Kensington Publishing Corp., 119 West 40th Street, New York, NY 10018, attn: Special Sales Department, Phone: 1-800-221-2647.

Dafina and the Dafina logo Reg. U.S. Pat. & TM Off.

ISBN-13: 978-0-7582-1773-2
ISBN-10: 0-7582-1773-1

First trade paperback printing: May 2007
First mass market printing: November 2008

10 9 8 7 6 5 4 3 2

Printed in the United States of America

To my mother, Mrs. Josephine Davis—
A true giver and a blessing to so many:
The person who dedicated me back to the Lord,
before I ever graced this place we call world.

Acknowledgments

To the only wise, true and living God—I thank You for choosing me before the foundation of the world to do what I'm doing right now.

To my agent, my publicist, my guide, and in truth, the best ghostwriter around—The Holy Ghost: thank You for being unsurpassed in all of these things and so much more in my life. Just look where You've brought me from.

My mother, Josephine Davis, is and always has been my greatest supporter. Mama, you've gone above and beyond the call of motherhood. A billion thank-yous wouldn't make a dent toward all you've done for me. I pray I have somehow made you proud. To my father, James Davis Jr., for the pep talks you've given me when I needed to know you believed in me and what I've been called to do.

My husband, Jeffery; and my children Jeffery Marques, Jeremy Dewayne, and Johnathan LeDavis; grandchildren Asia and Ashlynn—through the good and the bad, we've endured and pressed onward. We are truly a family, through everything, still standing strong. My life has been enriched because of all of you!

To my sister, Danette Dial: thanks for being the special *you* that you are; my brother, Terence Davis, and sister-in-law, Cameron, (you guys have gone above and beyond when it's come to supporting me and no, I've not forgotten!); my sister, Arlinda Davis, who's always telling somebody about my books; and my brother, Emmanuel Davis, who appreciates what it takes to write a story—all of you have made this journey called life and the faith we've employed in order to do what we do, so much more exciting.

Rosetta Moore: you're one special sister-friend indeed. To Vanessa L. Rice: you never fail to remind me who I am in the literary world. Thanks to my cousin, Mark Davis, who believed enough in the early days of my doing this to really spread the word (and some books) in the Maryland/D.C. area. Marie Primas-Bradshaw and Vina Lavendar: both of you have blessed me in ways like a mother caring for their own child. Thanks Wanda Lawson for your special thoughtfulness and true desire to bless me by planting a seed in what I've been called to do. Zelda Oliver-Miles, Linda H. Jones, Ryan Phillips, and Stephanie Perry Moore: I am so proud to know each of you and to call you fellow authors and friends. You hold a special place in my heart; I wish you the best in whatever you do.

Now comes the hard part. I wish I could name each and every person, every book club, online Web site, bookstore, library, newspaper, magazine, radio and television personality who has touched my life in a positive way. God knows, it hasn't always been easy. To list everyone would be a book within itself. So to those of you who were kind enough to choose my books and/or reached out to let me know how you were affected by my work; to individuals, book clubs, church organizations, and companies who brought me into your setting or extended an invitation for me and your group to have face-to-face fellowship (like Ella Wells, Ora "Polly" Mathews, Barbara Bryant and The Ladies of Distinction and Ladies Divine Book Club in Raleigh-Durham, NC; Long Branch Baptist Church and Book Club in Greenville, SC; Greater Beallwood Baptist Church and Book Club in Columbus, GA; the Sensational Readers Book Club in Rogersville, AL; Delta Sigma Theta Sorority Birmingham Alumnae, AKA Omicron Omega Chapter, Miles College, Bethel Baptist Church Prime Timer's in Birmingham, AL to name a few): May God bless you exceedingly, abundantly, above all you can ever ask for or think of!

To those who have e-mailed me, signed my guest book

with such positive and encouraging messages, sent letters, called (some of you are quite resourceful), or made a special effort to visit with me when I was in your city: please hear my heart when I say, "You didn't have to do it but you did, and I thank you from the bottom of my heart!" What a blessed dilemma to find myself in—having so many to thank, there's not room enough to name (or contain) them all. That is so like God.

A special thanks to Stacey N. Barney who—with much love and respect—was responsible for me returning to the published world at this point in my life. I thank you for reaching out to me like you did. To the staff of Dafina Books, I thank you for all the hard work you do. My thanks to Selena James, Editorial Director, and Monica Harris for the wonderful work you both did to ensure my work was polished and an enjoyable experience for the reader. No author (or person) is an island, and I want you to know that your labor is not in vain.

Lastly, to you who have chosen *Blessed Trinity:* I pray this book blesses you as much as it—and you—have already blessed me. What I do means little without you being there to receive it once it's done. Thank you. Thank you. Thank you. And thanks for continuing to help me spread the "Word." If you like what you read here, then be a blessing to someone else and tell them about it (just don't tell them too much and ruin their reading experience)!

Vanessa Davis Griggs

www.VanessaDavisGriggs.com

Prologue

Now Faith is the substance of things hoped for, the evidence of things not seen.

(Hebrews 11:1)

Everybody wants to know how I, a nobody from nowhere, became a somebody about to sport the coveted last name of Landris. It just goes to show how people shouldn't judge another without knowing what's happening on the inside. And never, ever to underestimate the power of Faith!

Before I get ahead of myself, maybe I should begin at the beginning, since I've already told you the end. Don't you just hate it when people flip to the back of a book and read the end before they even crack the beginning and middle just because they feel they have to know how it ends? Well, that won't be the case here. The end is officially out, over and done with. Faith wins!

Now we can concentrate on the story, and how I managed to arrive here.

I am Faith. Not Hope—Hope is the timid one. You know, the one who crosses her fingers and wishes for the best. Not Charity. Sweet little Charity, the one who really believes love conquers all, and, if I'm truly honest, has been told she's the greatest of the three of us. Both of them give up too easily.

It's like they're not really sure what they want—a bit too wishy-washy for me.

But now me—I know what I want. And as a rule, I generally grab hold like a pit bull until I get it. Not by giving up at the first hint of opposition. Oh, no. You see, Faith recognizes the impossible, yet sees the invisible, and holds fast to the confession. I succeed because I stand by what I want as if I'm entitled to it.

And I am.

That's why I claimed dear, charming Landris as mine the first time I laid eyes on him. God knows, it should be a sin for any man—let alone a man of God—to be so fine, smart, and good-looking, all swirled into one. *Note to God: Needed— an 11th Commandment: Thou shalt not be so tempting.*

So I "named it" and "claimed it," right then and there. The man never stood a chance, not when it came to resisting me. Faith was at work; he was as good as mine.

"You can't claim somebody else's man," Hope said to me when I shared my confession with her. I didn't want to, but I had to tell someone. "You can't impose your will over someone else's. You just can't!"

Dear Hope—always the practical one. She does have her own desires, but she chooses to live her life cautiously, always hoping. "Just in case it doesn't work out," she says, "at least I won't be too disappointed." She knows nothing about men, and if I'm honest here, even less about the power of Faith. That's who I am: Faith Alexandria Morrell, and by tomorrow, the new Mrs. Landris.

From the beginning, it was the three of us: Faith, Hope, and Charity. Like water, steam, and ice—the same, but different. Water—easy and fluid, can flow anywhere, yet it's strong enough to form a Grand Canyon. Steam—vapor like a spirit, practically invisible, yet leaves undeniable evidence of its existence. Dare I say, able to open, without detection, what some believe to be sealed for good, and create power never imagined probable, let alone possible. Ice—solid, steadfast and firm, can be grasped, handled, touched. Each the same, only a different form.

There's one thing I would like to clear up here and now: Johnnie Mae Taylor Landris had her hands full even *before* she met me. There was her mother's memory problem, and four siblings, three of whom were routinely uncooperative. She had a young daughter to raise within a brand-new marriage plus the demands of a writing career that required her to travel.

Her husband, the Right Reverend (and very handsome) Pastor George Landris, presided over a new ministry growing so fast it was making heads spin, especially for a church in Birmingham, Alabama. Now don't get me wrong—I'm not putting down Birmingham. It's just, who would have expected such a phenomenon to take place here? There were people who sold everything and moved from other states just to take part.

Can you blame them? Pastor Landris is a great teacher of the Bible. He definitely knows how to break down the Word of God. He's unconventional and sure of himself. How else could he wear dreadlocks and get away with it? He's the type who'll rarely back down when he believes in something. Pastor Landris is the kind of man of God whom people will literally uproot their lives to follow.

Like Sapphire and Angela Gabriel. Although from what I heard, Miss Angel Gabriel (Angel is what she prefers being called) didn't originally move from Asheville, North Carolina, to be part of this newfound ministry.

"Actually, I was supposed to be running a radio station," Angel said with a smile. She and I worked closely on Johnnie Mae and Pastor's marriage seminar material. We ended up talking, and that's when I found out some interesting information. It turns out Pastor Landris had supposedly bought that same radio station in a deal that, incidentally, ended up blowing up in several folks' faces. I'm talking big-time blowup! Of course, most people (including Miss Angel) quietly blame that costly misstep on Thomas, Pastor Landris's older, yet equally good-looking and, might I add, talented brother.

So when Hope, Charity, and I showed up at the church in 2003 and inserted ourselves in these folks' lives, things were already crazy. To our credit, we did try to help. And were you to ask Johnnie Mae, she would admit that I really was a blessing. And even if she were to deny it, I was—no . . . I still *am* a blessing.

Don't believe me? Okay, then you be the judge. Man can, and should, plan all he wants, but there are times when God has His own thoughts about the matter.

Romans 8:28 states, "And we know that all things work together for good to them who love God, to them who are called according to his purpose."

Yes, for *good* to *them* who love God and who are called according to His purpose.

And I *do* love God.

Chapter 1

*For I know the thoughts that I think toward you,
saith the Lord, thoughts of peace, and not of evil,
to give you an expected end.*

(Jeremiah 29:11)

Pastor George Landris watched her as she walked gracefully to the other side of the banquet hall of the church.
He couldn't help but smile; she had that effect on him. She
had to be the most beautiful woman he had ever laid eyes on.
With the passing of time, that belief had only intensified.
Knowing it would be inappropriate for him to act on his true
impulse, he casually strolled closer.

"I hope you won't think badly of me for saying this," Pastor
Landris said in a low voice only she could hear, "but you are,
without a doubt, the loveliest woman I've ever seen."

"Careful there, Pastor—I happen to be spoken for." She
held up her left hand and wiggled the three diamond rocks
that adorned her ring finger.

The two of them were standing near an empty table.
Many of the people who had attended the banquet were chatting in groups as they prepared to leave.

Pastor Landris moved in closer and began to whisper
softly in her ear. "Well, your man is indeed one blessed man,
if I say so myself. Tell me . . . honestly. What are the chances
of the two of us getting together later tonight after this thing
is over?" he asked—his voice deep, velvety-smooth. "You
know . . . to talk?"

"To talk, Pastor?" Skepticism laced her voice. "Just to talk?"

"Madam, I am a man of God, and I assure you, where the Lord leads, I have vowed to follow." He leaned back to be able to admire her better, then began shaking his head. "Mmm-mmm."

She tried, but failed—she couldn't help but smile. "Okay, Pastor. You know, it's hard to say no to someone like you, especially with that irresistible charm. How can one be so good, and yet be so bad at the same time?"

Pastor Landris bit down slightly on his bottom lip and grinned even more. He touched the back of the chair, as though he needed to do something to keep that one hand occupied. "Well, now, *Mrs*. Landris, I must confess—I have it bad for you. Only for you."

"Landris, you need to stop," Johnnie Mae Landris said, fanning at him while trying to keep her voice in check. "You would think after being married for three years—"

"It won't officially be three years until Wednesday." He grinned, his eyes again performing a quick scan of her petite body from head to toe as he slowly shook his head.

She smiled at him as he watched her before she swatted him playfully. "I told you, you need to stop."

"What?" he asked innocently.

"Flirting with me in public." Johnnie Mae continued to blush. She waved at someone walking out of the door who waved good-bye to her. The crowd that had originally filled the room earlier that night was now down to a handful.

"But you're my wife. It's perfectly acceptable for me to flirt with my wife, isn't it?" Pastor Landris rubbed his well-trimmed goatee. He looked down at his black patent leather Prada boots before looking back up at her.

"There's also a time and a place for everything."

"'To every thing there is a season, and a time to every purpose under the heaven . . .'"

"Yes, Mr. Walking Bible, and there's 'a time to love.' In a church facility, in front of people, immediately after a lovely banquet given by members and friends of the church, is neither the time nor the place," Johnnie Mae said as she began to sashay away in her beautiful Prussian-blue, beaded evening gown. She needed to hug a few more people and thank them for their contribution to such an unforgettable evening.

"I suppose this means we have a date for later tonight, then?" he yelled at her, a little louder than he'd intended. Quickly, he looked around to see if anyone had overheard him. His eyes were immediately met by those of a woman who had recently become a member of their congregation.

"Good evening, Pastor Landris."

"Sister Morrell."

"Oh, please—I've asked you several times to call me Faith. Sister Morrell just sounds so stiff and formal." She smiled.

"As you prefer—Faith."

"I just wanted to personally congratulate you and Mrs. Landris on your wedding anniversary." She pointed to the banner on the back wall that read: *September 8, 2001 to 2004—Only The Beginning of Something Beautiful*. "Three years is a long time to be with one person."

"Not really. Not when the ultimate joy will be celebrating our golden anniversary."

"Then I probably should say that three years would be a long time for me. But I suppose had I been as fortunate as Johnnie Mae to have married someone as wonderful as you—"

"Excuse me, but I believe you have it all wrong."

A puzzled smile came across her face. "I'm sorry. I have it all wrong?"

"Yes. You see, Johnnie Mae is not the fortunate one here at all—I am," he said with pride. "I am so blessed to have found such a woman to share my life—three years with her has been more like three minutes. 'Whoso findeth a wife findeth a good thing, and obtaineth favor of the Lord.' As far as I'm concerned, our happiness together now is merely a small hint of what is yet to come."

Faith's face quickly fell. "Oh," she said, a little disappointed, then recovered her pleasant demeanor. "That is so sweet!" Pure honey seemed to drip from her lips. "You two are blessed! So blessed. Congratulations again."

"Well, Sister Mor . . . I mean, Faith. Thank you. I'll be sure and tell Mrs. Landris."

"Please do. I was hoping to catch up with her before she left." She pretended to be earnestly searching, glancing at the few people still chatting in small groups. "I'm sorry we missed each other, but I must be heading home now. My sister, Hope, wasn't feeling well when I left, and I don't want her waiting up too late."

"Your sister is under the weather? I wondered why she hadn't come to the banquet. Hope worked so tirelessly, helping to put this together."

"Oh, it's nothing too serious. She was having some difficulty breathing earlier today. Probably just another one of the panic attacks that she's been known to have from time to time. Charity is keeping an eye on her until I get back."

"Please tell Hope we'll be praying for her speedy recovery. And that she was sorely missed tonight."

Faith maintained her smile. "Of course. I'll be sure and tell her. See you tomorrow at services."

Pastor Landris watched as she left. There was something about Faith and her identical twin sister Hope that really bothered him. He felt sure they loved each other, but something was going on between them. He just couldn't put his finger on what it was.

Pastor Landris and Johnnie Mae arrived home. It had been an enjoyable but long evening. Johnnie Mae had gone upstairs to step out of her evening gown—she loved Prussian blue and hoped to find a daytime dress in that color. Everyone had been so wonderful at the banquet tonight, the congregation having given them a lovely third wedding anniversary celebration. It had indeed been a glorious night, but she was exhausted. Tomorrow was Sunday and the start of yet another long day.

As she briefly closed her eyes, she couldn't help but reflect on all that had happened over the past few years that had brought them to this place . . .

Chapter 2

And they said one to another, Behold, this dreamer cometh.

(Genesis 37:19)

A few years earlier, Pastor Landris had been relieved of his duties as the pastor of Wings of Grace Faith Ministry Church in Atlanta, Georgia, a congregation that grew from some 37 members to over 4,000 under his leadership. Prior to his dismissal, he was asked to tone down his support of women in ministry. He didn't.

Pastor Landris and Johnnie Mae had just gotten married on September 8 of that year.

Johnnie Mae didn't immediately relocate to Atlanta, and as it turned out, she never had to. God spoke to Pastor Landris and instructed him to move to Johnnie Mae's hometown of Birmingham, Alabama, to start anew.

Thomas Landris, Pastor Landris's older brother, had made a mess of some investments he'd been in charge of on behalf of his brother. Fifteen years earlier, Thomas had invested money in Microsoft stock for both him and his brother. Thomas took his out early; Pastor Landris left his to grow.

And grow it did.

Pastor Landris became a multimillionaire, but when the IRS started looking for its share, he discovered his brother had cashed out the stocks, as Pastor Landris had instructed him to, but invested the money elsewhere without his knowledge or approval.

Thomas did end up recouping some of the lost money, and before Pastor Landris knew it, he was to be the owner of an FM radio station in Birmingham. Pastor Landris received this as further confirmation that he was indeed being led to relocate to the Magic City.

In December, Pastor Landris sold his house, packed his belongings, and moved to Birmingham.

He left without a church requesting him to come as pastor, to a home technically belonging to his wife, along with his brother and a few others who had also made the decision to relocate.

Thomas was to become the general manager of the radio station his brother was in the process of buying. Sapphire Drummond, a therapist, came along from Atlanta because she was dating Thomas, and she wanted a change of scenery. Sapphire and Theresa Jordan, Pastor Landris's ex-fiancée, had been best friends. Angela Gabriel, who preferred being called Angel, had been hired by the original owners of the radio station previous to the sale. In fact, she had no idea the station was even in the process of being sold when she accepted the job. Her beloved great-grandmother had just died, and this job was a great opportunity for her. She sure didn't know she had met the potential buyer when Pastor Landris visited her hometown of Asheville, North Carolina, earlier that year.

For Pastor Landris, everything seemed to be falling into place. Surely God was directing this move. But he would soon learn that things aren't always as they seem. What appears to be God's will one moment can end up looking totally different once things begin to unfold.

Pastor Landris would come to understand how Joseph the dreamer in the Bible must have felt. Joseph's father Jacob, later called Israel, loved him so much more than his other children that he made his beloved son the infamous coat of many colors. Joseph dreamed his family would end up bowing to him. He shared this dream with them—an announcement that didn't go over well with his brothers (or his father at first, for that matter).

"Shalt thou indeed have dominion over us?" Joseph's brothers and father wanted to know. Of course, they hated Joseph even more for his dreams and for daring to speak those dreams out loud.

Pastor George Edward Landris could definitely relate.

When Pastor Landris needed spiritual encouragement to get through the rough times—as he wrestled with feelings of rejection, being lied to and about—he would find comfort reading Genesis, Chapters 37-50, to help him go on.

As with Joseph, Pastor Landris believed God had given him a dream. *Somewhere Joseph must have believed God would bring it to pass or else he would have just quit.* When Pastor Landris needed a Word to help him, he would think about all Joseph endured before his blessings finally came to pass. He reflected on how Joseph was put in a pit by his own brothers, who had originally planned to kill him. And had it not been for his other brothers, Reuben and Judah, Joseph and his dreams might well have perished.

But God had His hands of protection on Joseph, and Pastor Landris knew God's hand was also on him. Pastor Landris's own "preach-brothers" in the ministry were not so happy to see him come to their city. They pretended they were whenever he was around, even as they plotted to get rid of him.

Not to physically kill him, although Pastor Landris wasn't one hundred percent certain about that at times. But he did realize they wanted to assassinate him—and his dreams—in a spiritual sense.

No one had called Pastor Landris to come to Birmingham. Who could say if he would ever have a congregation again? That paralleled Joseph being thrown in prison. On the plus side, Pastor Landris did have his new family: a wonderful wife in Johnnie Mae, along with her three-year-old daughter, Princess Rose. And there was Thomas and Sapphire, who had followed him to Alabama to lend their assistance.

Things would surely have to get better.

However, Pastor Landris—as did Joseph—would quickly discover that that's not always the case.

Faith Alexandria Morrell didn't care about church anymore. She'd had more than her fill of "church folks." One thing she could never understand was how the church pastor, who constantly hammered other folk about what they should and shouldn't do, could end up doing that same wrong thing, get caught, and the church would just forgive him and keep him on. It made no sense to her.

"They're all only human. He's just a man," her friend Dominique told her. Faith was still living in New Orleans then. She had questioned why the congregation hadn't kicked their pastor out on his holier-than-thou, self-righteous tailbone after they caught him messing around with all those women in the church. "Who are we to judge?" Dominique said. "Only God can do that."

Faith still didn't get it. She had witnessed him deliver a few sermons from the pulpit, getting the church all emotional as he began to sing and moan. The next thing she knew, hats and shoes were flying all over the place; people's glasses were landing on the floor or in the pews behind them; men were yanking off suit coats, ties, and jackets and running around, shouting. The women were dancing, unconcerned whether things she didn't care to see or mention were showing as they jumped or fell down, their dresses, blouses, skirts in disarray. Faith wondered—how holy could this be?

Those who weren't shouting were running up to the pastor and laying paper money at his feet, which only seemed to make him whoop and holler more.

Faith just did . . . not . . . get it. People claimed it was the Holy Spirit that had caused them to act that way, but she knew from scripture that the spirit was subject unto the prophet. She wasn't a Bible scholar, but that much she did know. This was emotionalism, pure and simple. It was the way they chose to react or express the way they were feeling, which was fine as far as Faith was concerned. She just wished folks would call it what it was and quit acting like they were being uncontrollably possessed or something.

Then this same pastor was caught having affairs with not one, not two, but three ladies in his congregation at the same time. What was worse, his wife was the one who finally caught him on tape. When she brought her audio evidence before the congregation during one Sunday morning's service, proving he was with this one woman, that caused two other women to pop up mad and argue there was no way this could possibly be true, seeing as he was with "her" exclusively. Talk about angry. They didn't seem to mind that he was cheating on his wife, but it was a whole other matter when they learned he wasn't being so faithful to them, either.

The pastor confessed to his loyal congregation a week later. Faith happened to be there that Sunday by special invitation from Dominique. They had front-row seats. He delivered a passionate, tearful plea, begging for forgiveness. He claimed Satan had him bound, using his godly gift of loving others against him. Apparently, he loved all the people in his congregation so much, he couldn't bear to see any of them in pain.

The pastor claimed he hadn't meant to hurt anyone, especially his lovely wife, who, incidentally, was driving a brand, spanking-new Mercedes-Benz and sporting a three-carat diamond ring. But he was only a man and not God, he said, and he was not perfect, nor, coincidentally, was any of them sitting there. A few people behind Faith were whispering that one or two of those women just might have put some type of voodoo on him to cause him to behave that way. Faith didn't believe in voodoo.

Then the pastor closed with a classic line: "He who is among you without sin, let him cast the first stone." As he looked over the audience, he knew there wasn't a person there who hadn't done something wrong. Maybe not that week, and maybe not to the extent that he'd done, but they were *all* guilty of *something*. "And a sin is a sin is a sin. There are no big or little sins in God's sight," he said, looking repentant, then upward toward heaven.

His closing defense was: "God uses imperfect people to do His work." Yes, he had fallen, but no one had a right to judge him when everybody there was guilty of something themselves. "Amen?" he said, jumping up as he got more "in the spirit."

Faith was a visitor and all the visitors had been asked to wait outside the sanctuary during the vote. Faith couldn't believe the congregation actually bought into what he had said and overwhelmingly voted to allow him to stay on.

"I just don't understand," Faith said to Dominique as they walked toward the parking lot. "Why in heaven's name would y'all vote to keep a scumbag like him as your pastor?"

Dominique had only said, "But girl, the man can preach! Do you have any idea how hard it is to find a *real* man . . . I'm talking about a *real* man who can preach *and* sing? Honey, hush! We're not letting the devil come in and mess up our good thing. Now, he came forward and asked for forgiveness. The Bible clearly admonishes us to forgive. How often? Seventy times seven. The pastor has been talked to about his behavior. He understands he can't do things like that anymore. So what more do people want?" She smiled, then popped her chewing gum three times.

And that was that.

Okay, so the man could preach and he could sing, Faith thought. But she couldn't help but believe these people needed a good reality check. Dominique insisted Faith was the one who was wrong, and the least she could do was give the church a real, honest try.

"Visit a few more times, Faith, and see for yourself. Everybody, including you, needs a good church home and family. Stop being so judgmental," Dominique said.

So Faith came regularly for a month. She had to admit, she did enjoy the services. She decided to join the church, even though she had been appalled by the pastor's behavior and the congregation's permissiveness. "There are no perfect churches here on earth—they all have something wrong," she'd been told on more than one occasion. Being a member, she did see how compassionate and loving the good reverend seemed to be. He indeed had compassion for his members, just as Dominique and the others had declared.

Almost a year later, the pastor pulled Faith off to the side and mentioned he needed to speak with her privately. There were things Faith's friend, Dominique, had come and talked with him about concerning Faith's well-being.

"Sister, I must be honest with you. I believe my office might be bugged, and I don't want to risk your business becoming known if that is the case," the pastor said.

He suggested an innocent place for them to meet: "Somewhere public, of course." He knew it wouldn't look right for him to visit Faith at her home—he wanted her to know he was on the up-and-up, so he took her to a five-star restaurant and bought her an expensive dinner. Right after dessert, he asked her to accompany him to his secret hideaway for some "faith healing," or, as he put it, "the laying on of hands."

"We must rid you of the demons inside of you, Sister Faith. And I want you to know—I'm committed to stick with you through this for as long as it takes," he said as he held his diamond-ring-laden hands in the air. "You see, I've been called to love everybody. I want to help you. These healing hands of mine are a gift from God. I must use my gift or lose it."

In August, 2001, Faith, along with Hope and Charity, left New Orleans, Louisiana, for Birmingham, Alabama, without looking back. Faith never bothered mentioning to anyone what the pastor had attempted to do.

What difference would it have made anyway? She'd learned very early in life that the woman usually took the blame, regardless of the details of what really went down.

Chapter 3

I know both how to be abased, and I know how to abound: every where and in all things I am instructed both to be full and to be hungry, both to abound and to suffer need.

(Philippians 4:12)

"Pastor George Landris," a tall, burly man with a deep, Barry White-like voice, called. "Good to have you here in the Magic City of Birmingham, my preach-brother. My name is Reverend Paul Knight . . . but all my friends call me Poppa Knight."

Pastor Landris looked at the man standing behind him who had walked up without having made a sound. He was dressed warmly enough in his wool, charcoal overcoat, thick, gray scarf, and black Banjo Paterson hat with a reed leather sweatband, perfect attire for the last day in January.

Pastor Landris was looking at a building he was hoping to rent or purchase so he could start conducting church services. Earlier this month, he and Johnnie Mae had discussed what he really wanted to do in his ministry. He told her he wanted to preach God's Word. God had called him to be a pastor, and he was sent here to start a congregation, but he would need a facility. His plan was to sell the radio station he hadn't really wanted in the first place, but according to Thomas, there was some snafu that was stalling the deal temporarily. And for some reason, he couldn't get his money back, at least not at this point. Pastor Landris planned to use the funds from selling the radio station or the refund to build a church.

Johnnie Mae had found forty acres of prime land she believed would be perfect to build a worship center. With the funds from the station sale, money wouldn't be an issue, but until that became available, Pastor Landris would have to make do.

God had spoken to Pastor Landris and instructed him to rent or buy a small building. This building was a bit run-down, but with some effort, it could be a nice place to get started. He was there checking it out when Reverend Knight had walked up to him.

"So Pastor Landris, what exactly are you doing here in this old place?" Reverend Knight asked. He took off his hat and looked at the walls and the ceiling in need of much repair.

"Looking for a place to start a congregation," Pastor Landris said.

"You thinking about starting it in this old dump?" Reverend Knight asked as he kicked a place in the floor and began to bounce his heavy frame in a spot that made an irritating, squeaking noise each time his body moved.

"I'm considering it. Why?" Pastor Landris said. "Do you know something I don't?"

Reverend Knight tried to hold back a smile. "Well, Pastor, I don't think this place is available for you to rent or to buy." He placed his hat back on his head.

Pastor Landris looked puzzled. He had seen the "for sale" sign outside when he walked in. He had called the listing agent and confirmed it was still available. She had come and let him in to take a look around as long as he wanted. He had enough money to buy or at least sign a lease for it, although three years was longer than he felt he would need it. He started to wonder what Reverend Knight was doing here, and how he happened to know someone, namely him, was even there.

"From everything I know, this place is available," Pastor Landris said, eyeing him more closely now.

Reverend Knight pulled out a business card and handed it to Pastor Landris. A photo of a skinnier, twenty-years-younger version of Reverend Knight graced the front of the card. The times of the church's Sunday-morning, evening, and Wednesday-night services were listed on the back.

"Pastor Landris, I would love to have you come join me in my ministry. I have over 2,500 members in my church. I know you realize how hard that big a congregation can be on top ministers such as ourselves."

"Excuse me," Pastor Landris said. "What do you mean by 'top ministers'?" Pastor Landris placed Reverend Knight's card in his coat pocket. "I'm not trying to be a big shot. I'm just trying to preach the Word of God. Being a top minister never enters my thinking. If people happen to have heard of me, that's fine. It just gives me a bigger opportunity to reach more people for Jesus. That's all fame is for me."

"Come on, Doc. Don't try to act so humble. Let me tell you what I'm thinking. Instead of you coming to the city and having to start from scratch, why don't you consider coming over to The Church of Revelation with me? I would be honored to have you on staff."

Pastor Landris tried to be polite. "Reverend Knight, I appreciate the offer, but God sent me here to start a new congregation, not to hook up with an existing one. In fact, He didn't even send me here to take over the congregation of an outgoing pastor. My specific assignment is to start anew."

Reverend Knight snapped his head to one side twice as though he had a twitch. He grinned. "Can I be frank with you, Doc?" He looked at Pastor Landris to gauge his reaction. "There are too many church buildings here in Birmingham. It used to be a running joke that there was a church on every corner. Now it's more like three to four churches on every street. What we don't need is any more churches. All of these places just siphon off members from existing congregations. Not many are going out into the fields to harvest those who have never heard of Jesus and bring in new converts. They wait for people to get mad and leave one place to traipse over to another, only to get upset or tired there and leave again.

"Now, my people are pretty stable. They don't leave too often. Were you to come on board, I believe we would double in size, quite frankly, and we could then build even bigger. Can you imagine a congregation of 20,000. Think of the power we would possess. With that many people, we could affect outcomes of elections. Politicians would court us. Sure, there are always challenges with that many people, but you expect that. When you become a church that size, you tend to attract the smartest, most successful and accomplished people in the area. Everybody would want to be part of our church so they can impress others. People want to be part of something alive . . . growing. So why waste your talent duplicating what's already in place? Let's team up." Reverend Knight shifted his weight. "There are only so many people in this town, anyway. Think of the money you and I could rake in together."

Pastor Landris shook his head. "Rake in?" He couldn't believe what Reverend Knight had just said.

"For the Kingdom, of course. All for the Kingdom. That's what this is all about. Raking in souls for the Kingdom. But let's not play games—it takes money to do anything worthwhile. And I assure you, at The Church of Revelation, all of your needs will be met. And I do mean ALL of your needs, if you catch my drift: spiritually, physically, socially, and financially." Reverend Knight glanced at his watch. He needed to hurry—the sun would be setting soon.

Pastor Landris nodded slowly. "All, huh?"

"Capital 'A', double 'L'—ALL. You're not going to find a better deal anywhere. I guarantee that. If you do, come back and see me. We'll renegotiate."

Pastor Landris smiled. "Is that right? Well, *Doc*, I'm afraid you're a little too late. I've already been offered, and accepted, a better deal. You see, I kind of feel like Paul when he wrote Philippians 3:7-8, 'But what things were gain to me, those I counted loss for Christ. Yea doubtless, and I count all things but loss for the excellency of the knowledge of Christ Jesus my Lord: for whom I have suffered loss of all things, and do count them but dung, that I may win Christ.' And Philippians 4:19 that says, 'My God shall supply all my need according to His riches in glory by Christ Jesus.' ALL my need. God handles each need as it arises. We might not see it, but it's there. Not *out* of His riches, but *according to* His riches. Not even *you* can top that."

Reverend Knight had a smirk on his face, then touched the rim of his hat. "I see you're truly as well-versed in scripture as people have claimed. That's good. Real good. I'm sure it will come in handy with the fight you're about to have on your hands."

"Fight?"

"Yeah," Reverend Knight said as he took out a handkerchief and mopped a bit of perspiration from his forehead in spite of the wintry January air. "Not that I'm one of them, but there are plenty of folks who don't want you or your teachings here. Righteous brothers and sisters, clearly under the radar, of course. Now I respect your gifts and I would welcome you with open arms. Then at some point, I would proudly turn over everything I have built up over the years to you. Everything. You see, I don't have a son to pass my church on to like some of the other preachers."

"Excuse me—*your* church? I didn't realize any church belonged to anyone other than Jesus. And what's this about congregations being passed on like an inheritance . . . some kind of legal birthright?" Pastor Landris said.

"Come on, Doc. Do you really think for one second these preachers who've built these huge congregations plan to let someone from outside the family just come in and take it if they have any say-so about it. Unless it's under certain umbrellas that keep that from happening, ministers like me have our ways of passing our churches on to our offspring. Or, at least, to a chosen one, especially when we've built something from nothing. I can see—there really is much I can teach you. So what do you say? Come on board with me. At least say you'll think about it?" Reverend Knight pulled off his skintight, black leather glove and extended his right hand to Pastor Landris.

Pastor Landris looked down at the hand waiting to be grasped. He looked up at Reverend Knight's hat and appreciated how his own dreadlocks somehow kept him warm enough that his head didn't need to be covered. He looked into the face of this older minister . . . a man who could easily have been his own father. Reverend Knight looked tired and worn, yet, he appeared sincere.

"Reverend Knight, thank you for stopping by, but as I said earlier, I've already accepted a better offer. Now if you'll excuse me," Pastor Landris said and nodded as he cautiously stepped over a pile of debris, "I need to finish checking out this place before it gets too dark to be able to see."

Reverend Knight lowered his hand slowly, then brushed it off on his pants as though it had been badly soiled. "Suit yourself," he whispered, almost to himself. Then he carefully made his way out the door, just as quietly as he'd made his way in.

Chapter 4

Being confident of this very thing, that he which hath begun a good work in you will perform it until the day of Jesus Christ.

(Philippians 1:6)

Pastor Landris had submitted an offer on the building he had looked at after taking one day to pray about it. According to the realtor, everything seemed to be a "go" but a few days later, he received a call from her saying the building was no longer available.

"What happened?" Pastor Landris asked.

"The owner decided they no longer want to sell or lease it. Quite frankly, Pastor Landris, I don't understand it myself. They have literally been jumping down our throats about finding a buyer. In fact, they've lowered the price more than a few times, hoping to find someone to purchase it. Then I received a call telling me it was no longer available."

"Do you think the seller possibly received a better offer?"

"It's possible, but if that's the case, I'm due a commission regardless. He had a contract with us, and if it sold, our office is entitled to something. All I was told was it is no longer on the market."

Pastor Landris thought for a second. "Is there any way I could speak with the owner myself?"

"We were asked not to divulge this information to the public. I'm sorry."

"May I ask you one other question? It will only require a yes or no answer."

"Sure."

"Would the owner happen to be a Reverend Paul Knight?"

The realtor hesitated for a full fifteen seconds. "Actually, Pastor Landris, the listed owner is a nonprofit organization."

"Oh," Pastor Landris said, disappointed with her answer. "Well, thanks, anyway."

"Pastor Landris?"

"Yes."

"Reverend Knight is the person handling the transactions for this organization."

Pastor Landris wasn't sure if he was pleased to hear this or not. "Thank you."

"I'll keep looking if you want me to. I'm sure there's something out there to meet your specifications. Unfortunately, there aren't a lot of vacant churches, but I'll keep my eyes open."

"I appreciate that."

Pastor Landris hung up and stared at the phone. He couldn't believe what was happening, but he wasn't going to let this deter him.

The phone rang just as he was about to go into the kitchen and find something to eat. Johnnie Mae and Princess Rose were out shopping, and Johnnie Mae hadn't said whether she planned to bring something home for supper. Thinking it was probably the realtor calling back, Pastor Landris didn't bother to look at the caller ID.

"Pastor Landris speaking," he said, cutting to the chase.

"Hey, man, why so formal today?" It was his brother.

"Thomas, I thought you were someone else." Pastor Landris took the cordless phone and walked a few steps away to the window. The Bradford pear tree in the front yard that was so beautiful during spring and fall was completely boring now. He saw his neighbor across the street walking his Alaskan

Husky, although it looked more like the dog was walking the neighbor. "What's up?" Pastor Landris said.

"I'm fine—thanks for asking," Thomas said to a question that was not asked.

Pastor Landris realized his big brother's meaning, but his mind was still reeling from his conversation with the real estate agent.

"Sorry, Thomas. My thoughts were somewhere else. No excuse. Please forgive me."

"Sure, I forgive you. We're brothers. And that's what brothers do."

Pastor Landris suddenly suspected something was amiss. "Okay, Thomas. What's wrong?"

Thomas knew it was best to get this over with. "It's the radio station money."

"Yes?"

"There's a problem . . . well, a major problem." Thomas let out a long sigh. "Listen, man. I probably should come over there and tell you this to your face, but I can't face you. So I'm going to tell you, and if you feel you want to come over here and beat the living daylights out of me, I can't blame you."

"What is it, Thomas?"

"You remember Sammie, the guy who was handling all of your deals?"

"You mean the hustler who handled the deals I never commissioned him to do in the first place? Those deals?"

"Yeah, those," Thomas said, deciding to come clean so he could finish. "It appears the money he had of yours for the radio station—"

"Ten million dollars worth."

"Yeah, that money. Well, it seems it's no longer there, and, of course, the radio station deal can't go forward without it. So that's what's been taking so long. Sammie was trying to fix it, but he sort of ran into a bit of bad luck, so to speak.

Other people he had deals with weren't as understanding about his investing ethics as—"

"Me and you?" Pastor Landris interjected with sheer sarcasm.

Thomas tried to laugh it off. "Yeah, you. Anyway, they filed criminal charges against him and have also filed several civil lawsuits. Any money he had in his personal and business accounts has been frozen. Can you believe that? They froze all his assets, including anything that may have belonged to other people, until his hearing comes up." Thomas sniffed a little. "That's messed up, if you ask me. He tells me they can't legally do that, so he and his lawyers are fighting this injustice tooth and nail."

"How long have you known about this?"

"I sort of knew a little about it back when you and I talked at the beginning of this year about selling the station. But George, man . . . I was praying it would all work out."

"Yeah, right, Thomas." Pastor Landris couldn't believe it. "So what does this mean for me?"

"It means that the radio station deal has fallen through because they have another buyer who has the finances and is ready to move on it. I've been trying to talk to them myself and work something out until this is all cleared up." Thomas spoke fast. "Come on, man. You know how much that radio station meant to me. Frankly, I can't believe something like this has happened! You know this is just the devil, right?"

Pastor Landris sat down in the blue recliner in the den. He ran his hand over his hair, then his forehead. It was dusk now. He turned on the Tiffany lamp perched on the table next to the chair. "What does this mean for my ten million dollars?" Pastor Landris asked in a slow, deliberate voice.

"You need a lawyer to file a petition in court against Sammie. I've spoken with one already, and he said you have a good case for getting your money released, provided you can prove it was yours to begin with. It's possible to have that part of the asset unfrozen and returned to you. It might be a bit expensive retaining the right lawyer, but that's better than losing the whole amount." Thomas paused.

"George, I'm sorry, man." Thomas continued. "I know this is all my fault. If I could go back and change things, I promise you, I never would have gotten involved with Sammie or any of his little get-rich-quick schemes. That was my mistake. I'm 44 years old—I should know better by now. But I'll tell you what. You and I are going to agree in the name of Jesus that Satan will not steal your money." He waited; his brother didn't utter a sound.

"George? I know you're still there," Thomas said. "Come on, George. Say *something*. Holler, scream, yell at me . . . just say *some*thing. Come on, man . . ."

Pastor Landris looked up at the ceiling. He knew God had called him to begin this work. It was good work. But for some reason, he just couldn't get anything started.

As he sat there and began to rock slightly in the chair, he heard a scripture in his spirit from Philippians 1:6. "Being confident of this very thing, that he which hath begun a good work in you will perform it until the day of Jesus Christ."

Pastor Landris stopped rocking and became totally still. He knew one thing for certain: he would have to trust God— now, more than ever.

Now, more than ever.

Chapter 5

How art thou fallen from heaven, O Lucifer, son of the morning! how art thou cut down to the ground, which didst weaken the nations!

(Isaiah 14:12)

Pastor Landris had been angry when he learned he wouldn't be able to purchase or lease the building he'd found for the church, but it bothered him even more when he realized Reverend Knight had been behind it.

"I just can't believe it," Pastor Landris said to Johnnie Mae as they stood in the kitchen. Johnnie Mae and Princess Rose had eaten while they were out, so he was searching the freezer for something to eat. "You remember that preacher I told you I met the other day named Reverend Knight?"

"You mean, 'Poppa' Knight," Johnnie Mae said, teasing him. When she glanced at his face, she immediately wished she could take that joke back.

"Poppa is right. He must think he's my daddy." Pastor Landris took three crab cakes out of the freezer, placed them in foil on the metal tray, and put them into the toaster oven. "Well, he's going to find out just how wrong he is. Somehow he blocked me from getting that building. I don't know how or why he did it, but the building is suddenly no longer available. And he just *happened* to show up the day I was looking at it. I knew something fishy was going on. He was trying to be all nice, talking about how much he respects me. How he wanted us to work together . . ."

"Landris, I know you're upset and disappointed, but I'm sure we're going to find a place to start a congregation," said Johnnie Mae. "The church is inside us, so it doesn't matter about the building. Wherever we are, the church is."

"It's not about the building. That place was in bad shape. It was going to cost about $300,000 just to fix it up. But it would have been a great place to begin. And to think that man stood there and looked me in my face . . ." Pastor Landris grabbed a plate out of the cabinet and set it on the counter, "knowing that place was under his control. Johnnie Mae, he was actually acting like he wanted to adopt me as his spiritual son so he could pass *his* church on to me. *His* church."

Johnnie Mae could see Pastor Landris was getting madder and madder. "Landris, just tell the realtor to keep looking. And if we can't find what we're looking for soon, we can begin services here in our home if we have to."

Pastor Landris stopped and stared at her. "You don't get this, do you? This man who calls himself a preacher is making a mockery of God—and he believes people are stupid. I see right through him. I'm sure other people can, too."

"I don't think people like Reverend Knight believe people are actually stupid," Johnnie Mae said. She put water in the copper kettle and turned on the gas stove. "They may just believe nothing will really happen to them. You know, like Adam and Eve did in the Garden of Eden. When God told them they would surely die if they ate from or even touched The Tree of the Knowledge of Good and Evil. But the serpent told Eve they wouldn't *surely* die. He then told her they would be as gods, knowing good and evil."

"Does this have any relevance to what I'm trying to say here?" Pastor Landris flopped down on the bench at the kitchen table.

Johnnie Mae smiled; at least she was getting him to calm down a little. "Eve knew from Adam what God said. They both knew God really existed because He walked and talked with them in the garden. Can you imagine the intimacy they shared with God Almighty at that level?" She smiled at the thought of it. "To be able to spend that kind of time and have that kind of a relationship with the Lord? Everything you could possibly need or want, God having already provided it . . . in advance. They didn't lack for food, because they had more than enough. Adam and Eve knew the good. They just never knew what bad was. Think about it—they couldn't have had a clue."

"Since you're bringing this up," Pastor Landris said, "you know what I've always found fascinating about Genesis 3:6? Adam was right there with Eve when she took the fruit off the tree."

Johnnie Mae pulled out the Bible they kept on the bottom shelf of the bookcase in the kitchen and turned to Genesis 3:6. She smiled. Landris never ceased to amaze her when it came down to recalling where a scripture was in the Bible. He rarely got a scripture reference wrong.

"'And when the woman saw that the tree was good for food,'" she read aloud, "'and that it was pleasant to the eyes, and a tree to be desired to make one wise, she took of the fruit thereof, and did eat, and gave also unto *her husband with her*; and he did eat.'" Johnnie Mae set the opened Bible down on the counter when she finished.

The kettle began to whistle. She turned it off and placed a tea bag inside each of the two coffee mugs. She poured hot water into each cup.

"Before they ate from the tree," Pastor Landris said, "they were naked and everything was good. Out of all the things God declared was good and very good, there was one thing he said that wasn't. In Genesis 2:18, God said, 'It is not good that the man should be alone.' I used to ponder about that tree. What was so special about it? Why did God put it there in the first place? Theologians have their own thoughts and opinions, but I don't necessarily buy what other people tell me. My thoughts are that God could have placed that tree anywhere else He wanted to, but He didn't. He placed the tree right there in the garden with them. I've come up with what I believe about that."

"You know, I would ask some of these same questions when I was growing up in the church, but no one ever wants to address them." Johnnie Mae set a cup of green tea in front of Pastor Landris and sat down with her own cup in her hand. She blew a ripple over the top of the tea to cool it. "People try to guide you away from asking any hard questions they either don't know the answers to or don't want to face. They merely avoid it by saying—"

"You shouldn't question God," Pastor Landris said, finishing her sentence as he watched her carefully take a sip from her cup.

"Exactly. So what's your take on it, Pastor?"

Pastor Landris smiled. "Oh, you're good. You think you're slick, too, don't you? I was talking about Reverend Knight and you have somehow managed to steer this whole conversation in a totally different direction. You are *good*."

She smiled back. "So is this your way of avoiding my question, Pastor Landris? Is that why you're trying to change the discussion back to Reverend Knight here? You do know what they say—if you can't stand the heat? You know . . . when things like the question I'm waiting for you to answer get too hot?"

Pastor Landris rubbed his chin and leaned in closer toward his wife as he teasingly leered at her. Raising his cup, he took a gulp of tea, and said, "You mean if you can't stand the hot water, you must not be tea?"

Johnnie Mae practically sprayed Pastor Landris with some of the tea she had just placed in her mouth as a laugh forced its way out. She grabbed a paper towel and wiped his shirt off, then dabbed at her mouth. "No," she said, not believing he'd just said that. "I was saying if you can't stand the heat, you need to get out of the kitchen. You're such a nut."

"Watch it, now. Be careful how you talk about God's anointed ones."

"*You'd* better be careful. I'm just as anointed as you are. Do you want to explain 'the hot water, then you must not be tea' quip you just made?"

"The tea changes the hot water to become more of what it is. So if you can't stand the heat, get out of the hot water. Too many people are like carrots going from being hard to soft while others are like eggs going from being soft to hard. But few are like tea bags that actually embrace the hot water in order to one, become all it's meant to be; and two, integrate its essence into what was first thought to be an adversity, only to change, enhance, and affect its immediate surroundings entirely. Which brings me back to Reverend Knight."

Johnnie Mae started clapping. "Before you go back to Reverend Knight, I'm still waiting on my answer. Why did God put The Tree of the Knowledge of Good and Evil in the garden, making it so easy for Adam and Eve to eat from it?"

Pastor Landris bit down on his bottom lip as he tried not to laugh at how cute she looked waiting for him to answer her. "That's a pretty simple one, my dear Johnnie Mae. You see, I figure it like this: God is omnipotent, omnipresent, and omniscient. Which means, in a nutshell, nothing has happened in the past or will happen in the present or future that God doesn't know about. Nothing. Which also must mean God would have had to know they would eat from the tree. Right?" Pastor Landris looked intensely at her as he moved in even closer.

"Careful, Pastor. You don't want to say something and find yourself in hot water."

"First, Peter 1:19-20 says, 'But with the precious blood of Christ, as of a lamb without blemish and without spot. Who verily was *foreordained before* the foundation of the world, but was manifest in these last times for you.' Hebrews 4:3, 'For we which have believed do enter into rest, as he said, As I have sworn in my wrath, if they shall enter into my rest: although the works *were finished* from the *foundation* of the world.' Please note that the words 'foreordained before,' 'were finished,' and 'foundation' are all my emphasis. And lastly . . ."

"How do you do that?" Johnnie Mae asked before he could finish. "How *do* you recall scriptures like you do?"

"And lastly," he said, smiling, not allowing her to derail him, "Revelation 13:8 says, and I quote, 'And all that dwell upon the earth shall worship him, whose names are not written in the book of life of the *Lamb slain from the foundation* of the world.' Verse 9, 'If any man have an ear, let him hear.' You see? *Before* the foundation and *from* the foundation, the Lamb was already slain! A very important fact, very important." He sighed. "Now that I've laid *my* foundation, please ask your question again. Go on. Ask it." Elbows on the table, he propped his chin on his fists.

She smiled and shook her head. "Why did God put The Tree of the Knowledge of Good and Evil in the garden, making it so easy for them to eat from it?"

"How did Princess Rose learn what was okay to do and not do when she was a toddler?" Princess Rose, Johnnie Mae's daughter, had recently turned three years old.

"We would tell her 'no' or 'stop' but mostly 'no' when she was doing something she shouldn't."

"Did you ever tell her not to do something before she did it?"

"Yes. Okay; I see where you're headed with this."

"And did she do it anyway?"

"Yes." She grinned and shook her head. "Can you possibly speed this along?"

"Okay. You told her not to do something, but as a baby she most likely didn't quite understand completely. After she did it, she learned what wrong was and the consequences that followed it." Pastor Landris leaned back in the seat and took a swallow of his tea. "Saying *not* to do something makes some people think more about doing it."

"I get it," Johnnie Mae said.

"So if you think about Adam and Eve, they really didn't

know what evil, death, or disobedience was because all they had ever experienced was good. They didn't know what bad or evil was, let alone what to 'surely die' meant. Prior to their act, nothing had ever been killed or died. It was only after they disobeyed God and ate from the tree that they became acquainted with *the knowledge* of good and evil." He drank the rest of his tea.

"They had broken fellowship with the only Father either of them had," Pastor Landris continued. "Think about it. That is death. They were literally banished from the Garden of Eden. Another loss. They discovered they were naked, then tried hiding themselves. God had to kill an animal to cover them—a blood sacrifice in order to cover sin. Being naked hadn't been a problem for them before, yet it was afterward." He looked at her and grinned. "Now, can we get back to Reverend Knight?"

"Okay, but I have just one more question for you that's generally off limits. At least, for any of the preachers I've tried asking in the past." Johnnie Mae took a cluster of grapes out of the refrigerator, washed them, placed them in a glass bowl, and set them on the table. Plucking off a few, she offered them to Landris. "This won't take but a minute. I promise. Then you can get back to Reverend Knight and whatever else."

"Go ahead," Pastor Landris said as he popped a big, black, seedless grape into his mouth.

"Where did evil come from?"

Pastor Landris thought for a minute. "I know you're expecting me to say, from Satan."

"If I get an answer, that's usually the answer I get." Johnnie Mae pulled a grape off the stem and took a bite. "According to what we were just saying, there was a tree in the Garden of Eden called The Tree of the Knowledge of Good and Evil. God put it there. My question is: Where did evil come from for there to even be the knowledge of it? We know Satan was once a top angel—beautiful, with jewels and the most melodious singing voice ever created."

"So you're saying Satan was the choir director?" Pastor Landris teased.

"Don't even go there," Johnnie Mae said, knowing full well the battle Pastor Landris had fought in the past with the choir director at Wings of Grace Faith Ministry Church. The choir director wanted to sing every song that came out as gospel, and Pastor Landris didn't believe some songs—old or new—fulfilled the requirements of gospel. Some were down-right depressing, playing mostly to emotions, and Pastor Landris just wasn't having those under his pastoral leader-ship. If a song didn't have a true gospel message, Pastor Landris refused to promote it at all.

"Okay, Johnnie Mae, back to your question." He knew his wife was only trying to keep his mind off what Reverend Knight had done by asking these questions, at least until he'd calmed down a little more. "Satan decided he wanted to re-volt against God and ended up getting himself and one-third of the angels thrown out of heaven. That's described, using Lucifer as the name, in Isaiah 14:12-14."

The phone rang. Johnnie Mae got up and checked the caller ID. Pastor Landris continued. "Now I don't exactly know how you're going to receive this but . . ." He saw John-nie Mae frown.

"This is Reverend Knight," she said, almost in a whisper as though Reverend Knight could actually hear her.

He waved the call away. "Let it go to voice mail."

"Landris, that's not right." As much as she wanted to di-vert his attention from Reverend Knight, she knew it was wrong for him not to answer the call.

"What's not right? I really don't want to talk to him." The phone rang a fourth time. It would automatically go to voice mail after the sixth ring.

"Hello," Johnnie Mae said, catching it on the fifth ring. "Yes, hold on." Johnnie Mae pressed the Mute button and walked the cordless phone over to her husband.

"I don't want to talk to him," Pastor Landris said, having

seen her press the button to mute their conversation. "What can he say to me at this point? I don't trust him, Johnnie Mae."

"Talk to him anyway. See what he wants. You've not talked with him since that building was taken off the market. Landris, you know what's the right thing to do here," Johnnie Mae said. "Be ye holy, Pastor. You know what's right."

"Yeah, I know. But knowing doesn't always make it easy—even for preachers." He took the phone.

"Pastor Landris speaking."

Johnnie Mae turned off the toaster oven, took out the crab cakes, put them on the plate Pastor Landris had taken out, and placed them in front of him. She walked out of the room, praying this conversation would settle some things for her husband so he would be able to do what he needed to do.

If nothing else, he needed peace about this in his own heart.

Cha

*I have been young, and now
not seen the righteous forsake.
begging bread.*

(Ps

"Pastor Landris, this is Reverend Knight. How are you?"

"Wonderful. And yourself?"

"Making it, or as my congregation loves saying every Sunday, 'Blessed of the Lord and highly favored!' " He cleared his throat, loudly in Pastor Landris's ear.

Pastor Landris pulled the phone away and looked at it while shaking his head in disbelief at the man's rudeness.

Reverend Knight continued. "I'm sure you're wondering what has prompted my call."

"It crossed my mind."

"Well, I was wondering if I might be able to interest you in lunch—on me, of course."

"And what would be the occasion? Celebrating my losing out on securing a building I was trying to get, maybe?"

"Oh, I can see you don't pull any punches. I like that in a man, and even more so in a preacher. You know, we've gotten so sanctimonious these days, we don't always say what's on our minds. That only leads to unnecessary speculation." Reverend Knight cleared his throat again. "Forgive me for the noise in my throat. I've almost used it up preaching for the Lord. You know, that's the way I want to go out," he said, as though he was preaching a sermon and coming to the

a second. "Listen, Doc, I want to get to-
you. Lunch, dinner, whatever you want. I just
have a real sit-down talk with you. I have an offer I'd
like to propose, and I don't care to discuss it over the phone.
So what do you say?"

"If I said I wasn't interested—"

"At least sit down with me and hear what I have to say. If
you're not interested, then you're the kind of man who will
flat-out tell me. But only a fool will turn down something
without knowing what he's turning down."

Pastor Landris only heard the word "fool," and that didn't
sit too well. "What if I want to think about it first?"

"Think about what? I'm asking you out to eat and talk—
I'm not proposing marriage. Besides, you're not my type!"
Reverend Knight laughed out loud at his own joke.

Pastor Landris was silent.

"Come on, Doc. Let's you and me sit down and break
bread together. You and me. We can talk and get to know each
other better. Who knows, you might find I have something
you're interested in. How's noon tomorrow looking for you?"

Pastor Landris already knew the whole day was open for
him. "Let me get back to you," he said.

"Sure, sure. Talk it over with the missus and get her okay."
Reverend Knight laughed again. "From more than forty-
eight years of marital experience, believe me, you don't want
to mess up there."

Pastor Landris decided not to even dignify that with a
comment. "What's your phone number?"

Reverend Knight gave him his number. "I look forward to
hearing from you shortly," he said. "Now don't keep me
waiting too long. You wouldn't want the cloud to move without you."

They hung up. Pastor Landris stared at the phone before
placing it back in its base.

He went to find Johnnie Mae. She was in the den folding
towels. A woman named Ms. Bertha came three times a week

to clean the house, but Johnnie Mae enjoyed folding towels fresh out of the dryer so much, she did that task herself.

"He wants to have lunch tomorrow," Pastor Landris said, watching Johnnie Mae smooth out and line up the plush, combed-cotton towel before triple-folding it.

"Wear something a little more casual than usual."

"Who said I was going?"

"You. He wants to have lunch and talk. I'm sure you want to hear what he has to say. Knowing you like I do, I'm sure you're planning to confront him. Instead of driving yourself crazy about what he may or may not be up to, call him back right now and tell him you'll meet him tomorrow. Regardless of what he ends up saying, you'll know for sure and have peace of mind."

"So what's on your mind?" he said, looking closer at her troubled, unsmiling face.

"Nothing."

He got up, squatted down in front of her, grabbed both her hands, and looked into her eyes. "Johnnie Mae, what's wrong?"

She released the towel and looked back at him. "I called over to check on my mother while you were on the other line talking with Reverend Knight. She's having a bad day today. Really bad. It's getting so hard. With Rachel home visiting, I now have Rachel, Marie, *and* Donald ganging up and badgering me about my decision to let Mama stay in her own house instead of putting her somewhere. But Mama doesn't want to leave her home yet. She loves her house . . . she loves her community. That's her comfort zone. How can I make her leave that?"

"I know. I just don't get why they won't trust your judgment. Your mother did—that's why she put you in charge of her affairs."

"Rachel spent the night at Mama's house this past week, and she says Mama gets up in the middle of the night and wanders around the house. She said Mama could leave the house and no one would know where she's gone. It's unsafe not knowing what her state of mind might be when she's wandering around unattended."

"I guess none of you would have known this otherwise," Landris said.

"No. We thought Mama just went to sleep and stayed asleep until one of us stopped by in the mornings to check in with her. Rachel asked me how I'd feel if something terrible were to happen to our mother just because I refuse to move her to a home. She says I'm being stubborn and reckless. I know she's the oldest and all, but I didn't ask for any of this."

"Stubborn and reckless—is that what she said?"

"Yes. And it hurts. I'm trying to do what I think is right. Landris," Johnnie Mae had tears in her eyes, "I don't know what to do. I know putting Mama in a nursing facility might seem like the right thing to do to them, but I can't manage to get something out of my head Mama said when we were little."

Pastor Landris moved the almost-empty clothes basket and sat next to her. He placed his arm gently around her. "What did she say?"

"That no matter what, we had better not *ever* put her in an old folks' home."

Landris pulled her in tighter, rubbing her upper arm. "I'm sure she didn't mean that."

"Oh, she meant it. Back then, she definitely meant it. Mama's brother had their mother put in a home. Here was this vibrant, active, alert woman, and Uncle Rusty had her put in a nursing home because he didn't want to be bothered. When we were little and Mama would talk about the awful things that happened to her mother while she was in that place, how rapidly her mother declined, she always told us we had better not ever send her to one of those places. She didn't care how bad she got—one of us ought to love her enough to fight for her and even take her in if we had to." Johnnie Mae laid her head on Pastor Landris's shoulder.

"You know, all that your mother said back then was before anybody knew anything about Alzheimer's. She didn't know what was coming, and how it would affect her."

"I know, but she thinks she's fine. Fifty-percent of the time she's her normal self. If we tried to put her in an assisted-living place or nursing home, she'd feel betrayed. I just know she would. Even now, she thinks all we want to do is put her away and take what's left of her money."

"Yeah, I know. She told me last week when I was over there that Rachel was only coming home to try and steal her money out of the bank. She asked me to take her to the bank so she could get it out and hide it. She accused Donald of taking things out of her house and thinking she doesn't know it. She said she's not crazy. She knows when things are missing." He stopped to see how Johnnie Mae was taking all of this. She seemed to be handling it okay, so he continued.

"She thinks Marie is the really sneaky one because she acts like she cares so much about your mother, when all Marie ever talks about is your mother going to a home just so she can commandeer her house. Your mother feels Marie is merely pretending to care about her. I tried to tell her all of you really do care about her. So naturally, now she thinks I'm part of the conspiracy."

"And me?" Johnnie Mae knew Landris was trying to spare her feelings. "What did she have to say about me?"

Pastor Landris looked at her. He knew he couldn't lie to Johnnie Mae, not even to protect her feelings. "She said you don't care anything about her. All you care about is that baby of yours, whose name she couldn't remember, and that jack-legged preacher you married. I guess that would be me." He tucked his wife's side-bang behind her ear. "She thinks most preachers are crooks and your smooth-talking husband needs church money, so she has to be careful around 'those two holy rollers.'"

Johnnie Mae cried silently as Landris held her close.

"I'm sorry you had to hear Mama saying all of that. I know it can't be easy for you to tell me this, either, but I need to know what she's thinking." Johnnie Mae dabbed her eyes with one of the hand towels. "And Christian? What did she say about my brother Christian? Did she mention him at all?"

"Oddly, she thinks Christian purposely stays in the army so he won't have to be bothered with her. She doubts if something were to happen to her that he would even take the time to come home and see about her."

"Wow, you certainly received an earful." Dabbing at her eyes some more, she tried to control her sniffles, then grabbed up the remaining four towels and began to fold them.

"Johnnie Mae, don't be hard on yourself. When your mother came back to herself again, which was about thirty minutes following her rant about all of you, she had the most wonderful things to say about each of you."

Johnnie Mae began to cry again. "Why is this happening to her? Why *my* mother?" She sat back and began to rock slightly. Pastor Landris pulled her close to him again and held her still. Johnnie Mae sat straight up. "I have to find a sitter for Mama, at least during the night. And that's that. The sooner, the better."

"Excuse me, Johnnie." It was Ms. Bertha. She was a tall woman, six-feet-one, and a few years younger than Johnnie Mae's mother. "I was coming to get the towels to put them away before I left for the day. I didn't mean to eavesdrop on your conversation just now, but did I overhear you saying something about needing a sitter for your mother?"

Johnnie Mae smiled and wiped her face completely, hoping to erase any visible signs of her distress. "Yes, Ms. Bertha. Do you happen to know anyone who might be interested and would be really good? I don't need anything major done for Mama, at least not at this point."

Ms. Bertha slowly placed her hand over her heart. "Yes, ma'am, I believe I do. In fact, I have the perfect someone in mind." She released a huge grin. "Me."

"You?"

"Yes, Johnnie. All my kids are grown and gone. There

ain't nobody left but me. It gets lonely being at a house by yourself," Ms. Bertha said. "So staying at your mama's wouldn't be a hardship on me. And you know I love your mama . . . I love me some Countess Gates. Truthfully, it wouldn't even be a job to stay there with her. I don't come here to your house but three times a week, so it wouldn't be too much on me to do both. I'm a light sleeper, so keeping an eye on her wouldn't be a problem a'tall."

"Ms. Bertha, I can't ask you to do this. I'm sure you don't want to be confined to sitting around during your off time. What about the bowling league and the other things you do with the people at your church? No, but I truly appreciate your offer—"

"Johnnie, you need a sitter. And I could use the extra cash. To be honest, I was thinking about looking for more work to supplement my income. Things keep going sky-high these days. It's getting harder and harder for us old folks to make the ends of our dollars wave at each other from a distance, let alone get close enough to meet."

"You're not old, Ms. Bertha."

"Oh, you're just saying that 'cause you're hot on my trail, seeing as you've hit your forties now," Ms. Bertha said with a chuckle. She was never one to hold back when it came to stating the truth. "I'll be sixty next month. My social security won't kick in for another two years at best. A woman still has to eat, even though you can probably tell I ain't missed any meals yet."

Ms. Bertha wasn't fat but what one might refer to as thick. She was solid through-and-through, with curves in all the right places topped off by a perfectly shaped, white afro she vowed would never even flirt with a bottle of anybody's dye. She was "all nat-u-rale," as she liked to say, and proud of it.

"It wouldn't be too much on you?" Johnnie Mae stared hard at her. "Ms. Bertha, are you sure about this?"

"Sure as my name is Bertha Ruff. Like I said, your mother was there when I needed someone; now I'd like to do what I can for her. She was the one who sent me to you for this job, which I appreciate more than you'll both ever know. I've worked in plenty of white folks' houses. Most of them now use maid companies to come in and do their cleanings and whatnots. Folks like me used to could count on this kind of work, but now it's become big business. There ain't a lot of places available for many my age." Ms. Bertha gathered the folded towels and began stacking them neatly inside the clothes basket.

"You pay better than anyone else I've ever worked for, but that ain't why I want to do this," Ms. Bertha said. "You know you could have gotten me for a lot less than you did, but you, being your mother's child, can't help but do more than right by people. And God's gonna bless you for that, too. I just know He is. Your mama is so proud of you. And I know I sho' am. We talk about you and all you've accomplished all the time at church. Countess and Jericho Gates did a fine job raising you. A fine job! You've done them proud."

"Well, thank you, Ms. Bertha. Okay, so I need to hire a sitter. And you definitely would be perfect for the job. If you really want it, it's yours."

"Thank you, Johnnie." She clapped her hands once, then picked up the basket of folded towels and started toward the arched entranceway. Turning back, she said, "We can hash out the details later." She winked, gave a quick nod, then left.

Johnnie Mae smiled as she hugged Landris. "Landris, I know everything is going to work out, but this is so much harder than people know."

"Well, I know," Pastor Landris said as he held on to his wife, enjoying every second of their embrace. "And you know God knows. People say that if God allows you to come to it, He's going to bring you through it. We just have to hold on to His hand. He's given us His promise and His Word that He won't let go."

Pastor Landris caressed Johnnie Mae's hands as he brought them, ever so gently, to his lips and lovingly planted them with a kiss.

Chapter 7

*Have we not all one father? hath not one God
created us? why do we deal treacherously every
man against his brother . . .*

(Malachi 2:10)

It was not so cold on Wednesday, that 13th day of February.
Pastor Landris had agreed to meet Reverend Knight for
lunch at a little restaurant on the east side of town famous for
its down-home, country cooking.

"Glad you decided to come," Reverend Knight said. The
two men were being escorted to their table by a tall, young,
reddish-hued woman whose hair, pulled up on top of her
head, swung and bounced like a real pony's tail with every
step, twist, and turn she made.

"Is this okay?" the young woman asked. She stood next
to a booth well away from the kitchen or any other distractions.

"Very good, as always," Reverend Knight said. "Thank
you, Sherry."

The woman blushed after hearing her name and smiled at
Reverend Knight, then Pastor Landris as she placed two tall,
laminated menus on the table.

Pastor Landris started to sit down when Reverend Knight
touched his arm lightly. "Say, Doc. Do you mind if I sit on
that side? It's just a thing with me."

Pastor Landris thought nothing about it and switched to
the other side of the table, his back now turned toward any-

one who might come up to them. "Looks like you're a regular here," Pastor Landris said as he picked up the menu.

"I like this place. It's family owned and operated." Reverend Knight placed his cell phone on the table. "A woman named Sophie started all of this. She passed her tried-and-true recipes down, and now her children and grandchildren run it almost the same way she did. Although I have come to the conclusion that good cooking is more than just knowing all the right ingredients. I can tell a slight difference in the taste from when Sophie was running things and now. Maybe it's all the health-conscious changes—banning hog jowls, ham hocks, fatback, and the like. But this is still the best soul food place you'll find anywhere around these parts." He leaned in and watched Pastor Landris scan the menu. "See anything you're interested in?"

"Everything looks good."

"Get whatever your heart desires. As I've said, this is on me."

"Any suggestions?"

"The seafood section is always great. You'll get your choice of three vegetables with every entrée. The slaw, with its special sauce, will have you begging for your own bottle to take home, which is why they had to start selling it. Now me, I lean toward the fried food section, but my doctor's been getting onto me about that. High cholesterol and Type II diabetes mumbo-jumbo—just the devil trying to steal my joy. My doctor says I need to eat more broiled and baked foods and lay off the grease. He doesn't know our people were raised on grease. I have to catch myself to keep from licking every one of my ten fingers. Grease virtually runs through our veins."

"He probably knows that, but we now know grease is not good for our health. You know what they say: when you know better you should do better," Pastor Landris said.

"Then I suppose you don't want to hear me suggest you

try the fried macaroni and cheese." He laughed. "It's to *die* for."

"Really? Well, I believe in life, so I may give that one a try and say it's to *live* for."

"I'd like to get some myself," Reverend Knight said. "But if I do, there goes my doing better right out the door before I even get started." He sat back, his attention vacillating from Pastor Landris to various people as they walked in. He acknowledged them with a slight wave or a quick nod.

Sherry came back and took their orders. "I'll be back shortly with your appetizers," she said with a smile.

"So," Pastor Landris began, "what did you want to talk to me about?"

"Direct and to the point." Reverend Knight nodded. "All right. That building you were interested in buying . . . I suppose you've probably figured out I have some vested interest in it."

"Vested, like head of the nonprofit organization that holds the deed to it? Yes, I figured it out, right after I learned it was no longer on the market."

"Tell me, Pastor Landris. Where are you and your family attending church these days now that you've moved to our fine city? I'm sure you must be visiting somewhere while you're in between assignments."

Pastor Landris paused as a plate of six golden brown, golf-ball-shaped items were quietly placed in front of him.

Reverend Knight eyed Pastor Landris's plate as a bowl of clam chowder was being positioned in front of him. "Now I wish I'd gotten some of those instead of listening to you about doing better. They look scrumptious. Even more than usual."

"Would you like me to bring you some, Reverend Knight?" Sherry asked.

"You're welcome to have some of mine," Pastor Landris said.

"If you could bring me a small plate, I think I'll take the good Pastor Landris here up on his offer and liberate him of some of his. This way, I'll be halfway doing better."

"Oh, my," Sherry said. "It really is you! You're Pastor Landris. Oh, my goodness! I knew it. I told one of my co-workers back there that you looked just like that Pastor Landris who used to come on television all the time. Dreadlocks and all! She said I was tripping. Wait until she finds out it really is you. You here visiting?"

"No—actually, I just moved here."

"You . . . are . . . kidding me! You actually moved from Atlanta to Birmingham? That's awesome. Are you the pastor of a church yet?" She was giving her full attention to Pastor Landris.

Reverend Knight looked at her as though he couldn't believe he was having to wait to get the plate he'd just requested.

"I'm working on starting a church congregation. But no, I'm not a pastor here as yet."

"Well, if I have my way," Reverend Knight said, "he will be soon. I'm trying to convince him to come aboard The Church of Revelation. You've been to our church."

Sherry looked at Reverend Knight and smiled, then turned back to Pastor Landris. "Pastor Landris, I *loved* watching you on television. A few of us wondered what happened to you. There was this other preacher who started coming on in your place. His name escapes me, and truthfully, he really wasn't that good. It didn't surprise me he didn't stay on TV long. Anyway, if I were to give you my name, address, and phone number, would you please let me know when you begin holding services? I know so many people who would love to come hear you." Sherry wrote her information down, tore off the sheet from her ordering pad, and handed it to him.

"I'll let you know," Pastor Landris said as he folded the paper and stuck it inside his jacket pocket.

Reverend Knight cleared his throat. Sherry looked at him. "My plate?" he said.

"Oh, I'm so sorry. I'll get that for you right now. Sorry." She left and came back in minutes.

"Enjoy," she said, her attention mainly directed at Pastor Landris. "It was so nice meeting you." She flashed a warm smile at them both, even though her last comment only applied to Pastor Landris.

"Same here," Pastor Landris said.

"See, that's what I'm talking about," Reverend Knight said after she was out of earshot. "Better not let your wife find that phone number on you." He shook his head and smiled. "Smooth," he said. "May we say grace now?" He bowed his head and prayed.

Looking back up at Pastor Landris, Reverend Knight took his fork and rolled two of the golden brown, fried macaroni and cheese balls onto his plate. "Mmm-mmm. These look divine!"

"Yes, they do," Pastor Landris said, slicing one of the four left on his plate with his fork. He placed it in his mouth. "You're right about this—they are good."

"Okay. Now, back to my question: where are you and your family attending church these days?"

"We have fellowshipped at my wife's home church in Edgewater. And we've popped in and popped out of a few other churches."

"But not mine?"

Pastor Landris placed another bite in his mouth and savored the warm cheese and macaroni alongside the fried, crusty taste of the crisp outside. "No, not yours."

"I extended a personal invitation to you in December as soon as you arrived. I thought you would come. Then I saw you last month and invited you."

"And you made me a proposition that I politely turned down."

"True. But you were also interested in that building I happen to be in control of. Have you located another place yet to get started with your church?" Reverend Knight ate a spoonful of his clam chowder. He shoved it away from him. "This is cold." He looked around for their waitress. When he got her attention, he beckoned for her.

"Yes?"

"Could you bring me some fresh, hot soup? This is cold."

She looked from him to the bowl of chowder. "Sure. I'm sorry about that." Sherry picked up the bowl—it was still hot.

Reverend Knight wiped his mouth with his white linen napkin and looked at Pastor Landris, still awaiting an answer. "A place—have you found one yet?"

"Not that it's really any of your concern—"

"Or business. You can go on and say it." Reverend Knight ate some more of the fried macaroni and cheese.

Pastor Landris couldn't help but smile at this man. "I'm still looking."

"What are your plans if you don't find a suitable place soon?"

"Careful, Reverend Knight —you might start to sound like you really care."

Reverend Knight ate his last bite. "You doubt that I do?"

"The thought has occurred to me a few times, especially after I learned my almost done-deal became a none-deal at your hand."

"Again. What are your plans?" His new bowl of chowder arrived. He tasted it and nodded his approval. Sherry smiled and left.

Pastor Landris finished off the last of his fried macaroni and cheese. He wiped his mouth. "Who knows? Since quite a few people are interested in me getting started, I might just begin in my home. I'm sure you're aware that's where the early churches in the Bible began—inside people's homes. There's no shame in that."

Reverend Knight began shaking his head. "Please don't do that. You have too much of a reputation to allow that to get around town. I can see the headlines now: *The Great, Magnificent, and Anointed Pastor George Landris, Reduced to Holding Church Services Inside His Home.*"

"Nothing embarrassing about it to me. As long as people are hearing the Word of God and getting saved, what difference does it make where a service takes place?"

Their entrees arrived. "Whoa, Nellie," Reverend Knight said as he watched both plates being placed before them. "I always forget how much food they give you here."

"Can I get you gentlemen anything else?" Sherry asked.

"What was I saying?" Reverend Knight said, ignoring her. His cell phone began to buzz and vibrate on the table. "Oh, yeah—I can't let you go out like that."

Pastor Landris smiled at Sherry and said, "We're fine. Thank you." He turned his attention back to Reverend Knight. "You can't let me go out like what?"

"Look, Doc, I like you. I like you a lot. I have more respect for you than you'll ever know. Why would you put yourself through things when you don't have to? I was even thinking maybe we could become something like preach-partners. We could take that building you were looking at, fix it up just like you envisioned, and it could become an extension of The Church of Revelation.

"One church; two locations: Westside and Eastside. You could be responsible for the East while I continue to lead the West." He tried to gauge Pastor Landris's face to see whether he should continue; his face gave up nothing. "So what are your thoughts?"

"I'm honored you think so much of me that you'd be willing to do that . . . but, it's not what God has told me to do."

"Okay, two weeks ago you told me you had received a better offer. I respected that, especially when it appears I was beat out by God. Arms are too short to box there. Maybe God is somehow in this, though—you and I meeting like we did in the first place had to be ordered by the Lord, don't you think? Let me ask you—do you still want the building?"

"I liked it and thought it would work for what I need short-term. But if I don't get it, I'm sure God will send something along as good or better."

"Well, here's my offer: the building—it's yours."

Pastor Landris sat back against the seat. "What's the catch? It's mine if what?"

"It's yours . . . if you want it."

"At the same price I offered originally that you—or should I say, your nonprofit organization—accepted before it was taken off the market?"

Reverend Knight shook his head. "No."

"I thought not." Pastor Landris leaned in. "So how much is it going to set me back?"

Reverend Knight tore off a piece of yeast bread. "I'm not interested in your money."

Pastor Landris looked at him and began a fake chuckle. "Yeah, okay. So what are you looking for in exchange—my soul? To agree to come on board with you, regardless of what I want to do? Oh, I know . . . we can pretend I'm in charge; meanwhile, you'll be the puppet master pulling my strings."

Reverend Knight leaned back and shook his head slowly. He turned down the sides of his mouth in a smirk. "No . . . strings . . . attached." He placed both hands on the table. "Nothing in my hands." He then turned them over, both palms showing.

Pastor Landris sat back and cocked his head to the side. "You must really believe I'm the most gullible person you've ever run across. First, you show up at a building I just happen to be checking out. I'm curious—how did you know I was there?"

"The realtor called and told me someone was going to look at it. Naturally, she was excited. We had been aggressively encouraging them, if you will, to hurry and secure a buyer. I don't own that building alone, just in case you're wondering."

"Okay, so she calls and lets you know someone is going to look at it. Did you know it was me when you happened to show up?"

He gave a short laugh. "Of course I knew. You don't honestly think I would waste my time showing up for just any old body, do you? Please." He placed a forkful of grilled salmon in his mouth, followed by a bite of heavily sprinkled, pepper-sauced collard greens. He closed his eyes, savoring the taste, and said, "Your food is getting cold, Pastor." His eyes opened. "At least eat while you grill me."

Pastor Landris dipped his jumbo shrimp into cocktail sauce and stuck it in his mouth. He chewed slowly. "So you specifically showed up to meet me?"

"If the mountain won't come to the sea, then the sea must come to the mountain. I believed you'd visit my church when you first hit our city. You didn't. Even though I had my secretary send you a personal invitation on my official stationery, there was no response. Not a peep." His cell phone buzzed.

"I've acknowledged I received it."

"So I figured it was divine intervention when the realtor called to inform me that this pastor was looking for a building to either buy or lease, and he was interested in ours. When I happened to ask who this fine minister might be, she, of course, blurted out your name—not even realizing who you were. She couldn't know that a building that size would only contain you, for what? A year? Maybe. She's so used to regular folks trying to figure out how they're going to make their payments. She had no idea that if you chose to buy the place, you most likely would be handing her a cashier's check for the entire amount without a mortgage."

"Who said I have that kind of cash to be dropping on a building?"

"You were buying a ten million dollar radio station. Cash, from what I heard."

Pastor Landris paused. "How do you know about the radio station?"

"I know about a lot of things—including the fact that the deal fell through, and that you're having a little trouble getting your cash back." He reached down and picked up his cell phone. "Pardon me. Someone appears desperate to speak with me."

He answered the phone, talking in code as far as Pastor Landris was concerned.

"Sorry for the interruption," Reverend Knight said when he finished. "Looks like I have to cut lunch short. I have a preacher friend who may be having a heart attack. He's one of those faithful friends. You know, the ones that start out with you and stay until the very end. I need to see him." Reverend Knight took a few rushed bites as he beckoned for Sherry.

"Yes," Sherry said, seeing his plate practically empty. "You two ready for dessert?"

"Duty calls, my dear," Reverend Knight said as he pulled out cash and handed it to her. "This should cover our meal as well as dessert, should the good pastor here decide he'd like to indulge himself." He looked at Pastor Landris, then Sherry, and grinned. "The rest is for your tip, madam, and for the fine way which you have served us today." Sherry was then summoned to another table.

"Pastor Landris, I highly recommend the peach cobbler," he said. "I'm somewhat of a cobbler connoisseur. And I've yet to find any that can touch this establishment's cobbler, including my own mother's—God rest her sweet soul—who was a champion cobbler cook, hands down."

He stepped into the aisle and slipped on his overcoat. "Doc, if you want the building, let me know. You have my number. It'll be available for as long as you want it at no charge. Think about it. Pray about it. Talk it over, but get back to me one way or the other. The sooner, it would seem to me, the better—for you." He placed his hat on his head.

"However, if you choose to pass on my offer," Reverend Knight said, "there are others right now who have—out of nowhere, it seems—lined up to purchase it. Two other groups must have heard you were looking at it. Now they want it and are willing to pay our asking price. I enjoyed lunch, I truly did. Maybe you and I can do this again soon."

"Thank you," Pastor Landris said. "And thanks for lunch. I'll be in touch."

Reverend Knight patted Pastor Landris twice on his shoulder as he left. He acknowledged various people as he made his usual showboat exit.

Chapter 8

Order my steps in thy word: and let not any iniquity have dominion over me.

(Psalm 119:133)

When Pastor Landris walked into her office, Johnnie Mae was working on the computer but actually waiting for him to get back from his meeting with Reverend Knight.

She looked him in the face to be sure she saw every expression. "So, what happened?" she asked. "Don't keep me in suspense."

"He offered me the building."

"How much does he want for it now?"

"He said he wants nothing."

"What?"

Pastor Landris took a deep breath. "He offered me the building. He wants to give it to me to use for as long as I want. Reverend Knight . . . the organization . . . whoever is doing this, wants to give me the building for nothing."

"Wait a minute. You're telling me he wants to let you have that building for free?"

"That's what he said—nothing. But he did try again to get me to come on staff with him." He told her about the Eastside/Westside congregation idea.

"I sincerely hope you turned him down," Johnnie Mae said.

"You know I did. I just don't get him, though." He shook

his head. "I haven't quite figured him out. On one hand, he seems to want me to join him. But on the other, it appears he's trying to set me up. For what, I'm not sure." He sat down.

"He knew about the radio deal."

"Who?" She threw him a hard frown. "Reverend Knight?" Her voice cracked.

"Yes."

"How?"

"I don't know how. I was just about to find out when he was conveniently interrupted by an emergency phone call. There's just something about him I don't get. But he wants me to pray about his offer. He said, 'No strings attached.'"

"You and I both know what's probably going to happen," Johnnie Mae said, shaking her head. She turned to her computer and clicked the Save button to make sure her last entry wouldn't be lost. "Okay. So he wants to let you use the building with nothing legal to protect your interest. Yet, you're supposed to sink $200 to $300,000 into something you really won't have any rights to afterward? Something that can be taken away at will? Nope."

"My sentiments exactly. But he's a preacher. So why should I question his integrity? If we acquired that building right now, it would still take two to three months to fix it up. We might be able to get one area completed enough to begin services in a month. The crew could possibly work on the rest without disturbing us. I don't know. Could this really be God at work? I'm just not sure what to do at this point. But he wants an answer from me pretty quickly." Pastor Landris sat back down in the chair.

"Then you know what? We need to kneel down right here, right now, and seek God's guidance and direction. Landris, you don't have to do anything until you hear from Him. I don't care what or who's pressuring you. When you don't know what to do, it's best not to do anything until you get clear direction about it."

Pastor Landris nodded and reached out his hand for Johnnie Mae to come to him. She walked around her desk, and they knelt down together beside the chair he'd been sitting in. As they held hands, Pastor Landris began to pray.

"Dear Lord, I come to You, not leaning to my own understanding, but acknowledging You in all my ways. Direct my path, O Lord. Order my steps. You've told me to wait on You and to keep Your way. In Psalm 37:34, You say if I do this, You'll exalt me to inherit the land. Lord, you know the hearts and motives of everyone walking on the face of this earth. I lift Reverend Knight up to you right now. I admit—I'm not sure whether he's for me or against me. Protect me as I do Your will. Not my will, but Your will be done. I'm committed to go where You tell me to go, to do what You tell me to do, to say what You tell me to say. Oh, that You would bless me indeed, and enlarge my territory. Let Your hand be with me, and keep me from evil, that nothing may cause pain. You've told me to wait on You; I'm waiting. You've told me you would supply my every need. You know what I'm in need of right now.

"Lord, we need a place for the ministry *You* sent me here to begin. You have begun a good work in me. I realize the enemy will use others to try to hinder or stop the work. It's up to us to keep pressing. Psalm 91:11-12 assures me that You will give Your angels charge over me, to keep me in all my ways. These angels will bear me up to ensure I don't even dash my foot against a stone. You say in Psalm 91:15 that we can call on You and You will answer, that You will be with us in trouble, You will deliver us, and honor us. Speak to me, Lord. Tell me what You desire me to do. This I pray and thank You in the name of Jesus. Amen."

"Amen," Johnnie Mae said. "Hallelujah, Lord. Thank You, Jesus. Thank You, Jesus for answering this prayer. We thank You that it's already done."

"It's already done," Pastor Landris chimed in with praise.

"Thank You, Lord. Thank You, Father, that You hear me always."

"Thank You, Jesus for being our advocate . . . for interceding for us as You sit on the right hand of our Father . . . forever interceding on our behalf," Johnnie Mae said in agreement with her husband. "Thank You for saving us. Thank You that You've already made a way. Right now, it's *already* done. Hallelujah to Your name."

"It's already done, in Jesus' name," Pastor Landris said as he realized that was his Word from the Lord. "It's already done."

Chapter 9

And when they saw him afar off, even before he came near unto them, they conspired against him to slay him.

(Genesis 37:18)

"Poppa Knight, how did it go?" a tall, slender man with hair cut low to his head asked as soon as Reverend Knight sat down in the recliner in the great room.

Five preachers were in attendance: Reverend Marshall Walker, Reverend Perry Grant, Reverend Moses Beam, Reverend Theodore Simpson, and Reverend Paul Knight.

"I think it went quite well. From the look on his face when I left him at the restaurant, he's seriously thinking about my offer," Reverend Knight said. He picked up a pastry from the platter—cream cheese with a pineapple filling. "Are these fresh?" he asked, poking it before taking a bite.

"Yeah, they've just been sitting out a while. We've been here waiting on you for over two hours now," said Reverend Beam, who was almost as round around the waist as he was tall. He picked up a pastry with raspberry filling and consumed it in three bites. "Taste fresh to me."

"So you left him wondering a little, you think?" the tall Reverend Walker asked.

"Your plan executed to perfection, Reverend Walker," Reverend Knight said as he looked straight in the eyes of his good friend Marshall. They'd known each other since elementary school and had been cut-buddies since middle school.

Reverend Walker had always been the brains of their group of five. Or, at least, that's what they let him believe. He was the one who devised this plan after learning Pastor Landris was pursuing the purchase of a building their organization owned.

The five took this information as a sign from God for them to put a halt to Pastor Landris's efforts before he got started. It was Reverend Walker's idea to send Reverend Knight. He made Reverend Knight believe it was his, since on paper, this was his organization. It was his place, by right, to take the lead in the matter.

"What about when the phone call came in of our dear preacher's heart ailment?"

"I think he was frustrated at the timing, Reverend Walker. Especially since I'd just dropped the bombshell about my knowledge of his defunct radio station deal. You called back just before he could get any answers to his questions," Reverend Knight said.

"That's how we planned it. I would call twice, back-to-back, as your signal to begin. At some point, you would bring up the radio deal. I'd call back repeatedly until you answered." Reverend Walker clapped his hands once with sheer delight. "And *voila!*"

"So what did he say? Come on, Poppa Knight," Reverend Beam said, "hurry up and tell us everything that happened. You know we've been sitting here waiting patiently. We were almost 'having a heart attack.'" Reverend Beam laughed as did the others.

"I'm certain two things are on his mind—the offer of the building for nothing for as long as he wants, and my knowledge of something I'm sure he believed no one knew about. Also, that it was a $10 million deal, and that the deal had fallen through, jeopardizing, or at least restricting, his cash flow." Reverend Knight looked at Reverend Grant. "Are you sure you didn't have anything to do with this fiasco?"

"Not a thing," Reverend Grant said, holding his hands up

as if to show he wasn't hiding anything. "You know that other group of businessmen I hang out with from time to time who are into all sorts of dealings? Well, they were the ones who told me about it. They thought it was too bad for the good reverend, but that's what happens when you don't do your own deals while playing with the big boys. You don't rely on others to handle important business. Pastor Landris never should have trusted his brother with something like that if it was out of his league. Word in the circle is, Pastor Landris's brother is bad business."

"So what exactly did happen with the radio station?" asked Reverend Simpson, the preacher with the thick, bushy eyebrows and mustache.

"Pastor Landris was about to buy that station over on the FM channel. The one that plays a variety of R&B and stuff," Reverend Grant said.

"You know . . . that stuff we pretend we don't listen to anymore," Reverend Beam added. They all laughed.

"There was something about him putting up $10 million dollars—cash—for it. But Sammie, that's the guy who was handling the deal for Pastor Landris's brother, does more than a few shady things alongside his legitimate dealings. All that caught up with the dude, and now everything in Sammie's possession has been frozen, including Pastor Landris's money. He can't get his ten mill back, which, from what I hear, he wasn't going to get back, anyway. It was this or nothing. Sammie has a reputation for playing with paper money and not the real tender after he pockets your cash," Reverend Grant said.

"You mean he matches up things people want and swaps those things like it's cash? Sort of like pyramid schemes people pay to get into?" Reverend Simpson asked.

"Exactly. And you know the scheme is fine if you get in at the right time. But if you're the last person coming in, you're usually the one left holding the bag."

"An empty bag," Reverend Beam said.

"And it looks like that's what happened here. That shady dude had access to the radio station sell. He didn't have Pastor Landris's money anymore, but if he could unload the radio station brought to him where they were asking for only $4 million when it was valued at $10 million, it would be like pulling $6 million out of nowhere. Paper money," Reverend Grant said. "The shady dude didn't count on having his operation shut down suddenly like it was. So in truth, he no longer had the cash—even if he wanted to—to refund to Pastor Landris or the cash to pay the radio station folks to complete the deal. The radio folks were desperate by the time they found out what was up. They ended up contacting one of my business friends about either buying the station or finding them a quick and reliable buyer."

"So who ended up buying the station?" Reverend Knight asked.

"A conglomerate that pretty much buys radio stations in trouble at a premium. So things worked out for all concerned," Reverend Grant said.

"All concerned except good old Pastor Landris," Reverend Walker said with a grin. "So Pastor Landris's money is tied up, and it appears he must not have much left to work with. Because if he did, he would buy some land and build a really nice sanctuary instead of trying to buy that run-down building of ours."

"Seems he has enough to pay $300,000 to fix it up," Reverend Knight said. "I did tell him I knew a guy who could do it for $200,000."

"Why would you tell him that?" Reverend Walker asked.

"Because I do know someone."

"Then you should have told him you know someone who could do it for $275,000, and we could have added the difference to our nonprofit fund," Reverend Simpson said.

"Let's get back to the building for now. Do you think he's going to take you up on your offer to let him use the building for nothing?" Reverend Walker asked.

Reverend Knight shrugged. "I don't know. He's sharp, that I do know. And he knows something is up. I told him to pray about it. I emphasized that there were no strings attached," Reverend Knight said. He didn't mention anything about his other offer to Pastor Landris to hook up with him. If Pastor Landris had already agreed to do that, this conversation wouldn't even be taking place right now.

"So we're really going to just give him the building?" Reverend Beam asked. "'Cause if we're just giving it away, I could use one. Y'all know we're leasing a storefront, and our congregation has been praying mightily for God to bless us with our own place. This would truly be an answered prayer."

"Do you have $200,000 to fix it up?" Reverend Walker asked, knowing the answer.

"No, but the bank might loan it to us now."

"Please. You can't get a loan for $100,000 to build new. You just need to stay where you are and see if you can't get that tired congregation of yours to add more than the six families that have attended since the church's inception some ten years ago," Reverend Walker said. "Exactly how many people do attend your services on Sundays?"

"About seventy-five . . . more or less. And two new families joined recently."

"More? Who are you fooling?" Reverend Walker said. "Most times it's less. I've never been there when it was more than fifty people. Maybe on a program day, you pull in seventy-five." Reverend Walker shook his head. "When you celebrate your pastor's anniversary and invite all of us here who have a good following, that's the only time you ever see more than seventy-five folks."

"Let's try to stay focused," Reverend Simpson said. "The fact is, we need to put a stop to these mega churches. There's that fellow talking about building a city of deliverance called 'Sought Out' or something like that. Then there's another guy with plans to build a city on the other side of town, only with a shopping center. All of them are getting on television trying to act like they're big shots. I'll have you know, I knew every single one of them back when. Back when they were broke."

"All they're trying to do is get more people to come to their churches," Reverend Beam said. "People want to feel like they're somebody, and these churches allow them to become a member of 'the club.' With more bodies in their pews, they can build bigger buildings while the rest of us are left struggling for people and money to survive." He looked at Reverend Knight and Reverend Walker, who both had a substantial number of members. "I'm not talking about you, Poppa Knight or Reverend Walker. I know what you two are about. You're doing God's work for sure. But too many of these folks are getting out of hand. Somebody needs to stop them; somebody's got to take a stand."

"Now, here comes Pastor Landris. Already been on national television, unlike some of these wannabe, little shots around here. Do you have any idea what will happen if he sets up shop—hangs his shingle out, stating he's open for business? We're all sunk! Sunk! That man has charisma. He's anointed," Reverend Grant said. "I used to watch him all the time on television before he went off the air. In fact, I've preached more than a few of his sermons, word for word. Of all places, he *would* decide to move here."

"This area can only support so many large churches," Reverend Simpson said. "I just have a feeling if Pastor Landris gets things rolling, he's going to put a lot of us slap out of business. I'm talking slap out, and that includes Reverend Walker and Poppa Knight."

Reverend Knight started shaking his head. "This is kind of sad, y'all. We're sitting here talking about a fellow preach-brother as though we were some gang members defending our territory. 'He's going to put a lot of us slap out of business'? Reverend Simpson, what's that all about? We're acting like he's the enemy. He's telling people about the Lord. He's bringing people to Christ. Isn't that the business we're all supposed to be in?"

Reverend Walker squared his body in front of Reverend Knight. "What's up with you? Sounds to me like you're starting to like this fellow. You backing out? Having a change of heart? If you are, let us know, and we'll be glad to let you out before you get in too deep."

"Out of what?" Reverend Grant asked. "Out of the group, or out of our plan?"

Reverend Walker looked hard at Reverend Knight. "That's entirely up to Poppa Knight here. Ain't that right, *Doc*?"

Reverend Knight looked back at him and stood up. "I know you're not stepping to my face with all that noise. I would suggest you take a few steps back and calm yourself down." He waited on Reverend Walker to do as he had just suggested.

Reverend Walker snickered a little and took two deliberate steps back. "Better?"

"Better," Reverend Knight said and sat back down. "Now listen to me. All of you. We are not thugs. Pastor Landris is still our brother in the Lord, regardless of what any of us think here. When I made that offer to him to give him that building at no charge, I meant it with sincerity. We are not about lying like that. After I spoke with him that first day, I admit, I did see something special in that young, dreadlocks-wearing preacher—"

"Don't tell us you're bonding with him and would like him to become a part of our group?" Reverend Grant said.

"I'm merely stating that what I said to him today, I mean for us to keep our word on. If he comes back and tells me he wants the building, I want to give it to him just like I said I would. He will be putting his own funds into fixing the place up. He can use it for as long as he wants—"

"Within a reasonable time limit," Reverend Simpson said. "We decided no more than five years."

"Five years, with a clause allowing us to rescind it at any time at our discretion with written notification, three months in advance," Reverend Walker said. "We've already decided and agreed that will be a nonnegotiable stipulation of his contract."

"Yes, Reverend Walker. Five years with an anytime out-clause for us," Reverend Grant said.

"The point is, I believe Pastor Landris is going to find the building's location is not the best place to ask people to come. He's not going to have that many people driving way out there to attend anybody's church—including his," Reverend Walker said. "More importantly, we'll still own the building. If Pastor Landris takes Poppa Knight up on this offer, he'll sink some big money into fixing it up, which will only increase the value of the building for later use. Better still, if we see things are getting too out of hand too soon, we can shut him down within three months. There's nothing worse than having a large congregation with nowhere permanent to fellowship. That'll scatter sheep pretty quickly." He smiled.

"So all we have to do now is to wait and see what Pastor Landris decides?" Reverend Beam said, looking from one preacher to the other. "Then go from there."

"I don't think it's going to take long, do you, Poppa Knight?" Reverend Walker looked at his friend. "And if you don't hear from him soon, I'm sure you'll follow up and impress upon him how this truly is a legitimate offer he'd be foolish to turn down."

"I'll do what I have to do," Reverend Knight said. "I told him to pray about it—we'll see which direction he takes."

Reverend Walker clapped his hands again. "Wonderful! Well, gentlemen, shall *we* pray?"

Three of the five picked up a dried-out pastry and nodded before taking a bite. They bowed their heads, sitting in their respective places, as Reverend Walker led them in a long and fervent prayer.

Chapter 10

Preserve me, O God: for in thee do I put my trust.

(Psalm 16:1)

Johnnie Mae and Pastor Landris had a long discussion about having more children. It was 2002, and Princess Rose would be four in December. Pastor Landris had no children of his own, and Johnnie Mae would be celebrating her forty-second birthday in August. Until she actually thought about the number 42, she believed she had plenty of time to adjust to being newly married before deciding whether or not she should have a baby.

In 1998, she'd become a mother when she hadn't expected to, then had become an author signed with a major publisher, coping with uncompromising deadlines. Two years following this, her husband died. On September 8, 2001, she became a wife again, marrying a man she'd been good friends with who ushered her into the position of a pastor's wife. Three days after their wedding, 9/11 happened, and she and Pastor Landris returned to Atlanta, only to learn he was officially being terminated as the pastor of a congregation he'd helped build and loved dearly. Now the couple was living in Birmingham.

She didn't even want to think about all that had happened with Sarah Fleming, Lena Patterson, and Theresa Jordan—or Asheville, North Carolina, and Montgomery Powell II. One of the good things that had come out of her two Asheville visits was her having met Pearl Black and her sweet great-granddaughter Angela Gabriel. Ironically, Angel, as everybody called her, ended up moving to Birmingham.

Angel had called Johnnie Mae a few days before Christmas in December 2001.

"Johnnie Mae, this is Angel. I'm so glad you're home." Her voice sounded shaky.

"Angel, what's wrong?"

"Nothing, I suppose. I don't know. You know, I started this new job back in late October working as a manager for this radio station. Rumor has it they're planning to sell it, and I'm not sure where that will leave me. I'm trying to be calm, but the truth is, I left my home and a secure job in Asheville, and I don't know what may happen to me if this rumor is true."

By this time, Johnnie Mae knew that Pastor Landris was the person buying the radio station, but she didn't want to say too much before everything was finalized. Johnnie Mae also knew that no one could predict with certainty how it would turn out in the end.

"Angel, do me a favor and don't worry about it, okay? God is still in control, no matter what might be happening in our lives, even when things look bad."

"I know. But sometimes things don't work out the way we feel they ought to, and bad things *do* happen to God's people. I know I don't have to tell *you* that. Just look at what happened with Pastor Landris and that church in Atlanta," Angel said.

"Yes, but you have to take an honest look at what happened. What Satan means for bad, God will use for good. Granted, Pastor Landris lost his position in Atlanta, and now he has moved to Birmingham. But see how God had His hand in the situation. I still had my house, so we didn't have to find a place to live when we came back here."

"Yeah, that's true."

"And we had no idea the first time you and I met that you would be moving to Birmingham, yet here you are."

She laughed. "Yes, here I am. I can see what happened to Pastor Landris was the reason he moved here. And if he hadn't moved, you wouldn't be here now, and I wouldn't have a soul in Birmingham that feels anything like family."

"See? Now had those seemingly bad things not happened, he and I probably wouldn't be *here*, for sure. So far, that part has turned out to be a good thing, even though it certainly looked and felt bad at the time."

"Is Pastor Landris ready to start a church any time soon? I am attending a church—it's okay as far as churches go, I suppose. But I've listened to a lot of Pastor Landris's tapes, and I really would love to worship under his leadership."

"We're working on it—things are looking good. Pastor Landris has a big project he's trying to complete first," Johnnie Mae said, referring to the radio station deal. "I'm not at liberty to say anything just yet, but I think you'll be excited when you hear about it. I also found a wonderful piece of property as a possible church site. It has 40 acres, and another 150 surrounding it that could become available to us. Pastor Landris has these grand ideas of where God wants him to go with this ministry. Besides the worship center, there will be a life center, activity center, drama theater, school, college, credit union, and other things I'm sure I've failed to mention. Not that Pastor Landris wants any glory— to God be the glory. It'll be a way to minister to God's people covering every area of their lives, spiritually, physically, socially, and financially," Johnnie Mae said with excitement.

"In fact," she continued, "Pastor Landris and I are waiting to hear back from the owners today regarding the cost of the land."

"I'll put in a prayer that things work out," Angel said. "Okay. So I'm not going to worry. It's like you often say: 'If you're going to pray, don't worry; and if you're going to worry, then don't pray.'"

"There you go. Use your energies elsewhere."

"Yeah, like doing a great job for this company so regardless of who comes in and takes over, they'll want to keep me on."

"That's the spirit—you're going to be fine. I'm sure the new owners, if that turns out to be the case, are going to be wowed by you. You're a lovely young person, with a good head on your shoulders. You have innovative ideas that could take their radio station to a whole new level."

Angel laughed. "I'm always encouraged and inspired after I finish talking with you. Always. I hate to bother you, knowing how hectic your schedule is, but I love our conversations."

Johnnie Mae smiled. "Don't ever feel bad about calling. I adored your great-grandmother, and I love you. I'll be your honorary aunt, and that means if you need to talk, ask my advice, or anything else for that matter, you can pick up the phone. Just remember what I told you: God is in control. We don't have to fret about what's going on around us because, ultimately, God is going to handle whatever comes down, good or bad. If it's good, praise the Lord. If it appears bad, praise Him even more. Praise Him for who He is: God Himself."

"You'd better quit—you're going to cause us to have church over the phone in a few moments," Angel said. "You've really gotten me fired up. I'll let you go so I can get my praise going before I start looking for something for dinner."

When Johnnie Mae hung up, she began to think about what she'd said to Angel. Words seemed to flow out of her, words she felt were intended to minister to her as well as Angel.

Words she would need a few weeks later to help her through all that Pastor Landris would find himself having to deal with: a failed radio deal and $10 million in legal limbo for who knew how long.

Words Johnnie Mae would repeat to her own spirit when Pastor Landris would locate a building to start a church, only to have it taken off the market completely without warning or cause. Now Reverend Knight had made a proposal regarding the building. If God told Pastor Landris to move forward and take it, but things turned out badly, would that mean Pastor Landris hadn't really heard from God? Would it mean he'd heard wrong? Or, would it mean that all of this was part of God's plan?

Maybe God had spoken to Reverend Knight, but could he go against God's instructions and do what he wanted? Would that mean this was still part of God's plan?

These were the questions Johnnie Mae watched her husband wrestle with.

Pastor Landris hadn't heard from God yet. Reverend Knight was calling him almost daily to get his answer. Regardless of Reverend Knight's true motive, Pastor Landris didn't want to miss hearing from God. He'd become almost paralyzed as he waited to hear a Word from God on this. Just one Word.

"Listen, Pastor Landris," Reverend Knight said after two weeks of relentless calling. "The others want me to move on this, one way or the other. We wanted to do this for you because God was leading us to. But if you don't have an answer by the end of the week, the committee has decided we're going in a different direction. I really wanted you to have the building. I just don't know what else to say or do to convince you of that."

"Well, Reverend Knight. You know what they say—you can't hurry God. I'm waiting on Him. So if He doesn't speak to me by your deadline, I suppose we'll both have our answers."

Chapter 11

Where no counsel is, the people fall: but in the multitude of counselors there is safety.

(Proverbs 11:14)

Johnnie Mae sat down. She had worked hard getting things ready for the first meeting they would have together as a possible congregation. About fifteen people met at their home to discuss what the next steps would be.

"Thank you all for coming out on this Saturday afternoon," Pastor Landris said. "Many of you have inquired as to when we would start a church. Well, this constitutes our first move. I know it's already March. Truthfully, I thought we'd be further along by this time, but things haven't quite worked out the way I would have liked. Before we begin anything, let's bow our heads for a word of prayer."

Everybody's head went down as Pastor Landris prayed.

"Let me again thank you for your interest in what God has called me and my wife to do. I realize this is my calling . . . and you don't have to be a part of it."

"Except my calling seems to be part of what God is calling you to do," Thomas said. "It appears I'm not the only one, based on the people assembled here today." He glanced around the room, nodding at Angel, an elderly couple named Watts, a young woman named Sherry Mason, and Sapphire. There were people from Johnnie Mae's family—her mother, younger brother Donald, sister Marie and her husband Phillip, and two of her friends, Honey and Sister, and about five other people who had come with Sherry.

Even though the radio deal was a complete bust, and he didn't have a job, Thomas was feeling somewhat all right about things. Pastor Landris had given him $10,000 to tide him over while he searched for a job.

It had been almost six weeks now, and he hadn't found anything that suited him. The money Pastor Landris had given him was almost gone, but he had faith things were going to work out. Unfortunately, Sapphire was starting to get on his nerves. She had too much to say about how he was handling his personal business.

"Thomas, you're spending a lot of money these days," Sapphire had said a few nights ago when she was at his apartment. She knew she had to be careful, or she would push him completely away. "Maybe you should slow down. Wait on buying things like genuine alligator shoes," she said.

"Will you chill, please," he said. "I know what I'm doing. These shoes go well with this new suit I just bought."

"That's what I mean. Look how much you're spending. You're still looking for a job, and maybe throwing money away like this is a mistake."

"Do you want to know what I believe was a mistake? Letting you know any of my business. Look, I know what I'm doing. I need to look sharp for job interviews, so consider my new outfits as investments in me." He took the latest suit he'd bought and went to hang it back up in his bedroom closet. "It's not like I've asked you for anything," he said, his voice fading as he left.

"That was a low blow, Thomas," Sapphire said as soon as he came back in the room. "I never said you were asking me for anything. I'm worried about you. Your thinking lately is just not logical."

"So I'm crazy now? Is that what you're saying?" He loosened his Joseph Abboud burgundy silk tie.

"No, that's not what I'm saying, either. It's just your be-havior lately has caused me some concern. You have sudden mood swings," Sapphire said as she waited for him to sit down beside her on the couch.

"Mood swings? Is that what you call them?" Thomas sat next to her. "My world came crashing down around me, Sap-phire. I'm entitled to be a bit moody."

"Thomas, I'm not talking about being moody. One minute you can be so up and happy, you're jumping around like you own the world; the next minute, you're totally on the floor. You're also extremely paranoid. That's what I'm talking about. When you and I went to dinner last week, you kept acting like someone was following you."

"How do you know I wasn't being followed?" He looked sternly in her face. "Do you have any idea how many people are after me? Sapphire, the government has spies watching me, and they're listening in on my telephone conversations. I don't want to even think about the number of folks Sammie may have on his payroll who want to keep me quiet, should I be called to testify against him at a possible trial."

"Sammie?"

"Yes. Sammie, the guy who messed up George's invest-ments. I know he's trying to set me up to take the fall for this. I just know it. I'll tell you what you do. The next time we're out, watch what people say and how they treat me. You'll see that people are put in strategic places to keep an eye on every move I make." He turned his body squarely to-ward her; one of his black leather, wing-tip Prada boots touched the side of her shoe. "Like when we were at the restaurant the other night. That lady behind the counter han-dling the vegetables—did you happen to hear what she said when we walked up?"

"You mean the little old lady with the shiny gray hair? She didn't say anything."

"See, that shows how much you pay attention. When we

came up, she looked dead in my face and said, 'It's good to see you out.' She wanted me to know I was being watched." Thomas waited for Sapphire's reaction.

"Thomas, that was nothing. She was only being polite."

"No, she wasn't. She knows you and I haven't gone out much because of my money situation. That was her way of letting me know that *they* knew I hadn't been getting out. Don't you see? That's why she said it was good to see me *out*. She wanted me to know."

Sapphire touched his arm. "Thomas, have you ever heard of bipolar disorder?"

"Nope. Never heard of it. What is it?"

"It's a condition of the mind, so to speak. It's a type of mental disorder that can be treated quite effectively with proper therapy and medication. You're exhibiting many of the signs—"

Thomas snatched his arm out of her touch. "You *are* trying to imply I'm crazy!"

"No, Thomas. That's not it at all. Bipolar disorder is a malfunction in the way your thoughts are processed—a disconnect of sorts. Being bipolar causes you to think things are okay and that you're acting normal when you're really not."

Sapphire took his hand. "You're out of control. As fast as you get money, it's gone. And most times you don't have anything to show for it. That's not normal behavior. That's a symptom of being bipolar. Most logical people—"

"You mean people who aren't crazy like me?" He stood up and started pacing. "I don't believe you have the nerve to come in my home and say this kind of junk to me! Someone you claim you love and want to spend your life with!"

Sapphire stood in front of him. "I'm not calling you crazy, Thomas. And it's not fair to put words in my mouth. There are so many people with this disorder. And that's exactly what it is—a disorder. I'm not saying this is what's wrong with you. You need a total evaluation."

"Oh yeah. I get it now. I guess that's why you wanted to

be with me—I was just a head case for you. What is it, Sapphire? You don't have enough patients, so you thought you'd mess around in my head?" He went to the hall closet and got her coat. "Well, guess what. It's not going to work. You're not my therapist. There's nothing wrong with me—"

"You have trouble sleeping through the night. You write constantly—you're writing practically nonstop. Those are some of the symptoms of people who are bipolar."

"I have trouble sleeping because I have a lot on my mind. You'd have trouble sleeping, too, if you'd messed up the kind of money I've messed up of my brother's. You'd write all the time, too, if you were trying to figure out a way to make some much-needed money." He handed the off-white wool coat to her. "I don't need this from you, Sapphire. I thought you were the one person I could count on to always be on my side."

"Thomas, I am on your side. That's why I'm trying to help you."

His eyes began to widen suddenly as he nodded. "You're in on this, aren't you? Yeah. Yeah. Well, don't be spreading your lies about me to my family and friends, trying to discredit me. Oh, yeah, you're in on it."

"In on what?"

He started nodding his head even faster as he picked her purse up off the floor and handed it to her. "Yeah, I see clearly now. It's late, Sapphire. Time for you to go. I have a lot of work I need to finish."

"Thomas, hear me out—"

"Good night, Sapphire. We'll talk later. You can see yourself out." He turned around and walked toward the kitchen.

Sapphire stood there and watched him walk away. His mind was deteriorating even faster than she'd originally suspected. She needed to talk with someone and get him some help before it was too late. But who? And did she have a right? Would he view it as a betrayal, especially if she turned out to be wrong?

* * *

Sapphire glanced back at Thomas as he made his comments about those who were in attendance at the church meeting. Pastor Landris was now saying that the church congregation's name would be Followers of Jesus Faith Worship Center. She couldn't help but wonder why the word "church" was not being included in the church's name. There was something that bothered her about a church that didn't have "church" in its name.

"Any questions . . . comments, so far?" Pastor Landris asked.

Sapphire raised her hand. She noticed Thomas shift his body away from her as soon as he saw her hand go up.

Chapter 12

A man hath joy by the answer of his mouth: and
a word spoken in due season, how good is it!
(Proverbs 15:23)

"Yes, Sapphire? You have a question or comment?"
Pastor Landris said, acknowledging Sapphire's raised
hand.

"Why are you calling it a center instead of a church?"

Thomas crossed his legs and arms and readjusted his
body again. Sapphire noticed his uneasiness. She hated that
he was still feeling so distant to her after their discussion a
few nights ago. She really did love Thomas; she was only trying to help him. She also understood that his bipolar disorder
was the very thing that was keeping him from admitting that
he had a problem.

"Good question," Pastor Landris said. "When people say
'church,' we mostly think of a building. We don't want people to think that the building is our church. The church is us.
Wherever we go, the church should always be there. God
doesn't reside in a building, waiting on us to come. Nor
should the building be a place where we have to invite God
to come in. The Holy Spirit should have come in with you.
God led me to call it a center, because the center of anything is
always the powerhouse. Case in point: my wife does something called Pilates."

A hand went up. It was the wife of the older couple. "Excuse me, what is Pilates?"

"Pilates is sort of an exercise . . . a workout routine where you engage certain muscles most people usually don't work on. Pilates can cause you to become leaner and, some people say, taller." He looked over at Johnnie Mae to see if he was explaining it well. She nodded, reassuring him. "When Sister Landris is doing this particular workout, most times she follows a woman on a DVD who coaches her on what to do and how long she should do it. I have often heard this woman say, 'Squeeze that powerhouse.' Sister Landris has shown me that the powerhouse is around the abdominal area—from the diaphragm to the pelvis. It's called the center."

He looked at various faces. "The principle is: the stronger the powerhouse, the stronger it will help the rest of the body to be. If these core muscles are weak, your body won't work as effectively as it could. This causes the other muscles in the body to pick up the slack. We want this congregation to serve as a center in the body. As we come together, we want to do what we can to strengthen the whole body. As for the words 'Followers of Jesus,' I felt it would best advertise who we are."

"Advertise?" one of the visiting people asked. "I thought this was church. So is this a business or what?"

Pastor Landris smiled and nodded slowly. "In a way, you could say we're a business. We are about our Father's business. You remember when Jesus, at age twelve, was found in the synagogue by his parents. They were upset because they'd left him behind. Jesus told them he had to be about His Father's business. God has given each of us assignments as part of God's business plan. We need to let people know more about the blessings God has for all of us. The words also describe our mission statement, our desire to be Followers of Jesus." Pastor Landris took a swallow of water.

"What did Jesus do when He was here on the earth?" Pastor Landris continued. "What did He instruct His disciples and apostles . . . His followers to do? That should be our question as a body . . . as followers of Jesus. We need to follow Jesus's lead. We must also ensure we're being guided by the Holy Spirit whom Jesus sent to us specifically for this purpose—our Comforter and our Guide."

"So what you're emphasizing is that we are to be followers of Jesus and not you?" Angel said.

"Correct. I'm following Jesus, and as long as I'm following Him, it's okay to follow me. But should I lose my way and go off on something you know is not of Christ and His teachings, then you or anyone else needs to confront me. Don't talk about me; come to me and lay it out with plain talk. If I'm not hearing the gospel truth, and you've taken the next step—gotten together as a group and confronted me—and I'm still wrong, then you need to break away."

People began to nod in agreement.

"I know some preachers who started out with a sincere desire to be, as you said, followers of Jesus," Sherry said. "I could tell they truly meant it when they began. But somewhere, it seems power, money, greed—I don't know exactly what happens, but they change. I question whether some of them even believe in God anymore. The way they carry on, you'd think they couldn't possibly fear or worship God."

"Or it's like they believe that because they're saved, they don't have to work their way to heaven, so if they do something wrong down here, it's okay," a friend of Sherry's said.

Pastor Landris smiled. "Yes, I know. And believe me, I've noted how some ministers can be. I can't speak for any of them. I won't even try to defend them. To be honest, even we ministers have to be careful of some who claim themselves to be called by God. You know the Bible tells us that some will say they are of Christ, but Jesus is going to say He never knew them. There are definitely plenty of wolves lurking out there in sheep's clothing."

"Sheep's clothing nothing," Mr. Watts said. "Many of them are so bold now they're wearing Armani suits."

"Does it bother you that they wear nice suits?" Thomas asked.

"No, I think we as Christians have a right to the best," Mr. Watts said. "Why would Jesus die for us to have life and live more abundantly? Why would the Bible declare blessings for the believers, and yet only Satan's folks get to partake of it? I'm just saying that a lot of preachers are in pulpits, plotting and scheming on how to get folks' money so *they* can have—and have more abundantly, while the rest of us are sitting in the dark because we paid tithes instead of our light bills."

"Many of these preachers have forgotten their first love," Mrs. Watts said in a soft voice. "They are wolves for sure, and they're not even bothering to hide it anymore. But they sure do dress nice, though."

"Okay, we don't want to get too far off the subject," Pastor Landris said. "The other parts to our name are Faith and Worship. I started to leave faith off, but we know that without faith it is impossible to please God. So we want this to be a place where we encourage the building up of faith. We really do want the kind of faith flowing in our congregation that can move mountains. But the core . . . the powerhouse of our mission will be to come together as a body and worship— praise and worship the only wise God. Thus—Followers of Jesus Faith Worship Center."

People started smiling and nodding. "I like it," a young lady said.

"Me, too," said another. The general consensus was affirmative.

"I'm still concerned that people may label this a cult because we don't have the word church in it," a man in his late twenties said.

Pastor Landris walked a few steps back and forth with both hands in his pockets before addressing that comment. "I've considered that. But you know, I can't get caught up in what other people think. Yes, I want everybody to get what we're about. I'm strictly going by the Word of God as well as listening to the Holy Spirit as He leads, teaches, and guides me. That's all I can promise any of you here, and any person who comes later. I realize we have collective bodies that decide, in some organizations, what truth is or is not, what's right or not. But I'll have to give my own account. I'll have to answer to God. I don't want to get to heaven and have a conversation with God about why I was doing what other folks said or thought was right, when He clearly told me what He wanted *me* to do. There is a life to come after we leave this place."

Pastor Landris smiled at the young man and walked back to the front. "We all will have to give an account not only for the things we've done, but the things we didn't do. God has instructed me to call this place of gathering and worship, a center. He may tell others to call theirs a church. Neither is wrong. But if God tells me one thing, but I want to establish my own thing, my own way, He's not going to bless it. I'm on my own, then. Trust me, this is not about me. There are plenty of other things I could be doing with my life, and probably with a lot less stress, headaches, and sad to say, less backstabbing. But this is what God is calling me to do, and I must be about my Father's business according to His instruction, not man's."

"You know, the Bible does ask: What is man that we're mindful of him?" Mrs. Watts said. "My husband and I are older than many of you. Gerald, here," she touched his arm lightly, "is 62, and I'm 60. Many of our friends are not going to be happy if we decide to join this ministry. They'll put us down and probably say we really are following a cult. But if we hook up here, as the young folk say, we're going to be doing what God has told us. The Bible says that obedience is better than sacrifice. We may lose longtime friends, but the Bible tells us that none of us will give up houses, land, family, or friends who won't receive it back a hundredfold and shall inherit everlasting life."

"Matthew 19:29," Pastor Landris said, identifying the scripture reference.

Johnnie Mae couldn't help but smile as she thought to herself: *Walking Bible.*

"And right after that verse it says, 'But many that are first shall be last; and the last shall be first.' We can't get caught up in this kind of stuff," Mr. Watts said. "We really must seek what God is telling our own, individual hearts to do. So can we join now, or do we have to wait?" He took his wife's hand in his.

Pastor Landris had a puzzled look on his face. "Join now?"

"Yes," Mr. Watts said. "This congregation. I know this was a meeting to talk about getting started, and I understand you're still working on securing a building. But personally, I'm content to come right here, if we have to, so why not get going? I know this is y'all's home, and you might not want to open your doors for services. But me and Eleanor here, we'll gladly open the doors to our home if needed. The early churches in the New Testament began in people's homes. There's no dishonor in starting out this way. I just want to start receiving some good Word from you. None of us are getting any younger."

Others began to say, "I'm in!" "Me, too!" "Count me in!"

"Hold up, everyone," Pastor Landris said as he tried to calm the swell of voices. "So you're telling me if we began services in our home, you wouldn't mind coming *here*?" He pointed where he stood. "You really wouldn't mind?"

"Absolutely not!" most of them chorused.

"Look, Pastor Landris," Sapphire said, "I've been privileged to learn from your teaching when you were in Atlanta. I've visited a few churches since my arrival in Birmingham. Please hear my heart: I'm not knocking any church or preacher, but I can't find the kind of soul food you were feeding us. Maybe I'm spoiled. I need the kind of Word that affects my life. I don't need to feel good for a few minutes, only to leave the same way as I came. I would rather come here on Sunday mornings and sit at your feet, than go to a quote-unquote 'church building' and leave unaffected and unfilled. When it gets warmer, we can meet at the park if we have to. Personally, I don't care. Meanwhile, I know God is going to open doors for Followers of Jesus Faith Worship Center."

"A temporary place to get started—that's all this would be," Thomas said. "Because I know God has big plans for you, little brother, and this ministry."

"I second that," Sherry said. "Oops! Sorry, y'all. I must have had a momentary flashback." At her old church, they would always vote on everything with one person making a motion, and another person seconding it.

A few people laughed.

Pastor Landris looked at Johnnie Mae. *Should we begin here this coming Sunday?*

She smiled at him and nodded as though she were reading his mind. "Yes," she mouthed, and continued to nod. "Yes."

Pastor Landris blew her a kiss as they all were rapidly exchanging various thoughts, opinions, and ideas.

"Well, people. For anyone interested, it appears the newly chartered Followers of Jesus Faith Worship Center will have our first service right here tomorrow, Sunday, March 10, at, let's say, 10:30 A.M."

Everybody clapped. It was all set. The first service would be held tomorrow in the house Johnnie Mae built.

Chapter 13

After these things the word of the Lord came unto Abram in a vision, saying, Fear not, Abram: I am thy shield, and thy exceeding great reward.

(Genesis 15:1)

"Do you want a baby?" Johnnie Mae asked. It was August 5, 2002, the day following, coincidentally, her forty-second birthday. "Because if you do, then we probably need to get started."

"Where did that come from?" Pastor Landris asked. They were sitting on the couch in the den, talking about the church building, when she changed the subject.

"It came from me honestly admitting how old I really am, and not the age I think I am in my head."

He frowned. "What? The age you *think* you are?"

"Yes," she said, letting out a sigh. "Somewhere in my mind I really think I'm still seventeen, I still think I'm young and can turn cartwheels and stay up late."

"Well, you are still young. Today's forty-, fifty-, and sixty-year-olds are not like our grandparents' ages."

"Good answer, but let's try to be realistic." She smiled. "I keep thinking I have enough time to do everything, but in reality, I really don't. When we got married, I thought you and I could wait another five years to think about a baby. But that would put me around forty-six. By the time our child turned twenty, I would be sixty-six. And you, you'd be sixty-eight. It's bad enough knowing if we start now I would still be sixty-two . . . sixty-three. Oh, it's depressing when I think that far ahead."

"Then don't think of it like that," Pastor Landris said.

"So what are you saying? You want a baby now?"

"No."

"No, you don't want one?" Johnnie Mae pressed the heels of her palms against her eyes. She quickly lowered her hands.

"No, I mean yes." He grabbed her wrist. "Johnnie Mae, sit down and slow down."

"What? I'm trying to find out where you stand on this." Johnnie Mae sat down and started chewing gently on her bottom lip. "Let's take this one question at a time," she said. "Truthfully, I want to know how you feel about this baby thing."

"Are you pregnant now?" Pastor Landris asked as his eyes drifted quickly toward her abdomen, then back to her eyes. "Is there a chance you might be?"

"No. I'm not, and I don't think I might be. I was just thinking about this gray hair that keeps coming. My hairdresser asked, again," she rolled her eyes, "if I wanted to dye my hair. I don't know. If I dye or streak it, I *would* look years younger."

"And all of this started you on a baby quest?"

"No, it didn't start me on 'a baby quest.' But it got me thinking." Johnnie Mae took a deep breath as he grabbed both her hands and held them tightly inside his. "My hair is turning gray," she said. "Daily. I could dye it, and it would make me look so much younger, and then maybe I wouldn't even be thinking about this baby question at all."

"Okay, J. M.," Pastor Landris said as though he was giving up. He still held onto her hands.

She snatched her hands out of his. "See, whenever you start calling me J. M. I know what you're thinking. I know this seemed to have come out of left field, Landris, but I need to know what your thoughts are about us—you and me—having a baby together. Do you want a child or not? I know you love Princess Rose like she was your own, but I know what it means, for some men, to have their own biological child."

"That's for men who want a child of their own," Pastor Landris said.

"See? See, now that's exactly what I'm talking about." She flung her hands close to his face in a staccato motion as she spoke. "I don't know if you want one or not. We talked about it during our premarital counseling, but your answer seemed to always come back to whatever I want. But I want to know what you want. And I'm not trying to be sweet here. If you don't want a child, and you feel strongly about not having one, especially at this late stage of the game—"

"My, you're making me feel like I have one foot in the grave and the other on a watered slip-n-slide with 'this late stage of the game'!"

"You know what I mean. Just answer the question, will you? Do you want a baby or not? You, Landris. Not what you think I want; do *you* want one? Yes or no?"

"Johnnie Mae . . ."

"Yes or no?"

"Yes," Pastor Landris said. "Yes." He kissed her hand, his voice escalating slightly. "Yes." He kissed her hand twice as his voice escalated a little bit more. "Yes!" he said in a loud, whispery voice, as he kissed her hand three times.

She let out a huge sigh. "You see now?" The tone of her voice was filled with frustration.

He looked at her, confused. "What?"

"What if I'm too old already? What if we've waited too long?"

"You? Too old? Oh, I don't think we're going to have any problems." He kissed her hand again. "In fact, I can almost guarantee this will be an assignment I can't wait to get to work on."

"Boy or girl?"

"Yes."

She purposely rolled her eyes so he would know she was doing it, then stared at him.

"What?" He chuckled. "You said 'boy or girl.' I think that's a great choice to choose between, unless you want to go for twins? That way, we won't have to have this discussion again."

"So you're saying you want two children?" Johnnie Mae asked, pulling her hand out of his.

He slipped off her shoes and began massaging her stockinged feet. "No, I'm not saying that. But if that's what you want, we can go for that, too. Now, are you telling me you want to take care of this with one pregnancy or two?"

"Like you have any say-so about whether we have twins or not," Johnnie Mae said with a tease in her voice.

"Is that a challenge? Are you saying there's no way I, George Landris, a man who has been called by God, can give you, my darling Johnnie Mae, twins?"

"One is enough. At least it's a start." She smiled, then became serious. "Thank you."

"For what?"

"Don't laugh. But seriously, we can get this going. In another month . . . two, tops, we can incorporate our little one in the other plans I'm sure we'll be pursuing full throttle. My due date would be around June . . . July 2003, and I'm sure we'll have to start thinking about the construction of our worship center building by then."

"I see you have this all mapped out."

She put her feet on the floor, reached down and grabbed his, swung them up across her lap, then peeled off his Bruno Magli cognac-colored leather sneakers, and began to return the foot-massage favor. "No, not everything. I still need to know: boy or girl?"

He laughed. "That tickles."

"Oh, really now." She began to truly tickle his feet. "Boy or girl?"

"Stop that," he said as he laughed between clenched teeth. "Stop it! It doesn't matter!" he yelled as he continued to laugh. "As long as the baby is . . . stop that, Johnnie Mae . . . healthy and happy!"

"Everybody says that," Johnnie Mae said, refusing to release his foot as he struggled to get out of her grip. She had stopped tickling him now. "I say a boy."

He was down to a slow giggle at this point. "Do you want a boy?"

Johnnie Mae stopped and looked into his eyes. "Honestly?" she asked as her eyes began to dance with adoration.

"Yes," he said, matching her now more serious tone. "Honestly."

"Honestly, I really don't care whether it's a boy or a girl. As long as, like you said, he or she is healthy and happy, and I'd like to add, knows the Lord the way we do."

Pastor Landris knew, at that moment, his wife meant just that.

Chapter 14

*I will praise thee; for I am fearfully and wonder-
fully made: marvelous are thy works . . .*

(Psalm 139:14)

Pastor Landris didn't know what to do to make her feel
better. After a year of trying, the frustration of not being
able to conceive was weighing heavily on Johnnie Mae's
mind and their relationship. What had definitely begun as a
happy endeavor had, within six months, descended into something more like a large-scale science project.

Johnnie Mae was taking her temperature and using kits to
predict ovulation days. There were constant doctor appoint-
ments for her and threats of possible ones for him, if it became necessary to know which of them had the problem.

Also, by August 2003, the church congregation had finally moved out of their house into a modern sanctuary, ac-
commodating 500 people comfortably. They had been able
to talk with the owners of the land Johnnie Mae found. All
63 members liked the location and the view, which was
breathtaking—almost heavenly. They negotiated to buy 5
acres with first options on purchasing the remaining 35. Pastor Landris had contributed a great deal of his remaining
funds, although the congregation insisted they considered it
a loan since the bank had turned them down for the required
financing. They bought three modular buildings because it

turned out to be the fastest way to get a building up and ready.

They had actually begun working toward getting a building that third Sunday in April 2002. Prior to that, they'd scouted for a building to rent, which didn't work out at all. That was when the suggestion came to reconsider the land Johnnie Mae had found.

Johnnie Mae explained to the congregation how much the entire forty acres cost. Mr. Watts was good friends with a banker—he felt confident the newly formed church could get approved for a loan. But even with Pastor Landris's money, along with the land as potential collateral, the bank turned them down. It was just too much money to risk on an up-and-coming church.

A young man named Brent Underwood came to visit the church the fourth Sunday in July 2002. "I must admit," he said, standing near the couch after services were over, "I almost didn't come. I didn't feel comfortable attending church in a house. Then I drove up and saw your place, which is lovely and large, and I couldn't believe you would actually choose to have services there. I don't know if I would be so open to having strangers in my house like this, even in the name of the Lord."

"We're glad you came anyway," Angel said, giving him a little bump with her shoulder. He was six inches taller than her five feet, three inches, even with her three-inch heels. Angel had invited Brent—they worked together at the radio station. Brent had been brought in to take over the job Angel was hired for, after the sale of the station went through. He had appreciated her attitude toward him—none of this was his fault. His father wanted to keep the business side under their thumbs, so Brent was appointed to manage things. Angel's job quickly became training Brent to do the job she was losing. She was demoted to programming manager.

"I'm thinking of the number of people I know who would

love to come but won't because they'll refuse to set foot inside a church doubling as a home or vice versa," Brent said. "We really need to find a less intimidating place to hold services."

"We, huh?" Pastor Landris said. "Does this mean you're coming on board?"

"Aye-aye, Captain," Brent said as he saluted Pastor Landris. "After that message today, definitely. But I don't just want to join. I have a lot to offer, and I plan to come with my sleeves rolled up, ready to work. The more people hear this Word you're preaching, Pastor Landris, the more they'll walk with God and His blessings," Brent said. "And that's really what church should be all about."

"We've tried to get a facility, but we keep running into roadblocks," Angel said.

"Why don't you rent a storefront if you have to . . . an empty house . . . something like that, then convert it to a church building even if it's just temporarily?" Brent said.

"We thought about that," Mr. Watts chimed in. "It doesn't feel right to any of us. We would really rather put the money into something that will belong to us instead of throwing it away on rent. Our heart's desire is to be good stewards of God's money, no matter what we're doing."

"I personally don't see what the fuss is all about," Thomas said. "It's only money. So we rent a place and fix it up, then leave it in, say, a year or two. What's the big deal? It's better than sitting around talking things to death." He shook his head and started laughing. "You should have taken that building that preacher was going to let you have. I still don't understand your reasons for not going with that deal. I would have taken it, myself."

Sapphire looked at Thomas. She knew he still wasn't getting enough sleep by the dark circles under his eyes. His condition definitely wasn't improving. She and Thomas were talking again as a couple, but he had become more withdrawn. He didn't want to talk about anything that concerned him or his erratic behavior. Not with her. He'd made it clear that his business was his, and not any of his brother's.

Yes, he had bought more things—lots more things. But he was working on starting up a production company now. He needed tools like that expensive video camera he'd purchased on credit that no, he couldn't afford. But it was portable *and* high-definition. So what if it cost a little over $6,000? When he got going with his company, he would make that chump change back in no time. He needed someone to support him and his dreams the way Johnnie Mae supported her husband.

"God is calling me into the television ministry," Thomas said last week when he excitedly showed Sapphire the expensive equipment for his latest endeavor. "There are lots of preachers out there who want to be on TV. With this, I can go out, tape them, and do an all-around professional job. Three good contracts will all but pay for this camera," he'd said.

So Thomas didn't understand what the fuss was about when it came to getting something as simple as a church building. His philosophy seemed to be: *If you have any money at all, spend it while you can, as quickly as you can. Life will take care of itself.*

"We discussed this," Pastor Landris said to Thomas, "and the majority decided the best thing would be to put that kind of money toward something that we owned."

"Have you thought about buying land and building a church?" Brent asked.

"Sure, we found a parcel of forty acres, but the price is astronomical," Angel said.

Brent thought for a second. "Have you checked to see if you can purchase a few of those acres instead of the entire forty at one time?"

"The owners want to sell the whole thing as a package deal," Johnnie Mae said.

"I see. I recall a company exec who once said the exact

same thing to my father. Our company proposed buying a good chunk of that land, and we signed a legally binding agreement with them to purchase the rest at a later date. Of course, the smaller amount of land will likely be a bit higher per acre, but it would get us started."

"You think that will really work?" Pastor Landris asked.

"It's worth a try. I'd be glad to help out—I'm pretty good negotiating deals."

"Pretty good, nothing," Angel said. "I've never seen anyone work miracles like Mr. Brent Underwood here."

Brent turned to Pastor Landris. "Here's my card. I'll be happy to see what we can do. If we can get them to sell a few acres, we could check into buying one or two of those modular buildings. In about a month or two, tops, we could have a church building ready for people to come worship. Large congregations use those buildings a lot. You might be surprised if I named some of them. Trust me— they're not cheesy-looking on the inside at all. And the best part is: you'll own the land and you can either lease or own the buildings. They could be used for future things down the road after a larger sanctuary is finally built on the other acres."

"I love this idea," Pastor Landris said. "You're pretty sharp, Brent."

"Thank you, sir. As I said, I'm sorry I have to run, but I have an appointment. And I detest lateness. Call me, Pastor Landris, and we'll get right on this. By October or November, we could be gathering in our brand-new sanctuary."

But things didn't go so smoothly. The company that owned the land wouldn't budge. It was all or nothing. It took three months of badgering to get them to consider the offer and another month to finally agree. Then there was the infrastructure requirement: water lines, electricity, gas, and roads that had to be developed. Inspectors took longer than Pastor Landris ever believed it would take to approve various steps in the process.

But with prayer, faith, and a lot of hard work, the congregation officially moved into the building the last week of July 2003. And on that first Sunday in August, 150 people came and joined the church. The following week, over 100 more did the same.

Pastor Landris could see that at the rate people were coming, he'd soon have to hold two services. People were steadily streaming in, creating problems Pastor Landris hadn't even begun to plan for. Never did he imagine more than 500 people would be attending services after just a few weeks in a building that could only accommodate 500. He had been fairly certain there would be plenty of time for them to grow into all of this. He was wrong. His reputation from his ministry in Atlanta, as well as having appeared nationwide on television while there, was drawing people more rapidly here.

Suddenly, Pastor Landris realized what a mess this could be if he didn't get a handle on things fairly quickly. He had the original ten people who joined that first Sunday back in March 2002—the Wattses, Sherry, Thomas, Sapphire, Angel, Tarsha, Simone, and Benjamin—Johnnie Mae made ten. During the months coming up to July 2003, membership had grown to a little over sixty.

Fortunately, Pastor Landris had begun various leadership classes, so there was some help amid the influx of people. He had a pretty good idea about who he could really trust out of that core sixty. However, other people were anxious to work in the ministry—he and his staff had to determine the best way to handle this. Pastor Landris immediately hired more staff. Things definitely changed in a hurry.

And so by August, things were going better than anyone expected.

But Johnnie Mae still hadn't conceived. She pretended she was fine, but Pastor Landris could see how this was affecting her. He didn't know if he should tell her it didn't matter to him whether they had a child or not. *Would she take it the wrong way?*

When he saw her spirits lower than he'd ever seen them

before, he decided to talk with her about it. They'd both been tested extensively; there wasn't anything the doctors could find that was keeping Johnnie Mae from conceiving. The doctor explained that stress could have an effect on a woman's ability to conceive, as can her age after forty.

With the marriage, relocating to Birmingham, starting a new church, and her mother's memory problems, Johnnie Mae was definitely stressed.

But in August, a woman visited the church. Johnnie Mae liked her the first day she met the timid woman walking alone, almost too withdrawn to strike up a conversation with anyone. So Johnnie Mae walked up to her and smiled. "Hi, I'm Johnnie Mae."

"Nice to meet you." She shook Johnnie Mae's hand. "My name is Hope Morrell."

"Hope. Are you a first-time visitor?" Johnnie Mae asked as she pointed to the red-colored badge Hope wore, signaling she was visiting for either the first or second time.

"Yes," Hope said with a smile as she dropped her head down, then looked back up. "I heard a tape of the pastor preaching. I had to come find this place, which is really out of character for me. But Pastor Landris is such a powerful speaker, I felt I would be blessed if I came to hear him in person, and I truly was. I've never heard anyone like him before."

"We all enjoy his preaching and teaching." Johnnie Mae watched Hope as she continued to look up at her, then added, "So you enjoyed yourself?"

"Oh," her face lit up and there was such a smile in her eyes, ". . . very much so! From the praise and worship until the final amen. I even took notes, which is also something different for me. I ended up having to write them on the back of my program. I didn't realize I should have brought a notebook. I'll know the next time, though."

"Hope, I have something I would love to give you—if you'd care to have it, that is."

No one had ever offered to give Hope anything for no reason at all. "Sure," she said. She couldn't believe this woman of obvious distinction was taking so much time talking to her and being so nice. People generally treated her like she wasn't there. "Thank you."

"If you'll wait here about five minutes, I'll run real quick and bring it back."

"I'll wait. Thank you again. You're so nice to do this. I'm going to stand over there, out of the way." She pointed toward a corner where there was less traffic. Hope couldn't believe how kind and friendly everybody was. She smiled back as folks nodded her way, waved, or came over and spoke. She felt so at home here.

Johnnie Mae touched her arm. "I'm back," she said, startling Hope. "Oh, I'm sorry. I didn't mean to cause you to jump."

Hope smiled. "It's okay. I'm known for being jumpy and nervous at times. I'm working on getting better, though. And hearing Pastor Landris speaking on all that I am in Christ really has given my confidence a boost. I'm fearfully and wonderfully made," she said. "I am not weak; I'm strong. I'm free—and whom the Son sets free, is free indeed." She let out a controlled giggle.

"Well, here you are," Johnnie Mae said as she handed Hope a purple journal with a raised, gold-foil design on the outside. "This is for you. And yes, Hope, you're all of those things and much more. You're also of a royal priesthood, a child of the Most High King."

As Hope took the journal, she covered her mouth with her hand, then looked into Johnnie Mae's eyes. "This is so beautiful! Thank you," she said as she hugged the journal close to her. "I don't know what to say. Thank you for everything. Really, thank you."

"You're welcome," Johnnie Mae said with a smile. "And Hope, you have a lot going for you. You need to start believing that."

Hope blushed and nodded without saying another word. Her head started to lower again, but she suddenly stopped, and with a certain pride, she held her head up high.

After Johnnie Mae walked away, Hope opened the journal where the purple ribbon marked a page to glance inside. That's when she saw an inscription.

Hope,

You're of a royal priesthood, a true child of the King. Keep your head up! God's blessings to you,

Johnnie Mae Taylor Landris 8/3/2003

Hope had no idea until that moment that she'd been talking not only to the pastor's wife, but to an author whose books she'd seen at the library and in the bookstore. Hope had been made to feel important today. She laughed out loud, did a quick half-spin around on her toes, and with a renewed bounce in her step and a newfound confidence, she headed for the exit.

She would be back. Oh, yes. Whatever it took to get here, Hope was determined—she *would* be back!

Chapter 15

And immediately Jesus stretched forth his hand, and caught him, and said unto him, O thou of little faith, wherefore didst thou doubt?

(Matthew 14:31)

Faith was in a pretty certain place when it came to her feelings about church. A few of her co-workers were always talking about this "walking on the water" Pastor Landris. Daily it was "Pastor Landris said this" and "Pastor Landris said that." She didn't want to hear about it. Then they started giving her tapes all the time of his sermons. To Faith, no pastor was *that* great. There had to be something in his closet, some thorn he was praying to God to remove from his side. She didn't want to go through that ever again.

All her life, many of the men she'd known had pretended to be good and true, but turned out to be wolves in sheep's clothing. Charity's job had taken her to Birmingham and Hope and Faith naturally followed. Faith was merely looking for a fresh start—somewhere new, where nobody knew any of them. Hope didn't like making waves, so she usually went along with whatever Faith and Charity decided. So things had worked out perfectly.

But the last thing Faith was interested in was attending anybody's church. And that included this one with the great and powerful Pastor Landris.

Then Hope happened to listen to one of Pastor Landris's tapes about peace, and she decided to go to the church.

That's when Faith had to see for herself what this man was all about, so she went, too. Pastor Landris was a handsome man—almost took her breath away. His voice was deep and so smooth when he spoke. She understood a little better what was drawing Hope there.

Pastor Landris was more of a teacher-like preacher. For the first time in her life, Faith actually understood what particular scriptures meant in the context in which they were written. She had become fascinated with this seemingly true man of God, though she had a few reservations.

Hope joined Followers of Jesus Faith Worship Center in September 2003.

Chapter 16

*For the perfecting of the saints, for the work of
the ministry, for the edifying of the body of Christ.*
(Ephesians 4:12)

Many people were shocked to learn that becoming a
member of the Followers of Jesus Faith Worship Center didn't require some of the same things as other churches.

"At the church I just left," a woman said to Hope as they sat waiting in the conference room for instructions on what would be required next, "we had to complete a fifteen-week new-member's class before we could even ask to become a member."

"Really?" Hope said.

"Girl, it was a trip. You had to go every week, and if you missed a class, you had to make it up. Making it up would have been all right, I suppose, only it wasn't like several classes were running consecutively. If you got sick or had an emergency, which was what happened with me, you had to wait until a new group was taking that class. When they informed me I would have to complete all my classes before I could receive the right hand of fellowship, I told them it was easier getting into heaven than getting into this church. I've vowed not to speak the name of that church ever again, but I bet if I said their little catch phrase, you'd know the church I'm talking about."

Hope shrugged, wondering if this woman would ever stop

talking long enough to come up for air. "I probably wouldn't know," Hope said. "I don't visit many churches."

"Oh, you wouldn't have had to go there. He's on television—I'm sure you've seen him."

"I doubt it," Hope said, looking back down at her unopened Bible. "I don't watch much TV, either."

"I'm feeling you. I flip through the channels—my old man calls it channel surfing. I happened to have seen that church on TV, and he was begging for money like many of them do these days. And to think folks used to make fun of Reverend Ike back in the day when he was doing what many of them do now. At least with Reverend Ike you got a prayer cloth." She popped her chewing gum. "Anyway, I was flipping through the channels, right? And I heard him say, 'If this program has been a blessing to you, please consider sending your financial support.' Well, I did enjoy his message that day—he can be quite funny. I bet you've heard of him, but I'm not going to say his name or the church's name."

The woman readjusted her body, shifting her weight to her other hip. "Anyway, I went down there, and all the people were being so nice to me and everything. Coming up and speaking, telling me how glad they were I came. Trying to act like they're so loving."

Hope smiled but said nothing as the woman continued.

"It was only after I joined that I found out people don't really care about you. If you're a visitor, they're told to be sure to love on you, but that's just to trick folks. After I didn't wear that visitor's badge anymore, hardly anybody ever looked my way. But now, you let a white person come in the church, and they act like gold has graced the carpet. I'm talking about these folk now. The rest of us had to sit where they made us, which usually meant you filled up the rows as you came in. But when somebody white came—and trust me, I don't have anything against white folk—there's an obvious difference. And the pastor was a black man." She looked to see if Hope was still following her.

"And the camera operators always put the cameras on them so it would look to the TV audience like white folk were in large attendance. That's the other white folks' signal that it's okay to come on down. Of course now, to be fair, those white televangelists do the same thing. They'll find a few black faces in the crowd and spotlight them so folks will think black folks are welcomed. I ain't hating, though. Folks got to do what they got to. And we do need to come together as the body of Christ." She stopped and looked at Hope again. "You don't talk much, do you?"

Hope looked back at her. "No. I suppose I'm just a better listener."

"Well, I'm a good listener, too, I guess, when somebody has something to say. That's why I'm enjoying this church with this pastor." She stopped and looked closer at Hope. "Forgive me, but what's your name?"

"Hope."

"Hope?" she said. "Well, my name is Regina." She reached over and shook Hope's hand. "Anyway, Hope, who knows what we'll have to go through to get into this place. You know Pastor Landris used to come on TV when he was in Atlanta. That's one of the reasons why people are flocking here in droves. He had a mega church. I hear they kicked him to the curb because he believes it's okay for women to preach. I was taught women shouldn't be preachers, and it's hard for me to believe differently. But I love this man's teaching, and he's not hard to look at, either. I'm excited about becoming a member. So Hope, what's your story?"

Pastor Landris walked into the room of about twenty-five people.

"Good afternoon," he said.

Regina nudged Hope. "Look! It's him. Up close and personal," she said with a whisper as she grinned from ear to ear.

"I'm Pastor Landris. I wanted to thank you for your desire to connect with this ministry. Trust me—we don't take your presence today lightly. I won't hold you too long, but we believe in giving information. I don't think you should join anything without knowing what that group believes, as well as its overall vision. Therefore . . ."

"Here it comes," Regina whispered to Hope, who was trying hard to listen to Pastor Landris. "He'll probably say twenty six-week classes."

"We offer a two-hour new member's class to explain our approach and give you an opportunity to ask questions or voice concerns. We've also created a new member's manual that's yours to keep. It provides you with all the information you should need about our long-range plans. You'll find out what we believe as a body, as well as information about staffing and various procedures which, I must admit, are subject to—and will likely—change. Many of the questions you have about Followers of Jesus Faith Worship Center should be addressed in this manual."

A woman began passing out white three-ring binders.

"These manuals are yours to keep. We provide two different opportunities for you to attend the class. There is one on Sunday mornings prior to second service, and one on Wednesday nights when the rest of us are in Bible study. Should either of these times be difficult for you, please let Sherry Mason here know . . ."

Sherry waved her hand as she continued handing out manuals.

". . . and we'll work with you. Our goal is not to make this a burden, but merely to enlighten you." Pastor Landris rolled his shoulders as though he were dumping a load off his back. "En-LIGHT-en you, if you will."

Everybody laughed. There were a few more moments of business discussion before Pastor Landris concluded.

After Pastor Landris left, people were talking among themselves. Regina turned to Hope. "He's a doll. I like him. He's so down to earth, not all full of himself like a lot of these preachers seem to be these days. Can you believe he actually came in here to talk to us himself? Most of them send their first-line lieutenants or an assistant."

"That was nice," Hope said, agreeing.

"Nice, nothing. That was genuine. I can't wait to become a member here. And we don't have to attend but one class for two hours and we're in! How smart and sensitive to others is this? They gave us this book to tell us all we need to know. I'm telling you, Hope, these people have their stuff together. I can tell you now—this church is going to be mega-mega. I'm talking double-mega."

Someone tapped Hope on her shoulder. She turned around.

"Johnnie Mae," Hope said with delight as she stood up and turned toward her.

"We're so excited to have you," Johnnie Mae said as she hugged Hope.

Hope smiled and hugged her back. "Thank you, so much. Thank you."

Johnnie Mae continued working the room, speaking to and hugging each person as she conveyed how glad she was to see them.

Hope started walking out of the room. She looked back at everybody chatting and laughing, then casually strolled out.

Chapter 17

> *These all died in faith, not having received the promises, but having seen them afar off, and were persuaded of them, and embraced them, and confessed that they were strangers and pilgrims on the earth.*
>
> *(Hebrews 11:13)*

"'Through faith we understand that the worlds were framed by the word of God, so that things which are seen were not made of things which do appear.'" Thomas Landris spoke loud and with enormous confidence as he read from his Bible.

Faith rushed in. She was so late. This was her second visit—she wasn't a member, so she wasn't as upset about missing the entire praise and worship segment of the service as those who knew what doing that truly meant.

She hadn't heard Pastor Landris teach on the importance of praise and worship to a service. "Regardless of what we might think we're giving God," Pastor Landris would say, "the only thing we can truly ever give God is praise and worship. Everything else belongs to Him anyway. Yes, you can praise Him in the comfort of your home, and you should. You don't have to be in a building with others for God to receive it. But the sweet aroma of praise that blesses Him when we come together—oh, it's wonderful."

She hadn't heard Pastor Landris say that our attitude matters to God. And even though God knows our hearts, He also knows when we can do better and don't. Pastor Landris would point out when people are consistently late and miss praise and worship service or have the wrong attitude, God sees that. "It's almost like we're saying, 'Here, God! You'd just better be glad I even came or did anything at all. I don't have to do anything, you know.' Do we consider what God really thinks regarding our attitudes?"

But for now, Faith had not heard any of this. She was just pleased she'd gotten there by the time she did.

Faith didn't have a problem with money and the church like some folks. She felt no guilt in letting the collection plate pass her by. So she didn't come late to deliberately miss that portion of the service like she knew some folks were prone to do.

Hope had made her late. They had argued over who would use the vehicle today.

Faith won, but she never stepped out of the house without her makeup and being dressed to bless. So she was late, but she looked good. She could tell that much from the many glances as she strutted in. And had she just been late and sat close to the back, that might have been fine.

Instead, she walked all the way to the front to sit next to Sister Bivens. She knew there was one seat there due to the good sister's tendency to sit her stuff on the chair next to her. Sister Bivens wasn't supposed to do that, but nobody ever challenged her. Faith sauntered right up to the front, stood and waited for Sister Bivens to take her sweet time to move the large purse, along with a notebook she likely never wrote a word in, onto the floor. Faith didn't care how long it took her, but she was sitting in that seat today.

As Faith sat down, she noticed Pastor Landris was not speaking yet. But another man, a bit older than Pastor Landris, was saying something about faith and how God formed the worlds. He was just as good-looking as Pastor Landris, if not more so.

She later learned that he and three other men had been chosen to speak on any topic they desired. This man had chosen to speak on faith and he was reading what he called "The Faith Hall of Fame" to inspire others as he'd been inspired by this list.

"Abel offered a more excellent sacrifice unto God," the man said. "Enoch was translated that he should not see death. Noah prepared an ark and became heir of the righteousness which is by faith. Abraham was called to leave one place to go to another he didn't know. By faith Sara received strength to conceive and had a child when she was well past childbearing age, just because she judged God, who had promised her this, to be faithful. By faith Abraham offered up his only begotten son Isaac, of whom it was said in him his seed would be called. By faith Isaac blessed Jacob and Esau concerning things to come. By faith a dying Jacob, leaning upon the top of his staff, blessed both the sons of Joseph."

Faith listened and read the scriptures this man sometimes only merely paraphrased out of Hebrews Chapter 11.

He had been quite good—almost as impressive as Pastor Landris during the five minutes he spoke. She wasn't sure if he could ever sustain a thirty-to-forty-minute talk, but she had to give him credit for holding her attention for five.

The man sat down next to a tall, dark-skinned woman with long dreadlocks. *Sapphire*. Faith had met her the first time she came to the church. Sapphire had made an effort to seek her out and welcome her, as well as let her know she hoped she'd come again soon. Faith hadn't been so receptive to Sapphire, though. First of all, she wasn't crazy about hair like that on women. *Dreadlocks*. She didn't understand why, in 2003, women especially were still sporting that hairdo. Faith concluded, from the way the two of them sat next to each other, that he and Sapphire must be a couple.

Pastor Landris stood and complimented all five men on a job well done. He called out their names and had them stand. "And last my brother, Thomas Landris, who just recited the list of some of the inductees into 'The Hall of Faith.' I'm a witness—my brother has come a long way. Don't tell me what God can't do."

Thomas Landris, Faith thought. *Good looks, intelligence, a passion for God, and fine taste in wardrobe must run in the family.*

She smiled, and after the service she made a special effort to go speak to Sapphire and Brother Thomas Landris.

"That was an inspiring message," Faith said. "You made me look at faith in a whole new light. It's interesting that you were moved to speak about faith. My name happens to be Faith. And I just happened to get here just in time to catch you." Faith looked at Sapphire and smiled. "I'm sure you must be so proud of your husband."

Sapphire moved a little closer to Thomas's arm. "I am proud of Thomas, but he's not my husband."

"Well, then surely you two must be engaged?"

Sapphire smiled. "No, just dating. Getting to know each other better."

"Sapphire, I just wanted to come say hello to you," Faith said. "You made me feel so welcome when I was here last time."

"So your sister Hope didn't come with you today?" Sapphire asked.

"Oh, no. We had a family situation come up, and one of us had to stay. Unfortunately for her, she lost out this go-round. But I am purchasing today's tape for her. It's the least I can do."

"Please tell her I asked about her, will you? Your sister is so sweet."

"Of course." Faith gave her a quick smile. "Again to you, Brother Thomas, I truly, truly enjoyed your presentation." She shook his hand. "Ta-ta, all. I *hope* to see you both again soon."

Faith couldn't help but laugh at that herself. *I . . . Hope.*

Chapter 18

But I see another law in my members, warring against the law of my mind, and bringing me into captivity to the law of sin which is in my members.

(Romans 7:23)

Hope went to church for three Sundays. Faith could see Hope changing, getting stronger, and beginning to act as though she thought she could keep her in check. Hope would refuse to tell Faith anything when she questioned her. She was coming out of her shell more after each visit. That was when Faith decided to go and investigate what kind of brainwashing cult activity was going on in that place. She was convinced it had to be a mind thing—Hope didn't normally have a lot of confidence and never had she been defiant. She was reading the Bible and writing in a purple journal who she was because of Christ, and what she could walk in and was entitled to as a child of God.

Faith had only attended a few times. In September— shortly after learning Hope had become a member—she decided it was in their best interest for her to also join.

Faith and the others who'd gone to the altar, conveying a desire for church membership, were taken to a conference room. Initially, the group was canvassed to see who needed to go in a separate room to receive salvation first. After that, they were told they'd be given instructions on how to officially become members. Faith was aware some churches were beginning to mirror exclusive social clubs when it came to membership. She couldn't help but wonder whether people had forgotten this was church. Faith could recall when people were grateful anyone even wanted to join the church, let alone make it more difficult to do it. Back then, coming forward was something to shout about. Now there were all kinds of rules and regulations about what someone interested in joining the church had to do. And for most folks, there was no reason to even *think* about being a leader. In order to be in leadership, most churches made it mandatory that leaders tithe. She'd overheard some people talking at work about how the leaders in their church were called in on a regular basis to testify before the pastor whether or not they tithed. If they didn't, they got kicked out of their positions.

The pastor said if they were leaders and weren't leading their people by their own example—going above and beyond—they couldn't be leaders. They were "sat down" until they came up to the standard that he himself was setting by giving beyond the tenth. Most of the people in the church saw this; they knew what was going on (enough for it to be discussed outside the church doors).

Pastor Landris came in and talked to the prospective members, thanking everyone for their interest in wanting to become a "supplying joint" to this body called Followers of Jesus Faith Worship Center. *Joint nothing*, Faith thought. *If I'm part of a body, I'm a major part!*

Faith could see Pastor Landris had a lot going in his favor. He had good looks, charm, and he seemed sincere about his work and his commitment to God. She found that overwhelmingly appealing. His wife wasn't there. Faith overheard a few people talking about her after the meeting adjourned.

"They say his wife usually comes in and speaks to everyone after he finishes," a young woman with short-cut, layered hair said. "But I heard she's out of town this week on a book tour. You know she's a famous author."

"I didn't know that," another woman said.

She looks like Olive Oyl—Popeye the sailor man's love

interest, Faith thought. She couldn't help but notice how skinny she was. Faith was certain not even a dog would want that bone.

Faith casually walked over to the two of them. "Hi. I'm Faith Alexandria Morrell." She held out a limp hand.

"Hi, Faith," the young woman with the short hair said, shaking Faith's fingers. "My name is Patrice Stephens."

"And I'm Olivia," the woman Faith thought resembled Olive Oyl said as she forced Faith's whole hand into hers instead of just taking her offered fingers. Faith couldn't help but smirk at the irony of the names Olivia and Olive Oyl.

"Patrice, Olivia," Faith said, smiling at them both. "I heard you guys talking about Mrs. Landris. So she's an author? A for-real author or just somebody who puts a book out herself that probably nobody except family and friends read?"

"No, she's pretty big. She has a top publisher. I'm surprised you haven't heard of her. She's been on radio, television, in the newspaper. Of course, she goes by Johnnie Mae Taylor instead of Landris."

"Johnnie Mae Taylor?" Faith asked, then frowned. "You mean she doesn't use her husband's name at all?" *Now there's a marriage in trouble or headed for trouble if I ever saw one.*

"No. But what difference does that make?" Olivia said.

"None, I suppose. I just wonder what it is about women who don't want to be associated with their spouses. Pastor Landris seems like a wonderful man. At least from what I've heard and seen so far. I would be honored, if it were me, to sport his last name. I'm excited about just becoming a member here, in fact. He has absolutely impressed me. I would think his wife would be ecstatic to share his last name."

Patrice laughed. "You really have strong opinions about this, don't you?"

Is she laughing at me? Faith hoped not. She wasn't Hope or Charity. "Excuse me. I see someone interesting I'd like to chat with," she said and turned up her nose at both of them as she strutted away. She was certain she'd left them gawking. *Eat your hearts out, ladies. What I'm wearing makes you two look like hoi polloi, in lay terms—peasants.* Faith walked over to another group of, quite frankly what she viewed, better-looking people—two women and two men. She made it her business to talk longer with them and laugh loudly. *Miss Patrice and Miss Olive Oyl, I hope you can see just how boring the two of you really are.*

Faith was curious about Pastor Landris's wife. She wondered how she could leave her husband to handle the Lord's work like this while she was off doing some book tour or something. Since she'd never heard of her (not that she was into reading . . . that was intellectual Hope's and brainy Charity's thing), Faith contended she couldn't be *that* famous. She was determined to see what Johnnie Mae Taylor could have possibly written.

She searched her out on the Internet as soon as she arrived home from church, kicking off her too-tight shoes enroute to the computer in the den. After putting Johnnie Mae Taylor's full name in Google, Faith saw there were over 18,000 hits, just on her name alone!

Now Faith couldn't wait to meet her.

She finally got her chance in October during the covenant ceremony (another term for the-right-hand-of-fellowship), but they didn't get a chance to talk much. Right before the two embraced, Faith told her who she was, and that she was Hope's twin. Johnnie Mae commented on how she'd taken a double-look, thinking she *was* Hope. The next person in line was rushing Faith so she could get her hug time with the pastor's wife.

That was fine. Faith moved on. She knew her time would come again soon.

The church now held two Sunday morning services. Hope attended first service, and she was determined to be an active member. Faith, left waiting for Hope's return of their only means of transportation, usually attended the second service. Yet, unlike Hope, Faith wasn't planning on joining any auxiliaries or committees until she knew the members a lot better. She concluded that Pastor Landris's wife—the infamous Mrs. Johnnie Mae Taylor Landris—would be her best route to the truth about this newly formed ministry.

Pastor Landris seemed to be the perfect husband, father-figure, pastor, brother, son, and friend. However, if anyone would know the real deal behind the man, in Faith's opinion, Johnnie Mae would. Faith had determined the two of them were going to become fast friends. It was obvious Johnnie Mae could use some help. And Faith—different from all the other conniving women who may have had their eyes on Pastor Landris—would find a way to make herself indispensable to the present Mrs. Landris.

Chapter 19

Follow after charity, and desire spiritual gifts, but rather that ye may prophesy.

(1 Corinthians 14:1)

Charity unlocked the door and walked into the house. As she glanced around, she hated the way the furniture looked. The chaise longue was back near the end table again. Charity had complained before about the furniture being moved around without her permission. Now, she'd given up on saying anything more about it. Her decorating ideas were entirely different from those of Faith and Hope; she liked a lived-in look.

Hope's way was more practical. She would arrange the couch with the end tables on either side of the couch and the coffee table in front. Traditional—the way most people arranged theirs. Her reasoning was, no matter where a person sat, they would have a place to set a glass or plate in case they were eating or drinking while socializing.

Faith, on the other hand, would move the end tables away from the couch completely. *Why encourage people to put things on them and junk them up?* She liked having one end table next to the wingback chair and the other near the chaise longue, which she would bring up front from the back room where Hope normally put it. It was a beautifully carved piece of furniture, its design reportedly dating from Cleopatra's era.

Faith immediately rearranged all the other furniture to make it fit in the living room.

Charity's favorite places in the house were the den and kitchen areas. That was why she made sure everything her heart desired in a kitchen was included. The den was cozy and old-fashioned-looking, with a stone fireplace that added that homey touch she liked so much.

Charity had loved hanging around her grandmother when she was young. She was what her mother labeled a "dump" cook, just like her grandmother. Motherphelia didn't use standard measuring tools. It was "a handful" of this, "a pinch" of that, "a smidgen" of the other.

Motherphelia was Charity's grandmother on her father's side. Her real name was Ophelia. She moved in with them after Charity's father died, to help her daughter-in-law, who was having a difficult time coping.

Everyone called Ophelia "Mother." That was fine before she moved in with her daughter-in-law on a permanent basis. It became a huge problem afterward, having two women in the same house answering to the same name.

"Hold up," Ophelia said when Charity was crying "Mother" and both women answered. "This is not working. I'll tell you what: You call me Motherphelia and your mother, Mother. That'll fix that problem."

It worked out perfectly. So much so that everybody—including other family members, friends, and neighbors—started calling her Motherphelia.

Charity loved her grandmother. She was the only one who seemed to understand her. The two of them could always talk, and of course, they had their most enlightening conversations in the kitchen.

"Take down a box of dark brown sugar for me, Love," Motherphelia said to Charity. She was the one who had been responsible for Charity's name. Indirectly, of course. Actually, Ophelia had suggested to her son that they name their new baby Lovey.

Her daughter-in-law, Dorothy, was not pleased. "I'm not going to name our baby Lovey," she said to her husband in the hospital room after the baby was born. "You can tell your mother to forget that one."

Jeremiah sighed. "Dot, you know I'm not telling my mother that. I'm her only child. If she had been able to have a little girl, she would have named her Lovey—after her mother."

Dot smiled. "Jeremiah, I didn't mean to be so harsh, but you have to be careful when you give a child a name. I don't like the name Lovey. It's probably a fine name for someone else, but not this child. Have you looked at her? Really looked at her?" Dot asked.

"Of course I've looked at her. She's beautiful, just like you. She reminds me of how much I love you every time I see her. I can understand why my mother wants to name her Lovey. Love is in the name Lovey."

"Love is also in the name Charity. Maybe not in the same way—"

"Charity?"

"Yes, Charity. It's the same as love."

"Yeah. Remember, Dot, when we all had to learn the entire 13th chapter of First Corinthians?" Jeremiah said. "Remember it?"

"Yes. 'Though I speak with the tongues of men and of angels, and have not charity (love), I am become as sounding brass, or a tinkling cymbal. And though I have the gift of prophecy, and understand all mysteries, and all knowledge; and though I have all faith, so that I could remove mountains, and have not charity (love), I am nothing. And though I bestow all my goods to feed the poor, and though I give my body to be burned, and have not charity (love), it profiteth me nothing.'"

"'Charity suffereth long,'" Jeremiah said, "'and is kind; charity envieth not; charity vaunteth not itself or does not brag, is not puffed up or arrogant, doth not behave itself unseemly or rudely, seeketh not her own, is not easily provoked, thinketh no evil; rejoiceth not in iniquity, but rejoiceth in the truth.'" Jeremiah smiled. He could see by his wife's face, she was getting it . . . the name . . . Charity—the name meaning Love.

"'Beareth all things, believeth all things, hopeth all things, endureth all things. Charity never faileth . . .'" Dot said.

Her husband picked up with the eleventh verse. "'When I was a child, I spake as a child, I understood as a child, I thought as a child: but when I became a man, I put away childish things. For now,'" he went over to the crib, "'we see through a glass, darkly,'" he picked the baby up in his arms. "'But then face to face: now I know in part; but then shall I know even as also I am known.'" He laid the sleeping baby in her mother's arm.

"'And now abideth faith, hope, charity, these three,' " Dot said as she brought the baby up next to her face. "'But the greatest of these is Charity.'" She kissed the baby as she began to cry. "Charity. Jeremiah, we can name her Charity."

Jeremiah smiled. "I think Mother will like that name just fine," he said.

Dot smiled. "I know I do." She cuddled the baby and softly planted a kiss on the top of her head. "Hello there, Charity," she whispered with a smile. "Charity Alexandria Morrell."

Charity and her grandmother shared much time and love in the kitchen. She would get the dark brown sugar as instructed, and listen to Motherphelia explain things about the three Ls: Life, Living, and the Lord. Charity remembered one special moment.

"You know why God gave us brown sugar, don't you?"

Five-year-old Charity knew the answer by now, but their routine called for her to shake her head so Motherphelia could tell her. She loved hearing her say the words.

"Because of sweet little brown children like you, of course.

God wanted you to know he was thinking about people like us, too. You know you're special, right?"

Charity nodded. *Of course she knew.* Motherphelia was the best, and she was giving her time and undivided attention to her. She had to be special.

"Now we need to put some sugar in our cup to make caramel icing. Get our special cup down," Motherphelia said.

Charity climbed up on the red stepstool and located the white-and-blue cup in the cabinet. She was so careful with it. "This one, Motherphelia?" She slowly handed the cup to her grandmother.

"This is the one." Motherphelia put the brown sugar in the cup and began to push it down with a spoon. "What lesson does this teach us, Charity?"

"Give, and it shall be given unto you," Charity said.

"Very good. And how will it be given to you, Love?"

"Good measure, pressed down," Charity said as her grandmother pressed hard, poured more brown sugar into the cup, and packed it in some more.

"You see how much we're able to get in here?"

"Uh-huh," Charity said, nodding her head as she watched.

"It's not just lightly put in here, it's what?"

"Good measure, pressed down."

Motherphelia picked up the cup and carefully handed it back to Charity, who held it as though it was fine china. She knew this was "The Lovey Cup." It meant a lot to her grandmother. She wrapped both her little hands around it now that it was full and heavy.

"How is it given to you?"

"Shaken together," Charity said as she shook the brown sugar out of The Lovey Cup into the saucepan. Motherphelia put half a cup of butter in the pan with the sugar. She turned the gas burner on low and made Charity stay back, far away from the stove, as she began to stir constantly.

When the butter and brown sugar melted, she let it boil

for about two minutes, then began to stir in a quarter of a cup of evaporated milk, again not using a real measuring cup.

"Tell me when to stop," Motherphelia said to Charity as she slowly poured. Motherphelia knew just where it needed to stop, and she would usually cheat if Charity didn't yell on time. "Now?" she asked as she began to taper off the flow.

"Now!" Charity yelled.

"Very good. You're such a great little helper. I don't know how I ever managed to do this without you." She smiled as she watched her granddaughter grinning back at her. She then stirred the mixture again. As it boiled, she stood next to Charity, putting away the various ingredients.

As if on cue, the mixture on the stove began to make a hissing sound.

"Oh my," Motherphelia said. "What's happening, Charity?"

"It's running over!" Charity sang. "It's running over! Running over!"

This seemed to happen every time they made caramel icing. Always, right before her grandmother turned off the heat and allowed the mixture to cool. Always.

"How did you say people will give to you?" Motherphelia said, turning off the heat.

"Running over!" Charity sang loud again, then laughed, because it did appear to occur every single time.

"Now what's our whole song about giving?"

"Give, and it shall be given unto you. Good measure. Pressed down and shaken together. Running over, running over, running over," Charity sang their made-up, special song as she demonstrated the running-over part with her hands.

Motherphelia would then beat the mixture with two cups of powdered sugar (two "dumps" from "The Lovey Cup"), and add a bottle cap (1 teaspoon) of real vanilla extract.

"For with the same measure that you use, it's going to be measured back to you. Is that right, Charity Love?"

"Right, Motherphelia!"

"And how's this, a truth to be true that we know?" Motherphelia asked, doing what was known as the call.

"Because Luke 6:38 in the Bible says so," Charity said, providing what was called the response.

Those were special times for Charity, times that lasted until she was around seven. That's when everything changed . . . when the bad . . . evil things began to happen. Things she had managed to blot out of her memory. Shortly after that, Motherphelia got her wings and went home to glory to be with Jesus. Charity didn't understand; she felt she needed Motherphelia down here far more than Jesus needed her up there. Her mother tried to explain how Motherphelia was in a better place now. She was with Charity's father.

Charity only knew that her heart missed Motherphelia. If only she could have stayed just a little while longer.

Chapter 20

Can two walk together, except they be agreed?

(Amos 3:3)

Although he was only thirty at the time, Brent Underwood turned out to be a true blessing to Pastor Landris. Back in mid-2002, they met with the owners of the land the church was looking to buy. They were turned down flat.

Brent and Pastor Landris began trying to buy land for their church and were working closely together, strategizing on various options. It took them three months to talk the company into granting them a hearing before the decision-makers.

Brent was the one who compiled the complete business proposal, showing in black-and-white where the church planned to be in the next twenty years. Getting the information out of Pastor Landris, Brent became familiar with Pastor Landris's intentions. He broke it down into five-year increments, just as Pastor Landris had directed. The executives were so impressed, in one month's time the church was allowed to purchase five acres to get started, with a contract allowing them first option on the remaining thirty-five acres within the next five years.

A year and a half later, Followers of Jesus Faith Worship Center had to begin holding two services just to accommodate the overflow of people "from the east, from the west, from the north, and from the south."

Pastor Landris realized two services were hard; three, if they had to, would be even more taxing on the workers. He and Brent decided to rework the five-year timetable and begin building the new sanctuary ahead of schedule.

In the midst of all this, Johnnie Mae's oldest sister, Rachel, called.

"Listen, Johnnie. I've come to a decision," Rachel said.

"Well, hello to you, too, Rachel."

"Yeah, well, listen. I've decided I'm going to move back to Alabama to help take care of Mama."

"You have? For how long?"

"For as long as you're going to let Mama remain in her house instead of agreeing to put her in a place where people are equipped to take proper care of her. She has Alzheimer's; she's not going to get any better."

"Rachel, I understand your position. Something else. Since you were here last, Ms. Bertha has been staying with Mama at night. I've cut back on a lot of my traveling to make sure I'm there more, doing what I can. Besides, if this is Alzheimer's, which the doctor hasn't totally said that it is, she's not that bad off, yet—"

"Not that bad? What planet are you living on, Johnnie? Are you hearing and seeing the same things the rest of us are? She's not going to get better!"

"Rachel, I know. I hear and I see where she is. But she has some good days where she's perfectly normal. When she has her spells and becomes disoriented, they don't usually last long," Johnnie Mae said. "I just can't see putting her in a home just yet."

"And what do you call 'last long'?"

"If she's disoriented, it's generally not the whole day. Rachel, I don't think you need to move back here for that reason. You still have two children at home, and you're raising your three grandchildren. How is Jasmine doing?" Jasmine was Rachel's middle child.

"Still on drugs and still talking about trying to get herself together. I don't know what else to do for her, but I'm not letting the state come in and take her kids away, so I'm doing what I have to do."

"I admire you, Rachel, for doing that. So many grandmothers today don't want to take on the responsibility of raising their grandchildren."

"Yeah, but there are a lot of us who do. It can be hard, but we're committed to do what we must. Now, back to Mama. It's worrying me being here, not knowing if she's getting the proper care. I don't mean to put you down or question your decisions. I don't know why she chose you instead of me to handle something like this. I'm the oldest, and I don't know why she would pass me over and give this to you. But then, that's neither here nor there."

"Rachel, she probably appointed me because she felt I had the least going on. You were caring for five children on your own after you and Trouble split up and even your grown children had drama. Marie has a husband and four offspring. I only had Princess Rose then."

"That's not it, and you know it. You're just trying to take up for Mama. Everybody knows you're Mama's favorite. She thinks the world revolves around you, but that's okay. She chose you to handle this, and we all have to respect her wishes and your decisions—whether we agree or not."

"Okay," Johnnie Mae said. "I've got it loud and clear. You think I'm wrong. But still, you don't have to worry about trying to move—"

"I've already decided. You may have all the say-so about whether Mama is admitted to an assisted-living facility or nursing home, but I can still decide what I'm going to do for her. There is one thing I need from you, though."

"What's that?"

"Mama's house is too small for me and my bunch to live in for any extended period of time. Marie's house is already maxed out. Donald . . . well, we won't even discuss Donald. You, on the other hand, have that huge house with a guest house in the back—"

"The guest house is small. It will only hold two to three people comfortably."

"I know that, Johnnie. What I was thinking, though, is that you have all that room in your house. Here's my idea: I could let my two teenagers stay in the guest house, and me and the three grands stay in your house."

"You want to come live with *me*?"

"This way, I could go to Mama's every day and help take care of her. It would free the rest of y'all from having to do some of it. You said you hired Ms. Bertha—she can continue what she's already doing. I could treat this like a job, you know? In fact, instead of you paying someone to come in during the day, you could just pay me. Not that I'm doing this for pay, because this is our mother, and that's all I care about. But what I'm saying is, if you *were* looking to pay a daytime sitter, who better for the job than me?"

Johnnie Mae held the phone in silence. Where Rachel was, drama was sure to follow. Instead of her taking care of their mother, before it was over, Rachel would likely be the one looking for someone to take care of her.

"Johnnie, are you still there?"

"I'm here. I'm just processing things. So you're telling me you're willing to pack up and move back here after all these years. And you want to come live with me?"

"Temporarily."

"How long were you looking to stay with me?"

Rachel laughed. "Well, I suppose I hadn't thought that far ahead. I'm sort of playing all of this by ear. It could be two or three months. It might be a year."

"Will you be looking for your own place while you're here with us?"

"Why should I worry about moving into a little dinky apartment or try to lease a house—?"

"You could buy a house if you don't want to rent or lease."

"Of course, you would say something like that. News-flash, Johnnie. My FICO score is shot. Not everybody has A-1 credit to buy a house like you do. And those who do, still have a hard time getting approved for a loan. I'll see what I can do when I get there, but I'm telling you upfront—I'm not really in a hurry. You have plenty of room in that big old house, and it makes sense for us to come and stay with you."

"You do remember I got married not long ago."

"I know it's been two years—the honeymoon should be over by now."

"Well, I'm sorry to have to disappoint you, but it's just gotten started," Johnnie Mae said with a snap. "Our honeymoon is a long way from over."

"Ooh, did I push a button? Usually when someone is that defensive, it means something's not right in paradise. That's it, isn't it? You aren't excited about me coming to your house because you think I'll find out you and the good pastor are having some marital problems?"

"No, that's not it at all." Johnnie Mae paused. "But I do need to discuss this with him before I give you an answer."

"Discuss all you want. What are you going to do when we show up? Turn me and the children away? Now, I can go over to Mama's and stay, but you know good and well these children are going to get on her nerves in a hurry. I'm trying to figure out the best solution for all concerned, and I think this is the best way. Regardless of what you decide, Johnnie, about me staying with you, I *am* packing my stuff, and I'll be arriving in Birmingham in two weeks," Rachel said. "Get back to me so I'll know whose house, yours or Mama's, to pull the moving truck up to once I've unloaded my other be-longings to a storage unit."

"Okay, Rachel. I'll let you know."

When Johnnie Mae hung up, she sat and stared at the phone. She knew Rachel was sincere about caring for their mother, but she also knew Rachel was making a point by deciding to move back now. Coming to live with her was just an additional dig. Johnnie Mae would gladly pay rent for her sister if she wanted a place to stay while she was here. Rachel's plan was about being in her face, every day, to remind her of what a mistake it was for her to insist on allowing their mother to stay at home instead of putting her in a facility.

Johnnie Mae couldn't explain it. Whether it was a black thing, a southern thing, for some perhaps an economic thing, or just the way people cared about their loved ones, she wasn't the only one choosing to wait until the last moment to put a loved one in a nursing home. Physically, her mother was fine, so a nursemaid wasn't needed around the clock. At this point, her mother preferred staying in her own house. They merely needed to ensure while she was there that she didn't wander off.

Of course Johnnie Mae knew the struggles her mother was having; she couldn't help but know. She had experienced them just like the rest of them had. And like them, it broke her heart, too.

Chapter 21

His seed shall be mighty upon earth: the generation of the upright shall be blessed.

(Psalm 112:2)

Johnnie Mae planned to talk with Landris about her sister's proposal after he came home later tonight. She was definitely not looking forward to this discussion. Landris already felt she allowed her family to run over her at times, although Johnnie Mae didn't agree. She had always been a pretty strong personality, but being a Christian—and now the wife of a pastor—placed her under more scrutiny.

It did hurt her a little when no one from her family chose to become a member of the church she and her husband started. Her family came to the initial meeting, but after that, not one—other than her mother—ever came for one of the services. Her former good friends, Honey and Sister, had also chosen not to visit, either.

"I just feel like I'm supposed to stay where I am," Johnnie Mae's second-oldest sister Marie had said back in February when the two of them were over at their mother's house. "I'm praying for you and George, though, Johnnie Mae. But my family and I have been members of our church for fifteen years."

"Yeah, but weren't you the one complaining, just the other day," Johnnie Mae said, "about how you're not learning anything at your church?"

Marie smiled. "Yes, I was. But that's even more of a reason why I need to stay there. Those people need me. I study the Word and many of them wouldn't know anything if I wasn't there to teach them. I listen to George's tapes over and over again, and pass on what I learn to them."

"All you teach is a Sunday school class. How many people are usually in your class?" Johnnie Mae asked.

"That's beside the point."

"No, I'm making a point. How many . . . roughly?"

"Three," Marie said smugly. "Give or take a few. But they're faithful. You never know who your words are reaching, Johnnie Mae. Those two or three folks could end up going out and saving the world one day."

"Okay," Johnnie Mae said. "I'm not trying to get you to come. I was merely pointing out how you complain, but you're not doing anything to change the situation. Landris serves an all-you-can-eat spiritual feast, and my own family won't even come and taste anything. But you'll order carry-out . . . listen to his tapes religiously."

"Don't take it personally, Johnnie Mae. Let's change the subject. Are you pregnant yet?"

"No."

Marie looked disappointed. "I was thinking for certain you would be pregnant by now. How long have you been trying? Six months?"

Johnnie Mae counted quickly in her head. It had indeed been six whole months. "Yeah, six."

"It's all this pressure. I keep telling you—you're probably worrying too much. You need to learn to relax more. And I'm sure this church stuff is not helping matters any."

"What do you mean?"

"You have to set up the chairs and do other things every week for Sunday services. I'm sure you're the one who's doing all that. Didn't you tell me you drape a purple-and-gold cloth over that mammoth entertainment center in the den so it looks like a curtain behind the lectern? That's got to be work, putting all that up and taking it down every single week."

"Landris puts out the chairs and helps drape the cloth. It's not that much on me."

Marie hunched her shoulders. "If you say so. I know the situation with Mama has got to be weighing heavily on your mind, too."

"We're all doing what we can. I'm sure you're just as concerned as I am about her. You've been great, doing your part for her. I appreciate that."

"Well, it's a lot of work for all of us. This can't be helping when you're trying to get pregnant. I could be wrong, but George probably couldn't care less whether you get pregnant or not anyway. He's likely praying that you don't."

Johnnie Mae frowned at Marie. "Why would you say something like that?"

Marie cocked her head to one side. "Johnnie Mae, if I were you and George, a baby would be the last thing on my mind. I would be working to get Princess Rose all grown and gone, and then enjoy my time to myself."

"Landris and I both have had plenty of time to ourselves. I think having a baby would be perfect. At our age, we're more settled. Some things, I've noticed, don't bother me the way they did or would have when I was younger."

Marie finished softening the last lemon she was rolling on the kitchen table. She took out a knife and sliced off the top, then started squeezing it into the glass pitcher. "Running after young children, at your and George's age, is going to be a challenge. Maybe you should leave well enough alone. You and George are able to travel without having to worry about a child. Maybe God has plans for the two of you, like missionary work, that doesn't include a newborn."

Johnnie Mae got up and stirred the pot of pinto beans, her mother's favorite. "And maybe this is the devil trying to deter us from a blessing God has ordained for us."

"Yeah, okay. If it's ordained, then no devil in hell will be able to stop it. If I were you, though, I would pray to God about a lot of things. Mama being tops on your list. Johnnie Mae, she's not getting better, and you and I both know she's not going to. At some point, you're going to have to let go."

"When that time comes, I'll know."

Marie looked at her watch. "Well, it's time for me to go." She leaned over and kissed her sister on the cheek. "Just as a heads up—Mama's having a bad day today."

"Really?"

"Yeah. I ran her bath water and she went in and undressed as usual. The next thing I know, she was yelling my name. I ran to the door and answered her. She said, 'Marie, was I getting in the tub or out of the tub?' It just hurts to see her this way now."

"I know. The other day she was at my house and started playing with Princess Rose. She grew tired and decided to retire to the room I fixed up for her. Just like with you, she started calling me. I didn't know what was wrong, but when I got there, she stood . . . paralyzed, halfway up the stairs."

"What happened?" Marie asked.

"She said, 'Johnnie Mae, was I going up the stairs or down the stairs?' I'm not being naïve about what's happening with her, Marie. But honestly, how many of us have gone to do something and found ourselves looking around, trying to remember what we went in to do? It's part of getting older. But there are days when her mind is sharp, and she really is back to being her normal self. She can tell me things I did when I was a little girl, recalling some things I only remember after she starts reminding me about it."

Johnnie Mae was thinking about these things as she sat with her mother. They were having a nice conversation, and Johnnie Mae debated whether she should mention the call she'd gotten from Rachel earlier that morning. Her mother suddenly became quiet, which typically was an indication that her mind was shifting to another time or place. The doctor had told them to try and keep her current whenever she started having her episodes.

"Mama, what's wrong?" Johnnie Mae asked calmly.

"Nothing," she said as she began looking around the room.

Johnnie Mae watched her mother fidget and continue to lean forward as though she was looking for someone to come through the door.

Johnnie Mae's eyes traveled from her mother to the doorway. "Mama, are you expecting someone?"

"Sort of."

"Who are you looking for?"

Her mother smiled. "I'm sure she'll be here any minute. She's usually always on time. You can almost set your watch by her."

"Who? Who's usually always on time?"

"My daughter."

"You mean Marie?" Johnnie Mae was baffled because her mother knew Marie had just left a little while ago. Marie had kissed her good-bye.

"Not Marie. Marie was here earlier. I'm talking about my other daughter."

Johnnie Mae wondered if Rachel had called and told her she was moving back. If so, she wished Rachel hadn't done that. Mrs. Gates had difficulty gauging time, especially during episodes.

"Are you looking for Rachel, Mama? Did Rachel call and tell you she's coming to visit you?"

"Rachel?" Her mother looked at her like she was crazy. "No, not Rachel. Rachel lives in . . . in . . . well, I can't remember right now exactly where, but she lives somewhere out of town. I'm talking about my daughter the author. Do you know my Johnnie Mae? She was supposed to be here by now." Mrs. Gates started looking toward the door again, then stood and looked out the window. "I pray nothing's happened to her. Johnnie Mae is never late. She's dependable like that. Did you know she's famous?"

"Mama, I'm Johnnie Mae."

Her mother looked at her. "Oh," she said. She then became silent and sat back down.

"Mama, you okay? Do you need anything?"

Mrs. Gates smiled, shook her head, and once again, started looking toward the door.

Johnnie Mae went over and hugged her as she wiped away a tear.

"Are *you* all right?" Mrs. Gates asked. "You're crying. Why are you crying?"

"Yeah," Johnnie Mae whispered, "I'm all right."

"Did you know I have a daughter who's an author? She's famous. Did you know that? She'll be here any minute. I don't know what's keeping her. Maybe you'll tell her why you're crying when she gets here."

Johnnie Mae managed a smile and wiped another rolling tear off her face. "She's famous, huh? Wow, that must be something," she said.

"Oh, it is. It really is. I'm so proud of her. Proud of all my children, if I can be so bold as to say that to you." Mrs. Gates nodded her head and rocked back and forth a few times. "All of them. Bertha will be by later. She's such a dear. I just love her so much. Only, she's gotten a bit old-looking of late. I don't know what happened. She went downhill mighty fast. We have so much fun, though. We play a game of concentration. I'm not too good at it anymore. Not too good. She claims it's my memory. I just think Bertha cheats. What did you say your name was again, dearest?"

"Johnnie Mae."

"Wow, what are the odds of that? I have a daughter named Johnnie Mae. She's an author. She'll be here any minute." She started looking at the door again. "Any minute now."

"I'm sure she will," Johnnie Mae said. She touched a strand of her own graying hair.

Chapter 22

Where no counsel is, the people fall: but in the multitude of counselors there is safety.

(Proverbs 11:14)

Johnnie Mae and Pastor Landris discussed Rachel's plans to come and stay with them.

"Did she say for how long?" Pastor Landris asked.

"Not exactly."

"Bad idea, Johnnie Mae."

"What? That my sister is coming, or that she wants to live with us?" Johnnie Mae looked up at him as she continued to chop an onion, causing tears to sting her eyes.

"Listen, I would never tell you your sister or any other family member or even a friend couldn't stay here. In truth, this is your house."

"Landris, don't do that. You and I agreed we weren't ever going to go into the 'my and your' thing."

"I know. But I'm just being realistic here."

"If I didn't respect your feelings about this, I wouldn't have asked. I told Rachel I needed to talk with you before I gave her an answer."

"Great," he said. "Make me out to be the bad guy. That's okay. If you decide to tell her she can't come here, I don't mind if she thinks I'm the reason."

"I wouldn't do something like that, and you know it."

He touched her hand to halt her chopping, took the knife,

and laid it down on the butcher block. "Johnnie Mae, wash your hands and let's you and I talk about this without any distractions."

"I'm fine. I need to finish making dinner."

"Dinner can wait. I'll help when we're finished talking, but this is important."

Johnnie Mae washed her hands and she and Landris sat side by side. He took her hand and held it softly but firmly.

"Johnnie Mae, if you want your sister and the children . . ."

"We're talking about two teenagers—one sixteen, the other seventeen—and three grandchildren all under the age of seven," she said.

"If you want all six of them to come here and live, that's fine with me. Am I crazy about the idea? No. But then again, I'll be all right. I'm not going to lie. I love having the house to ourselves—just me, you, and Princess Rose. Of course, we were working on that baby project, but I guess we'll just have to keep things quiet around here while we work."

Johnnie Mae slapped his hand. "Stop that," she said, smiling. "You're just being mannish."

"I'm keeping it real. You're my wife, and what we have is beautiful. I refuse to act like it's anything other than that. Now here's what I suggest. If they're coming to live with us, you need to establish, up front, for how long."

"But she doesn't know, Landris. And honestly, I'm not sure I even want her to come here. I just know she and I are going to get into it over Mama. I know it."

"Johnnie Mae, listen to what I'm saying. Rachel might not know now, but you still need to set a time frame up front. If you tell her three months, then both of you will know what's expected. If you don't set a time limit, she could be here forever. You'll want her to leave, and she'll feel like you're throwing her out."

"You're right, Landris. I know what you're saying is right. But I feel guilty because we do have this house with plenty of room, and it seems selfish if I tell her she can't come, especially since she's coming to help with Mama. They're already upset with me because they think I'm being contrary."

"Diligently pray about what you should do. If you want Rachel here, I'll be fine with it for as long as I have to be. If you decide you don't want her to stay, that's fine, too. But—"

She rolled her head around in a half-circle and sighed. "I know—if I say yes, I need to set a general, agreed-upon, time period."

"Exactly. And if you want to extend it later, you can always do that. There's no rule that says you'll have to put her out by the time you've set if you don't want to."

"She probably won't leave regardless. Landris, you don't know my sister."

"Oh," he smiled, "I think I got a pretty good idea the last time she was here."

"She was pretty hard on you that day. But you handled yourself in a very gentlemanly manner. I'll give you that much."

Johnnie Mae called Rachel back that night. They talked for over an hour. Rachel would stay with them for six weeks while she looked for a place of her own.

"So we agree, then?" Johnnie Mae asked her.

"Whatever you say, Johnnie," Rachel said. "After all, it *is* your house."

Chapter 23

There is that scattereth, and yet increaseth; and there is that withholdeth more than is meet, but it tendeth to poverty.

(Proverbs 11:24)

October 1, 2003, Rachel moved in with Johnnie Mae and Pastor Landris. By the end of December, she was still there, with no plans to move.

"Look, Johnnie, my money is funny right now," Rachel said. "I'm not trying to take advantage of you. You know that. I know I told you we would be out of here within six weeks, but the move here was more expensive than I first thought. Then Christmas cost us more than I'd expected. It's hard raising children. You wouldn't understand because you only have Princess Rose. I understand better than anyone why you and Pastor Landris have chosen not to have any more children. Smart. Smart!"

"We haven't chosen not to have a baby," Johnnie Mae said.

"So you really *are* trying?" She frowned. "Marie told me that, but I just knew she had to be joking. You're forty-three years old, Johnnie. Back in the day, we made fun of people your age who got pregnant. We'd say they got 'caught in the change.' Nobody in their right mind would purposely try to have a baby this late in the game. With the exception, of course, of rich, white movie stars."

"I'm perfectly in my right mind, and I'm trying like you'll

never know to have a baby. My doctor says the next step would be fertility treatments. But for now, we've just been praying and believing I'll conceive naturally."

"All right, then. So you're *praying* to get pregnant? Which, incidentally, were you to get pregnant say, today, would mean the baby would be due . . ." she began counting quickly, using her fingers, "around July or August. In August, might I remind you, you'll be forty-four." She placed emphasis on the number. "I know you didn't ask my opinion, but I think you should forget this nonsense. If you really want another child to raise, I have three little ones in there—you can take your pick."

Johnnie Mae shook her head. "In the first place, you know good and well you wouldn't let me have one of your grandchildren."

She grinned and jutted her chin. "Yeah, you're right. I'd never live that down. Besides, I've kind of grown attached to them, no matter how mad they make me sometimes."

"And in the second place—"

"I knew there had to be a second place," Rachel said. "You always have to run down a list."

"In the second place," Johnnie Mae continued, "Landris and I would like to have a baby of our own. Together."

"Well, if you do that fertility stuff, you're liable to have four or five of your own. Together. All at once. You've seen those folks on TV. And you can forget about asking me to help with any of them. You do the deed, you deal with the consequences."

"I would hope by then, you'd have found your own place and that wouldn't even be a topic for discussion."

"Woo, is it getting a little chilly in here or is it just *you*?" Rachel pointed her index finger at Johnnie Mae. "I know we're getting on your nerves, Johnnie. But hopefully I'll be able to move out in another two . . . three months, tops," Rachel said. She got up and opened a bag of cookies, and started mindlessly eating them, one right after the other.

"Landris just bought those cookies. They're his favorites."

Rachel laughed and bit into another one. "Sorry. I didn't know he was a chocolate macadamia nut kind of guy. Well, at least Mama appreciates me being here, even if no one else seems to."

"Is that right?" Johnnie Mae said as she took the bag of cookies off the table and put them back up in the cabinet.

"Yes, that's right. I don't know how you, Donald, and Marie did this every day like you did. She's wearing me out. I try to get Ms. Bertha to keep her up later at night so she'll tire out earlier during the day and give me time for a nap or something. But you know all most people want these days is to be paid without having to do too much work. I know you're paying Ms. Bertha well." Rachel picked up an orange from the fruit bowl and started peeling it, allowing the peels to fall on the table. "She's essentially being paid to sleep while Mama sleeps."

Johnnie Mae looked at her, then shook her head slowly. She tore off a paper towel and placed the orange peelings from the table onto it. "Ms. Bertha is doing a wonderful job. She and Mama play Concentration and work various seek-and-find puzzles. The doctor says games like these can help people with memory problems."

"Well, I've put a stop to *all* that. I told Ms. Bertha to quit playing Concentration with her, because she was looking for me to play it all the time during the day. I threw away all those puzzles as soon as I found them stacked up every-where. Mama was getting frustrated trying to work them. She doesn't need the aggravation, and neither do I."

"Rachel, you're not helping if you take away things from her that can aid her. Her doctor provided us with tools to use to help stabilize, if not minimize, her memory loss."

Rachel fanned her hand at Johnnie Mae as though she were shooing a fly. "Mama will be fine. I'm trying to get her interested in soap operas again."

Johnnie Mae placed her hand on her hip. "See? None of

us turn the TV on to watch those things when we're there. That's one of the worst things you can do, Rachel. Television is a passive activity. She needs active things to keep her mind stimulated. You're doing this on purpose. I suppose you're not walking with her, either?"

Rachel popped an orange slice in her mouth. "Nope. I don't do walks. I've found it to be bad for my health."

"I know what you're doing, Rachel." She sat down across from her. "But it's not going to work. If you want to help Mama, you'll have to stick to the program that's been established for her by her doctor. You know, I can just hire a home health aide to come in a few hours a day to do this."

"What more is an aide going to do than watch her like we're doing? It's not like Mama's condition is going to improve, Johnnie. And you know this." She pointed an orange slice at Johnnie Mae as she spoke. "Still, you insist on keeping her at home instead of placing her in a facility with a full-time staff. Okay, fine. I'm now watching her during the day. As for walking, Mama does that when you and Marie come over and go with her—twice every week is plenty for anybody. I don't want her to be miserable, doing things I know I wouldn't want to do if it were me." She ate another slice of orange. "You still haven't answered my question. How much do you pay Ms. Bertha to sleep at Mama's house?"

"Enough."

"Well then, enough sounds like plenty for me. You know—here's a thought. I could just move me and my five in with Mama. And what you're throwing away on Ms. Bertha and possibly an aide, you could throw my way. I'd be out of here—all problems resolved."

"You're kidding me, right?"

"No. I'm serious. You want me out of here—"

"Rachel, I did not say I wanted you out."

"Johnnie, you started this conversation off with, 'Rachel, it's been two months now. How's the new living-space hunting going?' That's a polite way of saying, 'Rachel, I know you're my sister and all, but you're getting on my nerves, and I'm wondering how much longer I'm going to have to put up with you.' I know how to translate polite talk, in case you've forgotten. I can't afford to get a job, Johnnie. Do you know what daycare costs these days? Besides, I moved here to help out with Mama. If I get a place, I'll need to get a job to pay for it. Which means I'll not be able to stay at Mama's but a few hours, a few times a week—if that much. That would defeat the whole purpose of my having moved here in the first place. I could have stayed where I was."

"Okay, Rachel. Stay here for as long as it takes."

"That was what I told you when I called you three months ago and informed you I was moving. But don't worry, I'm not planning on living with you forever. I'm not that insensitive. Besides, your precious little Princess Rose acts too much like a miniature diva for me and mine to be around for too long."

"What do you mean?"

"Don't take this the wrong way, Johnnie, because Lord knows I know how some of you newer parents are about your little darlings. But your precious Princess Rose is spoiled." Rachel got up and threw the orange peelings in the trash.

"Spoiled?"

"Yes, spoiled. I didn't stutter when I said it. I realize she's an only child, and she's had you all to herself for a good part of her life. But that child needs to learn how to share. Maybe you do need to have another child so you can change her attitude before she grows up." Rachel sat back down at the table.

Johnnie Mae snatched an orange out of the bowl and began to squeeze it hard in places. "Princess Rose is not spoiled."

"She doesn't share, Johnnie. I'm telling you, the girl won't let my grandchildren touch her precious little toys."

Johnnie Mae bit a hole in the top of the orange. "Maybe that's because your precious little grandchildren don't know how to take care of other people's stuff."

"Oh, I know you did not go there."

Johnnie Mae went to the counter and took down the

candy jar. She took out an old-fashioned candy cane and stuck it in the hole of the orange. "Yes, I went there. You know I'm telling the truth. Your . . . grandchildren have broken almost every toy my child has let them touch. In fact, I was the one who told Princess Rose to quit letting them play with everything they ask for. They don't listen, even when grown folks tell them to do or stop doing something. They're hardheaded."

"Oh, you're just saying this because of what I just said about your little princess. I'm sorry I brought it up, okay? Let's just drop it. I was wrong."

Johnnie Mae was about to say something when she stopped herself. "I'm not going to let you do this. You used to do this when we were growing up, and you haven't changed a bit. You always find a way to get the attention off what *you're* doing wrong. But Rachel, you and those kids don't need to live at Mama's house. Not unless I can get her to move in here with me."

"That's not going to happen. You said yourself—Mama wants to be at her own house. She's not coming here to live. Ever. But on the serious side—"

"I thought we were on the serious side already." Johnnie Mae sucked orange juice through the candy cane like it was a straw.

"'On the serious side' is just an expression, Johnnie, okay? Anyway, Mama is getting worse. You're going to have to do something soon. Think of me as your conscience. I plan to make sure, in the end, you do the right thing."

"I don't mean to be ugly, Rachel, but when Mama has lucid moments, she and I talk. She has told me she does trust me to do the right thing. She's counting on me to do it."

"Yeah . . . sure." Rachel got up. "Well, I think I'll go watch a little TV."

Johnnie Mae looked at the messy table Rachel left. She threw away the stray peelings, then got a wet dish towel and wiped the table clean.

Chapter 24

Follow after charity, and desire spiritual gifts . . .

(1 Corinthians 14:1)

January 2004

Johnnie Mae walked hurriedly, waving randomly to folks as she passed by following Sunday's second service. Forever poised and composed, she appeared to be the ideal wife one would expect of a prominent pastor.

"You're the pastor's wife," Faith said as she smiled and shook her hand that cold day in January. Faith had only been a member of the church since September. In that time, she and Johnnie Mae had only spoken once before—nothing resembling a real conversation, though. Johnnie Mae had a stack of books entitled *Walking in Divine Favor* that she was handing out to people as they filed by. "Why on earth are *you* passing these out?" Faith asked.

Johnnie Mae tilted her head slightly and squinted her eyes. Her smile was warm. "Well, why not me?"

"You're the First Lady," Faith said. "I'm sure there are people here who can handle something like this for you."

"So you don't think I should be doing something like this?"

"Honestly? No."

"Because I'm the 'First Lady'?"

"Precisely."

Johnnie Mae started laughing. "First of all, please don't call me the First Lady. I'm honored to be a helper to the pastor, but he and I have agreed we are, first and foremost, servants of God and servants to His people."

"So you don't buy into that First Lady thing at all?" Faith asked. She couldn't believe this woman could possibly be real.

"My name is Johnnie Mae. If you would like to help me pass these out, I would appreciate it. But no, I don't buy into the 'First Lady thing', and I don't think myself above doing something like passing out books if I believe they are a blessing." She held out one of the *Walking in Divine Favor* books to Faith.

Faith took it, but wasn't quite certain whether or not Johnnie Mae had been serious about her helping her. "My name is Faith Alexandria Morrell." She always said her entire name when introducing herself—a habit, perhaps—or maybe she just loved hearing it. "You probably don't remember me with so many members, but I briefly met you when I officially joined this church back in October." Faith looked at the stack of books. "Do you really need help?" she asked.

Johnnie Mae smiled. "Need? No. But if you would like to help, I'll gladly accept your assistance with appreciation, Faith."

Faith thought a minute. Helping wasn't exactly her strong point. She delegated well, though. Faith knew Hope would have jumped in head first without ever having to have been asked. And Charity was all about showing love. Nothing that needed to be done or anyone Charity met was beneath her. She actually believed love really *could* conquer all. Faith knew that's why her presence was so necessary. Faith felt Hope and Charity allowed people to run over them entirely too much. She, on the other hand, only allowed people to *think* they were getting over on her—but they really weren't.

Johnnie Mae looked at the long line of people waiting patiently to receive their copy of *Walking in Divine Favor.*

Faith's eyes followed the direction of her gaze. She could clearly see that with two of them working at this, things would probably *move* faster, if nothing else.

Faith walked around to the other side of the table, set down her purse, Bible, book, and lesson journal on the chair behind her, and positioned a stack of the seventy-page books in front of her. Johnnie Mae flashed a smile her way. That's when it dawned on Faith: there was a payoff in doing this. She realized Johnnie Mae, the pastor's wife, appreciated her gesture, and that this could be the way "in" she'd been looking for.

After Faith arrived home, she thumbed through the book Johnnie Mae and Pastor Landris had written together. They'd printed several thousand copies, not to sell, but to give away. Faith admitted that Johnnie Mae undeniably was a great writer. She could see from this book alone why publishers were after her. Faith retrieved her purse and located the business card Johnnie Mae had given her. Rotating it around in her hand front to back, she smiled. *Mrs. Johnnie Mae Taylor Landris gave me her card with her personal phone numbers on it.* Faith had offered to help her in the future and Johnnie Mae had offered to help her should she need it. Faith was convinced all of this had to mean something.

"Johnnie Mae, I would love to help you more. I like what you said about being a servant of the Most High," Faith had said after there was no one left in line. *"I'm sure with your busy schedule I could be of assistance to you. And if you're ever looking for an assistant—part- or full-time—I'd love to apply."*

"Do you have a job presently?" Johnnie Mae had asked before Faith left.

"Yes. But honestly, I would consider leaving to help you and Pastor Landris with the mission you've been given by God." Faith liked the way she'd phrased that: *the mission.*

"I'm sure a lot of grunt work is necessary in getting a new church off the ground—even more work and responsibility once it's up and going." Faith was working this angle, even though she didn't completely trust either one of them. She believed if they were up to no good, she'd find out one way or the other.

"First off, a church is not a place. It's not a destination. The church is the people of Jesus Christ. That's why we named this particular fellowship Followers of Jesus Faith Worship Center. The church is the people; we're followers of Jesus, we stand on faith as we come together to this particular center to build up and further increase our faith, and to worship God in spirit and truth. God the Father, the Son, and the Holy Ghost." Johnnie Mae abruptly halted her speech. Faith wasn't sure if it was because she had suddenly noticed the smile on her face after she'd said the word "faith."

"Faith—your sister's name is Hope, correct?"

"Yes, and a younger sister, Charity."

Johnnie Mae stopped again. "I haven't met her. Does Charity live here?"

"She lives here—she just hasn't come for a visit to *this* church yet." Faith was sorry she'd somehow allowed this slip and mentioned Charity's name.

"Is she at least a member of someone's congregation?" Johnnie Mae asked as she stacked up the remaining books and placed them inside an empty box on top of the table.

"No, she's not. But she's visited The Church of Revelation and Divine Conquerors."

"Reverend Paul Knight and Reverend Marshall Walker's church?" Johnnie Mae wrinkled her nose and smiled, like she'd just smelled something foul and was trying to pretend that she hadn't. "Everyone needs to belong to a spiritual family. Maybe we should work on getting her to come visit us."

Faith felt at this point that Johnnie Mae should mind her own business. *It's bad enough having to deal with Hope want-*

ing to be here every chance she gets. I don't need to have to deal with Charity, too. People didn't have the first clue how complicated Faith's life was, or could be if she wasn't extremely careful how she handled things.

"Faith? May I ask you a question? Is there something going on with Hope? I miss seeing her when she's not here. She always makes a point to at least come and speak when she does attend. I realize with so many more members in attendance and two services, it's more difficult to tell when a person is absent or merely attended a different service. But there are times when I'm sure Hope is not here, and it's not because she just didn't want to. When I ask her about it later, she won't necessarily say what happened. Although she has told me a few times it just couldn't be helped."

"Has she ever told you why it couldn't be helped?" Faith asked nervously. She was aware Hope could talk a little too much sometimes. Faith often compared her to an unplugged refrigerator—*can't keep a thing*.

"Well, no," Johnnie Mae said. "I generally let her know she was missed, and she usually responds that there are things that hold her back over which she has little or no control. I don't know. I just feel like there's something going on she's not telling, but she wants desperately to get off her heart. She did say she's trying to overcome these obstacles."

Faith began to nod. "That's true," she said, admittedly proud of Hope for that answer. It was a good and honest answer—almost. Faith couldn't help but wonder what Hope had meant by "little control" though. *Who is she trying to fool?* "That's Hope. I'm sorry; I can't help you with that one."

"Maybe you should bring Charity with you one Sunday and see if this is a place she might feel comfortable coming to. And, if there's anything I can do to help with any of you," Johnnie Mae handed Faith her business card, "I'll be more than happy to." Johnnie Mae looked at her.

Faith instantly recognized that look—Johnnie Mae was trying to read her. Faith smiled and nodded again. "I'll see what I can do—about Charity. But you know how some people are. Charity is the sweetest, kindest, most loving person I've ever known. She gets hurt a lot, though, because she puts herself all the way out there. She doesn't know how to hold back or do anything halfway. She trusts too easily, too much, and generally too soon. I'm just not sure if a large church would work for her."

"What do you mean?"

"The more people in attendance, the more people you have to be careful of. I'm sure you're aware that everybody who comes to church isn't there for the right reasons. Someone like Charity will put her heart out there, and some of these wolves in sheep's clothing might try to swallow her whole. That's why she didn't continue visiting Reverend Knight's church."

Okay, so that wasn't totally the truth, Faith thought.

"This church is small enough right now," Faith continued. "But we all know Pastor Landris is poised to take off big. People all around the city are *all* talking about him and what's going on here," Faith said. "Folks are being delivered, healed, and set free. Before this year is out, I'm certain there will be over a thousand members, if not more. And this building will be way too small to hold everyone."

"You're right. We're growing at a tremendous rate. But you're saying you're afraid for Charity to attend here because of people? Being around too many people?"

Faith stopped and thought a second. She knew whatever she said had to be right and honest. One thing Charity wouldn't tolerate was flat-out lying. Faith had seen Charity's reaction whenever she lied. Faith knew there would be consequences if she didn't speak the truth about her. And Charity would somehow know; she always knew whenever Faith had been untruthful. "Charity is great with people. But people will take advantage of her if she's not careful." Faith suddenly wanted to hurry and get away from this line of conversation. "That's all I'm saying."

"Is she a teenager or something?"

"No, she's thirty-one—two years younger than me."

Johnnie Mae smiled. "I was just wondering why you feel it necessary to protect your sister when it seems she should be old enough to look out for herself."

Faith didn't really care for that comment at all, or what Johnnie Mae was implying. Nobody knew what was going on with the three of them. And Faith planned on it remaining that way. "Don't misunderstand me," Faith said. "It's just that the genuine love she has for others can blind her to a fault."

"Fair enough. But I think she'd be fine here. A congregational body should start from the head and work its way down. Pastor Landris is leading us as he follows Jesus. Some things, I can assure you, he won't tolerate here. Maybe I should talk to Hope and see what she thinks about Charity possibly coming."

Faith knew this was a bad idea. She knew there was nothing more Hope would love than to have Charity come to this place. Then the two of them would likely start feeling strong enough together to aggressively challenge her as well as her decisions. She definitely couldn't have that.

Faith put Johnnie Mae's business card safely away in her purse. "I'll let Charity know the welcome mat has been extended by none other than the wife of the pastor. If she comes, she comes. If not, we'll just have to accept that maybe this is not the place for her."

And that was how Faith left it.

If Faith had anything to say about this, there was no way Charity would ever step foot in that church. Faith would fight that idea to the bitter end. Charity wasn't like Hope. Faith believed Charity was just too open and caring. And if both Charity and Hope started believing any way close to the way Hope was already starting to, Faith knew she could be in serious trouble.

Faith had worked too hard protecting Charity all these years.

Hope knew the deal. Yet, here lately, she felt Charity had become much stronger than Faith was convinced she had. Faith didn't believe Charity was there just yet. She'd seen Charity's pain. She knew how devastating things had been for her. And Faith had vowed never again to allow anyone to hurt Charity as long as she was around.

Never!

If Charity were to come to Followers of Jesus Faith Worship Center, Faith felt she just might start thinking she could handle things without her. She just might believe she really could do all things through Christ. Faith had made a promise to take care of Charity, to protect her, and go to bat for her. And she planned to do everything in her power to keep that promise.

I am Faith. I believe it, and I act like I expect it to come to pass. Faith could see Charity was somewhat like her, only she didn't seem to care as much whether she got the things she wanted or not. All Charity seemed interested in was sharing love. When people hurt her, she forgave them in love . . . whether they asked for forgiveness or not. Charity had told Faith once, "Forgiveness truly is a gift that I give to myself."

On the contrary, Faith cared about being hurt, and she did keep score.

Charity was patient. She would give people time, realizing that everybody made mistakes, so she was not so judgmental. Charity was kind; Faith had never heard her say one harsh word to or about anyone. Charity didn't sit around envying what others possessed, but she was always grateful for what she had. Charity didn't go around boasting about what she had either, or all she'd done.

Frankly, Faith thought both Charity and Hope could take more pointers from her. Faith believed one should toot one's own horn sometimes. *How else will people ever know what you've accomplished if you don't tell them?*

Charity was proud, but not in a prideful way. She was proud of what God had done and was continuing to do in her life, but she wasn't the type to walk around acting like she thought she was all that. Faith believed if you had it, you ought to flaunt it. But then again . . . she was Faith.

Charity could never be rude to anyone. And she wouldn't dare ever interrupt a person while they were talking—no matter how boringly long it took them to get their point across. Charity would merely sit patiently and listen. And walking out on someone the way Faith had done with Patrice and Olivia that time? Charity would *never* have done anything as discourteous as that.

Charity didn't get angry easily. Not to imply she didn't get angry, but it was hard to get her to that place. And when she did get angry, she chose not to sin doing it. Charity didn't believe in keeping a record of the wrongs people had done to her.

Charity wasn't the type to celebrate when bad things happened to people who had wronged her—even those she knew probably deserved it.

Faith, on the other hand, considered something of that nature to be poetic justice and was known to have performed a celebratory dance when those who had wronged her felt the sting of pain in their lives. Faith didn't necessarily pray for bad things to happen to them, but when it happened . . . .*Oh, well*.

Charity could be most protective—Faith felt they had that in common. The difference being: Faith's focus of protection extended only to those she cared about, whereas Charity's was not that limited.

Here again, this was why Faith believed she was so necessary. Charity trusted too much. She had a tendency to put herself out there to get hurt. Faith's job was to make sure Charity didn't get hurt again. Faith knew Charity would persevere, though. That was what she loved most about her. Some of the things Charity had experienced would have taken a weaker person out totally—but not Charity. She always found a way to cope, and she was still going strong. Charity had never failed because love never fails.

Although Faith would never admit it aloud, there were times when she wished she could love unconditionally like Charity.

Faith was still not convinced that visiting Pastor Landris's church would turn out to be the best thing for Charity or herself, for that matter, in the end. If Faith were to be truthful about this, she'd acknowledge how afraid she was that her position in Charity's life just might be the thing that came to an end.

And that—she didn't think she was ready for . . . just yet.

Chapter 25

But when they deliver you up, take no thought how or what ye shall speak: for it shall be given you in that same hour what ye shall speak.

(Matthew 10:19)

Pastor Landris and Brent scheduled a meeting with Dexter Iron and Steel, the owners of the thirty-five acres the church was looking to purchase. The church was holding two services now. It wouldn't be long before both would be filled to capacity. The board members of Followers of Jesus Faith Worship Center had met to decide the next course of action. There was discussion about adding another modular in an effort to open up more room in the main sanctuary. They had also considered the idea of making the new addition into an overflow room equipped with a large television screen to broadcast the service while it was going on, but that idea was tabled for the present.

They agreed that the best plan would be to purchase the remaining acres and begin building the new worship center sanctuary. The people who were attending presently were giving generously toward the ministry, evidenced by a 10,000 percent spike in finances.

"You want me to do *what* now?" Mr. Busby, the owner of Dexter Iron and Steel said.

"We'd like you to sell us the remaining thirty-five acres we previously agreed to purchase, only at a ten percent discount off the original asking price with consideration of this amended proposal," Brent said, tapping the folder containing his copy of the proposal. He looked at Pastor Landris, who nodded approval of Brent's summary of the previous hour-long presentation.

Mr. Busby looked at his financial advisor, then back over at Pastor Landris and Brent. "You do realize I'm a very busy man? And I don't have time to play games. I like to 'hit it' and 'quit it,' as some people say. This idea . . . this new proposal you two have just brought to me," he said, shaking his head, "is absolutely fantastic! I mean, I really love it." As the owner, his decision carried the weight Pastor Landris and Brent needed. "So . . . when can we get started? I'm ready. Let's get these papers drawn up." He glanced at his right-hand man.

"And Wilson," Mr. Busby said, "I don't want any of your usual red tape nonsense. In fact, I want you to draft it just like Pastor Landris and Mr. Underwood here have proposed it. Let them then take it to their lawyers to make sure it's exactly what we're agreeing on today. I mean, I don't want any unnecessary delays."

"But, Mr. Busby, I think we should discuss this a little more in depth, privately," Wilson said. His head slid downward slowly as an additional signal to slow things down.

"What more is there to discuss? We sell them the remaining thirty-five acres at the price they have proposed—the ten percent reduction of our price, which, looking at the figures, is still pretty high. We then take the 250 acres we still own surrounding their 40 acres and divide it up: 75 acres into an upscale housing division section of 3-acre plots, 30 acres into a middle-class housing development of one-third of an acre for each plot, and the other 145 acres go toward a shopping center, retirement housing community, possible business unit, and other projects the church is proposing. Like their future college campus, maybe. I think it's brilliant! Imagine the good will feedback this is going to generate. And we'll be doing something that's giving back to the community. Can't you just see those subdivisions? That proposal alone will more than make this entire deal worth it."

"But sir," Wilson said. "Might I point out—there are other churches already proposing to do this exact same thing or something similar? Other . . . *black* . . . churches. I *really* think you and I should sit down and talk about this further. Privately. We can then get back to Pastor Landris and Mr. Underwood as quickly as tomorrow."

"So you say other black churches are proposing this same sort of thing?"

"Yes, a few have mentioned this publicly. It's on record."

"Good! Then it sounds to me like an idea whose time has come," Mr. Busby said. "Talk is one thing; we're about to see something start to manifest in a matter of a few months, I do believe. These people here are ready to move. Pastor Landris, if you can get the money for the land within the next sixty days, plus what the two of you have personally agreed upon to purchase property to begin building your own new homes, we, gentlemen, will have brokered ourselves an awesome deal." He looked at Brent and Pastor Landris. "Wilson will have the contract in your hands in two to three days."

Wilson started to open his mouth, but Mr. Busby raised his hand and shook his head. Wilson's mouth closed.

"Sixty days to closing," Mr. Busby said to Pastor Landris and Brent, "after the contract has been signed."

Brent looked at Pastor Landris and smiled. They shook Mr. Busby's and Wilson's hands. Wilson wasn't at all as happy about this as the three.

Brent laughed, when he and Pastor Landris were secure in Pastor Landris's Denali and on their way back to the church to get Brent's car.

"Can you believe what just happened?" Brent asked.

"God is awesome, isn't He?" Pastor Landris said.

"If I hadn't been there to see it for myself, I wouldn't have believed it was possible. That man agreed to the whole thing! All of it," Brent said.

"Yeah." Pastor Landris shook his head. "Now, we just need to come up with six million dollars for the church land, and we'll be well on our way."

"And, of course, there's also the money you and I agreed to pay for the land to build our new homes," Brent said. "That was something, wherever it came from. Truthfully, I wasn't looking to build a house just yet. I thought I'd wait until I married to worry about that kind of long-term commitment. And you already have a nice home, Pastor Landris. So I know you did this totally for the new worship center's benefit."

"Both of us just made a sacrifice for the sake of the worship center that's to come. God placed those words in my mouth at that precise moment. It just happens that's what appears to have sealed the deal for us in the end," Pastor Landris said as he glanced at Brent. "Brent, I need you to be honest with me. The check you just wrote—can you cover it?"

"You mean the check I just wrote with my mouth, or the one I'm about to write out of my bank account for that property?"

"Both."

"Yeah, Pastor. I got it. I have some money put away. And this is actually a smart investment. So don't be totally impressed with me for agreeing to buy three acres of prime property for myself. Can you imagine? A subdivision as nice as these with a shopping center, theater, possibly the school and college you envisioned, all close to our new sanctuary?"

"Yes—in fact, I *can* imagine it. That's how God works. He says we have to see it before we can see it, then we'll see it. I've seen this from the beginning. After God sent me to Birmingham, He showed me this very thing in a vision. Now, thanks to you and the talent you've chosen to invest in the Kingdom of God through our ministry, we're on our way. Everybody will be able to see it."

Pastor Landris turned the music down. He was listening

to an Israel & New Breed CD. "Can I ask you something? It's kind of personal."

"Go ahead."

"Angel Gabriel. Is there something going on between the two of you? I've noticed you two when you're together. Am I getting something wrong here? Or is this just plain none of my business?"

Brent laughed. "Angel is . . . I know this sounds like a cliché, but she truly *is* an angel." He started grinning uncontrollably, the kind of grin a person tries to stop but can't.

Pastor Landris looked at him. "That's definitely the smile of a man who has fallen hard. So I'm on the right track." The light turned green. "Oh, yes, I remember that look well. I've seen it once or twice in a mirror myself."

"I don't know if I'd go as far as to call me fallen, but Angel is something special, for sure. To answer your question, she and I aren't actually dating or anything. We catch a movie together every now and then, get a bite to eat once or twice a week, or on occasion work late at her apartment. But that's pretty much the extent of it."

"Oh, but you're not dating? Uh-huh. I see."

Brent smiled. "Angel only seems to care about work. When she's not working at the station, she's working at the church. She really believes in what you're doing, and she's committed to doing her part. I saw that when she first began inviting me to the church."

"Well, Brent, when it comes to work, you're no slacker yourself. That proposal you put together was nothing short of . . . what's the word Mr. Busby used? Brilliant!"

"I like what I do, and I put my whole heart into anything I commit to. That's why dating has never come up in my conversations with Angel. She and I are too busy working to date anyone. Including, I suppose, each other."

"But hypothetically, say if you *were* interested in dating someone—"

"If I were, it would definitely be someone just like Angel.

In fact, I can't wait to tell her how our day went. She'll probably want to buy a piece of land to build a house herself, knowing her. Angel is just as committed to this idea as I am, if not more."

Pastor Landris smiled. "Maybe she can help you with your house for the time being. You know . . . help pick out a floor plan, colors of brick, roof, walls, carpet—stuff like that. There's a lot to building anything, believe me."

"Yeah," Brent said. "And she would be great with that. If she wants, I may just let her handle all of it for me." Brent glanced over at Pastor Landris and grinned. "So, what's Sister Landris going to say when she finds out you two are about to build a brand-new house?"

Pastor Landris laughed and threw his head back. "I'm not sure. It isn't like we've discussed this or anything. But one of her sisters has been living with us for a few months. Without saying too much, this just might turn out to be a real blessing in disguise. And Mr. Busby did offer his rolodex and any of his resources we might need to make things happen faster than normal, including the actual building of our houses. They say God works in mysterious ways."

Pastor Landris had money from the sale of his Atlanta house, which turned out to sell for $1.2 million. There was the alexandrite necklace and the rare-coin money, which had netted him $3 million. He'd used $2 million for the five acres of land and modular building. They had determined the land for the upscale subdivision would likely sell at $350,000 for the three-acre lot. The houses built in this area would have to have a required minimum value of 1.5 million dollars. This house would, for certain, drain all the money he had left.

And the church still had to come up with $6 million for the thirty-five acres of land it was buying, to be paid in full in sixty days.

"Okay, God," Pastor Landris said after dropping Brent off at his car. "We've done all we can do. Now the rest is up to You."

Chapter 26

A friend loveth at all times, and a brother is born for adversity.

(Proverbs 17:17)

Thomas had been going through thousands of dollars every few weeks. He was not any closer to finding work than when he first started looking. Pastor Landris didn't have a clue what was wrong with his brother, but he'd been acting really strange the entire year. When Pastor Landris arrived from his talk with Mr. Busby, he came home to find Thomas's car in his driveway.

"Hey, George," Thomas said as soon as his brother walked in the den. Rachel's grandchildren were in there playing—her two children were supposed to be watching them while they played video games. The room looked liked a tornado had hit it.

Pastor Landris nodded. "Thomas."

"Justin, stop it!" Chevon said. "Gimme back the gamote!"

Justin started laughing at his little sister as he ran around the room holding the television remote control high above his head. "It's not a ga-mote. It's a re-mote!" he said. "If you can't say it, little baby, then you don't need to hold it."

"Keisha, tell Justin to stop!" Chevon yelled to her sixteen-year-old aunt. She started crying. "I was watching that show and he snatched the gamote out my hand."

"Boy, I told you to leave her alone one time," Keisha

yelled. "Don't make me have to get up and come over there. You know you don't want me to have to do that," Keisha said, momentarily taking her cell phone away from her ear before returning to her conversation seconds later.

"Still got a houseful, I see."

Pastor Landris looked around. "Yeah." *What else could he say?*

"Look, I know you're busy. I wanted to come by and pay you back some of the money I've borrowed."

"Really," Pastor Landris said with skepticism, but with a pleased expression.

"Yeah. I thought I would have had more of it by now, but I have this project I just signed on to do. I've started my own business. I'm doing tapings for preachers who want to be on television and sell their own tapes. In fact, I just signed a huge contract with this pastor who has a pretty large church. You may have heard of him—Reverend Walker?"

"I've heard of him. Never met him, though."

"He's a pretty sharp guy. In fact, he was so impressed with me, he offered me a job. I told him I really wanted to do my own thing. He respects that, but money is hard to come by when you're starting your own business. I know you can appreciate that," Thomas said.

"Absolutely," Pastor Landris said.

"Anyway," Thomas took out his billfold and pulled out some cash, "I wanted to give you something back on the money you've loaned me. I feel bad never returning anything. I was thinking today—that's probably why I'm having such a hard time getting more of the money I need. I should learn how to give in order to receive."

Pastor Landris nodded. He knew this was leading somewhere, and he didn't care to be sucked in too quickly.

"Well, thank you." Pastor Landris reached out to receive the money Thomas still held in his hand.

"Yeah, I really want to give this to you, because, George, you've been wonderful to me. I don't know many brothers who would have treated their brother the way you have me, especially considering all that's happened. I'm so close to my breakthrough. If I only had $2,000 now, by next week, things would be right."

"Thomas, do you need to keep that money?" Pastor Landris looked down at the dollars still gripped in Thomas's hand.

"Man, do I. But I want to do right by you."

"Keep it, Thomas. You can give it to me later."

Thomas let out a sigh. "For real? Thanks. You're the best, George. I mean that." Thomas stood up. It was an awkward moment as he and his brother were eye to eye.

"Is there anything else?" Pastor Landris asked, sensing there was more.

"Yeah. I kind of hate to ask, but you know the Bible says we have not because we ask not." Thomas put his wallet back in his pocket.

"What is it?"

"I was wondering if I could possibly borrow $2,000?"

"You want to borrow some money from me now? Right now?"

"Just until next week, George. I promise—I promise this will be the last time. I'm so close to my breakthrough. I feel the wind shifting. But my rent's due, and I have other bills I've got to pay this week. But next week, man, things are going to be right."

Pastor Landris shook his head. "Sorry, Thomas. I'm going to have to say no."

Thomas looked at him in total disbelief. "What? Did you just say no?"

"Yes. I said no."

"George, didn't you hear me? My rent is due. I'm on the verge of a breakthrough here. I know I've promised you your money back before, but it's been hard trying to find a job. But now this is working for me. I don't want to throw all my hard work away. Not when I'm this close." He rubbed his face. "How about $1,000? I can make that work." He looked at Pastor Landris. "Come on, man. What kind of a brother *are* you?"

"What?" Pastor Landris said. "'What kind of a brother *am* I?' Is that what you just asked me?"

"Okay, I can see I went too far with that one. But I'm desperate here, George. Okay, let me come totally clean with you. My rent is past due. I have this eviction notice I need to handle this week." The television was blaring and the children were getting louder. Thomas reached out and grabbed his brother by his wrist. "I told you I'll give it back next week. I promise. What more do you want me to say? Do you want me to beg? Is that what this is all about?"

Pastor Landris pulled his arm out of Thomas's grip. "It's never been about anything. Do you even stop and think about the amount of money I've lost because of you? The radio deal was not my idea. You and I both know I'll probably never recover a dime of it. Yet, you've been in Birmingham for two whole years now, and you haven't managed to find a job. Who's been footing your bills since then, brother?"

"I know . . . you, George." The noise was getting louder. Thomas looked at the children, then back at Pastor Landris. "Can we can get out of this room and talk about this somewhere else? I can't take this racket . . ." Thomas walked out of the den into the hallway. He started inhaling deep breaths.

"Are you all right?" Pastor Landris asked.

"Fine, not that you really care."

"Thomas, don't even start. I'm not going to allow you to make me feel guilty. I always bail you out, and what do you learn?"

Thomas looked into his brother's eyes. He laughed. "Yeah, I get it now. I'm responsible for my own self. Coming here was a waste of time. Trust me, you won't have to worry about me making that mistake again."

Thomas stormed toward the entrance door.

"Thomas! Thomas!" Pastor Landris yelled. Thomas slammed the door behind him.

Johnnie Mae came to the foyer. "Was that Thomas leaving like that?"

"Yeah."

"What's wrong with him?"

Pastor Landris shook his head. "Can we not talk about him right now?"

"But you're upset, Landris. I'm here if you want to talk about it."

Pastor Landris smiled at her. She had flour on her face. "What are you cooking?"

"Okay, I'll play along. Blackberry cobbler."

"For real?" Pastor Landris couldn't believe it. He loved blackberry cobbler.

He put his arm around her waist as they walked to the kitchen together. "How did your meeting for the land go?" she asked.

"It went exceptionally well, in fact. We're getting the land for the church."

"Yes!" She pumped her fist. "I knew it, I knew it. I . . . knew it!" she sang.

"And you and I will also be building a new house in a brand-new subdivision associated with the church's property."

"What?" she asked in a tone Pastor Landris wasn't sure how to appraise.

"We're getting a new house, Johnnie Mae. Our house."

"Landris, that's not necessary. This house is fine." She grabbed him and pulled him to a corner as she whispered, "My sister will be gone soon. I promise—this arrangement is only temporary."

He kissed her. "Regardless, we're still getting a new house. Our house. One that you and I will build together. And J. M., just for the record . . ."

"Yes?" she said, smiling. He rarely called her J. M. unless he was about to say something really significant or special. "For the record . . . I absolutely love you," he said.

She continued smiling. "Yeah? Well, I absolutely love you, too. I guess this means you're going to tell me the whole story eventually, just not right now."

"Yeah," he said with a devious smile. "Eventually, I'll tell you the whole story. You wouldn't happen to have an extra six million dollars lying around, would you?"

"Oh yeah—you're going to tell me the *whole* story before this night is out."

He kissed her again.

"Mommy!" Princess Rose called out from the kitchen. "I'm still waiting!"

"The blackberry cobbler," Johnnie Mae said. "Princess Rose is helping me in the kitchen."

He kissed her again before she left. "Yeah . . . blackberry . . . cobbler. The blacker the berry," he kissed her again, "the sweeter the juice."

She blushed as she walked into the kitchen. "Hey, baby girl, Mommy's back."

"Daddy Landris," Princess Rose said in her sweet little singsong voice as soon as she saw him. "We're making a blackberry cobbler."

"So I heard." He looked at Johnnie Mae and winked. "Is there enough room for me to help?"

Princess Rose giggled. "Sure, Daddy Landris. There's always room for Daddy-o!"

They all laughed.

Chapter 27

Pride goeth before destruction, and a haughty spirit before a fall.

(Proverbs 16:18)

"Brother Thomas, to what do I owe the pleasure?"

"Reverend Walker, thank you for seeing me on such short notice," Thomas said. "Your secretary wasn't out there, but the receptionist told me it was all right to come on in." He shook Reverend Walker's hand and sat down in the chair on the other side of the pastor's colossal desk. Thomas did a quick perusal of the room again. "Nice. Really nice."

"Thank you. My staff tries." He sat erect in the tall, jet-black office chair. "Again, to what do I owe the pleasure of your visit so soon after our last conversation?"

Thomas cleared his throat. "I've been thinking about your offer."

Reverend Walker leaned forward. "Yes, the one I made offering you a position to come work here for me. The one you turned down flat." He placed his fingers together and tapped them. "Don't tell me God has answered my prayer, and you've had a change of heart?"

"I don't know about God answering your prayer, but I have reconsidered." Thomas rubbed both his hands on his thighs in a quick, back-and-forth motion. "Look, this is kind of hard for me. You know Pastor Landris is my brother."

"I'm aware of that, but that fact has no bearing on the offer I made you." He leaned in closer to Thomas. "You're a talented man. Gifted. You have ideas that, frankly, blow the people presently on staff around me out of the water. I need someone like you on my team. How do you think your brother will feel about you coming to work for me?" Reverend Walker asked.

"My brother doesn't own me. George is not like that, anyway. He'll be happy that I'm doing something I enjoy and am being well-paid to do it."

"Great segue into the money part of the conversation." Reverend Walker smiled and nodded. "Yes, I can see you and I are going to get along famously. Famously. Okay, so let's talk dollars and benefits."

Thomas smiled and returned the nod. This was going to work out fine. When he heard what the good reverend was paying for this full-time position, he was even more pleased he'd come to this decision.

"One more thing," Thomas said. "As an act of good faith, do you think I could get an advance on my first check? There are some things I'd like to have for this new position prior to coming onboard officially. And since this is for your organization, I wouldn't want to take any of my money—"

"Or your brother's," Reverend Walker said. "I'm sure he has paid you well for the service you've provided."

Thomas snickered. "Yeah. He's taken good care of me this far. But now it's time I head in a new direction. As you know, I have some cutting-edge ideas. I believe I can help you and your congregation catapult into the next level."

Reverend Walker picked up the phone and buzzed his secretary. An older woman walked in, which surprised Thomas.

"Ms. Jeanette, would you please cut a check to Thomas Landris. Also, he'll be coming on staff, starting . . ." he glanced at Thomas, "tomorrow?"

Thomas gave a nod of agreement.

"Tomorrow," Reverend Walker said. "You can catch him on the way out to fill out all of his paperwork. And be sure he signs the standard confidentiality agreement."

"Yes, Reverend," Ms. Jeanette said. "How much should I cut the check for?"

"How's $2,000?" Reverend Walker said, looking at Thomas.

"That will work," Thomas said with a huge grin. *God is good all the time!*

"Make it $2500, Ms. Jeanette—equivalent to his first semi-month paycheck. We want to be sure we start our new brother here off right. He's part of the family now. We'll consider this seed money," he said to Thomas. "So of course you know—we'll be expecting a return when harvest time rolls around."

"Absolutely," Thomas said, sitting up even straighter.

Ms. Jeanette left the office.

"She seems nice," Thomas said, being polite.

"I know what you were thinking. You thought I would have some young thing handling my secretarial functions."

"Well, in truth, I did expect someone like I thought you would have. The receptionist is something else. She's the one who has always announced me when I've visited. Your secretary was away from her desk both times I've been to see you. This is my first time meeting her."

"The receptionists are all volunteers," Reverend Walker said. "I never know who'll be guarding the door from one day till the next. But Ms. Jeanette has been with me for a long while. She's good, and I need people around me who know their stuff. I don't mind teaching folks, but successful people surround themselves with people who can handle their jobs with minimal supervision. Ms. Jeanette runs this place." He leaned in to whisper to Thomas. "In fact, she's really the brains behind most of this operation. If she ever left, we'd be sunk." He snickered. "But don't tell her that, though."

"Your secret is safe with me," Thomas said, mockingly zipping his lips.

"I'm liking you more and more," Reverend Walker said. He stood and extended his hand to Thomas. "Welcome aboard, Brother Landris. We're going to be a better organization, I do believe, because of you."

Thomas stood and, with a firm grip, shook Reverend Walker's hand. "Thank you. To be honest, I was a little apprehensive about doing this at first. But now, I'm glad I made this decision. You won't be sorry."

Chapter 28

As sorrowful, yet always rejoicing; as poor, yet making many rich; as having nothing, and yet possessing all things.

(2 Corinthians 6:10)

"George, how are you?" Thomas asked.

"Great, and you?"

"I'm happy and excited. I just wanted to call you and say, about last night—"

"Thomas, look. I'm sorry about that—"

"Oh, don't apologize. It was the best thing you could have done for me. Sometimes cutting a person loose, like you did me last night, can work out for all concerned."

Pastor Landris was quiet a minute. He could sense that something didn't feel right. "Well, I'm glad you see it this way."

"Also, my brother, I wanted you to be the first to know—I've gotten a job. Full-time, with great pay, and a great benefit package. In fact, they were so excited about getting me, they wrote me a check today—in advance, mind you—for $2500."

"Wow, that's great, Thomas. I'm really happy for you. I really am. Things seem to be working out for you, after all. So what company did you hire on with?"

"It's not really a company, per se, although you could say I'm technically still working in the family business. I accepted an executive position over at Divine Conquerors Church with Reverend Marshall Walker."

"Really," Pastor Landris said. He didn't know how he was supposed to feel about this news.

"Yes, really. And since this is a full-time position, I will no longer be able to help out with your church. In fact, I'm also required to become a member. They don't believe in filling their jobs with outside people. So, I start working officially tomorrow, and this coming Sunday, I'll join their church and begin a 15-week New Member's class. Can you believe they'll be paying me to attend that class? I'm getting paid for what some people volunteer to do."

Pastor Landris was stunned into silence. He tried to think of something to say, but he was not prepared for any of this.

"George, I know this is a shock to you, and I'm sorry that it's taking you a few minutes to process it. I do want to thank you for everything—and I do mean absolutely everything. You're a great brother, and I'm honored to have been able to serve under your leadership. In fact, much of what you've taught me over the past few years is probably what helped me land this awesome job in the first place. With that said, I love you, I thank you, and I ask the blessings of the Lord for your life and your continued ministry."

"Thank you, Thomas. But are you sure about this? I mean, there's something not setting right."

"Of course you're not feeling too good about it. I'm leaving you, and I'm sure you're concerned about how this might look to other people. But don't you be concerned about other folk and what they might think. You and I know we're still cool. There's no rift between us. We're brothers, we always will be, and we still love each other. You also know if you need me, I'll be there for you."

"Yeah, Thomas. I know."

"Well, I'm going to get off the phone now. I have some more calls to make. I have to let Sapphire know what's going on. And George, in case you're wondering—I won't try to take members from your church along with me. If Sapphire chooses to go, you know it's only because she and I have this special relationship."

"Sure."

"I'll talk with you later," Thomas said. "And George, thanks again. For everything, and I mean that from my heart."

Pastor Landris hung up the phone. Johnnie Mae walked in and looked at him.

"Okay, what's wrong now?"

"Thomas accepted a job with this preacher at Divine Conquerors, and he's planning to join the church this Sunday." Pastor Landris sat down.

"You mean Reverend Walker's church? Oh, Landris, I'm so sorry. Please don't let this get to you." She came over and took his hand.

"It's not about me," Pastor Landris said. "I just hope he knows what he's doing."

"This is Thomas we're talking about," Johnnie Mae said. "Thomas."

Pastor Landris looked at her. "We'd better start praying and covering him with the blood of Jesus right now."

"I'm already way ahead of you," Johnnie Mae said.

Chapter 29

Better is a dinner of herbs where love is, than a stalled ox and hatred therewith.

(Proverbs 15:17)

Johnnie Mae was taking care of more of her own housework since she told Ms. Bertha she'd much prefer she work those three additional days at her mother's instead of coming to her house. There were enough bodies around already without Ms. Bertha being there, trying hard to get something done. With six additional people underfoot, it was becoming almost impossible to keep anywhere clean for long anyway.

Rachel was supposed to be making her crew pick up after themselves. They did sometimes. Johnnie Mae felt her mother's house needed the help more now.

Her mother wanted to wash her own clothes and clean her own house, but things were going from bad to worse when she was left alone. Having her "sister-friend" Bertha around made it easier—Bertha was great at making her friend, Countess Gates, feel she was doing the work, when, in fact, she really wasn't.

Johnnie Mae had been invited to speak on a panel along with other authors from around the country—she would only be gone for two days. With Rachel and Ms. Bertha there to watch her mother and Princess Rose, Johnnie Mae felt okay about leaving.

There was an author at the conference on another panel who attracted Johnnie Mae's attention, a woman named Fern Reiss.

Fern was there to share some information from three of her latest books: *The Publishing Game: Bestseller in 30 Days; The Publishing Game: Find an Agent in 30 Days;* and *The Publishing Game: Publish a Book in 30 Days.* She was also promoting a newsletter that Johnnie Mae would soon discover was becoming all the rage with a lot of people.

But what really captured Johnnie Mae's attention was when Fern touched briefly on her battle with infertility. She'd published a book back in 1999 entitled *The Infertility Diet: Get Pregnant and Prevent Miscarriage.* Fern had spoken briefly about her book when Johnnie Mae visited a writing/publishing/promotion workshop in Denver, Colorado. Fern had just published this book and had candidly mentioned how the information it contained had changed her life. As proof, Fern had become, by then, the mother of two.

An honors graduate from Harvard University with a degree in government, Fern also studied cooking and nutrition at the Culinary Institute of America and the Kushi Institute for Macrobiotic Studies in Massachusetts. She now owned her own publishing company. Johnnie Mae walked over to her and pointed to *The Infertility Diet: Get Pregnant and Prevent Miscarriage.* "Excuse me—I don't want to take up too much of your time, but this book . . . I'm really interested in it. I've been trying to get pregnant for almost eighteen months now. My doctor can't find anything wrong with me or my husband—I hope something you've written in here will help," she added, picking up a copy.

"My husband and I tried for years to get pregnant with no success. The doctors couldn't find a reason for us, either. You know, there are foods a woman should eat before and during this crucial time, and there are foods she should totally avoid."

"Like?"

"Like—you're around what age now?" Fern asked.

"I'll be forty-four, six months from now."

"Okay, I would say to you—not knowing any of your specifics, of course—you should avoid eating pickled ginger at sushi bars. Ginger has been linked to miscarriage, and in China, it is used to abort."

"I'd never heard of that. I'm not a sushi kind of person, though. But I've had ginger tea a few times, although I much prefer green tea," Johnnie Mae said. She noticed others in the line who, rightfully so, were growing impatient.

Fern saw them as well and smiled to let them know she wouldn't be much longer. "Yams are a food I would recommend."

"You know, I've heard about yams from my mother. In fact, she said eating yams was the best way to produce a girl."

Fern laughed. "I have girls."

Johnnie Mae shook her hand, thanked her, and walked toward the exit.

Johnnie Mae started reading portions of the book she'd bought on infertility while on the plane home. She wasn't sure how much of this she'd actually do, but there were interesting points about many different foods.

As soon as she saw Pastor Landris waiting for her near baggage claim, she could tell by the look on his face that something horrible had happened while she was gone.

"Landris, why are you looking so distraught? And where's Princess Rose?" Pastor Landris was supposed to bring her with him.

"Four words: Rachel and her crew. We're going to have to do something, and soon." He took her suitcase from her. "We can talk about it after we get home. I know you're exhausted from your trip—and Princess Rose was just too upset to come along."

"Landris, except to see my baby, do I even want to go home?" Johnnie Mae asked.

He looked at her. "Not really. Just keep saying to yourself: they're only things. Just things."

Johnnie Mae stopped walking. "It's that bad? Maybe you should tell me now instead of later."

"Trust me on this, sweetheart. Even later will be too soon."

Chapter 30

So the poor hath hope, and iniquity stoppeth her mouth.

(Job 5:16)

"Okay now, Landris. We're almost home. I've had a long two days. I don't want any surprises. Tell me—what happened?"

"For starters, the walls and the carpet," Pastor Landris said as he drove and alternated his gaze between the road and Johnnie Mae.

"Go on."

"There are huge holes in some of the walls, compliments of Justin. Katie decided she wanted to color and paint the little one, Chevon, with permanent magic markers and her paint kit she got for Christmas. Chevon was very pretty, though. At least, she matched the walls and the floors perfectly. And Chevon stuffed the toilet upstairs with all of her favorite toys . . . or, should I say, all of Princess Rose's favorite toys, as she tried flushing them individually. She'd watched a television show and happened to see a character flushing toys down the commode as he sang the toy's name and the words 'down the hole.' Chevon did the same and enjoyed seeing these toys circling downward, right before they disappeared 'down the hole.'"

"Please, don't tell me any more."

"Oh, but you need to know the rest, since a few of the

toys refused to go 'down the hole.' It flooded the upstairs—
messed up the carpeting, some walls, and a few other things.
Your sister was asleep at the time, but as she puts it, 'Even
had I not been, I wouldn't have known how to shut the water
valve off.' So the ceilings in a few rooms are also in pretty
bad condition now."

When Johnnie Mae arrived home, it was even worse than
Landris had described. With the exception of Chevon, who
was almost marker-and paint-free. Almost.

"I don't believe this," Johnnie Mae said as she surveyed
the damage.

"Johnnie, now don't go getting all upset. I'll have all of
this fixed in no time," Rachel said. "I know it looks bad right
now, but we can plaster those holes right up. Buy some
paint—you know you can match up existing shades really
easy nowadays with the computers these home places have."

Johnnie Mae just looked at her. "Plaster the holes? Have
you seen those holes, Rachel? I mean, really—have you
looked at them at all?"

"I've seen holes bigger than those before. Somebody who
knows what he's doing can have that looking good as new in
no time." Rachel turned toward Pastor Landris. "You should
be pretty handy. I'm sure even you could fix something like
that."

"Rachel," Johnnie Mae said, "those holes are big enough
to throw a basketball through. What was Justin doing?"

"I'm not sure. As I'm confident your loving husband has
already informed you, I happened to be resting my eyes at
the time. I was having one of my headaches, and I decided to
lie down for a few minutes, just a few. I suppose I must have
dozed off. Princess Rose came running in the den like somebody was trying to kill her or something. That child really
does need to be around other children more than just at
kindergarten. The girl is five years old and practically scared
of her own shadow. She's hiding somewhere now."

"She's not scared of her own shadow. And she was doing

just fine until your grandchildren came here and started terrorizing everybody," Johnnie Mae said, looking at them as they wrapped themselves around Rachel's legs.

"See, Johnnie? Now you're scaring them. They're terrified of you. They think you're mean."

"They're not terrified of me. They know I'm not going to let them run over me like you do."

"They don't run over me. There are just ways to discipline children now other than hollering, fussing, and whipping on them," Rachel said. She began peeling them from her legs and sitting them on the couch.

"I don't advocate fussing and whipping, either. In fact, I can count on one hand the times Princess Rose has gotten a spanking from me," Johnnie Mae said. Princess Rose ran in and gave her mother a bear hug.

"Mommy, Chevon flushed my stuffed animals down the toilet—even Mr. Ears. I told her to stop, and she just laughed at me and said, 'Fluffy go down the hole.' I tried to go tell Aunt Rachel, and that's when Justin took the bowling ball and tried to throw a strike while I was walking down the hall. It crashed into the wall. He started laughing, and I told him I was going to tell on him. He took the bowling ball and starting swinging it and hitting the wall with it on purpose."

"Princess Rose," Rachel said sweetly. "What has Auntie Rachel told you about tattling so much?"

Johnnie Mae looked at Rachel almost crossed-eyed. She raised her hand and pointed it at Rachel. "Don't you dare!" Johnnie Mae said. "Don't you *dare* try to make my daughter feel bad about telling what shouldn't have ever happened in the first place. Look at this house! You mean to tell me you slept through all of this commotion?"

"This is a really big house, Johnnie. Besides, I'm used to tuning out noises." Rachel walked over to Johnnie Mae. "I told you I'll pay for whatever damages were done."

"With what, Rachel? Do you know how much it's going to cost to get this house right?"

"Johnnie Mae, let's go upstairs and get you unpacked," Pastor Landris said. "I've taken your suitcase up to our room." He grabbed her by the elbow and steered her as he held out his hand for Princess Rose, who reached up and placed her hand inside of his. "Come on," Pastor Landris said to them both. "I know, it's been a long day. We can deal with this later. It's going to be all right. I promise."

Johnnie Mae clenched her jaw and shook her head.

"I'm sorry, Johnnie." Rachel hollered after her. "And I'm going to figure out a way to pay for this. I promise you—I'm going to make this right."

"Keep walking, Johnnie Mae," Pastor Landris said in a soft voice. "This is going to be fine. They're just things, remember? Things. Only things."

The floor made squishing sounds from the water in the carpet as they walked down the hall to their bedroom. Johnnie Mae stopped and just stared at him. "Things," she said between clenched teeth. "Just . . . *things*."

Chapter 31

Except the Lord build the house, they labor in vain that build it: except the Lord keep the city, the watchman waketh but in vain.

(Psalm 127:1)

"Johnnie Mae, let's look at floor plans for our new house," Pastor Landris said, attempting to direct her thoughts away from all the damages that had occurred earlier at the house. "I'll go put Princess Rose in her own bed."

Johnnie Mae was sitting in bed; Princess Rose was sound asleep next to her.

"I don't know if I really want to look at any house plans tonight, Landris."

"Why not? You've put this off for the past two weeks as it is. The builders are going to need these if they're to build the house of our dreams."

Johnnie Mae wiped her eyes again. She had been crying since she came upstairs. She could hear Rachel downstairs, cleaning up. She knew Rachel was feeling bad about what had happened, but it was still hard for her to get over it.

"Why is it that people don't seem to care as much about other folks' things as they do about their own? Rachel would never have allowed those kids to tear up her house like she let them tear up ours today," Johnnie Mae said. "I'm sure she probably *is* tired. It's hard raising children—little ones, big ones, and especially the grown ones. Her teenagers are over in the guest house acting like they think they're full-fledged adults."

"I know. But I don't think we'll be having any more prob-lems out of them in that area. Not after I showed them the se-curity cameras that identify every person entering and exiting our property," Pastor Landris said.

"And when you told them you'd be turning over the tape to the police if you found any more unauthorized people on our property—that stopped all the traffic in a hurry." Johnnie Mae dabbed her eyes and smiled. She touched one of Princess Rose's pigtails. "Chevon flushed Mr. Ears down the toilet, and now he's gone. Her father gave her that mini bunny on her very first Easter. Look at her . . . sleeping so peacefully."

Every night, Princess Rose had made sure Mr. Ears was in the bed next to her and her favorite doll, whichever doll that happened to be at the time. Johnnie Mae would hand-wash him often, trying to keep him clean. Wherever Princess Rose went, Mr. Ears was usually in tow. People had tried giving her a new bunny to replace it, but no matter how large or beautiful the new one was, Princess Rose would say, "Thank you, but I don't need another bunny besides Mr. Ears. He's family. My daddy gave him to me." She would then hug him that much tighter.

"I won't wake her," Pastor Landris whispered as he scooped Princess Rose softly up in his arms and carried her out of their room.

When he came back, Johnnie Mae was reading a book.

"What are you reading?" he asked.

"A book about infertility and how certain foods can affect a woman's ability to get pregnant."

"Johnnie Mae," he took the book out of her hands and laid it on the nightstand, "if you and I don't have a baby, it's okay. I'm fine either way. I believe God will have His way in this matter when He's ready."

"So you believe there's nothing wrong with me?"

"I believe," he reached over and picked up the book of house plans, "we have enough on our plates to keep us busy while we wait on the Lord. And again," he began as though he was preaching a sermon, "I say—Wait on the Lord!"

She shook her head and took the plans out of his hand. "Have you seen anything in here you like so far?"

"A few things. But I really want us to do this together. I don't want it to be my house or your house. I want it to be our house."

"I still can't believe you agreed to do this. We have a house. We didn't need a bigger house—a minimum one point five million dollars worth of house, at that."

"Johnnie Mae, this was one of the things that cinched the deal for the remaining church property. Brent and I both agreed we'd be the first to build houses in this new subdivision. That's going to let people know we're really serious and committed. And honestly, I kind of wanted us to build a house together anyway."

She stopped turning the pages. "So you have a problem with this house?"

"This house is the home you built with Solomon," Pastor Landris said. "I know it has special memories for you and Princess Rose. I respect that. I wasn't planning on doing this right now, but since the opportunity arose, I'm ready to do it. The bank approved the $18 million loan for the thirty-five acres to start phase one of the church building. They were actually swayed by the new subdivision idea as well. I think Mr. Busby may have also called in a few favors to make this loan happen for the church. We all have a lot riding on this."

"I still can't believe they did things so quickly."

"What quickly?" Pastor Landris said. He took the plan from her and started turning the pages. "We took the bank the business plan and proposal, along with Dexter Iron and Steel's commitment and recommendation letter. It took all this time and a ton of discussion and paperwork for them to approve us, but they did. Of course, Mr. Busby calling in some favors to make things happen faster for us didn't hurt either. You can definitely see the hand of God on this. It's the favor of God."

"The congregation is really excited about the new building. People are giving from their hearts because they love God and believe in this work. No pressure from you, no scriptural manipulation—just because they love God." Johnnie Mae watched him turn the pages of the book. "Brother and Sister Watts have made arrangements to buy a lot in the new subdivision, as well as about ten other families."

Pastor Landris handed the book back to her and popped a page with his hand. "What do you think of this one?"

She looked at the floor plans and specs. "Nice, but do we really need six bedrooms?"

"Let's see . . . there's you, me, Princess Rose, the new baby—"

"You're just saying that, trying to make me feel you really want one. I don't think you do, and the more I think about it lately, maybe we don't need any more children."

"And miss out on a possible 'mini me' running around, driving you crazy?"

She started laughing even though she really didn't want to. "Landris," she placed her hand on his face and caressed it. "You're so wonderful to me . . . and Princess Rose . . . my mother . . . and even my sisters, who aren't always so nice to you."

"Believe me, it's fairly easy," Pastor Landris said. "Having you in my life and knowing that nothing that comes up, good or bad, gets past our all-knowing Father. Johnnie Mae, I wouldn't trade our life for all the money in the world." He kissed her. "Now, back to the house. I need to tell the builder something by the end of this week. Think of it this way: if Rachel doesn't move out soon, at least *we* can. Problem solved."

She laughed. "It's funny how things work out, huh?" She turned the page and stopped. "Landris, what about this one?"

He leaned over and studied it, then frowned a little. "So you really like that one?"

"Actually, I do. It has casual elegance, sort of reminds me of Oheka Castle, yet it's more practical," Johnnie Mae said, comparing it to the place where she and Landris had exchanged their vows.

"Do you want to go with this one or would you rather look some more?"

"Were there others you looked at already you want me to see?" Johnnie Mae asked.

He smiled and turned to the back of the book, pulling off a sticky note and handing it to her.

Johnnie Mae started laughing. "Landris, you'd already picked out that house plan! Why didn't you tell me that when I said I liked it?"

"I guess I just wanted you to see how much we really do think alike. So, it seems like this is the one. If you get a chance between now and Friday morning, jot down any changes or additions you'd like so we can have the builder incorporate them into the blueprint." He pulled out a scripture he'd also written down and had placed in the back of the book.

"Johnnie Mae, here's a scripture I found. You know I believe the answer to whatever we need is in the Word. This is a specific scripture, just for us."

Johnnie Mae took the scripture and read it out loud. "'He maketh the barren woman to keep house, and to be a joyful mother of children. Praise ye the Lord.' Psalm 113:9."

"Commit it to your heart, Johnnie Mae. If you really want to be a joyful mother of children, commit it to your heart. For out of the heart, the mouth speaks. And one more thing: when you say it, make it personal. Say: He maketh *me* to keep house, and to be a joyful mother of *children*. Just like that."

"You really do want a baby, don't you? I'm not the only one?"

He smiled. "Yes. I didn't know how much until the other day. I don't want you feeling any pressure from me one way or the other, but I can't help but wonder what our child will look like."

"And if I can't have one? How will you feel then?"

"We're not going to believe for that. You really desire a

baby. That's what I'm believing God for. I'm not going to compromise. You and I will mix our faith and God's Word together. I'm doing that daily for so many things: our spiritual growth; our family, both home and the congregation; the church building; our new house; and our baby."

The builders started framing the Landris's new house. Pastor Landris held Johnnie Mae's hand as they walked the land. He repeated Joshua 1:3 as they walked. "'Every place that the sole of your feet shall tread upon, that have I given unto you, as I said unto Moses.' Johnnie Mae, these were the words I spoke as Brent and I walked the place where the church will be going up soon. I also spoke them on this property as I chose the land we were to build our home on. God is so good. Look at where He's brought us from. He's given us the land."

She laid her head on his shoulder, and he knew the one thing missing right now for sheer happiness was the baby they both desired.

"If we get good weather, I anticipate we'll have your house completed no later than the first of July," Max, the building foreman, said as he walked up to them.

"You startled us," Johnnie Mae said, popping her head up suddenly.

"Sorry about that. As I was saying, with the house you chose, I believe it'll be ready to move in by July if we work at full capacity. It'll be tight, though. My boss has made it clear he wants this done as quickly as we can manage it, with our highest standard of quality, of course. You folks must have friends in high places."

Johnnie Mae smiled at him. *Yes, we do. And what a friend we have in Jesus.* She now had a due date. Not for a baby yet, but a due date nonetheless.

Chapter 32

Cast in thy lot among us; let us all have one purse.

(Proverbs 1:14)

Sapphire, Angel, and Faith were sitting in the publication room at the church, waiting for Johnnie Mae. She'd called to say she was running a little late. The three of them sat and chatted to pass the time.

"We haven't had much of a chance to really talk, Faith," Sapphire said. "I see you in passing some Sundays. I see Hope more—she always makes an effort to speak. I thought she volunteered to help with this project. I'm surprised not to see her here."

"Yeah, Hope discovered at the last minute there was a slight conflict. Both of us volunteered, but Hope won't be able to do this after all," Faith said.

"My name is Angel. Angela Gabriel, but everybody calls me Angel. I've met Hope, but not you. Is there a problem maybe we can help with?"

"Nice to meet you, Angel. I've heard a lot about you. Hope seems to think the world of you. And no, there's nothing you can help with."

Angel looked closer. "It's amazing how much you two look alike. I mean, in the face, that is." Angel gave her another quick once-over. "You dress differently, and you have very different personalities."

Faith noticed the way Angel was looking at her. "We get that a lot. I suppose that's why they call people who are identical twins, identical." Faith faked a smile. "So—Sapphire, where's that hunk of a man of yours? I haven't seen him around church lately."

Sapphire looked at her a second before answering her. "He doesn't attend here any longer. He joined another church."

"He joined another church? What is that all about? His brother is the pastor here, and he joined another church? Well, I mean, I know this place is not for everybody, but this is his brother," Faith said as she leaned in closer to Sapphire. She hoped Johnnie Mae would be late enough for her to get all the information.

"It wasn't anything like that," Sapphire said. "He went to work at Divine Conquerors Church and one of their stipulations for employment is a person has to be a member."

"He went there for a job?" Faith made a smacking sound. "What, there wasn't enough work for him to do something here? As talented as he is?"

"Why are you so concerned?" Angel asked.

Faith turned and looked at her. "Actually, Sapphire and I were discussing this, but since you asked, I'm just concerned about how it looks. Pastor Landris is his brother, and he leaves here and joins another church. I'm sure that's given people a lot to talk about. I just hadn't heard about it, that's all."

"That's because Pastor Landris doesn't like gossip. You may not know this about him," Sapphire said, "but he's really good at keeping his mouth shut about things that aren't everybody's business. He's not a tell-all pastor like some."

Faith looked at Sapphire. "Excuse me. I was just interested in knowing what was going on. I'm not planning to gossip about it or anything. So, Sapphire, why didn't you go with him? If it's okay to ask *that*, that is. I don't want to cross the line again." She flashed a look at Angel.

Angel got up and walked over to the computer, turned it on, and waited for it to boot.

Sapphire looked at Angel and back at Faith. "Thomas did what he felt he needed to do. He and I are not married, and I prefer Pastor Landris's teaching."

"What are you planning to do when the two of you do marry? Again, I'm not trying to be nosy, so if it's none of my business, I won't be offended if you tell me so."

Sapphire smiled. She glanced out of the side of her eye and noticed Angel was laughing to herself. *Angel's really enjoying this.*

"I'm not sure he and I are going to go down that path, at least not for a while. Thomas is working some things out within himself."

"Hey, look. I'm sorry. I didn't mean to pry," Faith said. "I just noticed I hadn't seen him around. Usually, you and he sit together, although everybody's been so busy since so many people have been coming here. Good thing we're expanding our space. That property for the new sanctuary is gorgeous! In fact, I'm thinking seriously about buying some land to build me a house. Probably not in the rich-folk section like Pastor Landris and some of the others, but I love the area and the whole concept."

Faith turned and looked at Angel. "What about you and Brent? Is that his name?"

"What about me and him?"

"Are you two planning to marry soon? I heard you were helping him with his house plans," Faith said. She stood up and walked over near Angel. She could see Angel was working in a program called Photoshop, playing around with two different graphics. "That looks nice. Did you do those?"

It was a picture of an angel holding a sword with the words SWORD OF THE SPIRIT engraved on the blade and BIBLE on the handle and one of a shield with FAITH inside it.

"I helped," Angel said.

"You and Brent make a nice couple. Anything happening there?"

"Just friends. We also work together professionally," Angel said. "Who told you I was helping him with his house?"

Faith acted like she was trying to recall. "You know . . . I don't remember. I'm sure wherever I heard it, it was in passing. I don't talk to many people. I like staying to myself mostly—less folks getting into my business that way."

"Oh, I feel you," Angel said as she closed the graphics off the screen.

"Sorry I'm late," Johnnie Mae said as she rushed in. "It's been one of those days." Johnnie Mae hugged all three women and set her purse down on the table in the corner.

"How's your mother?" Sapphire asked.

"She has her good days and her bad," Johnnie Mae said. "Today was a good day. Although I believe my oldest sister is really starting to try her nerves. We had a nice talk today, my mother and I. She realizes she's getting worse, and she and I have had to consider certain options that will probably be necessary sooner than either of us wants to face it."

"I just love sitting and talking with her," Angel said. "She's even a lot of fun when her mind travels back in time. Johnnie Mae, your mother was a mess as a young person." She laughed.

"Yeah, remind me to stop letting you visit her," Johnnie Mae said, teasing her. "You two have too much fun together. It's no wonder she prefers reminiscing when you're around. You're probably encouraging her so you'll have somebody to hang out with."

Sapphire swiveled her chair. "I suppose we should get started," she said. "We have a lot to do."

"Oh, I'm sorry," Johnnie Mae said. "That was very inconsiderate of me. First, I have you three waiting for over fifteen minutes for me to arrive, then I come in talking when

I'm sure you have other things to do." Johnnie Mae took out the notebook with her ideas for the marriage seminar.

She shared her thoughts with them, and they each decided which task they would take on. Angel would handle the layout after everything was finalized. Sapphire would work with Johnnie Mae on ensuring the accuracy of the information, and help with the research. Faith volunteered to type what Johnnie Mae and Sapphire wrote and pulled the information from the Internet, books, and magazines into one word-processing file. Johnnie Mae preferred typing her information, so if Faith got a copy of it on a disk, she would only have to incorporate other information as directed. After that, Johnnie Mae would edit, correct, change, add, or delete as needed. Faith would make those corrections and hand the word file over to Angel for typesetting and layout.

"We're going to have to work closely to get this done," Faith said. "Especially you and I, Johnnie Mae. I'm available at your beck and call. We'll knock this out pretty quickly, don't you girls think?"

Sapphire and Angel rolled their eyes at each other.

"And as a thought, Angel," Johnnie Mae said, "most people don't know this, but our own Pastor Landris is quite the artist. If you need something drawn—nothing big or time-consuming, of course—let me know, and I'll see if I can't get him to draw it."

"He's quite the talent?" Faith said. "Does he happen to have a brother?" She looked over at Sapphire. "I mean, other than Thomas, of course."

Johnnie Mae smiled. "No. Thomas is it."

Faith grunted. "Mmm, too bad."

"I didn't know Pastor Landris could draw," Sapphire said.

"Oh, he's quite good, in fact. He drew a portrait of me, and it's rather lifelike. I was taken aback the first time I learned he was that talented," Johnnie Mae said.

"I'll keep that in mind," Angel said. "I believe I'll have all

I need, though. But if you'll just jot down ideas in an outline form, I can get started. I figure it will take me about two weeks to lay the whole thing out. I'll get it to you to proof, make your corrections or changes, and give you the final proof copy when I'm finished. After that, we should be good to go to final print and copy."

"Sounds like a plan to me," Johnnie Mae said. "I believe with all of us contributing our individual parts, we'll make this work and end up with one great workbook and one blessed thirteen-week marriage seminar. Let's schedule it to kick off in June."

"Saturdays in June may not be convenient for most people," Sapphire said. "A lot of people have their weddings in June."

"Then, what about Friday nights?" Johnnie Mae said.

"I think Fridays will work," Faith said. "I'm usually not busy at all on Fridays."

Sapphire looked at Faith. "I don't think you're supposed to be here for this. Unless, of course, you plan to be married by then?" She looked at Faith as though she expected an answer. "This is a marriage seminar. And unless I'm mistaken, that means it's for married people only," she said.

Faith looked at Sapphire. "You never know. A lot can happen between now and June. There are plenty of men out there—a woman just needs to know where to look, the right bait to use, and how to reel the right one in." She threw Sapphire a stoic grin.

"Ladies," Johnnie Mae said, "I think we're getting a little off our agenda here." She flashed a stern look at both Sapphire and Faith.

"Sorry," Faith said, lowering her head for a second. "We can come if we're not married, though, can't we? I mean, married folks need a seminar to make their marriages better, but wouldn't it be better if singles learned these principles, too?"

"You know . . ." Johnnie Mae thought for a moment, then

continued speaking, "maybe it would be okay if you guys came to the seminar. I don't want to open it up to every single person just yet, but Faith has a point. I can see us possibly expanding this marriage seminar to something similar for single people who want to be married someday. If you three were present, you could take notes to suggest what we can expand upon for a singles' workbook and seminar."

Johnnie Mae looked at Faith and smiled. "We'll start with the married couples first, then move on to the SIP: Singles In Preparation. And eventually we'll expand it to include young adults. Too much is left for the world to teach our own. We need to quit sticking our heads in the sand, thinking people are going to just 'get it' the godly way without us teaching the information. Our folk are learning it from somewhere—it ought to be from us. The truth, but the Bible way of truth."

Sapphire nodded. "It *is* a good idea."

"I like it," Angel said. "I'll be there. You can count me in."

Faith smiled. "I can't wait. This is going to be such fun!"

"Angel, will you type up what we decided here and print a copy for each of us? Then we can pray, adjourn, and go home," Johnnie Mae said.

Chapter 33

Come unto me, all ye that labor and are heavy laden, and I will give you rest.

(Matthew 11:28)

Johnnie Mae saw Hope coming down the corridor. "Hope, hi," she said in a soft voice. "How are you?"

Hope hugged her and smiled. "I'm so much better—thank you for asking."

"I've been a bit worried about you lately. Is there anything you need? Anything I can do?"

"I'm fine—why do you ask?"

"It's just I know you volunteered to help with the marriage seminar."

"I'm sorry about that," Hope said. She began lightly touching Johnnie Mae's arm. "I didn't mean to volunteer and not be able to make good on my commitment but—"

"Hope, please don't. I wasn't bringing it up to make you feel guilty. I'm just concerned about you. Can you and I set a date and go out to lunch or something?"

"You know, things are so busy these days. And honestly, I'm not a real meet-for-lunch kind of person. I hope you understand. I do apologize for not being able to help with the seminar the way I promised, but it just can't be helped. Look, I really need to run." Hope started walking away.

"You're not sick or anything and not letting us know, are you?" Johnnie Mae asked. "I don't mean to pry, but I care about you. I want you to know that, Hope. I just want to be sure you're all right."

"I'm fine. I sometimes have these little episodes, but they don't last long. When they happen, I may lose track of time. I usually rest, and in a little while, I'm back to myself again. I've been dealing with this since age seven or eight," Hope said. "I've learned to manage it."

"Forgive me if I'm out of line, but it doesn't sound to me like you're fine," Johnnie Mae said. "Maybe you should go see someone about it . . . a doctor—"

"I have seen someone about it. The best thing that seems to work during that time is to lie down and wait until it passes." She smiled. "I've grown quite accustomed to it, and generally, it hasn't been a concern. I suppose it's because I've never actually put myself out there like I've done here. Maybe I should back off trying to work in the church for now until I get a better handle on things."

Johnnie Mae grabbed her by the hand. "Please don't do that. That's the worst thing you can do. Whatever is going on with you . . ."

Hope nodded. "It's okay. I know you're worried about me, and I appreciate that. I don't know if I've ever had anyone care specifically about me—it's always Faith or Charity, but never me."

"Don't let what I've just said or done keep you from doing what you can," Johnnie Mae said. "My husband and I really appreciate whatever you're able to do here. Your spirit is wonderful, your work impeccable. In fact, I was looking forward to you putting together the marriage workbook for me. You seem to understand what I want without me having to explain it. That's such a rare quality. Whatever you can find the time to do will be received happily."

"I could still type the work for the seminar—I like doing things like that. Why don't you get it together and give it to me—"

"Oh, Faith didn't tell you?" Johnnie Mae said.

"Tell me what?"

"She came to the meeting the other day and volunteered to type it after Sapphire and I finish."

"Faith? Faith volunteered to type the work for you?"

"Yes. I thought you knew. I'm sorry . . . I never would have brought it up like that had I known you didn't know."

Hope put on a smile and hunched her shoulders. "No biggie. Faith will make sure it gets handled one way or the other. She'll probably bring it home. And knowing her like I do, she'll let me help just because she knows this is my forte."

"I didn't know you were a twin until she showed up. I had no idea you both had a younger sister. Charity. I believe that's what Faith said her name is."

"Charity. Of course Faith told you about Charity."

"Not a lot, just that she's your younger sister. And that she wasn't attending church or, at least, she wasn't attending one earlier this year when she and I talked about it. I don't know if that's changed or not. We haven't discussed it since."

Hope touched her head and started rubbing it slowly.

Johnnie Mae moved in closer. "Are you okay? Is it a headache?"

"I really have to go now," Hope said. "Just get the information you want typed to Faith. If she needs my help, you know I'll do what I can."

"Hope . . ." Johnnie Mae called after her, but Hope quickly scurried away.

"Lord, touch her right now. Please, Jesus, let her be all right. In Jesus' name."

Chapter 34

A double-minded man is unstable in all his ways.
(James 1:8)

Sapphire and Thomas hadn't spoken in over a week and she was worried. Since he had begun working for Reverend Walker, he'd really become distant with everybody who cared anything about him—including his own brother. Sapphire also knew his bipolar symptoms were probably active. She feared it would only be a matter of time before he would crash and burn completely.

"Thomas, if you don't get help, you're not going to get any better," Sapphire said.

"Look, I've told you, if that's all you want to talk about with me, you don't even have to bother calling or coming over."

"You're being unreasonable, Thomas. I'm not your enemy. You need help. If you won't let me do it, then find someone you feel comfortable with. I've seen people with this before. Everyone behaves differently, but it's never a pretty sight. I don't want that for you."

"It's not your problem or your concern," Thomas snapped.

"Talk to your brother, Thomas. Talk to Pastor Landris—"

"For what? He doesn't care about me. All he cares about is his family, his church, and his new house. Can you believe he's building a new house? Reverend Walker and I rode by there the other week. It's a disgrace what people do in the name of God."

"What are you talking about, Thomas? You know his heart. Pastor's a good man—"

"Good ain't always godly."

"See, that doesn't even sound like you. It sounds like something that pastor you're running around with would say. What does he know about Pastor Landris? Has he ever talked with him?"

"He doesn't have to. He and I talked when I first started working there. He was interested in what George was doing— genuinely interested. He was talking about Divine Conquerors giving a large donation toward the church facility." He continued to walk as he talked. "When he learned about the shopping area, the subdivisions, and all that other stuff, he became suspicious of the real motive behind all of this."

Sapphire grabbed Thomas by the hand and sat down on the couch. No longer in the small apartment he'd lived in since he moved to Birmingham, he was now in a house with three bedrooms and two and a half baths. They were in the great room with the gas fireplace. She looked around the room. It was furnished with all new furniture.

"I see. Suspicious in, like, the way you're living now? It's okay for you to move into something bigger and better, get all new furniture? But if Pastor Landris gets something bigger and better, he's no longer godly?"

Thomas surveyed the room. "This house is a blessing from God. Because I was obedient, and came out from among those heathens that were blinding me to the true light of God. Reverend Walker arranged for me to have this place. And do you know how much I'm paying to live here?"

"How much, Thomas?"

"I know you think I spend money like crazy, but I get to live here now for free. That's right. This is one of the houses the church owns, and Reverend Walker appreciates my talents and abilities so much, he arranged for me to live here for nothing for as long as I want. Now, what did George do for me?"

"Thomas!" Sapphire bore her eyes into him. "I do not believe you're about to say anything negative about your brother. Do you realize all you've done to Pastor Landris over the past years? And he forgave you. He tried to help you by giving you money when the radio deal fell through." She frowned as she spoke. "The radio deal *you* arranged with his money. That wasn't any of his doing."

"You know what? I don't have to let you put me down in my own home. Yes, I've made some mistakes. So have you. So has my dear, perfect brother. If it weren't for me, he wouldn't have had any of that money to lose. None of it. George forgave me—big deal. When I really needed him, what did he do?"

Sapphire calmed her voice. *A soft answer turns away wrath.* "What did he do, Thomas?"

"He closed his wallet up to me. He told me to fix it myself. I didn't have any money or anywhere else to turn, and he left me hanging. My *brother*. If it wasn't for Reverend Walker and his congregation—they may not be perfect, but at least they aren't trying to show off by building the biggest 'this' or the biggest 'that' just to entice people." Thomas stood up. He was jittery. "Sapphire, I've enjoyed our time together, but I'm in a different place now. And the Bible tells us not to be unequally yoked with unbelievers."

"Thomas, if you're going to quote scripture to make a point, make sure it applies," Sapphire said. "I'm not an unbeliever."

"Well, however you want to believe, it's on you. There are women out there praying for a man like me. Reverend Walker is talking about ordaining me a minister."

"You're kidding."

"See, that's exactly why you and I don't need to be together."

"I'm not trying to be with you right now, Thomas. I want to get you help."

"I have all the help I need. If I am bipolar, God can heal me if He chooses for me to be healed. I have faith in God," Thomas said.

"I do, too. But God works with doctors. Don't you know you can take all the pills you want, you can have all the operations, but without God, it won't be successful? If you need to take medication to help with your problem, God can work through that until your healing manifests. It was God who gave man the knowledge to develop these medicines. Everything still comes from God, so you're not a sell-out if you get the help you need through doctors."

Thomas walked over and opened the door. "I can't have all this negative talk polluting my home. You've got to go. I wish you the best, and when you see my brother, tell him I'm praying for him," Thomas said.

Sapphire stood up, in shock. She looked in Thomas's eyes as she walked past him—they were blood red. She knew he wasn't getting hardly any sleep. He was in need of help. And Sapphire realized she probably wasn't the one to do it.

Chapter 35

Say unto wisdom, Thou art my sister; and call understanding thy kinswoman.

(Proverbs 7:4)

Sapphire and Johnnie Mae were meeting to complete her part of the workbook. It was coming together beautifully. Johnnie Mae was concentrating on using many of the principles and a few actual scriptures found in the Book of Proverbs, chapter 7.

"One of my Bibles," Johnnie Mae began, "contains subheadings, summarizing what certain passages in a section will be. Proverbs 7 has, 'The wiles of a harlot.' Sapphire, I believe there's a reason God inspired this chapter to be included in the Bible. Pastor Landris and I feel if we glean the real jewels from these passages of scriptures here, it will bless so many marriages but especially those in the household of faith."

Sapphire scanned a few of the scriptures. "Wow, verse 5 says in essence that if this is done, it will keep the men from the strange woman." She read, "'from the stranger which flattereth with her words.' I don't know. Are you sure you want to use this?"

"I'm not encouraging women to be harlots outside of their marriage, but things like verse 13: 'So she caught him, and kissed him.' What husband wouldn't want his wife to catch him and lay one on him like that?" Johnnie Mae flipped through the pages of her notes. "In verse 15: she's looking for him, seeking his face, and happy that she's found him. Do you know how many women, after they get married, can't stand seeing their husbands come through the door? But when they were dating, they were diligently looking for their future husbands to show up. This needs to be put back into marriages."

"Oooh, Mrs. Landris. I can't imagine you acting like that at any time in your life, let alone with Pastor Landris. You're always so cool and collected. Looking for him . . . seeking his face?" Sapphire shuffled through the pages she'd pulled off the Internet and copied from books and magazines that discussed how a woman should be excited about her man. She handed those pages over to Johnnie Mae.

"Don't get this all wrong, now. There is balance to all of this," Johnnie Mae said. "Pastor Landris and I have instructions for the men as well. It's just that men are moved by sight. Women are moved by the heart . . . they're emotional. Women like to be talked to, to be made to feel like they're the only one who matters, even if it's not always true at the time. Women like to cuddle and be cuddled. So we'll be hitting the men with their section on *The Way to Loving Your Woman is Through Her Heart: Romancing the Heart.* But women have been told and taught so many things growing up about 'good girls'; they get mixed signals about how they should be with their men after they marry."

"I have to deal with this in the real world on a daily basis," Sapphire said. "Wives with low self-esteem. I find women are so confused. They aren't sure how they should act with their mates. The image they have been given of, as you said, a 'good girl,' doesn't match married life. I think it's great how you and Pastor Landris will be using the Bible to let women and men know what God has to say on the subject of marriage. How couples can add zest to their relationships, while keeping it holy. Like here in Proverbs 7, verse 16. The bed is decked out with a pretty covering and fine linen of

Egypt. Then verse 17 says, 'I have perfumed my bed with myrrh, aloes, and cinnamon.'" Sapphire started laughing. "Can you imagine a wife thinking like this for her husband? Thinking about what she can do in a marriage to *spice it up* like she did before she married?" Sapphire stopped and gasped. "Oh, my goodness . . . look at this!"

"You're reading verse 18, aren't you?" Johnnie Mae said with a knowing giggle.

Sapphire continued to laugh and nod vigorously as she read the verse aloud. "'Come, let us take our fill of love until the morning, let us solace ourselves with loves.' And this is all in the Bible! How many people even know this is in here? It's so perfect for marriages."

"We're not going to use everything, but I do think verse 18 is a good one for the husbands and wives to reflect on. Pastor Landris and I have also included a section on communication. It's important to see a marriage as a two-way street. The superhighway of love knows how to send and receive. Those on DSL and broadband may need to slow things down and go back to dial-up. We touch on how each spouse should be mindful of how they present themselves. You know, reminding the wife not to always wear rollers and flannel pajamas around her husband. Again, men are moved by sight. A wife needs to let her husband see what he has in his fearfully and wonderfully made, beautiful, and godly woman. That'll keep him at home."

"And the men?"

"Some of these men act like having a basketball under their too-little-tops is synonymous with wealth. In the first place, a big stomach is not healthy. Women like their men taking care of themselves, too. You know what else we have in the workbook that's absolutely spectacular? Romantic ways to exercise together."

"You have an exercise section, too?" Sapphire said.

"Indeed we do. It's called: *Exercising Your Right to Be Left in Love: Working Out the Romance*." Johnnie Mae smiled.

"I gave Angel a note to find graphics with two people partic-ipating in various exercises together. Can't you just see how romantic that can be? She's on the floor doing crunches; he's holding her feet or ankles, and every time she pulls herself forward, he meets her and gives her a peck on the lips and vice versa. They can do other things like rock-the-boat."

"Rock-the-boat?"

"Yes. You never rocked the boat as a child?"

"No, I don't think so," Sapphire said.

"You sit down and wrap your arms and legs around each other, then rock back and forth like a seesaw. There are so many things couples can do that will allow them to spend time together and keep the home fires burning. The man doing his pushups while she's lying on the floor with her face turned to him . . . peck, peck. He can't be weak, though, and do that. That's the major theme in this workbook: Couples should not get married and stop dating. Things should heat up even more after they become one. But it's hard with so much more responsibility, and most times, the work lands on the woman. Home-girl is too tired for loving; men have to see this if they really want to 'get it'."

"Like Thomas and I have stopped dating," Sapphire said suddenly.

Johnnie Mae stopped shuffling papers and looked di-rectly at Sapphire. "Sapphire, I'm sorry. What's going on with you two?"

"Let's not talk about it now. We'll talk later." She flipped through more of Johnnie Mae's notes. "Tell me more about this section: *Dating Your Mate While Mating Your Date*."

Johnnie Mae smiled. "When the seminar begins, we're going to give the couples homework."

"Of course. What would marriage be without homework and playing house?"

"Exactly. Each couple will have to date each other during the thirteen weeks. They'll have to bring in something for show-and-tell regarding their date, but keeping it holy. I want them to remember why they wanted to marry that person in the first place. Men, especially, act like their work is over after they're married. They want to sit at home while the wives now wait on them. For these thirteen weeks, if anyone was doing this, it will have to cease," Johnnie Mae said. "They'll be graded on their homework assignments, with each—unknowingly—grading the other."

"You're making this into a serious seminar," Sapphire said.

"Yes. Those signing up will also have to sign a contract." Johnnie Mae showed Sapphire a copy of what the contract will look like. "And there will be a graduation ceremony and celebration for those who successfully stick with and complete the course."

"That sounds so nice."

"The ceremony is going to be really special. They won't know this when they begin, but the final ceremony will be a weddinglike setting where each will ask their spouse to marry them on that day . . . again. Those who say yes will get to renew their vows."

"That's really beautiful."

"I need help getting that all set up. I want the arch and candles, maybe a ring bearer and a flower girl to serve for all the couples. It's going to be a blessed event." Johnnie Mae took all the papers and stacked them back together. She put the ones she had, along with what Sapphire had given her, and placed them inside an expanding folder in her briefcase.

"Now that's done," Johnnie Mae said. "So, let's talk about you and Thomas. That's if you want to."

"What's to talk about? He and I aren't together anymore. And quite frankly, there's something going on with him that I probably should let Pastor Landris, or at least you, know so maybe y'all can get him the help he really needs. Especially since it appears that I'm not the one."

Chapter 36

And Jesus answering said unto them, They that
are whole need not a physician; but they that are
sick.

(Luke 5:31)

"Johnnie Mae, I believe Thomas is bipolar." Sapphire said
it in one breath.

"Bipolar?"

"Yes. He has many of the symptoms of bipolar disorder:
episodes of depression, difficulty sleeping, mood swings . . .
He'll go from thinking he's all that and being extremely talk-
ative to being antisocial and depressed.

"He thinks people are out to get him and that he's being
followed. It doesn't matter that you tell him differently; he
thinks the things he's seeing when he's hallucinating are real.
I probably shouldn't tell you this, but Thomas spends money
like crazy. He doesn't have much, but as soon as he gets
some cash, he has to spend it. He'll spend every dime he has,
and most times, has absolutely nothing to show for it. I really
believe Thomas has been going through what professionals
call 'rapid cycling,' meaning he's had quite a few bad
episodes in one year. I've personally witnessed a few myself
in the past twelve months."

"Why haven't you said anything to us before now?"

"Thomas doesn't like people talking about his business. I
thought I could convince him to get the help he needs, but I
couldn't. He doesn't believe anything is wrong with him.

Truthfully, I believe one of the reasons he left our church was his disorder. He's not thinking logically. There is medication available he can take once a doctor has officially diagnosed him and prescribed it. It's not a cure, but it does help the part of his brain that's having problems."

"I had no idea, and I'm sure Pastor Landris doesn't, either," Johnnie Mae said. "I knew something wasn't right with him. Just didn't know what. I'll let Pastor Landris know what you said, and see what he thinks we ought to do. If he would like to talk with you personally about this, will you?"

"You know you don't have to ask. Thomas is going to be upset when he finds out I've said anything to either of you. But he's not my patient, so I'm not under any doctor/patient confidentiality agreement. He needs help, and soon." Sapphire fidgeted with her necklace. "He's going to totally lose it soon, and I don't want to see that happen if it can be avoided. It's so hard on families. And it can take weeks to get the right medication."

"Could you also give me his new home address? I'd like to give it to Pastor Landris just in case he needs to go over there. From what you're telling me, Thomas might not even respond to his own brother. Pastor Landris will do whatever is necessary to get Thomas some help."

Sapphire wrote down Thomas's home address and handed the slip of paper to Johnnie Mae. "One more thing: if Thomas won't voluntarily agree to get the help he needs, there is one other option for a family in a situation like yours."

Johnnie Mae looked up. "What's that?"

"Go to probate court and file a petition to have him involuntarily put in the hospital."

"Have him committed?" Johnnie Mae's mind immediately went to thoughts of her mother, and how much she'd fought against putting her mother in a place she didn't want to go.

"They don't call it that anymore. Hospitals are legally obligated to protect the patient's right to privacy. No one has to know he's even in that section . . . the psychiatric ward, I mean. A person has to have a pass code to get in to see those patients. But the doctors there can help him get right before it's too late," Sapphire said. She looked away as she wiped away a few tears.

"Thanks, Sapphire. I know this is hard on you." Johnnie Mae touched her hand.

"It's terrible watching someone you love deteriorate like Thomas has been doing. Knowing there's help for him, but not being able to get him to accept that help. Do you know what's really sad, though?"

"What?"

"People on medication will inevitably decide to stop taking it because they think they're okay and can manage their disorder on their own. They end up worse off than before and have to start from scratch, taking their medicine."

"I'm almost speechless. I've learned so much about something I've only heard about in passing. I had no idea the depths of something like bipolar disorder. I'll speak with Pastor Landris today, and we'll try, as much as possible, to keep you out of this. I don't want to ruin anything you and Thomas might still have once he gets the help he needs. I'm sure there's a way to handle this."

Sapphire hugged Johnnie Mae. "Thank you. Please get him some help. I probably should have said something sooner. I thought I could get through to him—I was wrong."

Chapter 37

*Therefore to him that knoweth to do good, and
doeth it not, to him, it is sin.*

(James 4:17)

"Pastor Landris, this is Reverend Knight."

"Yes, Reverend Knight. How may I help you?" Pastor
Landris said.

"No idle chitchat for me—just straight to the point. I
won't keep you—I know you're extremely busy these days,
with the new sanctuary. And I hear you're also building a
new house," Reverend Knight said.

"Nothing gets past you, I see." Pastor Landris changed
the phone to his other ear so he could type on the computer
easier as he talked. "What's up?"

"You and I need to talk."

"About?"

"About your future plans, your growing number of enemies, the work of the Lord . . ."

"I don't think there's much for us to talk about there,"
Pastor Landris said. "My plans are God's plans, so any changes,
additions, or disagreements you have should be directed to my
Father in Heaven. As for my enemies, you know what the Bible
has to say about them . . . we will have them with us always,
as long as we're doing the will of our Father, and the work of
the Lord. I have plenty of assignments to keep me busy, but if
there's anything I can do to help you, all you need do is ask."

"I appreciate the offer," Reverend Knight said. "I must admit, I'm a little surprised. I would think I'd be the last person you'd want to help. Personally, I believe you have me pegged all wrong. I think you feel I'm your enemy. Pastor Landris, I assure you, I am not." There was a certain sadness and sincerity evident in his voice.

Pastor Landris softened a bit when he heard it. "I meant every word of it."

"I believe you. But again, you and I still need to talk. If not about your plans, enemies or work for the Lord, then about your brother."

"What about my brother?"

"He's working for Reverend Walker."

"Yeah, I know. For the past three months or so," Pastor Landris said.

"I take it you and he aren't talking much these days," Reverend Knight said.

"Is there a point you'd like to get to?" he said, feeling impatient.

Reverend Knight coughed hard and cleared his throat. "There's something going on with your brother and Reverend Walker."

"Exactly what are you implying?"

"I'm not implying anything. I've known Marshall Walker most of my life. I know his good points and bad. Reverend Walker doesn't care much for you. And I know he'll do anything when he wants something or somebody out of his way bad enough. You recall Matthew chapter 16, verse 6? Let's see if you're really as good as people claim. You wouldn't happen to know that scripture right off the bat, would you?"

"'Then Jesus said unto them, Take heed and beware of the leaven of the Pharisees and of the Sadducees.' And for the record, I don't appreciate being put to the test about how much scripture I can quote off the top of my head. I know scripture because I study, and because I desire to plant scriptural seeds in my heart," Pastor Landris said.

"Well said, Pastor Landris. Point taken. But as you'll recall, further in that passage, Jesus emphasized that people should beware of the doctrine of the Pharisees and of the Sadducees, the religious sector of the body. Interestingly, I find that Jesus would focus so much on the hypocrisy of the religious leaders who should have been the ones the lay folks could truly look up to," Reverend Knight said. "There are so many instances where Jesus pointed out problems with the religious folk, especially those having the most authority. It's no wonder they wanted to rid themselves of him. 'Crucify him' indeed."

"Reverend Knight, I'm certain there's something you're trying to tell me in all of this. I appreciate your concern for me and apparently for my brother. But Thomas is an adult. He's capable of making his own choices and decisions. I can give him my input, but ultimately, he's the one who will decide."

"Granted," Reverend Knight said. "I just don't know if you know how much trouble your brother may find himself in if he doesn't get out soon. Or at least, break ties with someone who has had an agenda against you from the very start. This time, Reverend Walker is playing for keeps. I respect you more than I ever believed I would." He was suddenly laboring hard, just to speak.

"That's fine," Pastor Landris said. "Reverend Knight, are you all right?"

He paused and regained control of his breath. "Pastor Landris, I have one request of you, and I'll be happy to answer that question."

"What is it?"

"Could you and I meet to talk for once without there being anything between us?"

"I'm sorry?" Pastor Landris asked. "What do you mean, 'between us'?"

"In the past, there always seemed to be something happening between us. I met you the very first time because of the building you were interested in. The second time, for that same building which you, incidentally, were offered, and wisely turned down."

Pastor Landris started laughing.

"What's so funny, Pastor Landris?"

"Forgive me. I was not laughing at you. I was actually laughing because, until this moment, I never really knew for sure if I had made the right decision or not. Now, it seems you're confirming that I did."

"God is truly on your side," Reverend Knight said. "Even right now. I shouldn't be talking with you, and I definitely shouldn't be warning you about Reverend Walker. The man is powerful and relentless. You must be vigilant and continue to listen and respond to the voice of God."

"When and where would you like to meet?" Pastor Landris asked.

"I know this is probably an inconvenience, but if you could come by my home, anytime that's good for you, I'll be here. Tomorrow . . . later this week. I'm not planning on going anywhere soon," Reverend Knight said.

"Give me your address."

Pastor Landris wrote down Reverend Knight's address and directions to his house.

"One last question before I hang up," Reverend Knight said. "How much longer before the new sanctuary is completed and ready for the first service?"

"It's going to be really cutting it close, and the sanctuary section will be the only part completely ready for use by then, but the builder is promising by the first Sunday in December."

"Do you think I might be able to finagle an invite?" Reverend Knight said.

"I happen to know the pastor pretty well," Pastor Landris said. "I believe we can arrange that. Reverend Knight, I'll probably be over tomorrow."

"Thank you for agreeing to come."

After Pastor Landris hung up, Reverend Knight dialed another number.

"Hello," the male voice said.

"Reverend Grant, I just got off the phone with Pastor Landris."

"Did he agree to come see you?" Reverend Grant asked.

"Yes. He said he'd be here tomorrow." Reverend Knight began to cough. He took a swallow of the water he kept beside him.

"Would you like me to be there when he comes?"

"No. I can handle this one fine, but thanks for offering. You're a good man."

"If you change your mind, or if you need me, just call. I'll have my cell phone on."

"I won't need you, but I appreciate you. You truly are a good and loyal friend."

Reverend Knight hung up, took a pill out of his medicine bottle, and chased it down with water.

Pastor Landris called Thomas on his cell phone after Sapphire told Johnnie Mae what she suspected. Basically, Thomas told Pastor Landris to mind his own business. And he meant for him to do just that.

"Thomas, I want to help you," Pastor Landris insisted. "I've read up on bipolar disorder. You really do have pretty much all the symptoms. But there's medication available that can help you. A good therapist can talk with you and help you learn to cope—"

"I'm doing fine." He sighed. "Have you not heard a word I've been saying? And I'm doing it without you or your help, George. That's what's eating away at you right now. I don't need you, or your church—or your wife, for that matter—doing anything for me."

"Thomas—"

"Listen, man. You're just jealous because you thought I

would fall on my face and you could continue looking like the good Landris. Yeah, 'Thomas is the one who screws up. Thomas is the one who's always looking for a handout. Thomas is the one who'll never amount to anything.' Well, guess what? Thomas is proving everybody wrong. In fact, Reverend Walker thinks I'm a great asset. He trusts me, George."

"I trusted you. Remember?"

"See, that's what I mean. Everything you define me by is in my past. That's the old man, George. He's passed away. All things have become new. I'm a new creature in Christ, but you're just like the devil: You always want to bring up my past when we're talking about my future. I have great ideas, George. You know that. Okay, so I make some missteps in the process. But if you don't try something, how will you ever know if it will work? That's what life's all about—trying so you can learn."

"I'm sorry, Thomas. I don't mean to make you feel I bring up your past like that. But I also don't appreciate the way you act like I've not been supportive and trusting when you know that's not the truth."

"Yeah, okay. You trusted me. You said you forgave me. That's the past, George. Where you and I parted ways was in the present. I needed something in the present, and you based your decision to help me or not on my past."

"Thomas, if you need me, will you promise to let me know? I mean it. You call me, and I'll be there."

After Pastor Landris hung up, he ran things over again in his mind. This was Thomas's life, and if he chose to go this route, who was Pastor Landris to disagree? If Thomas really was bipolar, what could Pastor Landris do to help him? Did he even have a right to interfere? Maybe he *was* feeling a bit slighted because Thomas had gone to another church and seemed to have found a place there.

A place he obviously had not found with his own blood brother.

Chapter 38

But Joshua the son of Nun, which standeth be-
fore thee, he shall go in thither: encourage him:
for he shall cause Israel to inherit it.

(Deuteronomy 1:38)

Pastor Landris went to see Reverend Knight as he promised. Keeping his word was important to Pastor Landris, even when things were falling apart. And that's what it
looked like: everything that could go wrong was doing just
that.

His brother was in a bad way, according to Sapphire. He'd
called and found out she was correct. Reverend Knight had
said something about Thomas during their conversation on
the phone. He wasn't sure what Reverend Knight's angle
was this time, but there was something in his voice that
caused Pastor Landris to believe things were different. He
didn't know what, but he would soon find out.

"Did you have any trouble finding the place?" Reverend
Knight asked when Pastor Landris came in and sat down in
the den. Reverend Knight was sitting in an easy chair. He
looked different—smaller, sitting down like that.

"No, your directions were really good," Pastor Landris
said.

"Should be good—I've given them out enough. Do you
know how many people want to come by and see you when
you're a pastor?"

"I have some idea," Pastor Landris said. "Of course, when

I started my ministry here, knowing where I lived was important for those coming to our service."

Reverend Knight gave a short laugh. "Yeah, that's right. You were over at your house holding church. That was ridiculous, you know? I told you that you could have had that building for as long as you needed it."

"But what was the catch?"

"Catch?" Reverend Knight started laughing again. "Oh yeah, *the* catch. We knew you would fix that building up, so the appraisal value would have tripled—that's what I figured, anyway." He started coughing and grabbed a paper towel to hold up to his mouth. Pastor Landris saw him spit something out, wrap the paper towel around it, and throw the towel in the trash can beside him.

"Are you all right?"

Reverend Knight looked over at Pastor Landris. "No, Pastor. Actually, I'm not."

Pastor Landris sat back in the chair. He could tell something was headed his way, and he would need to be braced to receive the full brunt without being completely knocked over.

"I have lung cancer."

"Do you smoke?"

Reverend Knight shook his head as though he was in deep reflection.

"Did you used to smoke?"

He gave another short laugh. "No. I never smoked a day in my life. But I hung around plenty of folks who did when smoking was allowed everywhere."

Reverend Knight took a swallow of water. "I'd gone in for my routine, annual checkup. They did the whole workup. You know, heart, blood pressure, prostate, colon, and my lungs. It was my throat and a hacking cough that had them worried; I couldn't get rid of this cough. My throat was starting to irritate me, too. I'm sure you notice how often I've needed to clear it when I talked."

Pastor Landris leaned in and situated his body more comfortably. "Is this why you wanted to see me?"

"Oh, you think I'm trying to make peace before I check out?" He laughed and shook his head. "Is that what you think my asking you here is all about?"

"I don't know. Why did you ask me to come?"

"I like you, Pastor Landris. I like talking to you. I like hearing you speak. You remind me of what I intended to be when I became a preacher. I don't know how your calling came about, but mine was so clear. I used to hear people say 'God spoke to me' or 'God called me to preach,' but I never knew what they really meant. Was it audible? Was it just a feeling down inside? What?" He coughed again.

"Marshall and I were tight back then—that's Reverend Walker," Reverend Knight said. "Marshall was getting into all kinds of trouble. I didn't want to look like a wimp, so I went along with him. We did something that was not only stupid, but illegal. Something that Marshall and I have always held over each other. We knew after that incident, we'd always be in each other's corner because one of us could always do the other one in," Reverend Knight said. "That building that I offered you—I told you there were no strings attached. But I wasn't completely honest about that."

Pastor Landris chuckled. "Go on."

"Oh, it's not what you think. I was straight up in the offer to you. I later learned, though, that Marshall was planning to mess you up in the worst way possible. And believe me, there's no doubt he would have done that, and then some. But I had my own personal strings. I looked at you, and I really did see the son I never had. My wife already had three girls when we married. She and I chose not to have any of our own. Or, should I say, she chose for the both of us. I regret that now."

"Why?"

"Because I often wonder what it would feel like to have my flesh and blood come and sit here with me, and just talk. The love between us would be so strong," Reverend Knight said. "I love my stepchildren like they were my own. But I've never told another soul this: I long to know what my child might have looked like or been like had I fathered one."

Pastor Landris began thinking about Princess Rose. He did love that little girl as though she were his own, but she wasn't his biological child. Biologically, she was Solomon's and Johnnie Mae's. Johnnie Mae had been trying to get pregnant for almost two years now. The doctor told them that other than trying fertility drugs or in vitro, they might have to accept that having a baby of their own wasn't going to be.

Johnnie Mae had been attempting to convince Landris she was fine with that. Neither he nor Johnnie Mae wanted her to take fertility pills. He had not let her know, though, just how much the two of them having a child together really meant to him.

At first he wasn't sure he wanted a child other than Princess Rose. After they talked, and he saw how excited Johnnie Mae was, it was okay with him if she did get pregnant. But he didn't think he would be that upset if she didn't. Somewhere along the line, things changed.

And it wasn't because his mother was upset about having two sons, neither of whom had blessed her with a grandchild yet. It wasn't because it would make him feel better as a man, knowing he'd passed on his DNA. It was the feeling of partnering with God, creating a life that only God can cause to live and move and have its being. It was being a father and understanding even more how God sees things as our Father. He wanted a child more than he'd ever expected because he wanted a baby with the woman he loved. It was as simple as that. What a gift to give, to share with each other: a child to call their own.

As Pastor Landris sat and listened to Reverend Knight, he understood him so much better now.

"I have something I want you to have, Pastor Landris," Reverend Knight said. "I don't know how much longer I have here on this earth. None of us do, really. Believe me,

I'm fighting with all I have to extend my stay. On Sunday, I plan to turn in my letter to the church to officially retire as senior pastor." He cleared his throat and placed his hand over his heart. Reverend Knight was visibly choking up. Tears began to form in his eyes. "I've been there for a long time. I love those people more than anyone will ever know. There's a minister there I hope the congregation chooses as my replacement, but I've made the decision to stay out of that whole process."

Pastor Landris watched him struggle to get something out of the drawer next to his chair.

"You know, before I met you," Reverend Knight said, "I might have decided differently, even about the church where I'll no longer be the pastor. It's our way, sometimes, as the old going out, to handpick our successors. Moses chose Joshua. I've watched how you've handled yourself through all the adversities you've had thrown your way." He pulled out a large gold envelope from the drawer. His hand shook as he held it.

"You are my Joshua. I'm not trying to pick you to take over my church." He smiled. "Funny, huh? How often I've said *my* church over the course of my life?"

"I know. I've heard you a few times just since we met," Pastor Landris said.

"Well, I was wrong about that. You've taught me this is not about me or mine. It's God's church. Those are God's people. We're not even the true shepherds, huh?"

"I preached on that about a month ago," Pastor Landris said.

"Jesus is the true Shepherd; I'm just an overseer under Him. They're still Jesus' flock. That's why He told Peter if he loved Him to feed His sheep." Reverend Knight took another sip of water and set the glass back on the table as he contin-ued to hold the padded envelope in his other hand. "Pastor Landris, I've preached about feeding Jesus' sheep. I heard you say it on a tape I was listening to—"

"You listen to my tapes?"

"I'm a regular fan of yours. I signed up for your life-partner special deal. You know, the one where we get a cassette a week. I don't know how long my contract will last, since my doctor gives me only about six more months to keep whipping this thing or let it whip me."

"You're going to be all right," Pastor Landris said.

"Is that a prophetic Word or just you being kind to an old man who one time was not so kind to you?"

"It's one of those Second Corinthians 5:8 messages," Pastor Landris said. " 'We are confident, I say, and willing—' "

" '. . . rather to be absent from the body, and to be present with the Lord.' " Reverend Knight finished the scripture for him. "But we can't stop there—verse 9 says, 'Wherefore we labor, that whether present or absent, we may be accepted of him.' Then verse 10—"

" 'For we must appear before the judgment seat of Christ; that every one may receive the things done in his body, according to that he hath done . . .' " Pastor Landris said it with a quiet voice.

" '. . . whether it be good or bad.' That was a good Word, Pastor Landris," Reverend Knight said. He handed the envelope to Pastor Landris. "Well, Joshua, I have been to the mountaintop, I have looked over into the Promised Land. I won't be able to take the people there, but I know you're going to lead them well. That envelope there . . ."

Pastor Landris turned it over in his hand without attempting to open it.

"That envelope contains something of mine I want you to have. You can open it."

Pastor Landris unclasped the metal part and looked inside.

"There is a white envelope inside with <u>Personal and Private</u> on it. I don't want you to open that one unless you're absolutely forced to use it. That's the secret that will keep

Reverend Walker in check. It's the proof you'll need, should he ever try to bluff his way through. He knows I have it, but the last thing he'd ever expect is for me to have given it to his sworn enemy."

"Sworn enemy? But I don't even know Reverend Walker except that my brother went to work for him," Pastor Landris said.

"You don't always have to know your enemies for them to hate you with a passion. I've kept my good friend Marshall in check against you. He knows I'm not well now. He thinks when I'm gone it will release him to come after you. He will learn, if he chooses to do that, it will be a big mistake. Put that envelope in a safe deposit box, and don't let anyone know you have it." Reverend Knight took another drink of water and released a sound that indicated a lifelong thirst had been quenched. He rested a minute, then began again.

"There's an envelope in there with your church's name on it," Reverend Knight said, twirling his hand in a winding motion as if to tell Pastor Landris to find it and take it out.

Pastor Landris pulled it out, opened the white envelope, and looked at a check written to Followers of Jesus. "Twenty thousand dollars?" Pastor Landris said with obvious surprise.

"That's my gift to the church. I believe in what you said about sowing into good ground. I believe the work you're doing is good ground. I asked God to give me seed to sow. There was a time I used to teach the idea that people needed to sow to get seed. You made me see how backward that really was. How can you sow what you don't have to get what you're hoping to eventually possess? God has the seeds; all we have to do is ask Him to bless us with the seed so we can sow it. That's pure scripture. The principle behind planting takes care of us having more seeds from sowing what God blesses us with. Another good Word from you, Pastor Landris."

"You asked for this seed to sow?" Pastor Landris put the

check back in the envelope. "You went to God specifically asking Him for this seed to sow into what I'm doing?"

"Yes. I asked God to give it to me, and He did. I'm not taking this from anywhere that I can't afford to take it from. He gave me this seed for you, just as I asked. He also gave me extra seed while He was giving me that for you," Reverend Knight said. "As old as I am and as many times as I've read that scripture, I've not taught it right or lived it right. Think of all the blessings I've missed because I was teaching people to find seed to sow to get seed from God. I should have been teaching like you: Ask God for seed, and He'll give you seed to sow. But we have to ask Him. You can do it the hard way, but why, when God has made it so simple."

"I don't know how to thank you. You have no idea what this means to me, spiritually," Pastor Landris said. "This was the last thing I expected."

"From me," Reverend Knight said. "You can say it. You know I've always told you I like the fact that you don't play around, and you get to your point. Don't go getting soft on me now because we're here bonding." Reverend Knight's words were becoming labored.

"You're getting tired," Pastor Landris said.

"One more thing and you can go," Reverend Knight said. "There's one more thing in that envelope. See that box in there?"

Pastor Landris looked again in the envelope. "Yes."

"Take it out and open it."

Pastor Landris did as he was told. Inside the small box was a man's ring.

"That was my father's ring. I loved and respected my father so much. He had that ring specially made. I used to think of it as our kingdom signet ring, as if I was the son of a real king. When my father gave it to me, I was so proud to own it. I cherished it with all my heart. It always made me feel like he was still with me just because I had his ring. If I had a son, I would have passed that ring on to him in hopes that he'd feel the same. I'd be honored, Pastor Landris, since I don't have a son of my own, if you'd accept this symbol of kinship on behalf of a son in whom I am well pleased."

"Reverend Knight, I'm honored that you would even consider doing something like this, but I know how much a family heirloom like this can mean to other family members. Don't you have any brothers or sisters or other relatives who might want it?"

Reverend Knight laughed. "In fact, I have plenty. But my father gave that ring to me. It was a gift I could do with as I chose. My intent was to pass it on to my son when I had one. I have now chosen to pass it on to you."

Pastor Landris wiped his face with his hand. This was weightier than anything he'd anticipated when he agreed to come here.

"I'm truly, truly honored," Pastor Landris said, looking Reverend Knight in his tired eyes. "I mean that."

"No, I'm the one who has just been honored." Reverend Knight reached on top of the table and picked up his Bible. He started turning the pages. "I know I said I only had one last thing. But there's a scripture—I want you to read it for me. I won't even try to see if you know this one by heart. You probably do. I just want to hear you read it for me." He handed Pastor Landris the Bible already opened to the book of Deuteronomy. "Read from Deuteronomy 1:35-38." He closed his eyes as Pastor Landris began to read.

> *Surely there shall not one of these men of this evil generation see that good land, which I sware to give unto your fathers. Save Caleb the son of Jephunneh; he shall see it, and to him will I give the land that he hath trodden upon, and to his children, because he hath wholly followed the LORD. Also the LORD was angry with me for your sakes, saying, Thou also shalt not go*

in thither. But Joshua the son of Nun, which standeth before thee, he shall go in thither: encourage him: for he shall cause Israel to inherit it.

Pastor Landris ran his hand over the page, closed the Bible, and handed it back to Reverend Knight with a nod as he found himself fighting back his own tears.

Chapter 39

*But Nineveh is of old like a pool of water: yet
they shall flee away. Stand, stand, shall they cry;
but none shall look back.*

(Nahum 2:8)

Faith and Johnnie Mae were working in an office at the church. Faith didn't want Hope to try to help her do the typing of the workbook Johnnie Mae had written. Faith was the one who'd suggested she and Johnnie Mae work together at church. She felt things would go faster, and if she needed clarification or saw a problem that needed to be addressed, the two of them would already be there to handle it.

Faith could overhear Johnnie Mae's conversation on the phone. She soon learned Johnnie Mae was busy with all kinds of problems Faith had no idea about.

There was the new house she and Pastor Landris were building. It was stressing her out more than she'd expected. The contractor had ordered the wrong things—they had erroneously put double-crown molding in the rooms for which they had specifically requested triple-crown. Johnnie Mae had picked out the carpet and paint colors, but they'd misplaced the information for the carpeting and needed an answer quickly since the house was getting close—or so they claimed—to being finished.

"Tell you what—just put white carpet upstairs in all the rooms except the ones with hardwood floors," Johnnie Mae said.

Faith couldn't believe she was getting white carpet. *That's a nightmare waiting to happen, for sure!*

Johnnie Mae's present house had just finished having extensive work done—Faith learned the work on the old house was because of damages caused by her nieces and a nephew a few months back.

"I'm glad, Rachel, it didn't cost as much as it could have," Johnnie Mae said that day at church on the phone. "I know, God is good. No, Rachel, I'm not letting you have this house just because we're building a new one. I'm not being stingy, it's my house. I do have a right to do with it as I please. What am I going to do with it?" Johnnie Mae sighed. "I don't know for sure, but there's no hurry. Yes, Landris paid for the new house with his own money. I really don't see where that's any of your business whether or not he's paying cash for the whole thing. Look Rachel, I'm working. I need to go." She stopped for a second. "What's wrong with Mama? Why do you feel you have to sit and discuss my problems with her? She doesn't need to be bothered with what's going on with me, Rachel. I hear what you're saying, but she doesn't need to hear you claiming that I'm depressed about not having gotten pregnant yet, when it's not true. I am *not* depressed! No, Rachel, I'm not. I'm not upset, either."

Faith got up and walked into the office. She stood patiently waiting.

Johnnie Mae placed her sister on hold. "Yes, Faith?"

"I wasn't sure if this is what you really meant to say right here. It sounds funny. I just wanted you to look at it before I typed all this." Faith primped her pin curls while Johnnie Mae looked at the page. Faith felt it was actually too dressy for work in a church, but she had something special she was planning to attend tomorrow and this style was perfect for that.

"Yes, I want it just like I wrote it there." Johnnie Mae waited to see if there was anything else.

"Thanks. Sorry to have bothered you."

"That's okay. That's why we're here." When it came to work like this, Johnnie Mae missed Hope—she always appeared to understand exactly what Johnnie Mae was trying to do. She did appreciate Faith's willingness to want to do something like this though.

Johnnie Mae returned to her phone call. "Rachel, I said for you to hold on. No, I didn't hear what you just asked. Landris is not upset with me because I can't have a baby. Why would you tell Mama something like that? Look, I would prefer you not talk about my business with Mama. No, I don't have anything to hide. It's just she doesn't need this, especially when it's not true. I don't care what *else* the two of you talk about, just don't make it about me and problems you perceive I'm having with my husband, my marriage, my career, or anything else you know nothing about. Is that clear?"

After she hung up with Rachel, Johnnie Mae began to repeat her daily baby confession to herself. "He makes *me* to keep house, and to be a joyful mother of children." She'd been saying the same verse for almost two months now. Nothing seemed to be working. Her phone rang again.

"Rachel, what did you do? You did what?! You fired Ms. Bertha? For what? You had no right to fire her. Oh, you didn't really fire her—she quit, huh? What happened?" After Johnnie Mae heard the whole story, she placed the phone back on the cradle.

Faith walked in Johnnie Mae's office again.

"Is something wrong? You sound like you're really upset," Faith said.

"Nothing," Johnnie Mae said and tried to shake it off with a false smile.

"It has to be more than nothing. Look at you. If you don't want to tell me, I won't bother you about it. I just wanted to help if I could. Sometimes having a set of ears to listen can be a blessing. That's what Motherphelia—my grandmother—used to say," Faith said.

"Motherphelia was something," she continued. "She loved to dress in the latest styles. I get that from her, I suppose. She's why I'm such a stickler for fashion and looking good." Faith struck a vogue pose. "She was always saying, 'Love . . .' she called us 'love' sometimes. 'Love, always wow them. A house may be old, but it doesn't mean you can't keep up the maintenance, spruce up the place, and keep it looking good on the outside.' Motherphelia's hair was always perfect and in place, even when she stayed in the house all day. She'd wake up every morning and put on some makeup. She taught me all the tricks of being pretty." Faith sat down in the chair in front of Johnnie Mae's desk when she saw Johnnie Mae had relaxed a tad and seemed interested in what she was saying.

"When we needed to unburden ourselves," Faith said, "Motherphelia would be there and ready to listen. We do miss her." Faith could tell her spirits were starting to wane as she revisited this part of the past. She changed the tone of her voice and got back on track. "Do you want to tell me about what's going on with you, or should I get back in there, keep typing, and tend to my own business?"

Johnnie Mae looked as though she was weighing whether to talk to Faith or not.

"I had a sitter, Ms. Bertha," she began. "Who was coming in at night and a few days through the week to care for my mother. The doctors believe my mother has Alzheimer's. My sister, who moved back here in October, just got in to it with Ms. Bertha. Now, it appears, Ms. Bertha has just quit."

"She's probably upset for now," Faith said. "After Ms. Bertha thinks about it, I'm sure she'll reconsider. She wouldn't leave you in a bind like that."

"You don't know my sister. I'm sure she and Ms. Bertha have gotten into it plenty of times I've not even heard about.

This was probably the last straw. And Rachel is not going away anytime soon. So even if I convince Ms. Bertha to come back, she'll probably not stay much longer. Now, I'll likely need to find a new sitter who won't disrupt things too much for my mother at this stage. Someone who's great with older people. Someone sincere."

"I'm sure you're going to find someone you'll be pleased with," Faith said. She could practically hear Charity's voice saying how perfect she'd be for the job. "What do you think you'll do to replace her?"

"Call some agencies, maybe post something here on the bulletin board, then start the long, in-depth interview process. So if you happen to know someone who would be good and really cares about the elderly, and not just someone looking at this as merely a weekly paycheck, please let me know."

Faith stood up and rubbed her head.

"Are you okay?" Johnnie Mae asked.

"All of a sudden, I'm starting to get a massive migraine headache."

"Hope had something similar happen to her once when she and I were talking. Both of you should go get that checked out."

Faith pressed her palm harder to her head. "Would you mind if I take this work home and finish it there? I need to lie down and rest for a little while. They don't ever last too long. But what seems to work best is to completely let go . . . relax until it passes."

"Sure. No, go on home and take the work with you. I want to go over to my mother's and see what's going on, anyway. Maybe I can do some damage control with Ms. Bertha."

Faith started to walk away. Johnnie Mae noticed she walked differently. Not the usual, diva-like swag she was known for. *She must really not be feeling well.*

"I hope you feel better," Johnnie Mae said.

Faith turned around. "Before I go, I could type up that job information requirement sheet about a sitter for your mother."

"You don't have to worry about that," Johnnie Mae said. "Maybe I won't need it."

"I was thinking, I may know someone who'd like the job. If I had the information before you posted it, you might find you like this person as well. Then you won't need to go through a long process. I don't want to sound pushy or anything, just wanted to help out if possible. I really think you'd like her, should it turn out you really will need a replacement." Faith looked at Johnnie Mae as though she really cared.

So unFaith-like, Johnnie Mae thought. She'd originally felt Faith didn't have a real-concern-for-others bone in her body. The expression on Faith's face was starting to convince Johnnie Mae—maybe she'd misjudged her. Faith looked genuinely sincere.

"Why don't I just write out the information for you, and if the person you're thinking about turns out to be interested, we can see where it goes." Johnnie Mae wrote the qualification requirements and her contact information on a note paper, tore it off, and handed it to Faith.

"Thank you so much. I really do appreciate this. And I'll be praying for you and your mother. I know something like this can be hard on you and your family, but God is with you. I know He is," Faith said.

"Thanks . . . Faith." Johnnie Mae tilted her head slightly. "You go home and take care of that headache, okay?"

"Oh, it's starting to feel better already. But thank you for caring. You're really a sweet person." She walked out and came back. "Excuse me again. I'm sorry to interrupt, but can you tell me the best way to get out of here?"

Johnnie Mae frowned a little. She wondered how Faith could be confused about getting out of a building she'd only entered two hours ago. "Out the door and to your left. That will take you out to the parking lot. Faith, are you sure you're okay? I can call someone to come get you or I could take you home—"

"I'm fine. Thank you, though. Thanks for the directions. I guess I'm a little turned around—you know how that can be. Again, I pray you find everything okay when you reach your mother's house." Faith smiled, left Johnnie Mae's office, gathered up her things and the information she was taking home to work on, and left.

Chapter 40

And when Jehu was come to Jezreel, Jezebel heard of it; and she painted her face, and tired her head, and looked out at a window.

(2 Kings 9:30)

"Okay, Faith, listen to me and I don't care to hear any arguments from you," Charity said as she paced the floor. "I really want this job. I don't care what you think is best for me. You know how much I love taking care of people, and Johnnie Mae Taylor Landris seems like a good person. She needs someone like me caring for her mother. There's no reason, if I love doing this and I want to do it, for me not to do it. I want to at least apply for it, and that's what I intend to do. I don't care what you feel."

Charity sat down and relaxed in the chaise longue that was in the living room area again. She was really getting tired of the furniture always being moved and could feel herself getting stronger now. Strong enough to decide for herself what was best for her, strong enough to stand up for herself if she needed to, strong enough not to be intimidated by people who seemed to intimidate others just for the sport of it.

Yes, she appreciated the way Faith and Hope always seemed to come to her rescue. How they'd stepped up to help her get through that devastating "situation." That's how they all referred to it whenever the subject presented itself about that day when Charity was only seven.

Oh, how she missed Motherphelia.

Faith was the first one who came in and took control of the situation. Hope might have been the identical twin, but she was different in how she handled things. Hope was not as strong as Faith, but she was the smart one . . . the practical one.

Faith didn't have a problem with their beauty; Hope preferred they toned their looks down. Faith liked to dress in the latest fashions. She got her hair done, liked makeup—the whole shebang. Hope would put on mascara and a little lipstick—and that was about it.

Charity laughed when she thought about how much alike they all really were, yet so vastly different. Charity didn't care for any makeup at all, not even lip gloss. She couldn't care less about clothes or fashion. She just liked people.

Motherphelia liked to look good, but never wore heavy makeup. She'd see others with too much rouge on and say, "Jezebel! Tramp!" under her breath. She would say, "Look at her. That's too much blue on her eyes to even appear natural. Her rouge makes her look like a clown. She must have gotten dressed without a mirror this morning."

"What's a Jezebel, Motherphelia?" Charity asked.

Motherphelia smiled. "Someone who has to do all this stuff to herself and act a certain way just to get men's attention."

"I don't want to be a Jezebel," Charity said.

"That's a good girl. You can dress nice and fix yourself up. Not too much, though, because you're only seven. But maybe when you get fifteen, I'll show you how to put on eye shadow and rouge the correct way. It needs to look like it belongs there. Not like you're a walking neon sign, advertising you're a tramp."

"Is that like *Lady and the Tramp?*"

Motherphelia smiled. "What's that, Love?"

Charity giggled. *Her grandmother knew everything. How could she not know this?* "It's a movie, Motherphelia. Me and Mother have seen it."

"Your mother lets you watch too much trash. You have to protect those ear gates and eye gates. Everything that comes on the radio is not appropriate for you to listen to. Some of this junk these young peoples listen to they call music is a shame and a disgrace. Rap, in my day, was when someone was saying something somebody wanted to hear. 'Let me talk to you.' That's rapping. This stuff y'all call rap and music, we'll just see how long it lasts. Keep yourself pure, Charity. You have to be careful out here in this world. Peoples ain't like they were when I was coming up."

"How was it when you were my age?" Charity asked.

"For one thing, we could leave our doors unlocked and no one would come into your house and try to take anything from you, let alone try to kill you for it. This world is going to 'h', 'e', double toothpick in a hand basket . . ."

"Oooh, Motherphelia," Charity sang, ". . . you just spelled a bad word."

"That's not a bad word. Not the way I used it. That's a real place. Just like heaven is a real place. But the word I spelled is bad in that it's not a place you want to end up in."

Motherphelia cupped both her hands around her granddaughter's face, brought her face down to meet it, and placed a quick peck ever so lightly on her lips.

"Now," Motherphelia said, smiling, "you have on just the right amount of lipstick for a girl your age."

"You put lipstick on me, Motherphelia?" Charity said as she ran to find a mirror so she could see her lips.

"You're a brilliant child—I hope you don't waste it. I'm looking for you to graduate valedictorian of your high school and whatever the highest thing there is in college. And you're going to go to college . . . on a full scholarship. I just feel it in these bones of mine. I've watched you since you were a little baby. I saw you in the hospital a few minutes after you were born. You're going to be somebody. And if you have to fight to get there and stay, you fight. 'Cause Motherphelia will always fight for you, Lovey."

"Lovey?" Charity laughed. "You called me Lovey, Mother-phelia, just like The Lovey Cup."

Motherphelia smiled and rubbed her knees.

Charity came over and massaged her grandmother's knee. "Is old Arthur acting up again, Motherphelia?" That was what her grandmother would say when her knees bothered her.

Motherphelia grabbed Charity and pulled her up onto her lap. "I love you, Charity. You're filled with so much love, faith, and hope . . . all inside of you. There's nothing you won't be able to do or handle in life. You just remember what Motherphelia has told you."

"Always dress nice, always look my best, always do my best, always be as smart as I can be, don't dumb myself down for nobody, show people what I can really do even if they get jealous, treat others right, and never, ever, give up."

Motherphelia laughed. "That's my Charity. You have so much inside you, all rolled up in one. Don't be arrogant, though," Motherphelia said. "God doesn't like peoples with haughty spirits. Me and God have that in common; I don't like uppity peoples neither. You can show pride without walking around with your nose in the air. Remember that."

Charity thought about all of this as she sat there in the chaise longue. That was the last conversation Charity remembered with her grandmother before that "situation" happened. The situation that changed her life and the way she viewed everything. Charity started to think back to what happened that day.

Her head began to pound. "My head hurts," she said, pressing her temples hard. She lay back on the chaise and closed her eyes, trying to make the pain stop.

"Don't, Charity. You don't need to even think about stuff like that." It was Faith's voice Charity heard as her eyes remained closed. "Tell her, Hope. Tell her that's not something she ever needs to think about. She'll listen to you. We all know what happened that day; we vowed to let it be buried when Motherphelia was buried. Let's not dig it up. Let it rest in peace, Charity, along with Motherphelia. That's what she'd want."

Charity drifted off to sleep with Faith's voice ringing in her ear. "Let it rest in peace. Okay. There's nothing remembering will do that will change anything. Things are what they are. Hope and I vowed to take care of you, to protect you, no matter what. We meant that, didn't we, Hope? Nobody's going to come between us. Not as long as I'm around . . ."

Chapter 41

But we have this treasure in earthen vessels,
that the excellency of the power may be of God,
and not of us.

(2 Corinthians 4:7)

Hope took the folder with the finished, typed marriage seminar information to church. Johnnie Mae wanted it by the end of April, and it was only the middle of April. There were three services now, and if the new sanctuary wasn't finished soon, the more than 1500 people attending were threatening to force Pastor Landris into a fourth, possibly fifth, service. He was considering a worship service on Saturday or temporarily suspending Bible study for a Wednesday night service just to alleviate the overflow crowd on Sundays. Hope always attended the first service whatever time that happened to be.

With three services, the time had been moved up and shortened. Everything was tight and on a strict schedule. The Praise & Worship Team could only sing for twenty minutes. Not a minute longer. Pastor Landris only spoke for thirty minutes, which was okay. He just left out any fillers, and the congregation received pure meat to chew on until the next time they assembled. There were lots of volunteer workers, but of course that required training workshops.

Hope loved being a behind-the-scenes worker. It didn't matter to her whether she received credit for what she did. That's where she and Faith truly differed. Faith loved getting credit, even for work she didn't do. Hope didn't mind if Faith got the credit, even for what she'd done. She just wanted the work done, and done right.

"Johnnie Mae, here's the workbook information for the marriage seminar," Hope said as she handed Johnnie Mae a folder. "All done."

"Hope!" Johnnie Mae said her name as though she was so happy to see her. "You have the workbook information already, and it's finished?" She took the folder and opened it, nodding her approval. "Impressive. This looks really, really good! Wow, I'm so impressed. But why are *you* bringing this instead of Faith? Not that I'm complaining."

Hope smiled. "We wanted you to get it as soon as possible. I always attend first service, so here it is."

"Faith did a great job," Johnnie Mae said in hopes that Hope would admit the truth: she'd actually typed this. Johnnie Mae could tell this was Hope's doing. She'd seen the little Faith had attempted to do when they were in the office together. Besides, she knew Hope's excellent handiwork.

Hope only grinned. "I know you're busy. I don't want to hold you. After you've read through it, you can let Faith know if there are any changes you need. And if Faith's not available, just let me know. I'll be happy to take care of it for you. I know where it's filed on our computer at home."

Johnnie Mae smiled back. "I'm just overwhelmed at how wonderful this looks so far. And on top of that, it's finished two weeks ahead of schedule."

"How's your mother?" Hope asked. "Faith mentioned you were having some problems . . . something about your sitter suddenly quitting."

"My mother is the same, but thank you for asking. I'm confessing more good days over her life than bad, and I was able to talk Ms. Bertha into staying. For now, anyway. My oldest sister and I have differing ideas about how things should be handled. Pray for me," Johnnie Mae said, laughing.

"I know how the oldest can be. I'm happy things worked out for you. I hope it continues to do so."

"Well, Hope, I don't just hope," Johnnie Mae said with a smirk. "I have to have faith it will. But however it works out, we all know—it will work out for good. Romans 8:28."

Hope nodded and looked down for a second before quickly lifting her head back up.

Johnnie Mae had noticed Hope had gotten better about not being so shy. She wasn't looking down at her feet quite as often as she had when she first arrived at the church.

Johnnie Mae closed the folder and placed the rubber band back around the folder to keep everything secure. "Thanks again, Hope. For everything. And I do mean *everything.*" Johnnie Mae touched Hope's hand to let her know she knew the truth, even if Hope wouldn't admit it.

Hope smiled. Feeling appreciated was so different from feeling used. Hope knew what feeling used felt like. Lately, she was learning more and more what it meant to be appreciated.

Chapter 42

The words of a talebearer are as wounds, and they go down into the innermost parts of the belly.

(Proverbs 18:4 & Proverbs 26:22)

Charity had been inside Followers of Jesus Faith Worship Center only briefly, but it had been long enough to make her want to visit during an actual worship service. Faith thought it was a bad idea, and she let Charity know how she felt. Besides, there was so much going on with the new building, if Charity was going to visit, the best time would be after they moved into the new sanctuary. The new sanctuary was being built to seat 5,000, so there would be plenty of room for everybody to sit.

When the committee was first designing the floor plan for the sanctuary, they thought 5,000 seats would take a long time to fill up. This was not Atlanta, where Pastor Landris had been able to draw more than 4,000 members. This was Birmingham, Alabama, where the biggest talk about a subway system seemed to be for one *between* Birmingham and Atlanta.

In Birmingham, Alabama—the home of the Civil Rights Institute and the infamous Sixteenth Street Baptist Church—churches were sprinkled all over the city. Congregations were meeting in hotels. Some bought or rented vacant storefronts and converted them.

Now it appeared, even with 5,000 seats, they would still not be going to one service as Pastor Landris and the workers had first believed. Over 2,000 people were presently in the database as members. The media was covering the new building and its surrounding developments, and the excitement was mounting with each passing day. At the rate things were escalating, as soon as they moved into the new sanctuary, a flood of people who had been held at bay would be released. It was highly possible that within a month's time, there would easily be some 5,000 people in their databank.

Pastor Landris needed help from every person he could trust. He and Johnnie Mae had begun the thirteen-week seminar in June. It was now September, and members of his staff and the congregation had put together a wonderful third-year wedding anniversary banquet in the fellowship hall for him and his wife. Pastor Landris had planned something special for their actual September 8th anniversary date, but he appreciated how much the members cared to do something like that for them.

Pastor Landris and Johnnie Mae had moved into their new home three weeks earlier, back in August. They loved the house—it was indeed a mansion, in spite of how much Johnnie Mae didn't want to think of it like that. The builder had exceeded in what they had imagined it would be. All of them—Pastor Landris, Johnnie Mae, and Princess Rose—had to get used to a place that size. Rachel was still at their other house. Johnnie Mae hadn't decided what to do about that now touchy situation. In October, Rachel's six weeks' stay at the house would officially become one year.

Some people had issues with Pastor Landris building a new house just as the sanctuary was also being built. There were even rumors making the rounds that he and Brother Brent had scraped money off the church's fund to build their homes in the expensive part of the new subdivisions.

A group of four women were sitting around talking at their weekly Thursday night get-together.

"They already had a house," one woman said as she shuffled the playing cards one final time before setting it down to be cut. "There are some of us here who don't know what home ownership even looks like. Theirs wasn't a little house, either, from what I heard. But I suppose that wasn't enough for them; they had to get a bigger house to show off."

"And it's not but the three of them," another woman said, cutting the cards by dividing the stack in half. "His wife is so selfish, she won't even give the man a baby. I feel sorry for him, really. As many women as there are out there who would love to carry his child."

"He is good-looking, ain't he?" a third woman said.

"Honey, hush! Ain't he, though?!" said the fourth woman at the table.

"Well, if she wasn't so stuck on her book career and herself, she might stop long enough to think about somebody else for a change," the first woman said as she dealt the cards. "That man is too good to be with someone who doesn't care about him."

"I bet you they don't make it. They gonna turn out just like some of these other preachers and their wives around here. I've seen plenty of these women who sacrifice their own lives and careers to support their husbands' ministries. And as soon as he gets there, you start hearing rumors about him beating on her, fooling around on her, and other stuff. Then before you know anything, the old model's out, and another model is in, calling herself the new first lady. Mrs. So-and-So," the woman who had cut the cards said.

"Some of those women don't play that, though," the third woman said as she arranged her cards.

"Well, if he kicks this one here to the curb, I bet you he gets himself one that will have a baby for him," the fourth woman said. She looked at the cards in her hand and smiled.

"Shoot, if he really wants one, I'll volunteer for the job, and he don't even have to marry me. Just pay me my child support. 'Cause I ain't playing that independent-woman mess. But at least he'd have his own child to carry on his legacy."

They all laughed.

Chapter 43

We then that are strong ought to bear the infir-
mities of the weak . . .

(Romans 15:1)

It was Saturday night, September 4, 2004. Pastor Landris was conducting three Sunday services. After two years, there were more than 1,700 names in the church's database with some 1,500 attending on a regular basis. People moved their membership from other churches for various reasons. Some were being saved and coming to church for the first time ever, or were coming back to church after having become disenchanted years ago. When people moved into the area, this was one of the churches they visited and joined. The building only seated 500 comfortably, although they could squeeze in 600.

"Tired?" Pastor Landris asked Johnnie Mae as she strolled back into the den wearing a red silk negligee. They'd had a long evening. The church had given Pastor Landris and Johnnie Mae a lovely banquet at the fellowship hall to celebrate three years of marriage.

Johnnie Mae smiled and slipped into her husband's arms as they sat on the couch together. "Yes. But I'll be okay." They had the whole house to themselves tonight—Princess Rose was with Johnnie Mae's sister, Marie.

"You know, you don't have to stay for all three services

tomorrow. Why don't you just pick one and let that be it for you," Pastor Landris said.

"You're preaching all three services, aren't you?" Johnnie Mae asked as she readjusted herself; she didn't want to become too comfortable and fall asleep right there on the couch.

"Yes."

"Why don't you let one of the other ministers help? Or better yet, let two of them each take one and you pick one of the three?" Johnnie Mae stood up and walked around to the back of the sofa. She began to massage Landris's shoulders as though she were kneading dough.

Pastor Landris closed his eyes and began to allow his body to fully relax. He had no idea he'd become so tense and tight. He'd already taken off his aqua paisley tie. He unsnapped the top two snaps of his white Collezioni shirt. "That feels wonderful," he moaned and got even more comfortable. "Your hands must be anointed."

"Would you like me to get you the phone so you can call someone before it gets too late?"

Pastor Landris didn't want to think about anything. Johnnie Mae definitely knew how to work out the kinks. He was melting even deeper into her capable hands.

"Landris?" She stopped and leaned down to whisper in his ear. "Are you listening to me at all?"

"Yeah, baby. I hear you. You want me to call one of the ministers to fill in for me tomorrow. I was thinking about it, but I don't feel it would be fair to any of them to do that." He moistened his lips and rotated both his shoulders at the same time, hoping Johnnie Mae would take the hint and start back with the massage. "Sure, as ministers, we should always be ready. But it's almost 11:00 P.M. How right would it be for me to call anybody this late to handle the 7:30 A.M. service when it's not even an emergency? Besides, I'll be okay tomorrow. God manages to give us brand-new mercy each and every day. Tomorrow, I'll be good as new." Pastor Landris sat up straight after he realized his massage had ended. He turned around and looked in his wife's angelic, but obviously tired, face. "You're finished?"

"Yes. I believe I am." She yawned and stretched, then started walking away. "I think I'll turn in."

"Oh, before I forget, Faith Morrell told me to tell you congratulations on our wedding anniversary. She thinks you're fortunate to have me," he said teasingly.

Johnnie Mae laughed a little. "Oh, really now?" She shook her head in disbelief. "She told you that, huh? So where was I?" She began turning off the lamps around the room.

"It was a little after you left to get your purse from my office. In fact, she only missed seeing you herself by about a minute." Pastor Landris stood up and started walking his wife out of the den and toward the stairs.

He loved the way the staircase's wrought iron, sculptured banister curved as it ascended. He and Johnnie Mae had designed it after Oheka Castle. He loved everything about their newly built house. It had taken almost six months for it to be completed, but it was definitely worth the wait. They'd only been in it a little over three weeks.

"You know, Faith really wants to be my assistant," Johnnie Mae said as they climbed the stairs, arms wrapped around each other.

"Yeah, you mentioned that. So what are your feelings about it?"

Johnnie Mae stopped when they reached the top of the stairs. The white carpet always reminded her of a field of freshly fallen snow. Everybody told Johnnie Mae that it was a huge mistake to put white carpeting in a house, especially one this size—six bedrooms and five full baths.

"You'll never keep it clean," Johnnie Mae's mother had said. "Marie, tell her."

Marie had only smiled and nodded. She knew better than to try and convince her younger sister of anything. Once

Johnnie Mae's mind was made up, there was no reasoning with her. Marie had figured that much out.

All four siblings had agreed—including Christian, now fighting in Iraq—that it was best to put their mother in an assisted-living home. She needed constant supervision. Everybody could see that except Johnnie Mae, who was the one with the power of attorney given to her by their mother.

All Johnnie Mae knew was that her mother wanted to remain at her own house, and she refused to put her away just because it would be easier on them. Her mother probably wasn't going to get any better, but she wouldn't get any better in a home either. It wasn't the right decision for everyone facing this dilemma, but it was the right one for her now.

Then, there was Faith and Hope. There was something that bothered her regarding them, but she couldn't quite put her finger on it.

"Johnnie Mae," Landris said, "did you fall asleep that fast?"

She was leaning back comfortably in his arms as they lay in bed. "No, I was just thinking. Faith *seems* okay. And, I admit, at times she's been helpful. Landris, I do need to hire an assistant. She did help with the marriage seminar typing—sort of, anyway. The truth is, I really love the work Hope does. But maybe I should consider giving Faith a chance. She's the one who keeps bringing the subject up. I just don't know—there's something about Faith that doesn't quite add up. I can't figure out what."

"I think," he turned her face toward his, "we have a long day ahead of us tomorrow, and we should table this discussion for later." He kissed her on the forehead. "We've had a wonderful night tonight," he played with her hair, "and I," he kissed her on one cheek, "don't really want," he kissed her on the other cheek, "to think," he gently kissed her top lip, "or talk," a kiss to her bottom lip, "about," a soft peck on both lips simultaneously, "work right now."

"Okay." She smiled and gave him a quick peck back.

She'd table this for tonight. But she was determined to get to the bottom of what was going on, in particular, with Hope. Johnnie Mae really liked Hope, and lately something just wasn't feeling right.

Chapter 44

Faith was at the Exhibition Hall along with Johnnie Mae, Angel, Sapphire, Tarsha, and Sherry as they finished the final touches for the marriage seminar celebration. Over two hundred couples attended the thirteen-week seminar. They had intended to have the celebration in the church fellowship hall, but with that many people, those plans had to be changed.

The previous Saturday, the church had celebrated Pastor Landris and Johnnie Mae's third wedding anniversary. Hope had worked hard helping out with that. She'd also done a lot for this marriage celebration, but as with the anniversary banquet, she would not be in attendance. Faith was excited about it because it gave her yet another opportunity to show off her latest new "do" and the burgundy chiffon, Vera Wang dress she'd ordered from a company called BlueFly.com off the Internet. The outfit looked and fit nicer even than she'd expected. But then, she'd heard Vera Wang's dresses were like that.

She'd also heard Beyoncé and her mother were about to launch their own clothing line, House of Dereon. Dereon was Beyoncé's grandmother, a private seamstress in Louisiana. Faith understood the love a grandchild felt for a truly exceptional matriarch. This was one label that Faith couldn't wait to try on. *Beyoncé's mother can throw down like nobody's business.* Soon enough, people like Faith would have access to Tina Knowles's styles.

The graduation and wedding-vow renewal celebration was set for September 11, at 7:00 P.M. Faith knew she would be the best dressed person there—hands down.

"Doesn't Sister Landris look gorgeous?" someone was saying as Faith walked in. "Did you see that gown? I'd love to go shopping in *her* closet. She can give me her hand-me-downs any day of the week."

"And her hair—she probably pays a fortune to her hairdresser."

"No—I once asked who did her hair, and she said a woman named Pam. I thought Pam might have been one of those exclusive, snooty stylists, but Sister Landris says she's really a down-to-earth Christian woman. She's been going to her for years."

"Hi, ladies," Faith said, giving an extra twirl and bounce to her movements. "I'm glad you were able to come. This is so exciting! Lots of surprises in store. If you need anything . . . anything at all, you see that woman over there?" Faith pointed to her right.

"You mean Sapphire?"

"Yes, Sapphire. If you need anything, you let her know. She's here to make sure you all have a wonderful time."

"Are you the hostess or something?" a woman with freckles asked.

"Me? Oh no. I'm one of the people who helped put all of this together for you guys. I've worked closely with Sister Landris on this whole thing, starting with the workbooks."

"Those workbooks were wonderful. People have been trying to get mine and make a copy of it. I told them I thought it was copyrighted, and they would be breaking the law if they copied it."

"You told them right," Faith said. "I believe Sister Landris is working with a publisher to have it available shortly for all married Christians."

"It's certainly going to bless a lot of people. I know me and my husband have gone to a whole new level in love because of it and that marriage seminar."

"Well, ladies," Faith spun around with flair, "I have to run. Busy, busy, busy." She smiled as she practically glided away.

Pastor Landris was sitting alone near the table where all the VIPs would soon assemble. Faith walked over to him.

"Pastor Landris."

"Faith," Pastor Landris said. "See, I got it right that time."

"Yes, I'm proud of you."

"This place looks beautiful. All of you did a fantastic job. Johnnie Mae hasn't stopped talking about the work that you, Hope, and especially Angel and Sapphire, along with others on the committee, have done over these past few months."

"It's been a labor of love, I assure you." She looked around the room to see if anyone was approaching them. Satisfied that they could pretty much talk freely without eavesdroppers or interruptions, she sighed loudly.

"Something the matter?"

"No. Well, maybe something. I was thinking about all the problems you and Johnnie Mae have had to deal with these past few months. And now it looks like things are getting better. Last week's anniversary celebration was special, and I hear the two of you have moved into your brand-new house."

"Yes. It's really nice."

"And now the new church is close to being finished. The first Sunday in December we'll be in there getting our praise on like nobody's business," Faith said, smiling.

"Absolutely. It won't be long now."

"Listen, Pastor Landris. I wouldn't bring this up, except I

really would like to do something to help out. I know your brother has been having some difficult times."

"Who told you that?"

"I've just been hearing things. At first it was just here around our church, but now people are mentioning things in other churches. You know, the fact that there must be something wrong going on at Followers of Jesus Faith Worship Center."

"Oh, you mean the one about 'If your own family isn't participating, they must know something other people don't'?" Pastor Landris said. "I've heard. I can't do anything about what other people say, but you can certainly help, though."

"How so?"

"By not spreading it any more than has already been done. Every time you tell someone, it's like you're part of the problem. Think about it: if people wouldn't keep passing that along to someone else, it would eventually die. Instead, we give things life with that one little busy-body member we call the tongue. That little weapon alone has destroyed too many lives, families, friendships, businesses, and church congregations."

"You're right," Faith said. "I've only brought it up to you, though. As a rule, I don't talk to many people. I'm a great listener, so sometimes I hear things. Like I know you and Johnnie Mae have been trying to have a child. I don't know quite how to say this, but I would be honored to carry your child for you, if you'd like."

Pastor Landris looked at her and frowned. "Excuse me?"

Faith saw the look on his face, but she was determined to get this out there. She had no idea when the opportunity might present itself ever again. She would plant the seed, and see where it led later down the road.

"I don't mean any disrespect," Faith said. "You know I love your wife like a sister, and I respect her position as your wife. The reason I want to propose this to you is because if you think it's a bad idea or that it will hurt you or her in any way, I know you will set me straight."

"I don't like the road this is going down. Maybe I'm missing something here, or maybe you should stop now before you end up really saying the wrong thing," Pastor Landris said.

"Oh, I think you have this all wrong," Faith said, laughing. "I'm not proposing anything illicit. I was suggesting that if you guys are in need of an egg donor . . . or a surrogate, I would love to do something like that for you . . . for both of you, really. I would be honored to carry your baby for you."

"Where did you get the idea that we're looking for an egg donor or a surrogate?"

"I overheard Johnnie Mae on the phone when she and I were working at the church office. She seems truly devastated that she can't give you a child. I'm young, healthy, and willing to carry your baby if it would bring the two of you the child I know—in your hearts—you desperately desire."

Pastor Landris stood up. "This is not the place for me to say what I'm really thinking. I think you're totally out of line to bring this up to me here without my wife being present. If you were really concerned about her, you would have mentioned this to her, and not me." He clenched his jaw even tighter.

"Pastor Landris, I believe you're getting upset unnecessarily. I haven't proposed that you and I sleep together or have an affair to produce your heir. I was merely thinking of what I might be able to do to give you two the baby you know you both want. Johnnie Mae knows how badly you want your own baby, and truthfully, it's eating her up inside. Don't you see that?"

Pastor Landris walked back toward her so he could speak without anyone overhearing. "You don't know my wife at all! And you surely don't know me." He rubbed the bottom of his chin. "Not that it's any of your business, but if my wife and I *never* have a child together, being with her is all I need in my life. I love *her*. I hope you understand *that*, Miss Morrell."

Faith cocked her head to the side. "I understand. I apologize. Trust me, I won't make a mistake like this one again." Faith stormed off.

"Faith," Johnnie Mae said as she passed her on her way to see Pastor Landris. When she finally reached him, she said, "What's with Faith? I saw you two talking just now—looked like it was pretty intense."

He smiled. "Later. I'll tell you about this one later." He let out a long, slow sigh.

"Well, I have some great news," Johnnie Mae said, clapping her hands together.

"Do tell."

"We have hired a new sitter for my mother. Rachel, Marie, Donald, and I all agreed—in fact, they called just as I was on my way down here to get all these decorations up for tonight. I didn't know what I was going to do when Ms. Bertha said she couldn't do this anymore. I was about to post something on the bulletin board when I got a call from, of all people, Faith and Hope's sister, Charity."

"Faith's sister?"

"Yes. Remember I told you about her last week after our anniversary banquet? I was going to talk with Hope about trying to get her sister to come visit our church. Well, it seems Charity found out I was looking for a sitter for Mama, and she called me. I had her fax her resume and some references, then called her back and had her come meet with me and the others yesterday. We were able to see how she interacts with Mama. We asked tons of questions, and she's perfect! I mean, she is so sweet, and so caring. Princess Rose even likes her, and you know children can usually see right through people. We offered her the job this morning, and she called back and graciously accepted."

"Are you sure about this? Do you know anything about her? Do you know whether or not she has a criminal record?"

"Landris, come on. Don't bring ants to our picnic. You're going to ask me to marry you again during the ceremony. If you start acting like this now, I might not say yes."

"Oh, please. Not that. Not the 'if-you-asked-me-to-marry-you-now-I-would-turn-you-down' threat."

Johnnie Mae threw her head back as she laughed.

"J. M., have I told you I loved you lately?" Pastor Landris said as he moved in closer.

She looked at her watch. "Not in the last five hours." She smiled. "Wow, that must have been a really good one," Johnnie Mae said. "Oh, yeah."

"What?"

"Whatever it was you and Faith were discussing." She grabbed his arm and escorted him to the VIP table. "Just let it go, Landris. Whatever it is or was, it's not worth ruining our evening over. We'll thoroughly check to be sure Charity doesn't have a criminal record. She gave us several references we've already verified. The people at the nursing homes she visits love her. The staff told us they were jealous that our mother would have such loving, excellent personal care. Charity is Hope's sister, and honestly, she's even sweeter than Hope. And I didn't think that was possible.

"We're in our new house, the church is almost ready. There's only one thing that hasn't happened, but we're not going to dwell on it tonight. I'm still saying my confession daily: *He maketh me to keep house, and to be a joyful mother of children. Praise ye the Lord.*"

Pastor Landris sat down and smiled up at her. "But we have each other, and Princess Rose, and things are getting better and better every day. And that's all that really matters."

She squeezed his shoulder as she started walking away. "I have to locate the others who are supposed to be up here with you. Faith was in charge of seating the VIPs. I guess she must have more important matters to attend to. So—I'll be back with the rest of your comrades, my darling." She blew him a kiss and winked.

He nodded and smiled as he watched her leave.

Chapter 45

Let all your things be done with charity.

(1 Corinthians 16:14)

Charity was working out wonderfully. She loved Mrs. Gates, who seemed to instantly improve with her. Charity knew how to get through to her in ways that even impressed her doctor.

Charity even figured out a way to settle Rachel down. She made everybody feel so at peace whenever she was around. And she was genuine. That was the number one word everybody used about her.

"I'm planning to come to your church on Sunday," Charity said. She was wearing a simple pink jogging suit with a hoodie top. "I can't believe I haven't been there already. I have visited a few churches, but I was having more fun visiting my usual nursing facilities and having church with them. I love the old songs. I miss them. People don't seem to sing them much in churches anymore. I'm not talking about the sad ones that make you cry—I'm talking about the songs that tell a story."

Johnnie Mae was excited as she sat talking with Charity. And to hear she was finally going to come visit the church after all this time was icing on the cake. "I like *some* of the older songs, too," Johnnie Mae said.

"Me, too," Mrs. Gates said.

Charity turned to Mrs. Gates. "What's your favorite song, Mama Gates?" She made it a point to keep her in the conversation and not ignore her like so many people did.

"I still love that song by Dorothy Love Coates. You remember it, Johnnie Mae?" Mrs. Gates said.

"Which one, Mama?"

"The one you and your sisters tried to sing when y'all started a singing group. Don't try to act like you've forgotten."

Johnnie Mae started smiling. "I remember doing that, but I can't remember the song you're talking about."

"Do you remember any of the words in the song, Mama Gates?" Charity asked. "Sometimes it helps if I can just remember one word. Then all the other words come back."

"Faith," Mrs. Gates said.

"No, Mama. Her name is not Faith. This is Charity. You know . . . Charity."

"Faith, Mama Gates?" Charity said. "Did you say faith?"

"She's probably getting confused now," Johnnie Mae said, almost in a whisper.

Charity started smiling. "*I'm Holding On, And I Won't Let Go of My Faith,*" Charity began to sing.

"That's the one," Mrs. Gates said as she joined in and started singing it, too. "Oh, I loved me some Dorothy Love Coates and the rest of those singers. Alabama produces some talented people. Most folk have no idea who all's from here. Take my Johnnie Mae. She's an author. Most folk she meets probably automatically assume she's from someplace else—one of those larger, popular cities. Not Birmingham, though."

"True, Mama Gates. People have no idea how much talent is here."

"And now we have Ruben. You know, he won on *American Idol*. And that black woman who won the first gold medal at the Winter Olympics. What's her name?"

Johnnie Mae was about to answer when Charity touched

her arm and shook her head. She nodded toward Mrs. Gates, who was struggling to find the name.

Charity waited and smiled. "Oh, you remember her name, Mama Gates. We were talking about her just the other day. She has twin boys."

"I know. It starts with a 'V'."

"That's good. Remember what I told you. Go through all the alphabet if you have to until one feels familiar. Then your brain will help you from there," Charity said. " 'V.' "

"Verletta. No. Voncetta. No, that's my cousin. Vonetta. That's it! Vonetta Rose . . . no, Vonetta Flowers," Mrs. Gates said.

"That's it," Charity said, laughing with her.

When Johnnie Mae was leaving, she was bubbling over with joy. "Charity, you're doing such great work with my mother. I haven't seen her like this in years. Years. And everybody thought she was pretty much gone, but in just three weeks, you have her closer to her old self."

"She loves listening to music, so I found some of her old albums. And I located a needle for the record player, which was hard. CD players have, for the most part, put phonographs totally out of business. But I did find one. In fact, I bought two, just in case we wear this one out." She laughed. "Songs store memories for her, as they do for all of us."

Johnnie Mae thought about that. "You're right. Certain songs make me remember certain people and times. I love Earth, Wind & Fire, and when I hear certain cuts from those songs, I'm immediately transported back to the memories I shared with that song."

"That's what has happened with your mother when we listen to songs. Only she's able to go there under her own power. It doesn't happen to her—she's the one making it happen. It changes how her mind processes things. There are songs that I already know will calm her, some that will cause her to be happy or sad, or reflective. It's like in the Bible when Saul had a troubling spirit. David was able to play music and soothe his spirit. That's what your mother and I do a lot."

"Well, you and she do more than that. You take her for walks and play games, help her around the house. You're just a godsend—that's the only way I can describe you."

"Thank you. I'm just glad everything worked out. I loved being with my grandmother when I was growing up. She taught me how to love and respect what older people have to offer. I still look for that. So every opportunity I'm blessed to be around an older person, I honor it for what it truly is. I learn as much from them as they get from me." Charity peeked around the corner to see what Mrs. Gates was doing. Her eyes were closed. "I think she's taking her nap now. When she wakes up, we'll have our tea."

Johnnie Mae smiled and shook her head. "I almost envy you two. I'm starting to think maybe I should drop in more often."

"We'd love and welcome the company anytime. I have nothing to hide. I told you and your sisters from my heart what my intentions were. To show love to someone who has shown love to others. Your mother deserves the best of care, and that's what I intend to give her. My grandmother, Motherphelia, and I used to cook a lot. And there was one recurring scripture she managed to use whenever we cooked."

"Cooking with scripture—what an interesting concept," Johnnie Mae said.

"The scripture was Luke 6:38. Would you happen to know it?"

"Oh, you must have heard I'm married to the Walking Bible," Johnnie Mae said.

"Pardon me?"

Johnnie Mae laughed. "It's an inside joke. My husband can quote scripture like he sat down and just memorized the Bible. I mean, he can tell you where a scripture is, chapter and verse. If you call out a chapter and verse, he can quote it as though it's embedded on a memory chip in his head. So I call him the Walking Bible. You know, a Bible that walks and talks."

"Yeah. I got it." Charity smiled slightly.

"Luke 6:38—I believe that's the one about giving and it being given unto you?"

"That's it. 'Give, and it shall be given unto you; good measure, pressed down, and shaken together, and running over, shall men give unto your bosom. For with the same measure that ye mete withal it shall be measured to you again.'"

"I've always liked that one. You give with a teaspoon; you get back a teaspoon of blessing. You give with a bucket; you get back a bucket of blessing. Charity, you certainly should get a downpour of blessings because you certainly give a downpour of love."

"Thank you. Well, you don't pay me to stand around talking . . . well, you do, but you know what I mean," Charity said. "Thank you for this opportunity. And I'm looking forward to church service on Sunday."

"I can't wait," Johnnie Mae said. "And you're coming at a pretty good time because in one more month, we will be in our new sanctuary. And I know that Faith was worried about you and there being too many people, but I think you'll find we're a pretty good bunch. Not perfect, by any means, believe me. Even Pastor Landris gets ruffled from time to time. Between me and you, he doesn't always react correctly. Do you think the three of you will come together on Sunday?"

"I don't think that's ever going to happen. It would be nice, but it's a challenge getting all of us in one place at the exact same time," Charity said. "We're close, just not like that. Personality conflicts we don't care to air in public."

"Yeah, I've sort of noticed that. When Hope is there, Faith isn't. When Faith comes, Hope either gets held up or she's not feeling well. I do see Hope on Sundays, first service most times, except for the last two Sundays. I've not seen Faith or heard from her since September 11, when she ran out on us before the celebration began."

"I don't know what Faith is up to." Charity shrugged and shook her head. "I have sensed she's extremely upset. But it may be because I've decided I want to work at what I enjoy doing and not what she or Hope think I should do. When Faith is mad, there's no telling what or who she's scheming against. But be assured, she's plotting something."

"Maybe I should try talking to her." Johnnie Mae shifted her purse to her other shoulder.

"Charity," Mrs. Gates said, "it's tea time."

Charity and Johnnie Mae laughed.

"I won't hold you any longer," Johnnie Mae said. "I'll see you on Sunday."

"If the Lord willing and the creek don't rise," Charity said.

"Since you were the one who just brought that up, I've always wondered. What is that really talking about?"

"I don't know. That's an old folk phrase. I speak the language; I don't claim to always know the interpretation. But I suspect it had to do with a person going to a place where they had to cross a creek. If the creek rose, they couldn't cross it, so they wouldn't be able to make it. The Lord willing probably had to do with them stating that if they were alive or physically able to make it, they would—If the Lord willing . . . and the creek don't rise."

"That works for me," Johnnie Mae said.

"Charity," Mrs. Gates sang her name again.

"Duty calls." Charity smiled and turned to go back in the other room. "Coming, Mama Gates."

Johnnie Mae smiled and quietly left.

Chapter 46

*For ye have not received the spirit of bondage
again to fear; but ye have received the Spirit of
adoption, whereby we cry, Abba Father.*

(Romans 8:15)

Pastor Landris hadn't told Johnnie Mae what Faith had
said to him, and he was glad because it would have only
added to the feelings she was experiencing already about not
having gotten pregnant. The last thing he wanted was for her
to feel in any way less than the woman he'd vowed to love,
honor, and cherish. It didn't matter what they faced, they
would do it together. And he was not about to spread hurtful
words to someone he cared about. Not if he could help it.

Pastor Landris had been to see his brother. Thomas was
not doing well at all. As much as Pastor Landris hated to, he
knew he was going to have to intervene if Thomas was to get
the help he needed. Talking to him wasn't getting anywhere.

Faith hadn't been back to the church since that night at
the marriage ceremony celebration. Johnnie Mae hadn't
spoken with her, either. Angel and Sapphire wondered where
she'd gone so suddenly without a word to anyone. She left
them in the lurch—not that she was really doing that much
to help, but it was the principle of the thing.

Sapphire had been visiting Mrs. Gates regularly during
the transition from Ms. Bertha's care to Charity's.

"I'll admit," Sapphire said to Charity, "I was a little concerned about how this would work. I knew whoever came in,

they would have to be strong, yet gentle enough to put Mrs. Gates at ease. You've done that, Charity, and then some. Her doctor is so very, very pleased with her progress."

"Thank you, Sapphire. I appreciate your words so much," Charity said.

"I hear you're coming to church this Sunday."

"Yes, and I'm excited. I just know I'm going to be blessed. Johnnie Mae is super nice and her mother is . . ." she placed her hand over her heart, "she's so precious to me. And she's lots of fun. I can't imagine them putting her in a nursing facility just yet. I can tell from the short time I've been here, not all of them feel she should still be here in her home. But she has too much life in her to be shoved in a corner, and only pulled out on visiting days."

"Yeah, but you realize not everyone is as equipped as you are to deal with her down times. Her medication helps a lot. She's great when she's herself, and even when her mind travels back in time, she can be a joy to talk with," Sapphire said.

"Oh, I know," Charity said. "It's like time traveling for real. Sometimes she'll say something, and it will transport me back to a time with my grandmother. Sometimes I have trouble distinguishing what's real and what's just part of my own mind."

"But when she's badly disoriented and agitated and wants to fight . . . when you have to cover the mirrors because she looks in them and the person looking back at her is a stranger to her . . . when she can't figure out why this older woman is being reflected back to what is, at that time to her, a younger self—that's when it's hard on everybody."

"Rachel has a difficult time when her mother wants to go home and she's telling her that she *is* home," Charity said, "and Mama Gates doesn't believe her. She's trying to get back to her home-house. I understand that. Memories are a tricky thing, and they can be quite a force to a fragile mind. Trust me: nobody understands that better than me."

"Why is that, Charity?"

Charity had been staring and smiling as she spoke. When Sapphire asked her why she understood, she suddenly realized she'd let her guard down for a minute in the wrong place at the wrong time. Faith had told her she always had to be on guard. One slip-up, and there was no telling what the consequences would be. Sapphire made her feel comfortable. That could be dangerous for the three of them.

"Don't you understand better when you're around other people and you think the way they think?" Charity said. "Even if what they think or believe is skewed? Who's to say what is real and what's not? You and I see this chair. It seems real, but somebody may walk in and not see it. Or maybe they see something we don't. Is something less real just because it's unseen? I've never seen God, but I know He's real. We can't discount or dismiss the unseen. We just can't."

"How do you know all of this?" Sapphire asked. "You sound like you've studied psychology in college or something."

"Or something. I didn't go to college. But I love the library, so I read a lot. In fact, reading is my favorite thing next to cooking and caring for people." Charity took the teacups into the kitchen and put them in the sink. "Tell me about church services. Do you honestly think I'll really enjoy myself?"

"Oh, definitely. Pastor Landris is an outstanding teacher and preacher. Have you not heard him? I mean, I would think with both your sisters attending, you would have at least listened to his tapes."

"He has tapes? Oh. Well, I suppose Faith and Hope must have kept those for themselves. There are some things both of them will refuse to share with me."

"I don't know why they wouldn't have at least shared some of his tapes with you," Sapphire said.

"It's probably because they know I prefer reading to listening any day. I don't much listen to books on tape. Now, if

Pastor Landris had a book to read, they might have brought that to me."

"He and Johnnie Mae wrote a book on *Walking in God's Divine Favor* about two years ago."

"Oh well, that explains it then. If Faith sees or has anything she cherishes, she'll put it away to protect it." Charity grinned, then started clapping her hands a few times. "But I'll get to hear him for myself in just a few more days. I'm so excited!"

Charity knew now how much opposition she'd face going to this church on Sunday. Hope wouldn't dare get in her way, but Faith had been visiting another church the past few weeks, a church called Divine Conquerors. She was truly upset about something, and it seemed to have had something to do with Pastor Landris. Charity hadn't been able to find out what had happened, but it would come out eventually. Things always did.

She was getting stronger and Faith knew that. Faith might not have liked it, but she'd have to come to terms with it at some point. Soon.

When Charity got home, she was glad to see the furniture was just as it had been for the week. The phone rang. She was not a phone person and started to let the answering machine get it. Faith was the one who liked talking on the phone, so anyone calling would likely be looking for her. After it rang again, she decided to answer it.

"Hello."

"Faith, how are you? This is Thomas. Why haven't you called me or come by in the last few days?"

"This is not Faith," Charity said.

"Faith, quit playing, girl. You know I know your voice."

"I told you, I'm not Faith. I'm Charity."

"Charity, huh?"

"Yes."

"Well, Charity, then why haven't you asked if I would like to leave a message?"

"Not to sound rude, but because you just said your name is Thomas and you're calling for Faith. Besides, I don't know when or even *if* Faith will be back anytime soon."

"Faith, if you don't want to talk to me, just say that. But don't be playing games. The thing that I liked about you from that first time I saw you at church . . . you remember: when you came over to tell me you liked my *Faith Hall of Fame* speech."

Charity held the phone and shook her head. She didn't know what she could say to this guy to convince him she wasn't Faith.

"I don't remember, Thomas, because I wasn't there. If you were talking to Faith when this happened, you need to be strolling down memory lane with her."

"Okay, so it's Charity, you say?"

"Yes, Charity."

"That means love, huh?"

"I'm hanging up now."

"Whoa . . . whoa, hold up! You're a little fireball, I see. Don't get schizo on me," Thomas said. "Okay, Char-i-ty. Would you please take a message for *Faith* for me?"

"Sure."

"Do you have pen and paper ready? This is a rather long message."

"Hold on, please."

Thomas laughed while she was away. "Charity . . . yeah, okay, Charity. You sound too much like Faith to me. Identical, in fact."

"I'm ready," Charity said.

"Faith, I'm waiting to hear from you. Please don't keep me waiting. I like kicking it with you. And I like kicking it to my brother even more. I hope to see you at church on Sunday, and I'm hoping you can go out to dinner with me. Reverend Walker wants to talk with us afterward about our wedding plans. He says the date we want is available."

"You think you're actually going to marry Faith?" Charity

said with a laugh. "What century were you planning on doing this?"

"Charity, you're not supposed to be making comments. You're supposed to be taking my message. And since Faith *isn't* there, according to you, then I need to be sure she gets all of this. Is that all right with you?"

"Well, Faith *isn't* here, just like I said. But I also know Faith is not marrying anybody, and that includes you. If Faith were getting married, trust me, I would know."

"Did you know she and I were dating? Did you know she's going through new members' class at my church?"

"No."

"Then I suppose you wouldn't know that she and I are planning a small wedding. It will be on December 4, in my home. We're only inviting some family—in my case, none—and friends. I can't speak for Faith, but since it's a little less than a month away, and you don't know about it, I don't know if she's planning to invite *her* family, either." He snickered. "Thanks, love."

"It's Charity."

"Yes, Charity. Thanks, Charity. Tell Faith to call me, okay?" They hung up.

"Faith? Faith," she yelled. "Who is Thomas? And I hope you know, you're getting married only over my dead body."

"Now that's not love, Charity," Faith said. "And Hope already knows, so Hope is not going to help you. As you can see, I need to go to church on Sunday. I certainly hope you don't have any plans. If you do, you'll just have to cancel them. I need the vehicle."

"I'm going to church on Sunday," Charity said.

"You're more than welcome to come with me to Divine Conquerors."

"I'm not going to Divine Conquerors. You have me going to these churches where you know I won't be blessed. I'm going to Followers of Jesus Faith Worship Center," Charity said. "Over there with Pastor Landris and Johnnie Mae."

"No, you're not. Didn't you hear what Thomas said? We have to go with his pastor or he might not marry us. And I don't want to go to the courthouse to get married."

"You're not getting married! So it doesn't matter if you miss going with his pastor or not. Hope, you tell her. She has to listen to me. Tell her, Hope," Charity said. "I'm going to church with Johnnie Mae. I told her I was coming, and I am. Do you understand me, Faith? And what have you done to Hope?"

"Charity, I don't think you want to do this. And Hope is a bit upset with me right now. But, she'll be all right. Now you . . . you need to think about what you're doing. You're out there taking care of someone five days a week. So it wasn't enough for you to go here and there occasionally to nursing homes, spreading your brand of love? Well, it's dangerous for you to be in one place like this. You're making a terrible mistake. You know I'm telling you right. You've always listened to me. Don't start messing up now."

"I'm not the one talking about getting married to some guy . . ." Charity stopped as she noticed she was stuttering. "How long have you known him, anyway?"

"I met him when I was first going to FOJFWC—"

" 'F' 'O' what?" Charity sat down and started rubbing her head.

"FOJFWC—Followers of Jesus Faith Worship Center. That's easier than trying to say all that other nonsense. DCC—Divine Conquerors Church. TCOR—The Church of Revelation, although that pastor resigned months ago, and I hear he has a one-way ticket leaving this earthly realm very shortly," Faith said. "That's what the Right Reverend Walker told Thomas. All those preachers are out there jockeying for Reverend 'Poppa' Knight's old job. Anyway, I met Thomas last year, so we've technically known each other for a while.

I ran into him again around the second Sunday in September. He and I have been pretty steady every since. I understand him, and he understands me. Unconditionally. What more is there to love?"

Charity's head was pounding hard. She got up, ran to the bathroom, and commenced to throw up.

Chapter 47

But thanks be to God, which giveth us the victory through our Lord Jesus Christ.

(1 Corinthians 15:57)

It was crowded at Followers of Jesus Faith Worship Center. People could tell something powerful was about to take place spiritually.

Johnnie Mae was hoping to see Charity. There were always so many people there. She'd told her where she sat, in the front row, generally the second seat, next to Pastor Landris when he was sitting down. Unless Charity came in before the praise and worship part of the service and waved as Johnnie Mae had asked her to do, she wouldn't know if she was there or not.

The Praise & Worship Team walked in singing "You Are Good" by Israel & New Breed. They followed that with "Here I Am to Worship." Praise was on another level on this day. Pastor Landris could only imagine what the first Sunday in December would be like if everybody was like this now. It didn't seem like it was scheduled, but suddenly they started singing "Yes" by Shekinah Glory. If they'd planned on singing any other songs, it would have to wait until next week. There was a spiritual joy that flowed throughout the church. People were bowing down, on their knees, where they were. Those who stood were lifting up holy hands and weeping with joy.

Johnnie Mae was a little disappointed after the service

was over. She'd hoped Charity would make it. Something must have come up. *Maybe the creek rose.*

"Johnnie Mae?"

Johnnie Mae turned around and smiled. "Charity, you're here!" She hugged her.

Charity was plain-Jane for sure. No makeup, which Charity had explained to Johnnie Mae she didn't wear because it got on people's clothing and was too much trouble and time-consuming. She wore comfortable clothes—mostly loose-fitting and easy-clean—because she hated feeling constrained. She wore flats because they didn't hurt her feet, and she could get from point A to point B faster than most people wearing heels. Her dress was pretty, just definitely not something you'd find in Faith or Hope's closet for sure. The hair was the only thing consistent among all three.

"I promised you I'd be here. I always try to keep my word."

"I appreciate that, but I know things come up unexpectedly sometimes. You hair is pretty. So why didn't you come up front and sit with me? I saved a seat for you before the service started. After it starts, they like to fill them, so someone came and sat in it."

"I saw you," Charity said. "I started to walk up there, but the Praise & Worship Team came in. I didn't want to be in the way—they were so good."

"I take it since you're here alone neither Faith nor Hope came with you?"

"Faith's not coming here anymore. She's decided to join another church along with some guy she's planning to marry in a few weeks, from what I hear. Hope is probably trying to stay out of Faith's way. She does things like that. But it worked out. At least neither of the two was in my way today. Faith did declare she was going over to that other church and make me miss coming here. She did her best to stop me, but as you can see, I made it."

"Why would Faith do that? I don't understand what's going on with her these days."

"We only have one mode of transportation. Don't worry about it—I'm here. I enjoyed myself. Pastor Landris gave me a Word about God's strength in our weakness. And I intend to keep coming here to get stronger and more in the Word. I'm looking forward to the series he said he'd begin teaching in January on Strongholds and breaking them from our lives. I know I'm supposed to be here. I know this from my heart. I'm sorry I've wasted all this time when I could have been here being taught the Word. I was *blessed* today."

"That's wonderful. I'm glad to know you were so blessed."

"I was, and I'm on my way to find the prayer room they were talking about earlier. I can certainly use all the help I can get. I do know what God can do, and I truly believe in the power of touching and agreeing. I just haven't had anyone to touch and agree with me lately."

"Would you like me to go in and pray with you, too?"

"Oh, I would love that!"

Charity and Johnnie Mae went to the room dedicated and anointed for prayer. And the prayers of the righteous that day availed much.

"Something is happening," Charity said as she cried uncontrollably on Johnnie Mae's shoulder. "I feel so light and so happy. I haven't felt like this in a long time. What is this?"

"It's the power of the Holy Spirit working in you right now," the other person who had prayed with her said. "It's the anointing that breaks the yoke. Just release yourself totally, and allow God to do His work. Yeah, I feel it. I feel something is shaking loose right now, in the mighty name of Jesus. You're being set free. Oh, hallelujah. I feel it." She started shaking her one hand fast, as though she'd touched something that burned.

"Just let go of every weight that so easily besets you. You've been carrying this weight for so long. I hear the Spirit of the Lord saying for you to release this burden over to Him. He's the potter. He says He's going to take your broken pieces and put you back together again and anew. I hear the Lord saying, 'Again' and 'anew.' He's putting the broken pieces of your life back together again and making you anew. I don't know what this means, but God says you shall be whole again. How long, Lord? He says, 'Not long.' I hear Him saying as He has inspired the words of First Corinthians 15:58: 'Therefore, be ye steadfast, unmovable, always abounding in the work of the Lord . . .' Oh thank You, Jesus. '. . . forasmuch as you know that your labor is not in vain in the Lord.' "

Charity cried hard and praised God as she kneeled down and worshipped God, bowing to Him with her face to the floor.

For the first time in decades, Charity felt free.

Chapter 48

For there are three that bear record in heaven,
the Father, the Word, and the Holy Ghost: and
these three are one.

(1 John 5:7)

Sapphire was making her rounds to check on Mrs. Gates. Charity was really good with her, and she was responding wonderfully. Charity and Mrs. Gates had the record player blasting. It wasn't a church song like Mrs. Gates usually wanted to hear. It was a song by Otis Redding.

Mrs. Gates was really into it. "*Sitting on the dock of the bay,*" she sang.

But Charity was in a chair, balled up like a fetus and rocking back and forth.

"Mrs. Gates, you okay?" Sapphire asked her, although she was watching Charity.

"I'm fine. Call me Countess. I said I was going to marry Jericho when I'm older, but I might change my mind, so I don't want you playing like he and I are married yet, just in case I don't end up marrying him after all."

"Jericho? Was that . . . is that your husband?"

"He will be. He is so cute. Have you seen him around? He's been hiding from me, and that's why I might not marry him after all. If he acts this way now, you know what he'll be like after we get married. He'll probably up and leave without telling me, and I'll be mad at him. But I do love him. He's the most handsome little sweet talker, though."

Sapphire hugged her. "Okay, Countess. Do you know what's wrong with Charity? Can you tell me what happened to her?"

"I don't know what happened with that girl. I think somebody left her, too, without saying good-bye. Go on and tend to her. I'm fine. I have to find another record that Jericho likes. If he hears his favorite record, he'll come out of hiding," Mrs. Gates said. "Go on and see about that other girl over there. She's a little too old to be acting like a baby, though, if you ask me. But nobody asked me." Mrs. Gates went over to the stack of records and albums and started shuffling through them as she sang.

"Charity, what's wrong?" Sapphire spoke softly into her ear.

"They're mad at me."

"Who's mad at you?"

"Faith and Hope. Not so much Hope, but she always does what Faith tells her, and Faith is really, really mad now. So Hope is not talking, either."

"What's Faith mad about?"

"She didn't want me to go to church Sunday. She still got to go to the church she wanted, but she doesn't want me to go to a place unless she says it's okay for me to go."

"But you're an adult. Faith can't make you do something, or not, unless you agree to it." Sapphire put her arms around Charity to stop her from rocking. "Sit up and talk to me, okay? Come on. Sit up."

Charity stopped rocking, but she wouldn't show her face.

"Come on, Charity. Sit up and talk to me. I'm a great listener."

"Faith told me I can't talk to anyone anymore," Charity said. "She says I've messed up already. I shouldn't have taken this job. But I did. I shouldn't have gone to church on Sunday. But I did. I shouldn't have gone into the prayer room and let people pray for me. But I did. Now she's really mad because I almost told Johnnie Mae a secret about her and her husband-to-be."

"Faith is about to get married?"

"Yes, and I told her she's not. She wants me to go away so I can't stop her. But I'm not going away. And Otis Redding is dead, and Motherphelia loved that song. She and I would listen to it for hours and hours. Then I didn't hear it anymore because she died, and everybody says it was my fault. But I don't remember. I just remember this man who thought I was cute, and Motherphelia told him he'd better not ever mess with me again. But he did, and she came inside the house. Secrets. Secrets. 'This will be our little secret.'"

"Did the man hurt you?"

"Everybody wants to keep everything a secret. Motherphelia said it was our secret until she could figure out what to do. She died, and left the secret with me. Faith and Hope showed up and said they would take care of things until I was better and stronger. Faith said she wouldn't let anyone hurt me ever again."

"Charity, what do you mean, Faith and Hope showed up?"

Charity sat all the way up and looked at Sapphire. "Faith has your man now."

"What? Charity, I'm not following you. I want to help you, but you're not making sense."

"That's what Hope said. That if I tell, and believe people will understand or do what they say, I was setting myself up for a lot of disappointments. Hope is good at handling things that might hurt if they don't turn out right. That's Hope's specialty—not getting her hopes up." She giggled, then quickly stopped.

"Charity, tell me about Faith and my man."

"See, that's what Faith said. People don't really care about anyone else. All they care about is what's best for themselves. They pretend like they care, but they won't be there for you if there's nothing in it for them. You don't care about me, do you? You just want to know about your man now."

"Of course I care about you. I'm trying to help you, but I need you to help me."

"You really want to know if Faith has your man."

"I don't have a man, Charity."

"Thomas."

"What about Thomas?"

"Faith is going to marry Thomas."

"Charity, honey, I think your mind is playing tricks on you. Sit right here. I'm going to call Johnnie Mae. Then you and I are going to see if we can't get some help for you." Sapphire went to the phone and hurriedly dialed Johnnie Mae.

"I need you to get over to your mother's right away," Sapphire said.

"What's the matter? Is Mama all right?"

"Your mother is having an episode right now, but she's okay. It's Charity. Something awful is happening."

"Is she sick?"

"Just get over here as soon as you can." She hung up and went back to Charity.

"I'm sure you think Faith is getting married to Thomas, but that's not possible."

Charity looked at her. "Thomas goes to Divine Conquerors Church. He's really good friends with Reverend Walker. Faith is upset with Pastor Landris, so she left your church and started going over there. She and Thomas started seeing more of each other. Secrets. Everybody has secrets." Charity grabbed her head and started holding it. "My head hurts so bad."

Sapphire slowly sat down on the floor. Charity was accurate about too much concerning Thomas, but she knew she had to remain calm as she spoke. She was a professional, and no matter how personal this was, she had to maintain her cool. "Thomas and Faith are dating?"

"We're more than dating, Miss Sapphire. Thomas and I are getting married on December 4 of this year."

"Charity?"

"No. Charity talks too much. I've always told her that.

She just had to go play that stupid record. I told her not to let that woman ever play Otis Redding's "Dock of the Bay." I specifically told her. Now I have to clean up her mess—once again."

"Who are you if you're not Charity?"

"Like you don't know. Faith . . . Miss Sapphire. I am Faith. Not Hope. Not Charity. But you can make it easy on yourself by calling me Trinity. Just know, I'm the one who won't let you make me think you're smarter than me because you have a degree in something you apparently can't use to help yourself." Faith stood and looked down at the dress she was wearing, then found a mirror. "Ahhh, this is hideous! How does she wear these ugly, unflattering things? And what does she keep doing to my hair? Charity would end up an old maid, but I'm about to fix all that real soon."

Sapphire stood up. "How are you going to fix it, Faith?"

"Thomas wants to marry me. Question—how long were you and he together?"

"That's really none of your business," Sapphire said.

"Oh yeah, that's right. You're all up in *our* business, but your business is off limits to us. If you want me to answer your questions, I'd suggest you answer mine. Do we understand each other, Miss Sapphire?"

Sapphire nodded.

"See, you might have been able to bully sweet little Charity, but Faith don't play that. I'll walk out of here in a minute. So let's try this one more time. How long were you and Thomas together?"

Sapphire took her dreadlocks and swung them around to her back. She moistened her lips by pursing them together. "I met him a few years ago, and we pretty much started hanging out from the first day we met at church in Atlanta."

"That is so sweet. You and he met at church; he and I met at church. I should write a book. I could call it *1,001 Places to Meet Your New Mate*. What do you think? Think it will sell? Don't answer that one. So you and Thomas had been technically dating for a couple of years. It's now about seven weeks until the end of this year. If we subtract the time he dumped you this year, what's that been now . . . about seven . . . eight months? I think he kicked you to the curb around April, maybe? Oh well, that's neither here nor there."

"What's your point?"

"My point is, he and I started dating in early September . . . on the twelfth, the day after we had that marriage seminar celebration or whatever y'all were calling it."

"Oh, you mean the event you showed up for to show off your dress and then did the disappearing act?" Sapphire said. She glanced at Mrs. Gates, who was sitting in her favorite chair, taking a nap. She must have fallen asleep when the record stopped.

"FYI, not that this is any of your business, and I sure wouldn't want to be labeled a talebearer or gossiper—," Faith said.

"Well then, maybe you shouldn't say it," Sapphire said, finding it harder not to lose it with Faith.

"Or maybe you shouldn't listen when I say it. How about that? I'll say it, and if you really don't want to hear it, stop up your ears. Pastor Landris and I had a few words, and he must have thought I was coming on to him. All I really was doing was volunteering to help him out by carrying his baby. But he's so sanctimonious and self-righteous, he didn't even want to discuss it. He acted like I said we should skip the middleman and get a room. I merely offered to be a surrogate if they needed one."

"You're kidding. You talked about that with him in a place like that and neither he nor his wife had said publicly or privately that they were even looking for a surrogate? And you wonder why he'd take that the wrong way?" Sapphire said, aghast.

"I can see your point, but he could have spoken to me in a kinder tone than he did. He made me feel like a child who'd done something wrong and deserved to be punished. I'm a grown woman. I don't have to stand for anybody talking to me that way."

"So you decided to get back at him by leaving Johnnie Mae in a bind and not doing what you'd volunteered to do? Then, on the following day, you visit another church, but not just any church—the church Pastor Landris's brother left him for," Sapphire said, nodding her head. "Yeah, I can see the logic in all of this. But what I'm missing is, why marry Thomas?"

"Of course you would ask that. You're the one spreading those vicious lies about him being mentally ill," Faith said, strolling around the room, lifting whatnots up to examine them and placing them back down with disinterest.

"Thomas is bipolar, Faith. It's nothing to be ashamed of. It's an illness. There are lots of people with this condition. Many of them have no idea that what feels like crazy has a name and, there's a way to, many times, successfully manage it and live a normal life."

"Well, I think Thomas is fine. He thinks I'm fine. So to get all of you off our backs, we're going to get married. Besides, we've laid the truth about ourselves on the table. We know what we're getting into, so why waste time looking for that perfect someone else? Thomas found out what wasting time can do when he was with you. When he needed you to defend him, you badgered him until he did what any red-blooded man would do in the same situation: got *rid* of you."

"You're a tough one, huh? No wonder Charity is scared of you. Hope, too."

"They're not scared of me. They respect me." Faith surveyed the room. "I've really got to get out of this place. I'm sure Charity will want to come back and finish the job she agreed to do, but to be honest, Miss Sapphire, I have my own plans. I don't have time for this sitting-around-taking-care-of-people stuff. I want to live life, not just exist."

"Don't leave," Sapphire said.

"Why not? Because you called Johnnie Mae, and you

think you're going to trick me into going to the hospital like you were trying to trick Thomas? Not going to happen. Not with me. If you can ever catch Charity again, which I seriously doubt, she might be willing to listen to you. But I promised to take care of things for her, and I mean to keep my promise."

Sapphire looked in at Mrs. Gates, who was still sleeping. She tried to calm Faith down.

"Faith, what happened with Charity and her grandmother? Do you know the secret?"

"Of course I know it. But I also know how to *keep* secrets, even from Charity."

"If you love Charity, you'll get her some help. I can help her, but you're going to have to help me. And Thomas, if you want to marry him. I don't have a problem with that, but Thomas was in a bad way when I last saw him. He needs help as well. You're in a position to help two people you say you care about: Charity and Thomas. Please, help them before it's too late."

Faith looked at Sapphire and picked her purse up off the floor. "Maybe I'll see you around sometime," Faith said and walked out the door.

She was gone ten minutes when Johnnie Mae arrived.

"Sapphire, what's going on? Where's Charity?"

"Charity," Mrs. Gates said, having awakened from a nap. "It's teatime!" She walked in where they were. "Well, hi there, Johnnie Mae . . . Sapphire. Where's Charity? It's time for our daily tea. We make eyebright tea. So where is she?"

Johnnie Mae looked over at Sapphire for an answer. "Faith came and took her away," Sapphire said to Johnnie Mae.

"What? Was Charity sick?" Johnnie Mae asked.

"She's got some serious . . . issues," Sapphire said, choosing her words. "Mrs. Gates, I'll be happy to make your tea for you. Johnnie Mae, will you come help me in the kitchen?"

"I don't want you to make my tea. I want Charity to do it,"

Mrs. Gates said. "She knows how to make it just right. Most folks steep tea too long or too short. That child has tea-brewing down to a science."

"Mama, let me and Sapphire make your tea. Don't hurt our feelings, okay?"

"Sure, baby. I'll go work a couple of my seek-and-finds while you and Sapphire 'make my tea.' I just hope you two aren't talking about me behind my back."

"Mama, behave," Johnnie Mae said, trying to make things lighter. She kissed her mother on the cheek.

Johnnie Mae and Sapphire talked while they were making the tea. Sapphire told Johnnie Mae every detail of what had just happened.

Johnnie Mae was shocked, angry, hurt, disappointed, and crushed—all at the same time.

"She called herself, or the three of them, Trinity?" Johnnie Mae said. "Faith, Hope, and Charity—they're three persons in one?" Johnnie Mae found a chair and sat down. "They're Trinity?"

Chapter 49

So ought men to love their wives as their own bodies. He that loveth his wife loveth himself.

(Ephesians 5:28)

"Why didn't you tell me?" Johnnie Mae said as soon as Pastor Landris walked in the house.

"Tell you what?" He leaned down to kiss her; she dodged him, so he missed. "What's wrong with you today? Bad news? You called me and said I had to get home pronto. I'm here. Let me in on what's going on, Johnnie Mae."

"Back in September, after our wonderful anniversary banquet and the special night out you planned for our actual anniversary date, we had the marriage seminar celebration at the Exhibition Hall downtown," Johnnie Mae said.

He spread his opened hands out to her as if to say: *Give me a little more of a clue, please.* "Yeah, so we're going all the way back to September, and I suppose whatever you're upset about is tied in with all of that? That's not good."

"Faith Alexandria Morrell."

"Oh. So you found out what she and I talked about? I wanted to tell you, but I didn't want to upset you or make you feel like you weren't enough. I'm happy with us just like we are. I don't have to have my own child to be fulfilled. I have you and Princess Rose. Who could ask for more without being just plain greedy?" He made a funny face to try and get her to smile. "How did you find out? Did Faith approach you with the same offer she made me?"

"What offer are you talking about, Landris?"

"Maybe you should tell me what you know, and we can go from there."

"Maybe we should go sit down and get all of this out on the table. I can't believe you've held something back from me, Landris. I'm getting all kinds of revelations today."

They went to their master bedroom suite and sat in the sitting area.

"I don't guess you'd like to go first," Pastor Landris said.

"Truthfully, I would; but I think it's best I find out the information you have so I can process everything together." Johnnie Mae folded her arms across her chest.

"Faith offered to carry my baby for me . . . well, actually, our baby for us."

"Oh, she did, huh? And you didn't think that was something you should have shared with your wife?"

"I thought about it, but I didn't think it was something I needed to dump on you. I didn't want you feeling like you were inadequate because you haven't been able to conceive. I knew if I said something, you might think I was entertaining the idea because I really wanted a baby that bad. But I don't want another woman carrying my child."

"Okay. So another woman approaches my husband about carrying his baby and you didn't want to bother me, your wife, by telling me. Didn't you realize there was a possibility I might happen to hear about it and it could come out totally different from what you're saying? All because you didn't want me, your wife, feeling inadequate because obviously I can't produce a child for you, my husband, although another woman can. Does that about sum it up, Landris?"

"See, now when you say it like that, you make it sound worse than when I was thinking about it—in a short amount of time, mind you." He grabbed her hand.

"Landris, I do understand what you were trying to do. I know this baby thing has been hard on both of us. I thought I didn't want to get pregnant, but I really did. At first I thought you didn't care whether I did or didn't, then I could see that it meant a lot to you as well. And that did bother me, because it's not fair for you not to have your own baby just because I've waited too long, or something's not working right inside of me. How do you think I feel? I have thought about what your baby would look like, and if I can't have one, then you really wouldn't ever know unless you have one with someone else—"

"Then I'll never know. I only want a baby with you. I don't care about some other woman, even someone you might know, being an egg donor or a surrogate for our child. I want to listen in on what the baby is doing inside your stomach. I want to place my hand on you when I feel the baby kick or move around. It's about me and you. Together."

"Landris, I know what you're saying. And on some level, I understand your reasoning. Let me tell you what I just learned today." She turned her body more toward him while allowing her hand to remain in his. "Charity has some real problems. She's not going to be able to take care of my mother anymore, that's for certain. I don't know how I'll ever replace her. What she has already accomplished with Mama is a miracle from God, and I know this."

"What happened? Is Charity sick? I know you called and said you had to go over to your mother's and you were in a hurry. Did she have to go to the hospital? What?"

"Let me, if I may, just tell you everything. Then we can go back over it together. There are some things that involve you, Landris. And you're going to have to make some hard decisions, I believe, once you hear everything."

Johnnie Mae took a deep breath and released it slowly. She retold the story of Charity, Faith, and Hope.

"Multiple personalities . . . Sapphire called it Dissociative Identity Disorder. She believes whatever happened when Charity was around seven, traumatized her to the point where she developed two other distinct personalities named Faith and Hope."

Pastor Landris threw his hands up. "Wait—give me a minute to process this. Faith, who dresses to the max, is pretty much a diva, and can be pushy and rude, is also Hope, who is quiet and prefers to fade into the background, out of the limelight and attention, as well as Charity, who will get down on the floor and play jacks with Princess Rose, couldn't care less about how she looks, and dances around the room with your mother as they sweat to the oldies. And all three of these people are the same person?"

"Trinity. That's how Faith refers to the three of them."

"Trinity?"

"Yeah. It gets worse."

"Is that possible? I mean, this sounds pretty bad so far."

"Faith was upset with you about whatever you said to her that night at the marriage celebration. She left our church and now attends Divine Conquerors Church."

"She's over there with Thomas now, huh? Well, there has to be something good happening to draw so many people in. At least she's still in church."

"Yeah, she's over there with Thomas, all right. According to Faith, she and Thomas are getting married December 4."

"I doubt that. Faith has to be delusional about that one. I know my brother, and if he were ever going to marry anyone, which I'm starting to doubt he ever will, he would have married Sapphire. Look how long they were together. Sapphire moved here mainly because of him. As much as I would like to think she came here to help me in the ministry, we all know if she hadn't been dating Thomas, she would still probably be in Atlanta."

"You do know Sapphire and Thomas broke up? Sapphire says people who are bipolar don't process things the way most people normally do. It's very possible Faith is telling the truth."

Pastor Landris stood up and started pacing. "I've got to hurry and get him some help. They can't get married. From what you're telling me, they both need help. That's the classic 'blind leading the blind' if I ever heard it. Faith or Hope or Charity or Trinity—how do we even classify them?" He stopped walking. "Who is the real person of the three?"

"Sapphire believes Charity is. And you know, we did do paperwork and a background check on her prior to hiring her. Her birth certificate and all the other information had Charity Alexandria Morrell on them." Johnnie Mae stopped. "Alexandria Morrell. Why didn't I notice that before?"

"What?"

"Whenever Faith would say her name, she always said her whole name: 'Faith Alexandria Morrell.' With Hope, all I ever knew was Hope Morrell, which was not unusual since sisters who haven't married often still have the same last name. When I saw Alexandria on Charity's information, I felt it odd their mother would give them the same middle name, but then there's George Foreman—all of his sons are named George."

"I'm going over to see Thomas and put a stop to this marriage nonsense." Pastor Landris started pacing again. "There has to be a way I can get through to him. He can't marry somebody like Faith."

"He's an adult, Landris. Truthfully, he can marry her if he chooses."

"Then I'll do whatever I need to do to keep that from happening."

"Do you think you should just go over there unannounced in your present frame of mind and spring all of this on him? If he's not processing things logically, do you think he'll take this very well?" Johnnie Mae said.

Pastor Landris picked up the phone. "Well, I'll see what his mental state is right now before I go over there."

"Thomas, hey, this is George." Pastor Landris looked at Johnnie Mae and watched her as she slowly pumped her hands—palms down, her way of telling him to calm things down.

"Look, Thomas, I want to come over and see you. You know, just to chat, brother-to-brother." Pastor Landris looked at Johnnie Mae again. She smiled and nodded.

"I know you're busy, but I really need to talk. You know we have the church's first service three Sundays from now. I miss you. I thought maybe we could kick it tonight like old times." He walked toward the fireplace mantel and rubbed his temple.

"I understand. I'm not planning to take up a lot of your time." He looked up at the ceiling. "When then? You can come over here, if you'd prefer. That way you can leave when you get ready. I just really need to talk, that's all."

Pastor Landris balled his fist and gently pounded his forehead. "Thomas, you can't get married. And you especially can't marry her. There are things about Faith you don't know . . ."

Johnnie Mae stood up and walked over to Pastor Landris. She placed one hand on his upper arm. He started bouncing with frustration as he tried to listen patiently without interrupting.

"I don't care what Faith told you I said or did, she's not telling you the whole truth. Thomas, Faith has some serious problems . . . no, you don't already know about her problems. Thomas, nobody called you crazy, and nobody's calling her crazy. You have a mental illness—it's just like a person who has hypertension, diabetes, cancer . . . it's not anything you've done that made you or made Faith sick. But you both . . . need help."

Pastor Landris walked away from Johnnie Mae.

"I'm not going to let you get married to her. At least, not now. Get some help, get better . . . then see if you really want to marry her. If you do, I'll come be your ring bearer if you like." Pastor Landris tried to laugh.

"Thomas, I know you think you're making sense lately, but you're not. You're messing up your life, and it's hard for me to sit here and just let you do it. Don't hang up . . .

Thomas, don't hang up. Thomas . . . Thomas!" Pastor Landris clicked the phone off and threw it on the sofa.

"He hung up," Pastor Landris said as he sat down next to the phone.

"I could tell you weren't getting through to him at all."

"He told me not to come over. He thinks I'm just trying to keep him from being happy the way I am. I have you, and he wants someone who will put him and his needs first the way you do mine."

"Oh, he doesn't have a clear picture of our relationship, I see," Johnnie Mae said. "You and I put each other's needs ahead of our own, which is why our marriage works. If the two of them go into this marriage lopsided, it's definitely not going to last."

"Faith told him or led him to believe that I made a slight pass at her. She didn't make it sound like I physically tried anything, but that I sort of insinuated some things. Then I turned it around and tried to make her out to be the bad guy, when all she was doing was trying to help the two of us out. That's why, she told him, she had to leave the church like she did. She couldn't face you after you and she'd become so close."

"Okay. So you're going to have to go a different route to reach him. And you don't have a lot of time to do it. Sapphire said you could go through probate court and file a petition, but the waiting list to pick a person up and get them in the hospital is about sixty days now. She had a patient they were trying to have involuntarily admitted to the hospital, and the family was told it could be sixty days before they would even have a bed available."

"That's not good. He's getting married in three weeks."

"Maybe if you go down there, you can convince them this is an emergency and they could move him to the top of the list," Johnnie Mae said. She laid her head on his shoulder.

"I'm sorry. I'm so wrapped up in Thomas and Faith, I forgot there are other things involved with this. You really liked Hope a lot. Now, at least we know the reason why she was missing so often during certain times. It was because of Faith."

"Faith loves the spotlight. Hope was content to do the work that needed to be done, including what I told you a few months ago about her typing that marriage workbook—"

"That you were sure Hope had done it?" Pastor Landris said, nodding.

"Funny, though. I guess Faith could get credit for doing it if Hope did it and she and Hope are really part of Charity and they're all one and the same."

Landris reached over and pulled Johnnie Mae into his arms. "I love you so much. This must be so hard for you. I know you adored both Hope and Charity."

"Charity is special. I can't imagine what she's going through right now. My mother was doing so great with her. I don't know how she's going to take losing Charity. By the way, Rachel is thinking about moving to Columbus, Georgia. And my brother Christian is due back to the states in January— they've stationed him and his family there for about eighteen months. Really, I think Rachel is just looking for a way out, and now that Charity is gone, she doesn't want to have to deal with Mama like she said she was coming here to do."

"What are you going to do about your mother? Now you need a new sitter since you've lost Charity."

"I'll have to keep praying and listening to God. If I need to get another sitter or hire full-time nurses because I decide to leave Mama at her house, I'll do that."

"And if you have to put her in a home?"

"I don't want to think about that yet. For now, Mama's not declining any further. In fact, she seemed to have been improving. I'm sure her medication helps. I'll probably tell her about Charity tomorrow. But I need to find out how to help Charity, too. Sapphire really respects Charity. We're going to see what options we have and whether or not we can get Charity—or, I guess for now, to simplify we'll just say Trinity—to let us help her."

Pastor Landris took his arms from around Johnnie Mae. "One thing for sure: we're not going to resolve all of this anytime soon. But I'll go tomorrow to probate court and see about filing a petition to have my brother put in a hospital. You should hear how he sounded when I was talking to him on the phone. He doesn't want me to come over, because his house is probably a mess—"

"He's a guy. I'd expect his house wouldn't be all that clean."

"No, you don't understand things about his bipolar disorder. He cleans all the time, but cleaning to him is pulling everything out of the drawers and on top of things onto the floor. That's a symptom of his disorder. I took a picture with the camera on my cell phone when he wasn't looking the other week when I was over there." Pastor Landris pulled out his phone and found the shots.

"Oh, my goodness! It looks like a tornado went through this house," Johnnie Mae said. "Are you sure he was cleaning and not bulldozing it?"

"He couldn't talk with me long that day because he said he was cleaning, and I was keeping him from finishing up. I asked him how long he'd been working on it, and he said for the past two or three weeks. That was his results. On top of that, he had a broom, trying to sweep this pile down the hall."

"Sweep it? That's impossible. Anybody can look at this and tell you can't sweep it."

"That's what I'm trying to tell you."

"Yes, you need to hurry and get him help," Johnnie Mae said.

"I just have to do it, and pray I can do it before his wedding takes place. Because if he gets married, she has the legal say-so about whether or not he's admitted into a hospital."

"And do you really think Faith will allow that to happen if she marries him?"

"Of course not. But even worse—what happens to Charity if the two of them go ahead with this marriage?"

Chapter 50

Therefore shall a man leave his father and his mother, and shall cleave unto his wife: and they shall be one flesh.

(Genesis 2:24)

Thomas and Faith were set to be married the following day. Pastor Landris was trying to stop it. He'd even called Thomas the night Faith had left Mrs. Gate's house, exposing the whole truth. Faith was sure Sapphire had told Johnnie Mae everything. She could just hear Sapphire saying, "Faith is crazy. She's planning to marry my ex!"

Faith wondered why women who lost out couldn't merely slink away gracefully. She hadn't gone after Thomas; they'd met each other halfway.

Truthfully, Faith did go after him . . . a little. And she worked that thing. Faith was a firm believer in what the Bible said. Specifically, that *Faith without works is dead.* She was simply letting the world know that Faith was very much alive. And Faith didn't play!

The first time she ever saw Thomas Landris, he was in church, speaking on faith. She knew right then and there— he was the man for her. Faith could now see how God was working things out from that very first day, even if the two of them hadn't known it at the time. Admittedly, Faith didn't like it when she learned Hope was visiting Followers of Jesus Faith Worship Center. But now, she could see that had it not been for Hope defying her and going anyway, she and

Thomas might never have met. And they wouldn't be about to come together like Velcro®. Faith couldn't help but smile when she considered everything. All things really did work for the good.

Having overheard Johnnie Mae calling Pastor Landris by the name "Landris" a couple of times (she later learned that was her term of endearment), Faith instantly fell in love with it. She decided she would call Thomas "Landris" as well. However, after only a few times doing it, Faith found that it set her teeth on edge. It was too sugary for her taste. She ditched it and changed her loving term for Thomas to TL. She liked that much better; it wasn't as sweet. She needed something that would be all her own, anyway.

Faith recalled how fine Thomas had looked that first day, standing there in his tailor-made suit. She adored a man who thought enough of himself to care about how he presented himself when he stepped out in public. It did pain her to see Thomas looking a bit shabby these days. But that was due to his recent mental state—so much pressure.

Maybe he was *a little depressed. But in this day and age, who doesn't get depressed from time to time?* Faith didn't totally buy into him being bipolar like people were trying to say he was. And so what if he was? Maurice Benard, who plays Sonny on her favorite soap, *General Hospital*, is bipolar and nobody was trying to put him away.

Sapphire irked Faith. *She can tell everybody else what's wrong with them, but can't see she has problems of her own.* Faith couldn't understand how Sapphire could be over forty, never married, still holding on to her virginity; yet, running off a potentially great husband by inferring that he's crazy . . . mentally unstable. *Now, that's what's crazy.* Faith figured the virgin story was solely a ploy on Sapphire's part to get Thomas to marry her. *Don't give away the milk for free; make him buy the whole cow.* In Faith's opinion, it might have worked, too, had Sapphire not been such a nag. Faith knew Thomas wanted her, which was why they were getting married tomorrow. And it hadn't taken a long courtship or her having to give away free milk for Faith to land him at the altar, either.

Faith could tell lots of women at Divine Conquerors wanted Thomas. But she had stepped up in there that first day with her hair laid perfect as always, dress hitting and fitting in all the right places, perfume perfectly applied (*not too much—a man still needs to be able to breathe when you're around*), her heels (*name-brand, of course*) high enough to cause her behind to hypnotize a man if he was foolish enough to look. Her makeup was applied just right as her brown eyes drew in anyone who dared look into them, her lips sparkling wetalicious (a word Faith made up) with hints of glitter that Alexis Vogel had been known to slip into her Feisty red lip gloss, and her legs (which Charity always made her business to cover up) so toned and shapely even Faith had to stop from time to time to admire herself.

When Thomas saw her walk in, he never stood a chance. Faith knew he'd come find her as soon as the service was over. She knew that in the way he had leaned to the side, as though he wasn't sure it was her, but was praying it was. Reverend Walker preached a good sermon, although Faith felt he had nothing on Pastor Landris. Folks shouted, but for the life of her, she couldn't see how anything he'd said would honestly make one iota of a difference in anyone's life. For certain, Faith didn't go back to that church the following Sunday because of the service. It was the one fringe benefit they had that had hooked her.

Faith came back because Thomas wanted her there with him. And she'd told him from the get-go, "I don't play games. If you have something you want to say, I'd suggest you say it. I don't read minds, and I don't care to try to figure out the message between the lines. If we have an understanding, we can proceed. Otherwise, there's the door."

Thomas told her she was his kind of woman. And they made a deal to lay everything out on the table. She told him all about Hope and Charity. Well, not the fact that the three of them shared the same body. Charity often called it sharing a vehicle . . . their one mode of transportation. Faith thought that was cute. But anything she felt was relevant, Faith had told him. He knew the other two existed, even if Thomas still never quite believed he had been talking to Charity instead of her when he'd called that time.

"Charity sounded *too* much like you, but in a fake way," Thomas had said after she returned his call. "I realize sisters can sound alike, but that was just *too* much alike for me to believe it wasn't you just not wanting to talk to me. I tell you what: put Charity on the phone and both of you talk at the same time."

Of course Faith couldn't do that.

Thomas had told Faith that he knew something wasn't right all the time inside his head, but that he was praying and believing God that he'd be able to manage it without having to take medication. Reverend Walker had told him he just needed more faith.

"I don't think Reverend Walker was referring to me when he told you that," Faith said, teasing him.

"Woman, you know I know *that*. I just believe that was a prophetic Word. I needed more *faith* to be able to cope, and God sent me *more* Faith to be able to cope," he said.

"The first time I saw you I 'named it' and 'claimed it.' I had a Word we would be together. And you were a man of God on top of all this." Faith touched his face and straightened his necktie. "I knew you and Sapphire weren't going to last. And having spent more time around her self-righteous self, I can see why you sent her packing."

"To be honest, I thought you had your eye on my brother," Thomas said.

"Who are you talking about? Pastor Landris? You mean, Mr. Henpecked himself?"

"He's not henpecked, although I did say that to him once. Johnnie Mae is a good woman. I see why he's like he is about her. George is totally, madly in love with her."

"Listen, your brother doesn't have anything on you. You're fine, smart, and good-looking all swirled into one. I'll let you in on a secret. I told Hope you were going to be mine when you were with Sapphire . . . that I claimed you for myself. She said I couldn't claim somebody else's man . . . that I couldn't impose my will on someone else's."

"She's right, you know."

"She might be right in theory and principle, but in reality, you're here with me now. So whatever." Faith threw her hand up in the air and laughed.

Now Faith was about to become Mrs. Landris. One more day and Thomas wouldn't have to worry about fighting his brother—or anyone else, for that matter. Faith would be the one who would decide whether he went into a hospital or not. With her standing by his side, Faith knew he wouldn't have to worry about being betrayed. She couldn't help but wonder: *Why is it that people always think they know what's best for someone else?*

Faith couldn't see how Thomas was hurting anyone—the torment he was going through was all his own. Faith truly believed Thomas would know if and when things were too much for him to bear. And if he needed help, he could now feel confident in coming to her, with the assurance that she would help him without judgment.

Likewise, she believed he'd do the same for her. She also believed when she and Thomas said "I do" tomorrow in front of their pastor, Reverend Walker, Charity and Hope would go away for good and leave her in peace to be with her new husband.

To Faith, it only made sense.

Chapter 51

*There hath no temptation taken you but such as
is common to man: but God is faithful, who will
not suffer you to be tempted above that ye are
able; but will with the temptation also make a
way to escape, that ye may be able to bear it.*

(1 Corinthians 10:13)

Pastor Landris had gone down to probate court to file a petition, essentially to have his brother committed. That's
not how people referred to it in this day and age, but that was
what he was trying to do. And on top of everything, he didn't
have a lot of time left.

Therein was the problem.

There were things Pastor Landris would need to know to
fill out the form. And because Pastor Landris wasn't Thomas's
legal guardian, they admitted they wouldn't be so quick to
approve the petition, have him picked up by the police, then
brought to a hospital against his will. Pastor Landris was
told that because he wasn't the legal guardian, it could take
months longer.

"Then who would be the best person?" Pastor Landris
asked the woman as they sat in the small conference room.
Three days had already been lost.

"A spouse."

"He's not married. In fact, that's what we're trying to stop
him from doing now, which is why time is so crucial."

"If he gets married before this is approved, you realize
this application becomes null and void. His wife would have
to file the petition in order for us to proceed."

"But he's not married right now. In this particular case, who would be considered his legal guardian?"

"A parent."

"My mother can come do this quicker than myself?" Pastor Landris asked.

"Of course. She's still considered his legal guardian until he transfers that right to someone else, be it via a legal document or marriage, which technically is a legal document."

"If my mother filled this out, is there any chance we could expedite the process and have him put in a hospital before December 4?" Pastor Landris asked. "This is important."

"Get his mother to come in, and we'll see what we can do. I can't promise anything because it still has to be approved by the judge. Keep in mind—we will be closed for the Thanksgiving holidays, too."

Pastor Landris left the courthouse. He called his mother from his cell phone and explained everything that was going on with Thomas.

"I felt it the past few times I've spoken with him," his mother, Virginia LeBoeuf, said. "He talks a lot lately—almost nonstop. And he jumps all over the place about subjects that aren't related. He wrote me a letter a month ago telling me about this woman named Faith. I suppose that's the one he's trying to marry now. The letter was eighteen pages long! And he had the nerve to stuff it in a regular-size, white envelope. When I got it, I thought he was sending me a piece of clothing or something, the envelope was so big."

"Can you fly here immediately and file this petition?"

"Well, I have a doctor's appointment later this week. I have to go—it can't be changed. My doctor says it's a must."

"Are you okay?"

"We'll talk about that some other time. Right now, we need to help Thomas. I'm so sorry all of this is happening. It's hard when you see your children suffer and you know you can't do much to make things better."

"But there is something that can be done to help Thomas.

He won't do it for himself, so we have to do what we can. I'll get your ticket to you. The courthouse is closed on the weekends. Would you prefer to fly in Saturday, Sunday, or wait until Monday morning?"

"I'd like to spend time with you and Johnnie Mae. I can't wait to see your new house. And the church . . . you're moving into the new church, not this Sunday, but next Sunday, aren't you?"

"Yes, and we're excited. It's kind of stressful around here, though, so I don't know how much I'm actually appreciating the experience."

"Then fly me in Saturday. That way I can go to church with you in the old place, and stay for your first service in the new sanctuary. Hopefully, we'll get things squared away with Thomas on Monday, and they can get him in a hospital room by Tuesday."

"I hope you know Thomas is probably not going to appreciate this," Pastor Landris said.

"He might not now, but one day, I believe he will. I have faith that he will."

Chapter 52

Though I speak with the tongues of men and of angels, and have not charity, I am become as sounding brass, or a tinkling cymbal.

(1 Corinthians 13:1)

Faith and Thomas were ready to take their vows. The ceremony would not be at his house as originally planned. Faith had gone over there to see what would need to be done the day before, and she couldn't believe how wrecked the house looked.

"I hope you know, I'm not cleaning this mess," Faith said as she stood outside the great room. "There's nowhere to even walk in here. And why are clothes piled up on the floor in here, of all places?"

"I was cleaning, and I haven't finished."

"This is not cleaning. This is demolition," Faith said, turning up her nose. "And it stinks in here." She pinched her nose and hurried back outside.

Thomas came outside with her. "I think something may have died in the piles, I don't know. When I finish cleaning, I'll find it and get the smell out."

"I'm not staying in this place. Not like this. And we definitely are not going to get married here."

"It's okay. I'll call Reverend Walker and see what he suggests."

"Do you have to ask Reverend Walker everything? Do you have to ask him if you can take a shower?" Faith leaned over and sniffed him. "How long has it been since you took a shower?"

"I've been busy this week, Faith. I told you, I've been cleaning. And you know I work a lot down at the church. They gave me three weeks off, starting this week. I know you understand vacations." Thomas rubbed his scrubby face. "I need to shave, too, huh?" He smiled.

"Yeah. You know how I am. If you're going to be with me, you have to be an asset and not a liability. I don't want people looking at you and wondering what's wrong with me that I have to be with someone who looks like I picked him up on his way to the homeless shelter."

"You do know people have been following me. It's just hard to take care of your business when you're under surveillance. My mother called. She's in town."

"I hope you didn't invite her over," Faith said as she placed her hand on her hip.

"Of course not. I'm sure George called her to come. She's trying to talk me out of marrying you. I'm glad she's here, though. I'd like to invite her to our wedding tomorrow."

"Do you think she's cool with you marrying me? I don't want any drama at our ceremony. That's exactly why none of my sisters will be there. Charity has been trying to rear her head, but she must have forgotten who she's messing with. I'm not letting anything or anyone stop me from marrying you. That includes your mother."

Thomas took her by the hand. "Are we doing the right thing? Getting married right now? We don't really have to rush, if you're not sure."

"What will we be waiting for? For you to see if there's anyone else you'd rather be with? For me to see? If we wait, why would we be waiting?"

"You're right. You're right."

"And this way, I can protect you like I've protected Charity. If they try to send you to a mental institution, I'll be your wife, and they will have to go through me to get to you," Faith said. She placed her hand on her head.

"Headache again?"

She nodded. "It will pass."

"Is it bad? Do you need anything for it?"

She tried to smile as she grimaced and pressed her lips tight. "I'm strong. I got this one," Faith said. She lowered her hand from her head and let out a long sigh. "You need to go call Reverend Walker right now so we'll know where we're going to have the wedding. Then you need to start getting ready . . . today. Haircut, shave, shower, make sure the suit and shirt you plan to wear are all in good shape."

"I bought new clothes for this. I want you to be proud of your man."

She patted him softly on his face. "I'm sure I'll be proud. I'll just be glad when this is all over, so I can breathe easily again."

He reached out and touched her hair.

"Don't touch my hair, okay? I'm getting it done tomorrow, so I'll be looking fabulous as usual. Let's just get through tomorrow," Faith said. She grabbed her head with both hands and pressed hard. "After tomorrow," she closed her eyes and let her head extend backward, "I believe we both will be home," she grimaced again, "free."

"Are you sure you're okay?"

"Yes. Charity is not going to get the best of me this time. Not this time. Not before tomorrow is come and gone. I'll fight her with every fiber I have left in my being. That much, I promise."

"What?"

She shook her head. "Just talking to myself." She managed a smile. "Merely talking to my . . . self."

Chapter 53

But now hath he obtained a more excellent ministry, by how much also he is the mediator of a better covenant, which was established upon better promises.

(Hebrews 8:6)

Pastor Landris had taken his mother down to the courthouse on Monday to file the petition on behalf of Thomas. She filled out the paperwork and signed it. The woman told them they would probably hear something by the next day—if it was approved. There was one quandary—they needed a doctor or therapist's evaluation. It was one thing to say a person was acting crazy, something else entirely to provide medical proof.

Thomas was not going to a doctor, which was why they had to go this route now. On the other hand, were he to have a total breakdown and go to the hospital or get picked up by the police, who would be able to see that something was going on mentally, or that he posed a danger to himself or others, that would be enough to commit him.

Having a mother who hadn't seen him in over a year, and a brother who was a pastor, stating that a person was bipolar was not enough for them to have him arbitrarily picked up.

"Sapphire is a therapist," Pastor Landris said to the woman in the courthouse office. "This is her field. She has spent time with him and was the one who diagnosed him as bipolar."

"That would work. But this will delay my being able to

hand it over to the judge for at least another day. Get the medical write-up, get it notarized, and we'll proceed," the woman said.

"We're cutting this close," Pastor Landris's mother said.

"I'm sorry, but this is how things work. There are rules in place for a reason. I know you care about your son, Ms. LeBoeuf," she said to Virginia, "and your brother, but he still has civil rights. We can't just ignore his rights because you think something is best for him. Today is Wednesday. We still have two more days until the week is over."

"We understand. I just pray this works out," Virginia said. "Otherwise, if this is not approved and done by Friday, on Saturday it's over anyway. It will truly be in God's hands then."

Late Friday afternoon, Pastor Landris and his mother got a call from the courthouse. It hadn't been rejected, but it hadn't been approved, either. It would probably be the first of next week.

"That will be too late," Pastor Landris said to her.

"I'm sorry. We did the best we could do. I'll leave it in the system, and if you're really a praying man, you might want to start now," the woman said.

Pastor Landris looked at his mother. She leaned over and started to cry.

She'd seen Thomas on Friday, just missing his fiancée by an hour. He hadn't shaved or showered. He'd reluctantly allowed her in the house because she needed to use the bathroom. That's when she saw all the mess everywhere.

She was so hoping to hear some good news by that afternoon. That's why they had called every thirty minutes for an update. It had gotten down to the wire, and the verdict was still out as to whether her son would get the help he needed in time.

"She said if you were a praying man, you should start now," Virginia said.

"I have been praying. I've been praying since Thomas left

my house and our church earlier this year. And when I knew he had really serious problems, I stepped up my prayers."

"Well, don't stop now," she said. "Don't stop now. Right now your prayer is our only hope."

"I have to get ready for Sunday," Pastor Landris said. "It has been so crazy, getting the final touches done on the building and the sound system, which is state of the art, up and running. The department heads have taken care of the details along with Sherry, who has become my right arm. Angel and Brent, who don't even realize they're actually dating the biblical way, have worked nonstop for the past three weeks coordinating everything."

"Are you preaching on Sunday, or will it just be praises, worshipping, drama, dance, all those things large churches generally do the first time they march into the Promised Land?"

"I have a short Word. It's actually in answer to a question Johnnie Mae asked me once. I never answered her. I'll speak for about twenty minutes. But at the beginning of next year, I'm starting a series on Strongholds. In light of Thomas and Faith, a.k.a. 'Trinity,' dealing with their strongholds, this is going to be a powerful series, I believe. I'm planning to touch on lots of things. I've already started praying for people to be delivered. There are so many things people don't even think of as strongholds."

"You'll have to send me the tape series of that one."

"But I'm praying, Mom, for Thomas and for Johnnie Mae and Charity and for you. Whatever is going on with you medically, I'm praying about it right now."

His mother smiled. "Let's pray your brother out of his situation first. Then we can work on mine. Deal?"

"It doesn't have to be either/or. We can pray for both of you."

"Yeah, but you know what? Sometimes dealing with something that may or may not be . . . can be draining. So for now, we'll work on those things that definitely are."

"Okay. Thomas first. Then you're going to tell me what's going on with you."

"Oh, me? I'm going to get my praise on. Come Sunday, I'm going to have a lot to shout about. You taught me that. Trust in the Lord. I'm trusting in Him on this one." She smiled, then looked up toward heaven. "I'm trusting You totally on this one, God. I've done all I can—now I'm standing on Your promises! I'm letting my yea be yea. Yes, I know somehow, You're going to handle all of this!"

"Amen," Pastor Landris said. "What a powerful prayer, Mom."

"Hey, I was just having a little talk with Jesus. And He has already worked it out."

"Already worked it out," Pastor Landris said.

"Already worked it out!"

Chapter 54

*God looked down from heaven upon the children
of men, to see if there were any that did understand, that did seek God.*

(Psalm 53:2)

"In Isaiah, Chapter 53, verse 1, it reads," Pastor Landris
said, "'Who hath believed our report? and to whom is
the arm of the Lord revealed?'" Pastor Landris looked out
over the crowd that filled the sanctuary. There was an overflow, so much so that people were standing along the walls
and sitting down on the floor.

Praise & Worship went to a new level. The dance team
blessed everybody with precision and grace. The drama team
performed a skit that touched on believing during unbelief. It
was so real and so fitting. Pastor Landris had faced that very
thing on Saturday as he watched the minutes tick toward his
brother's wedding hour.

Pastor Landris had driven his mother to the wedding.
Thomas had invited her, but not him or his wife. Johnnie Mae
went along for the ride or, in truth, to give her husband moral
support. If nothing else, they could sit in the Denali and pray
while the ceremony was taking place. Maybe the newlyweds
would seek help after they were married. This was still God's
business, and no one can ever dictate how, in the end, God
will handle things.

"How do you think your mother's holding up in there?"

Johnnie Mae asked as thirty minutes passed after the wedding was scheduled to begin.

"I don't know, but I know she's a strong woman. She'll do what she has to."

"Do you think she'll object, you know, when the preacher comes to the part about if anyone there can show just cause?"

Pastor Landris looked at her as he took his hand off the steering wheel and laid his arm on the armrest. "She's not going to do anything like that. One thing about my mother—she'll voice her opinion strongly from the beginning, but if you still insist on butting your head against a brick wall, she'll just get the bandage and alcohol ready and wait."

"Would you have objected had you been in there?"

"No. If I was going to do something that bold and disruptive, I would have just taken Thomas out before the wedding began and beat him up," Pastor Landris said.

She looked at her watch. "Ready for tomorrow?"

"I'm a little excited. You?"

"I'm so pumped. Isn't it something to see how far God has brought us? Three years ago, minus three months, we were having church in our house. It sort of reminds me of when that guy had the ark in his house . . ."

"Obed-edom the Gittite. Second Samuel 6:10-12," Pastor Landris said.

"Yeah, okay . . . him. He had the ark in his house for three months and his whole household started getting all these blessings. Then David showed up and asked for the ark back after he realized exactly how they were receiving God's blessings. We were having services in our home, and we ended up being blessed with a bigger and better house, and now we're about to move into a bigger and better church sanctuary."

Pastor Landris smiled. "You like our new house, I take it?"

"I love it. Absolutely love it. And getting out from under Rachel and those children? I had no idea how much I needed to do that."

"That's how God works. He begins a thing, and we have no idea how it will work out. He wants us to trust Him and move when He says move, without asking Him why and how is He going to make it work for our good. That's scripture." Pastor Landris reclined his seat a little. "When we moved from Atlanta, He didn't tell me we'd be buying 40 acres of prime property, building an $18-million church facility, partnering with the people who owned the property to build subdivisions, a shopping mall, a business district—"

"And the college you want to build that they want to be part of," Johnnie Mae said.

"See, that's what I mean. Some things look bad when they're happening, but you just have to trust God and know that He sees what's going on farther down the road," Pastor Landris said. "I hate to see Thomas marry Faith. I hate Charity needing help and we don't seem to be able to do anything *to* help her. All we can do is pray that God will do what we can't do, or for Him to tell us what to do next."

"Yeah." Johnnie Mae opened a bag of onion rings, offering the bag to Pastor Landris. "Want some?"

"No, thanks." He looked at the bag again. "I don't know how you eat those things. The thought of them makes me sick."

"They don't bother me. I can eat a whole bag."

Pastor Landris looked at the clock on the dashboard. "It's been forty-five minutes. It's not like they were having a full production or anything. According to Mom, it was going to be a few people and the minister. How long does it take to say, 'I do'?"

"It didn't take us long to say 'I do', but we had a production leading up to it and afterward, that's for sure."

"Our wedding wasn't that big."

"Maybe not the wedding party, but the things we read

and said to each other from the Song of Solomon—that took a while. They're probably doing something similar. Or maybe the pastor is doing that covenant reenactment. You know, how the man takes some salt from his bag and the woman takes salt from her bag and the preacher asks them to drop their individual salt into the one big bag that represents their new life together. Then the preacher shakes the salt up, and tells them they can't take back their individually owned salt because it would be impossible to separate it."

"Where did you see that?" Pastor Landris asked. *She really is going to eat that whole bag by herself in one sitting.*

"That wedding I went to back in October. The minister did that during the ceremony, and I thought it was so neat. I wish we had known about it—we could have done it at our wedding or, at least, at the seminar celebration." She had a funny look on her face. "Yuck," she said.

"What's wrong?"

"I don't know. All of a sudden, I'm not feeling so well. I must have eaten a bad one or something. I feel like I have to throw up."

"Well, open the door and step outside if you really have to."

"You're so cute. I think I'll go find a rest room." She opened the door and got out.

As tempted as she was, she didn't veer toward the sanctuary to look for the wedding ceremony. It was probably over by now, anyway. She found the rest room, and just in time. She was really nauseated. She'd never reacted that way to a bag of onion rings before.

After she finished, she went over to the sink and wiped her face with a wet paper towel. She wasn't feeling well at all. The cool water from the towel helped. The door opened, and someone slowly stepped inside. Johnnie Mae glanced to see who it was. She was shocked to see the bride standing before her—hair perfect, as always.

"Faith," Johnnie Mae said. She didn't know what else to say. Congratulations was out, since she wouldn't really mean it.

As Johnnie Mae looked closer, she saw how messed up Faith's face was. She'd been crying, and from the looks of it, it was one of those messy cries—the ones that leave mascara trails and foundation meltdown.

"What's wrong? What happened?" Johnnie Mae walked toward her.

Faith just stood there.

"Are you okay?"

Silence.

Johnnie Mae reached out and pulled her close. "Come over here. Let's get your face cleaned up." She wet a paper towel and gently wiped Faith's face.

"Where is Thomas? Is he okay?"

Nothing.

"I can't help you if you won't talk to me."

She looked up into Johnnie Mae's eyes as Johnnie Mae continued to gently but firmly wipe the remaining makeup off her face.

"It's Charity," Faith said.

"Charity, huh? Well, I sure miss her myself. I bet you miss her, too."

"I'm Charity," she said and bowed her head down.

"Charity. You're Charity? Oh, Charity!" Johnnie Mae hugged her tightly.

"Please, Johnnie Mae, will you please take me out of here," Charity said.

"Where do you want to go? Do you want to go to my house?"

She nodded blankly. "Anywhere but here. Your house would be fine."

Johnnie Mae kept her arm around her as they walked out and back to the SUV.

Pastor Landris saw Johnnie Mae coming, and she wasn't alone. He jumped out to meet them.

"Johnnie Mae, what are you doing? Have you lost your mind? You can't kidnap a person like that," Pastor Landris said.

"Hush, and help me get her in the SUV. Hurry," Johnnie Mae said.

He did as she said, but only because he didn't want them to be seen while he talked some sense into his wife. She obviously needed some kind of help herself.

Johnnie Mae got in and sat with Charity. Pastor Landris was in the driver's seat. Once they were safely inside the SUV, he turned around and looked at them. "Johnnie Mae, you can't do this. I know you love me, and you think you're doing this to help Thomas. Oh, Johnnie Mae girl, what have you done? We'll have our first service in our new sanctuary tomorrow, and I won't be there because we'll either be in jail or on the run. What were you thinking?"

"Landris, stop that," Johnnie Mae said.

"I don't want this. I get to choose, and I don't want this. You can't make me, and I'm not doing it," Charity said.

"See, she's going to press charges against us. She knows who we are. I can't believe you did this, Johnnie Mae. I should have left you at home and none of this would be happening. Or I should have made you stay in the SUV—"

"Landris, stop! This is Charity."

"What?"

Charity looked up. "Pastor Landris, can you pray for me? I really need someone to pray for me. I've got to get away from here. I need help. Please help me. Sapphire said she'd help." She turned to Johnnie Mae. "How is Mama Gates? I'm so sorry. I didn't mean to let her down like that."

Johnnie Mae held her. "We'll get you some help, Charity. I promise."

"I prayed God would help me. Faith was supposed to help

me as well as protect me. Something went wrong. She didn't want to let me come back. It's not right what she was doing to Sapphire. Sapphire is a good person. She's been wonderful to me. She's so good with your mother, Johnnie Mae. And Thomas . . . Thomas needs help. Faith was not going to help him, either. It was up to me to stop her. I had to stop her."

"Landris, can you call your mother on the cell and see if you can get her to come on out so we can leave?"

"Thomas's mother was there," Charity said. "She came for the wedding. Thomas looked really nice and all, but none of this was right. That preacher knew that. There is something evil about him. How could he not help Thomas when he sees how bad he is? Thomas's mother got sick. They laid her down on a pew. I thought she was dead. It freaked Faith out—just like back with Motherphelia. His mother asked to be taken to the hospital, but Reverend Walker wanted to finish the ceremony first."

Pastor Landris clicked off his cell phone. "She's not answering." He turned to Charity. "Charity, is my mother all right now?"

"She wasn't doing so well when I left and ran to the rest room. Faith and I got to fighting right there in front of everybody, including your mother. Faith didn't want to let me back, and I began to pray with all that was within me. What she was about to do was not right. I couldn't let her hurt anybody else anymore. She did it one time—I couldn't let her do it again. I called on the name of Jesus. You said there's power in Jesus' name."

Johnnie Mae shook her head to tell Pastor Landris not to pressure her. "Landris, go in there and see about your mother. I'll stay here with Charity."

"Turn your cell phone on, Johnnie Mae." Pastor Landris knew Johnnie Mae rarely had it on. "If I need you, I'll call. I'm going to leave the key in the ignition. If something is not right, and if you feel you have to, leave without me."

She nodded.

Just then Pastor Landris saw Thomas and his mother coming toward them. She was leaning heavily on him as he helped her to walk. Pastor Landris jumped out and ran to meet them. He and Thomas got her in the SUV.

"Mom, what happened?" Pastor Landris asked, after she was safely inside.

"Let me catch my breath. I'm all right, though. Just let me catch my breath."

"Thomas, what happened to her?"

"She needs to go to the hospital," Thomas said. "Don't listen to her talking about she's all right. She wouldn't let me call the ambulance. She said you were out here waiting, and she wanted to get back to you. She needs to go to the hospital, George."

"I said I'm all right. Now quit making a fuss over me, you two."

"Then what happened?"

"Can we please get away from this place? I'm so tired," Charity said, laying her head on Johnnie Mae's shoulder. "I just need a little rest."

"This girl's got a point," Virginia said. "Let's go to your house so I can get my heart medicine, and I'll be fine. I can't believe I didn't have it in my purse. It felt like I was going to die in there."

"Heart medicine?" Pastor Landris said.

"Yes, heart medicine. I told you we'd talk about it another time. This was not the time I envisioned, but I have heart problems. The doctor gave me some medicine that Friday after Thanksgiving, right before I came here."

"Mom, I'm sorry," Thomas said. "George, you should have seen her. Mom had me so scared. She passed out, and we had to lay her on a pew. She wasn't out but a minute." He looked at Charity. "You really are Charity? My goodness. Landris, I'll get my car later. Let's just hurry and get Mom to your house to get her medicine." He shook his head. "Charity."

Pastor Landris drove out of the parking lot.

Chapter 55

And the Word was made flesh, and dwelt among us, (and we beheld his glory, the glory as of the only begotten of the Father), full of grace and truth.

(John 1:14)

"My wife asked me once, where did evil come from," Pastor Landris said on the first Sunday in the new sanctuary. "I know there are some things some of us don't like to talk about. I'm not going to speak for long today, but I have so much to thank God for. So much. As we look around this facility, we can see the work of the Lord. If you look at the person sitting next to you, you can see the work of the Lord. We take so much for granted. We beg God for things, and when we get them, we can't stop long enough to tell Him thank you, for being too busy begging Him for more stuff.

"I'm not coming today to ask God for anything. I just want to stop and say, 'Thank you.' I know I'm not the only one here God has blessed—I'm not that naïve or foolish. You may not want to say it, but God has been good to you. Things might not have come about the way *you* thought they should have, but God does *what* He wants, *when* He wants, *how* He wants. I'm so grateful because around this time yesterday, my world was going through some real changes. Do you know, somebody sitting next to you today might have had a rough night last night, and you don't even have a clue? Then we walk around hating one another. For what? Just because somebody has more stuff than you? Because somebody has a few more friends than you?

"Then why be mad at them? Why don't you go to God and tell Him what you need? And mind you, I said need, not greed. There's a difference in desiring something for its own sake and desiring something because somebody else has it, and you don't think they deserve it, so therefore you ought to have it, too. But I've strayed a little off the subject." He smiled. "My mother is here for our first service celebration. Stand up and wave, Mom. Ladies and gentlemen, Ms. Virginia LeBoeuf."

The congregation clapped as Virginia stood and did the "Miss America wave" with precision.

"She gave us a scare yesterday afternoon, but I thank God that He is still in the healing business. Yes, she had to take some medicine, but scripture tells us that one plants, one waters, but only God can give the increase. Man can develop the medicine, ingest the medication, but only God can give the . . ." He did a quick little dance, spinning around once like a top. "God did some increasing yesterday.

"My oldest brother, whom some of you know, is here with us today. I'm thankful because I know that God not only heals, but He's also in the restoration business. There is no name under the sun that doesn't have to bow to the name of Jesus. Sickness has to bow. Cancer has to bow. Heart disease . . . has to bow. Division amongst God's people has to bow. Alzheimer's has to bow. Mental illness has to bow. Sickle cell has to bow. Diabetes has to bow. Poverty has to bow. Discord has to bow. Depression . . . has to bow. If it has a name, it has to bow to Jesus.

"We have other blessed folks with us. I'm only pointing out a few because I saw the hand of God move in a powerful way yesterday. I want God to know, I thank Him. I'm like the Samaritan woman at the well. 'Come see a man who told me all things that ever I did. Is not this the Christ?' I must tell it because there is somebody here today who needs to know: God is still in the mind-regulating business!" He paused for the shouts.

"I'm only going to call her by the name of Trinity. After what she's been through, today she is truly a blessed Trinity. And God is not finished with her yet. As He did with her, God can take the broken pieces of our lives and make us whole again. I know, without a doubt, there is nothing too hard for God. Hope is good to have in life. So hear me: I'm not knocking hope. Faith is good and necessary to have in life, especially if we want to please God; I'm not knocking faith. We teach on faith. We believe faith without works is dead. But without charity . . . without love—hope and faith are nothing. Have hope. Have faith. But not without charity. First Corinthians 13:13 says, 'And now abideth faith, hope, charity, these three; but' . . . 'the greatest of these is charity.' " He smiled at Charity, sitting near Johnnie Mae. "Whatever we do, know this: Without love, to God, it means nothing."

"Amen," the congregation said as they raised the roof with shouts of praise.

"I would also like to recognize another guest for coming to celebrate with us on this day: Reverend Poppa Knight." He nodded at Reverend Knight as they lightly applauded.

"I suppose you're saying, 'Pastor Landris, I thought you were going to answer the question your wife asked.' Well, I'm going to do that right now. In Genesis, chapter 1, verse 2, it says, 'And the earth was without form, and void; and darkness was upon the face of the deep.' Over in the book of John, the first chapter, beginning at the first verse down through the fifth, it reads, 'In the beginning was the Word, and the Word was with God, and the Word was God. The same was in the beginning with God. All things.' " Pastor Landris paused a minute and scanned a sea of faces. "What kinds of things?"

"All things," the congregation said.

"What kinds of things?"

"All!"

Pastor Landris continued. " 'All things were made by him; without him was not any thing made that was made. In him was life; and the life was the light of men. And the light shineth in darkness; and the darkness comprehended it not.' " He closed the Bible and glanced around the magnificent edifice, now filled past capacity with God's people.

"Where did evil come from? If all things were made by Him, without Him was not *any* thing made—then who is Him?"

"God," the congregation said with a weak voice.

"Who?" he asked. He wanted them to say it as though they were sure.

"God!" they shouted louder.

"I know you're probably thinking 'Pastor, are you saying God created evil?' Well, I'll tell you what I *am* saying, and please hear me and get it right. I don't want you out there spreading lies about what Pastor Landris said. What I am saying is, God is not surprised about anything that was, is, or will be on this earth. I know this may come as a shock to some of you, but God was not surprised when Adam and Eve ate from the tree. Not the omniscient, omnipresent God I've grown to know.

"Having said that, I'm struggling not to touch on this subject since I promised I wouldn't be long, but here's what I want you to know about evil. Evil is darkness. That's why people refer to evil as 'the dark side.' Darkness was here *before* the world was formed. Darkness is merely the *absence* of light. When we think of light, we think of the sun. In Genesis chapter 1, the very first thing God spoke into existence was light. That's in verse 3. Not the sun, which came in verse 14. Evil is darkness, and darkness is the absence of light. Church, Jesus is The Light. When you get home, read the entire first chapter of John to verify it for yourself. Where there is light, there can be no darkness. If you don't believe me, prove this scientifically as well when you get home. Equally, where there is darkness, there is no light. The knowledge of good and evil is to know a world *with* The Light—good, and a world *without* The Light—evil.

"We know the sun gives light and warmth. The sun is essential for life to exist. Without the sun, there is no *natural* light. Without the S-U-N, there is no light. And without the Son S-O-N, there is no Light. Therefore, evil is a condition, position, or place without the Son . . . S-O-N. So where did evil come from? It was here before the world began. God called forth The Light, 'Come here, Son S-O-N!' And God saw: it was *good*!

"There are scriptures throughout the Bible that show how God the Father, the Son, and the Holy Ghost worked together blessing the earth. There is evidence of the three from the beginning. Don't believe me? Okay: God Spoke, the Spirit Moved, and the Word Walked. Yes, all three, beginning in Genesis. The Word was walking on the earth back in the beginning. Genesis 3:8 says, 'And they' (referring to Adam and Eve after they had eaten from the tree) 'heard the voice of the Lord God walking in the garden in the cool of the day.' The voice of the Lord God *walking* . . . walking. The voice of the Lord God is the Word. In the beginning was the Word. And the Word was made—"

"Flesh!" the congregation shouted and began a thunderous applause.

"God the Father, God the Son, God the Holy Spirit. God in three persons—Blessed Trinity." He held one hand in the air to thank them as they gave him a standing ovation, lifted holy hands toward heaven to thank God, and sat down next to his wife and family.

Chapter 56

And let us not be weary in well doing: for in due season we shall reap, if we faint not.

(Galatians 6:9)

"Here, you can have this scripture back," she said.

Pastor Landris held the paper in his hand. *Psalm 113:9. He maketh the barren woman to keep house, and to be a joyful mother of children. Praise ye the Lord.*

"So, you're giving up?" Pastor Landris asked.

"After two and a half years, what do you think?"

"I think, Mrs. Landris, that you should believe God."

"For how long?"

"For as long as it takes."

"And if it doesn't happen, and it doesn't look like it's going to happen, then what?"

"You wait on the Lord."

"Pastor Landris, is waiting enough? What if God has merely said 'No'?"

"What if God is merely saying 'Not now'?"

"What if people look at you like you're crazy just because you believe in something so strongly, yet they don't see anything that even resembles triumph in your life?"

"So who are you going to be mindful of? Whose report are you going to believe?"

Johnnie Mae started grinning. She pulled a white stick the size of a pen from behind her back and handed it to him.

"What is this?" he asked, looking down at it.

"I suppose it's my way of saying to you, dear Pastor Landris: I choose, chose, have chosen, and will continue to choose to believe the report of the Lord."

"Come again? This is a plastic stick with a plus sign in a tiny window."

"Are you *positive* that's all it is?"

He was getting a little weary of this game. "Yes, I'm positive it's a plastic stick with a plus sign in a window-looking thing."

"If that's true, then we no longer need faith for Psalm 113:9. We're pregnant!"

He looked at the stick, then back up at her. She was jumping up and down the way Princess Rose does when she's about to get something she really, really wants.

"We're going to have a baby?" Pastor Landris asked. "We're going to have a baby?"

"Yes!"

"You and I . . . me and you . . . *we* are going to have a baby?" He jumped up off the couch, picked her up, and started swinging her around. He stopped suddenly. "Oh goodness. What was I thinking? I didn't hurt you, did I? I didn't upset the baby, did I?" He touched her stomach gently. "When is he or she due? When did you find out? I should have known something was up. You got sick Saturday while we were in the parking lot. I should have sensed something, but so much was going on. Then Sunday, we had our first service in the new sanctuary. Monday, we got Thomas into a hospital of his own free will. Charity started seeing Sapphire to get the help she needs. Mom went home Thursday morning . . . it's just been crazy. Well, tell me. Don't keep me waiting. When?"

She laughed at how he was carrying on. "I haven't been to the doctor yet. In fact, I just did the test. My best calculation is that it will be some time in August." Her eyes got wide. "Wouldn't it be something if the baby came on my forty-fifth birthday? That would be a grand present."

"I'm going to be a father?" Pastor Landris said. "My mother is going to have her first grandchild? You and I . . . we . . . together . . . we're going to have a baby! God is awesome! Oh, I'm so glad I'm saved and know the Lord for myself! And He makes it so easy for everybody, Johnnie Mae. All they have to do is say, 'Lord, I'm a sinner. I want to be saved. Come into my heart, Lord Jesus. God, I believe You sent Your Son Jesus. I believe He died on the cross for my sins. I believe You raised Him from the dead. I receive Jesus into my heart today.' They don't have to sit on a mourner's bench or turn cartwheels. Just believe in their hearts, confess with their mouths, and receive salvation.

"It's too simple to be saved for people not to be. Maybe they think they're going to miss out on something, but oh, the joys of the Lord . . . the things He blesses us with! There is no comparison. Turning my life over and allowing Jesus to be Lord of my life was the best thing that ever happened to me. Then he double-blessed me with you." He looked in Johnnie Mae's eyes as he saw tears begin flowing. "I just wish everybody knew all they were missing simply because they refuse to open their hearts. Jesus stands and knocks; all they have to do is open up and invite Him in. Just say yes."

"Just say yes," Johnnie Mae said, crying as he leaned down and softly kissed her. "Yes, Lord. My soul says yes. Yes to Your will; yes to Your way. We'll just say . . . yes."

Goodness and Mercy

Chapter 1

Come now, and let us reason together, saith the Lord: though your sins be as scarlet, they shall be as white as snow; though they be red like crimson, they shall be as wool.

—Isaiah 1:18

"If you're here today," forty-eight-year-old Pastor George Landris began, "and you feel there's something missing in your life. If you admit that although there are billions of people on this earth, you still feel like you're all by yourself–that sometimes it feels like it's you, and you alone. If you feel as though no one truly loves you. If you're *fed up* with being fed up." He paused a second. "If you'd like to be born again . . . you want to know *Jesus* in the free pardon of your sins. Then, I want you to know that your being here today is neither an accident nor a coincidence. I want you to know that it's time for a change! You see, I've been told that the definition of insanity is doing the same thing over and over again but somehow expecting a different result." He shook his head slowly, then took one step to the side.

"Well, to that someone who's here today, your change has come. If you're looking for change, change you can *truly* believe in, then the Lord is extending His hand to you today through me. He's asking you, on *this* day, to accept His hand. I know I'm talking to somebody today. In your life, it's time for a change." Pastor Landris nodded as he narrowed his eyes, then ticked his head three times to one side as he smiled.

"Oh, I know we heard the word change a lot last year. We

talked about change. Some of you even voted for change. Some of you voted for the first time in your life *because* of change. Well, on November the fourth, two-thousand and eight, change took a step forward in these United States of America . . . a change that's *already* had an impact on the world. But on *this* day"—he pointed his index finger down toward the floor—"on this Sunday, January the fourth, two-thousand and *nine*, sixteen days before that embodiment of change is to be sworn in as the forty-fourth president of the United States, it's time for your own personal change. A change, a wonderful change."

Many in the audience began to clap while others stood, clapped, and shouted various things like: "Change!" "A wonderful change!" and "Thank God for change!"

Pastor Landris bobbed his head, then continued to speak. "For those of you here who are tired of fighting this battle alone, let me assure you that there *is* another way. And in case you don't know or haven't heard, *Jesus* is the way! He's the truth, and He's the light.

"And today—just as Jesus has been doing since before He left Earth boarded on a cloud on His way back to Heaven where he presently sits on the right hand of the Father—He's calling for those who have yet to answer His call to come. Come unto Him all you that labor and are heavy laden. Jesus desires to be Lord of your life. Won't you come today? Won't you come? Come and cast your cares on the Lord, for He cares for you. Oh yes, He cares . . . He cares. He cares. He . . . cares."

Pastor Landris extended his hand. He looked like someone waiting on a dance partner to take hold of his outstretched hand in order to continue the next step of a well-choreographed dancing routine.

Twenty-six-year-old Gabrielle Mercedes heard his words. She felt them as they pierced through her heart. She doubled over as she sat there in her seat. Quickly, she felt the warmth wash completely over her, starting at her head. It felt as though she was being covered with pure love and peace, as though buckets of warmth were being poured out on her and were quickly making their way down to her feet. Her feet heard the music inside of the words "Come and cast your cares on the Lord, for He cares," and they began to move, to tap rapidly, all on their own.

The music that played on the inside of her was not the usual music one might expect to hear in church. It was music that no words she knew could aptly describe—angelic. Her body instinctively knew what to do; her legs summarily brought her upright to her feet. She hurriedly, but gracefully, started across—one-two, one-two, side-step, side-step—from where she'd sat, quietly excusing herself past those who shared the row with her. Then, forward she glided, with long, deliberate strides down a wide center aisle—flow, extend, now glide, glide, faster, faster—toward the front of the church building's sanctuary. Nothing happening before the right side of her brain was ever even able to effectively launch a logical and methodical discussion about any of this with the left side of her brain. She was moving forward, refusing to look back.

And when she shook the hand that continued to remain extended for any and all who dared to reach toward it, she didn't see the man of God's, Pastor Landris's, hand. All she saw was the Son of the living God called Jesus, Emmanuel, the Prince of Peace, the King of kings, the Lord of lords, the President of presidents. She began to leap—higher, higher.

And as she shook Pastor Landris's hand, at least twenty other people also came forward and stood alongside her. But she only felt the hand of God holding her up as she stood there and openly confessed she was indeed a sinner. She knew—without any trumpets sounding, any special effects, and any special feelings—that in that moment of her confession, she was saved. Saved by grace. Now.

Now faith is . . . now . . . faith is now . . .

And the feeling she had? It was the Lord leading the dance of her life, whispering throughout her every being that she now only needed to follow His lead. She needed to allow Him to take her to the next step, and then the next one, and the next one, without knowing what the next step might be. Fully trusting His lead. *One-two-three.*

Oh, how Gabrielle loved to dance! But until this day, she'd never known the true grace in dancing. That amazing grace. God's amazing grace. The feelings she had now were a by-product of the new knowledge she possessed: the knowledge of knowing Jesus Christ in the free pardon of her sins. All of her sins, every single one of them, Pastor Landris was saying, were officially pardoned. She was free!

"Pardoned—your slate wiped cleaned," Pastor Landris said to those who came up. "Your sins totally purged from your record. It's as though they never happened. God says your past transgressions have been removed as far as the east is from the west; the north from the south. All of your sins—the ones folks know about, and yes, the ones only God knows. Gone. Gone! Whatever sins were in your past, from this day forward, as far as the Lord is concerned, they're gone." Those standing were being signaled by a ministry leader to follow her to an awaiting conference room.

"Hold up a second," Pastor Landris said, halting them before they exited. "I want you to say this with me: My *past* has been *cast* into God's sea of forgetfulness."

They did as he asked—some of them leaping for joy as they shouted the words.

"You are forgiven of your sins," he said. "Look at me." He waited a second. "And God is saying to you, don't allow anyone . . . *anyone* to ever bring up your past sins to you again. Did you hear what I said? Don't let *anyone* use your past against you. If they bring it up, you tell them that it's under the blood of Jesus now."

The entire congregation erupted with shouts of praise as they stood to their feet.

Chapter 2

For I know the thoughts that I think toward you,
saith the Lord, thoughts of peace, and not of evil,
to give you an expected end.

—*Jeremiah 29:11*

"Do you have a Bible?" one of the ladies asked Gabrielle in the conference room where the new converts were taken after they let out of the main sanctuary.

"No, I don't. But I can buy one," Gabrielle said.

"Oh, we have one for you—a gift from the church." The petite woman smiled as she handed Gabrielle a six-by-nine-inch maroon Bible. "I'm Tiffany Connors. I'm part of the ministry that welcomes converts who come to Christ through Followers of Jesus Faith Worship Center. Our goal is to ensure that you have as many tools as possible at your disposal to get you started learning all you can about the Lord. Pastor Landris insists there's nothing worse than having something new and either *not* receiving or not reading the manual that comes with it—oblivious to its features, benefits, and the instructions to operate it. And of course, any good manual contains troubleshooting information to help in understanding when something is not working properly, and what is needed to correct it. We believe there's no better manual for Christians—novices and veterans alike—than the Bible." Tiffany tapped Gabrielle's Bible twice, then held out her hand to shake hers.

Gabrielle glanced at the Bible she'd been given. She smiled

at Tiffany as they shook hands. "I'm Gabrielle Mercedes, and it's a pleasure to make your acquaintance."

Tiffany tilted her head in a quizzical way. "Is Mercedes your married name?"

Gabrielle smiled. She wasn't offended or felt Tiffany was moving too quickly into her business. She knew exactly what was going through Tiffany Connors's head. It was what she found herself encountering a lot since she'd legally dropped her last name of Booker and adopted her middle name as her last. Most people could tell by looking at her smooth brown skin; hair that was, without fail or excuses, relaxed every four to six weeks to keep it from going back to its natural state of Afro-ishness; and a signature behind that defined many a black woman as a black woman (there always being an exception to any rule, as folks like J. Lo have proven) that she was not Hispanic, as her last name night somehow suggest.

The next logical thought was that she, being a black woman, must have married someone with the last name of Mercedes to have acquired it. She could have easily, but didn't bother to, explained how she ended up with it. But then that would defeat the whole purpose in her having changed it in the first place.

"No, I'm not married, and I've never been married," Gabrielle said. She just happened to look down and realized she was hugging her Bible. She let her arm down by her side, along with the Bible she held in her hand.

"Gabrielle Mercedes. Well, it certainly is a beautiful name," Tiffany said. She glanced at her watch and grimaced. "Listen, I hope you don't mind me having to leave so quickly—kind of drop the Bible and run—but I have to go pick up my children from children's church so the workers there can leave."

Gabrielle smiled as she tilted her head only slightly. "Forgive me, but did you say children's church?"

"Yes, We have a church for the children. They call it children's church even though it's still pat of this same congregation. There's also a teen church with activities geared specifically for the teenagers and their style of praise and worship. Today was my day to work in this ministry. And since Darius, that's my husband, didn't make it to church today, I'm the only one available to pick up my little ones by the cut-off time."

"How many children do you have?"

Tiffany appreciated Gabrielle for asking. She loved talking about her children. "I have three. My oldest daughter is Jade. She'll be eight this year. Dana, our middle daughter, turns six in a few months. And our son Darius Junior, we call him Little D., just turned two this past November. He's in the toddler's section of children's church."

Gabrielle nodded. "That's nice of the church to have a children's church and a teen church within the main church. I only went to church a few times when I was growing up, although I went all the time when I was a baby up until I was about three. My mother used to take me every Sunday . . ." Gabrielle could not remember anything from such a young age. So she discontinued, at least aloud, this train of thought.

Gabrielle smiled, pretending it was perfectly normal to switch topics and entire conversations in mid-sentence. "Suffice it to say, there was nothing separate for the children or the teens to do in the churches I attended growing up. And the preacher, when we *did* go those times, mostly put folks to sleep. I mean, they would be sleeping good, too. Until he reached the end of his sermon and started whooping and hollering— startling babies, men, and old folks alike, right out of their naps." She laughed. "I'm sorry. Here I am going on, holding you up when you clearly said you needed to go. Please, go on and pick up your children. And thanks for the Bible." She patted the Bible's cover. "It's beautiful."

Fatima Adams walked over to Gabrielle and Tiffany just as Tiffany was about to leave. "Well, hello. It's Tiffany Connors, right?"

Tiffany nodded. "And you're Fatima . . . ?" She frowned as though that would help her recall Fatima's last name.

"Yes, Adams. Fatima Adams," Fatima said as she politely shook Tiffany's hand.

"Well, Fatima, I must say that you have *impeccable* timing. I'm hurrying to get my children from children's church. Now I don't feel so bad leaving like this. Great meeting you"—she said to Gabrielle—"and great seeing you again," she said to Fatima.

Fatima turned to Gabrielle. "Well, hello there. My name is Fatima Adams, as I'm sure you just heard." She smiled and held out her hand to shake Gabrielle's, then suddenly leaned in and hugged her instead. "I just wanted to come over, introduce myself, and welcome you to the body of Christ, as well as to Followers of Jesus Faith Worship Center. We're so excited you've chosen to accept Jesus into your life. And believe me when I say that your decision is an eternal, life-changing, and life-saving one."

Gabrielle felt Fatima's hug had been sincere. Still, she'd quickly pulled away, and even took a step back. "Thank you. I'm Gabrielle Mercedes. And before you ask, I'm not married, so it's not my married name." She laughed a little. In truth, the hug had taken her a little off her stride. Gabrielle wasn't accustomed to being hugged. She hadn't been hugged much since her days with Miss Crowe, a teacher who had been a rock in her life. In fact, as she thought about it, the last time she'd actually allowed anyone to hug her, to really hug her, was the last time she'd seen Miss Crowe—some nine years ago. Right before the horrible accident that ended up dramatically changing both of their lives. Any other hugs didn't mean anything to her; they were merely perfunctory.

Miss Crowe was the only person who had really cared about her. She'd cared about Gabrielle's dreams and aspirations. Cared that Gabrielle was treated fairly and with respect. In a nutshell, Miss Esther Crowe had cared about what Gabrielle cared about. So, whenever Miss Crowe hugged her, she knew that Miss Crowe wasn't hugging her for what she could get out of her. She was hugging her because she knew

Gabrielle needed it. After Miss Crowe was no longer in her life, she didn't want or care for anyone to hug her.

But she had to admit, there was something different about Fatima's hug—a hug that quite honestly, she hadn't seen coming before it happened. A hug that felt rather sisterly, just one more thing she wasn't all that familiar or comfortable with.

"Thanks for the information, but I hadn't planned on asking if you were married or not," Fatima said. "Not at this point, anyway. I wouldn't want you getting the wrong impression about us here."

In fact, Fatima had noticed the slight cut above Gabrielle's right eye. She couldn't help but wonder what the real story was behind that. And that pukey green, bright sunshine yellow, hot fuchsia, orange, and red scarf carefully tied around her neck didn't seem to match the classy outfit. Fatima wondered if Gabrielle had possibly worn that scarf to cover up some infraction surrounding her neck. That cut above her eye had given Fatima plenty of reason to pause. And Fatima was leaning more toward some act of violence having been done to her than any act of love.

"Well, I wanted to come and personally welcome you to the body of Christ, as well as to Followers of Jesus Faith Worship Center," Fatima said, maintaining her upbeat manner. "I'd also like to give you my phone number and possibly get yours. That's if you don't mid me having it. With thousands of members, Pastor Landris wants to ensure any new people who attend here have at least one person they can easily reach, in case they need something or have any questions. A point of contact, if you will. And I am indeed delighted to say that I am your contact."

Gabrielle flashed Fatima a quick smile. *Indeed.* She'd caught Fatima's glance at the cut above her eye that honestly she'd forgotten was even there. And had she known she would end up going forward to be saved, ultimately placing herself visibly in front of other people instead of the come-in-and-leave-without-talking-to-anyone plan she'd originally thought she'd do, she might have put off coming to church altogether. At least, until her impossible-to-hide-without-big-shades cut above her eyes had completely healed.

Gabrielle touched the scarf she'd tied around her neck— happy now she'd chosen to wear it. Scarves were definitely not her thing. They were too old fogey for her. And she was not a scarf person. But leave it to her aunt on her father's side, Cecelia "Cee-Cee" Murphy, to give her something she didn't want, but would later possibly need. The only time Gabrielle ever considered wearing a scarf was on her job, and only then, if it was requested. Truthfully, even then, she didn't keep it on long enough for it to aggravate her the way this one was beginning to do. She pulled at the knot to loosen it a little more, careful that it not become *too* loose and expose the black and blue bruises on her neck.

After leaving the building, she slid into her pearl-colored, automatic five-speed, V6, 2008 Toyota Camry Solara SLE convertible. She draped her off-white wool coat on the passenger's side headrest. She then placed her new Bible and the Newly Converted/New Member's Handbook she'd received from another person, who came over right before she left the conference room, in the passenger's seat. She cranked the car, turned the heat on full blast, and pressed a separate button to heat up her tan leather seat. The seat began to warm quickly. When she'd bought this car, that was one feature the manual spoke of that she thought she'd never use, especially living in the south. But on a cold day like this, she absolutely adored this benefit of her car.

Gabrielle reached for the Bible, retrieving the handwritten card Fatima had given her with her contact information, along with a message she'd written. Gabrielle couldn't help but smile as she read it.

"You are now a new creature. Those old things are officially passed away. It's time to let go of past mistakes made by you and even those made against you. It's time for you to walk in your godly call. If you need anything, have questions as you embark upon this new and wonderful faith journey, or you just need a friend, please trust me when I tell you that I'm only a phone call or an e-mail click away."

Fatima had included her home and cell phone numbers, as well as her e-mail address.

Following that were the words "P.S. Read Jeremiah 29:11."

Gabrielle looked at the Bible and suddenly realized she'd never really opened a Bible before, and especially not to seek out a specific scripture. Those few times as child she *had* gone to church, the deacons usually read from their Bibles while the congregation passively listened, and nodded with occasional amens. When the pastor stood and read his selected scriptures before giving his text, the congregation was neither required nor encouraged to open their Bibles and read along with him.

Even her beloved Miss Crowe, who had told her some things about God, had never opened the Bible or read anything out of it in her presence. Miss Crowe merely quoted a scripture when she felt the need.

Starting at the front, Gabrielle turned in search of a table of contents. Most nonfiction books contained one. Surely the Bible had to have one. Surely it had to.

She smiled when she found it. Old Testament. Jeremiah. Page 1099.

Practicing What You Preach

Chapter 1

*And the hand of the Lord was there upon me;
and he said unto me, Arise, go forth into the plain,
and I will there talk with thee.*

—Ezekiel 3:22

The sunlight seemed to pour through my bedroom window even more than usual. I pulled my blanket completely over my head as soon as I realized the brightness was affecting my sleep. I didn't want to get up today. I just didn't. I was tired. Not physically tired (although working a full-time job while putting together an elaborate wedding is draining), but tired on the inside. Tired of people expecting things from me, tired of people asking if I can do things for them, automatically assuming I'll do it. T-i-r-e-d, tired! I sneaked a quick peek at the clock. Twenty more minutes until the alarm was set to go off. *Quick! Go back to sleep. Before there are people to please.*

I don't usually consider myself a people pleaser. In fact, I would describe myself as strong and independent. But lately, I've been taking on more and more. I don't know, maybe all of this can be traced back to my upbringing—the people-pleasing part, that is. It's what my mother prides herself on, although she likes to call it being a peacemaker . . . a unifier . . . a real leader. My mother, Ernestine, is the one everybody goes to when somebody needs something: time, help, money (especially money), and everything in between. She's the one who takes care of the family—immediate, extended, and those who merely call themselves family. She forever places herself last on the list, which normally means there's nothing left when her turn finally rolls around. And at fifty-two that's what's slowly taking a toll on her. It's not the high blood pressure and cholesterol her doctor has her taking pills for daily. Putting everybody else's needs and wants above her own is what's dragging her down.

Well, I've decided at age twenty-eight that my mother's fate will not be mine, no matter how much people claim I'm just like her. I want a lot out of life, and I don't intend to put my goals on the back burner. I just need to figure out how to say no to things I don't want to do and stick with it after I say it.

Those two letters—*n* and *o*—when knitted together form a definitive answer. But for some reason I've not been able to make them work for me effectively. Sure, I may start with the *n* but it will invariably come out as, "Now?" or "N . . . oh, you *really* want me to?" Or worse: "No problem."

Two days ago my friend Nae-nae called and gave me a chance to test just how far I'd come with this "saying no" business.

"Peaches, I have something I *have* to do that I absolutely can't change," Nae-nae began, calling me by the nickname reserved and used only by a few family members and my closest of friends. "Can you take my mother to the grocery store for me tomorrow?"

"No," I said firmly, fighting off my normal knee-jerk reaction to add something else to it in the form of some type of acceptable excuse.

"No?" she said as though I had no right to ever say that. "What do you mean, *no*?"

"I have some things I need to do myself," I said as I began to slip back into my usual role of not wanting anyone to be upset with me because I'd dared not please them.

She laughed. "Oh! Is that all? Well, you can just take her after you finish what you have to do. It's not like she has to be at the grocery store at a certain time or anything, although you know she is slightly disabled and shouldn't be out too late at night. Come on, Peaches, you know I don't have anyone else to help me out. I've always been able to count on you. Please don't start being like everybody else and let me down now. Pleeeaaase?" she whined.

"Okay, fine. I'll take her," I said even quicker than I suspected I would. She thanked me and hurried off the phone. I had caved in yet again.

What I should have said was, "Well, if your mother doesn't have to be there at a certain time then you can take her after you finish what *you* have to do." That's what I should have said. But no, that wasn't what I said at all. I'd merely given in once more.

It's so funny how later on you can always think of stuff you *should have* said. So my new goal is to learn how to say what I mean and stick with it no matter what. I just have a hard time telling someone I can't do something when honestly I know that physically I can. Just one more lovely trait I can attribute to my fine upbringing.

My mother never believed in telling lies, not even the little white ones folks basically say it's okay to tell. You know like, "No, you don't look fat in that." Or "Cute outfit." What about, "Oh, no; I really *do* like your hair. I was only staring so hard at you because it's so . . . *different.*"

Not my mama. It was "Girl, now you know you're too old to be trying to wear something like that." Or "Somebody lied to you. Go back and try again." Or what about, "That looks good, it just doesn't look good on *you.*" Still, she will do anything for you.

I started planning special events as a hobby about two years ago, but lately it appears this could someday become my real bread and butter if I continue to pursue it seriously. Everybody says I'm great at putting things together. That's what I was doing yesterday after work—taking care of some pressing business for an upcoming wedding. A wedding, incidentally, that's huge and could really put my name on the go-to-for-event-planning map.

I pushed myself to do what I had to do after work, then managed to take Nae-nae's mother to the store. It took her two whole hours to shop. Two hours I really didn't have to spare. She insisted on doing it herself. Seriously, she could have given me the list she'd already written out anyway, and I would have been done in fifteen minutes. Tops. Instead, she ended up riding in the mobile cart the store provided. She'd stand up, get an item, put it in the basket, sit down, then ride sometimes just to the next group of items, only to begin the slow and tedious cycle all over again.

I don't know, maybe I really am as hopeless a case as Cass said. Cass is my ex-boyfriend. His real name is Cassius, named after his father who was named after Cassius Clay the boxer before he changed his name to Muhammad Ali. If you ask me, I'd say Cass thought his name was short for Casanova. But truthfully, he was the one who got me started on this self-evaluating journey I've been on lately. Cass flat out said I was too easy and a real pushover. Well, he should know, since he treated me like a disposable pen, then pushed me over and threw me away when he felt my ink was all but used up.

And to think he had the nerve to break up with me and make out like everything was all my fault. He claimed I was too self-centered for him. *Give me a break!* So I was supposed to believe that I was too easy, a pushover, while at the same time believe I was self-centered. *All righty then.* Looking back, the best thing Cass ever did for me was to move his narcissist-self on. Now, you want to talk about somebody being stuck on himself, then that is Cass, the guy I dated last for a whole year, to a T. After Cass, I started listening to my pastor and decided to pray that God would send the right man into my life, because I sure wasn't doing all that hot on my own.